ABIGAIL SLOTER

The Stolen Rose

First edition

ISBN: 978-1-7344046-0-9

Editing by Cae Hawksmoor
Cover art by Jessica Bell/Jessica Bell Design

This book was professionally typeset on Reedsy.
Find out more at reedsy.com

"There is nothing impossible to him who will try."
—Alexander the Great

Contents

Acknowledgement

The Acknowledgments of a book have a special place in my heart. I enjoy flipping to this particular page and hearing the author thank everyone who helped them on their journey, and I'm excited to write my own.

Everyone here has my gratitude for their help, encouragement, and constructive criticism.

Mom, you encouraged me to keep writing when I contemplated giving it up and becoming a zookeeper (because that is how quickly my mind hops from one idea to the next). I may have started this story solo, but I couldn't have finished it without you.

Alex, you read the first renditions of this story and brainstormed with me on how to make it better. You were my very first editor, and I couldn't have asked for a better one.

Joshua, I will never forget how you always referred to this story as 'when' and never 'if.' That means a lot to me. Plus, you always helped me with the tech stuff, which, lets be honest, wouldn't have happened without you. Or it would have happened but been accompanied shortly thereafter with a hysterical breakdown. Not pretty.

Caleb, your logic helped make this book believable. Not only did you help me with math, but you also helped me figure out tricky situations and make them logically sound.

Billy, you helped me with my characters and situations, and together, you and Caleb always eased my stress—which was at crazy, vein-popping levels at certain times.

To the rest of my family: thanks for the endless support and interest in my fantasy world.

Thanks to Cae Hawksmoor, whose editing helped me find the best version of my story. I so appreciate your patience!

Thanks to Jessica Bell for the fantastic cover. I couldn't have asked for anything more awesome!

To my readers: thank you for reading this story. You could have spent your time watching television or listening to music, but you chose to spend it with Chasina. That means a lot to me.

Chapter One

C hasina dug a shallow grave.

The underground cavern was shaped like a half moon. People from the village aboveground shuffled across the cavern's spacious curve, staying away from the latrines at the cavern's rear. Those were the living quarters. The quarters for the dead lay at Chasina's feet: two graves and a third nearing completion. They lined the cavern's straight wall, the straight edge of the half moon.

Despite her calloused skin, blisters were beginning to appear on Chasina's palms as she labored over the latest grave. Yesterday, she'd dug two graves for elderly twin brothers, and the blisters were beginning to pop. She could have gotten someone else to dig the graves. More than a hundred people congregated in the underground cavern, many of them conditioned to obey her commands. But most of them were sick, and anyway, these graves deserved her attention. Three of her villagers would never draw breath again, and she needed to remember their faces.

The bloody lips.

The pale skin from weeks of confinement.

The caved chests.

Chasina carved each face into her memory before covering them with dirt. If the lung rot kept spreading, there would be many more faces to remember. And even without the blisters, digging those graves would be painful.

Theodoric toed the mound of earth beside the grave. "We need to give these people the respect they deserve and burn their bodies. Earthen burials dishonor them."

Theodoric was a powerfully built man and village elder in name alone. Theodoric hadn't held any power since Chasina had dethroned him a year ago. Listening to his advice was like sifting through dirt to find gold, only to find that the gold was fake. What else was Chasina supposed to do with the bodies? Dishonor or not, she wouldn't leave them rotting in the open.

"No fire in the cavern," she said, shoveling more dirt. "We will burn the bodies when it is safe to leave."

"And when will that be?"

"When the giants stop hovering outside our village, waiting to eat us the moment we pop out of the cavern."

Chasina dropped the wooden shovel and lifted the dead woman into the grave. She filled the grave with dirt and laid a hand on the earthen mound, silently blessing the woman's death.

Footsteps stopped behind Chasina, and a breathy voice cracked when it spoke. "Chasina, I need to talk to you."

Chasina traced a rose into the mounded dirt and kissed it. *Be at peace. I will not forget your face.* Rising to her feet, she faced the man who had spoken. He bounced from toe to heel, his face shining with sweat as he darted glances at the ladder rising behind Chasina.

Chasina angled herself to stand directly between the man and the ladder. Since gathering all the villagers into the cavern, she'd heard many complaints. But unless she was greatly mistaken, this man had transcended complaints and was about to do something foolish.

2

Regardless, she needed to listen to him speak. Venting might keep this man from acting on his stupidity.

Chasina inclined her chin, signaling her permission to speak.

The man licked his lips, his hands a blur of twitching and twisting fingers. "We are running low on water. The food rationing is getting smaller every meal. The latrines are full. None of us has seen daylight in a month. Please, we need to leave the cavern."

Silence descended on the cavern, broken only by uncontrollable coughing and the steady thumping of people pounding each other on the back. Without torches to light the pitch-black cavern, the whites of people's eyes hovered like miniature moons in the darkness. Most of those moons looked away when Chasina challenged their gaze.

It had been over a month since she had confined them to this cavern, and with the lung rot spreading through their midst, people were beginning to buck her control. It was only to be expected.

Chasina picked up her shovel and pointed it at the earthen ceiling. "There are giants aboveground, drooling over themselves for the chance to pounce on any human they see. They don't know where we're hiding because I haven't let anyone outside. We will all die if I let you go up the ladder."

"But we've been down here for a month without any sign of giants," the man said. "People are dying. We all need fresh air before the lung rot kills us."

Another round of coughing supported the man's statement. Chasina did not blame the villagers for wanting to go aboveground to escape the sickness, darkness, hunger, and thirst. She blamed them for yielding to the desire. The villagers knew what happened when giants captured humans, but their desire to exit the cavern somehow overruled their common sense. Lucky for them, Chasina was here to keep them alive.

Chasina pressed the flat of her shovel against the man's chest.

"We stay down here until we can be sure that there are no giants aboveground. Now, get back into the crowd."

The man pushed past Chasina and raced for the ladder. Chasina chased him, tackling him around the knees. She straddled his chest and socked him in the jaw. While he recovered, she reached into her left boot and pulled out a spara leaf. When the man saw the leaf, he stopped fighting.

"Please don't," he said, his head shrinking into his shoulders. "I'm sorry for trying to leave. It was desperation, nothing else. Please. I have a family. I'm a good person."

Chasina wrenched open his mouth and squeezed the leaf, trickling clear spara sap down his throat. His mouth sagged into a smile, and his whole body relaxed beneath Chasina.

"Hello?" Chasina asked quietly. The man moaned happily, caught somewhere between sleep and wakefulness. Spara sap was a powerful drug that dropped users into a short trance followed by sleep unless a loud noise or sudden stimulation woke them.

Chasina scooted off the man and tilted his face toward her, aware that the whole cavern was waiting for her to speak. No one said anything. Even the rampant coughing took on a softer edge. Everyone knew what she would ask because most of them had been in this man's position.

Chasina traced the scars on her lips before asking softly, "What is your worst secret?"

The man tilted his head from side to side, the happy smile pressing into his lips until it looked carved on his face. "I accidentally killed my mother."

"How did you do that?"

The smile almost slipped from the man's lips. It ghosted around the corners of his mouth, present because spara sap cradled his mind, ghostly because he was ashamed. He struggled to speak.

4

"I left her in Brundar after we foraged for edible plants. I thought she was behind me. I wasn't paying attention. By the time I realized she wasn't with me, and I went back to find her, she was dead. Slipped on a rock and bashed her head."

"What did you tell everyone about her death?"

His voice quivered. "I told everyone one of Brundar's animals killed her."

Good enough. Chasina shook the man awake, clicking her fingers until he focused. No one remembered what they did or said while under the influence of spara sap, but everyone knew what happened when Chasina drugged them. Being drugged and interrogated wasn't uncommon in the village, and everyone who came back from the interrogation was changed. More docile. More obedient. No one bucked Chasina's commands when she held their worst secrets, ready to announce them to the village.

"I know what happened to your mother," Chasina said, gripping the man's chin and forcing him to look at her. "If you ever disobey me again, I will tell everyone about it, starting with your father. Do you understand?"

Nodding emphatically, the man scrambled to his feet. Chasina caught his arm before he ran away.

"I just saved your life," Chasina said. "Doesn't that mean anything to you?"

He cleared his throat, inching away from Chasina. "Thank you. Can I go now?"

A sincere 'thank you' was probably too much to ask for, no matter what she did for the villagers. Keeping everyone safely hidden from giants didn't necessarily correlate with keeping them happy. *Still, though, if he wants to be unhappy, I can help with that.*

Chasina planted her shovel in the man's chest. "The latrines are full, so go dig a new one."

Clutching the shovel, the man dove into the loose crowd and hurried toward the row of stinking latrines. The crowd parted for him. People nonchalantly coughed into their fists as they shuffled away, pretending like they didn't want to know his darkest secret. Pretending like Chasina didn't know their darkest secret.

Chasina noticed one person who wasn't shuffling or hiding her face. It was Katie. She pushed through the crowd, heading straight for Chasina. Katie had a belt tied around her straight waist, hung with bandages and needles.

"What is it?" Chasina asked.

Katie's face, usually a mask of scowls directed at Chasina, was tense and tear-streaked. "It's your grandmother. Gran has the lung rot. She's dying."

Chapter Two

A rock dropped in Chasina's stomach and sent ripples quaking against her insides. Gran was one of the strongest women she knew, one of the herbwomen that tended the sick and wounded in the village. Sickness never touched Gran. It wouldn't dare.

"What did you say?" Chasina asked, realizing that several long moments had passed since Katie had spoken.

Katie sniffled as she spoke. "Gran is dying."

The words sucked the air from Chasina's lungs, but she tamped down her shoulders and nodded sharply. "Take me to her."

She followed Katie into the crowd of people scattered across the cavern's curvature. People shrank when Chasina neared them, ducking to avoid eye contact. The guilty people whose secrets Chasina harbored were easy to spot. They offered her limp smiles that died when they thought she wasn't looking. After a year of interrogations, Chasina commanded their obedience. She had yet to command their happiness.

Katie stopped at the upper edge of the half moon, where Gran rested against the wall, possibly asleep. Gran's long gray hair snarled around her face, and every breath sounded like a chorus of crickets singing in her chest.

Chasina knelt beside Gran and clicked her fingers at the nearest villager. "Get me some water."

"She drank her whole ration."

"Give her mine."

The villager scurried away, and Chasina brushed the hair from Gran's forehead, fingers catching on the knots of dried mucous. Gran was the senior herbwoman in the village. People came to her for healing, even Katie, who still had three more years on her apprenticeship before becoming a full-fledged herbwoman.

Gran arched her back. "That hurts, Katie. I told you to stop combing my hair."

Chasina's fingers twitched mid-groom. Katie already tried untangling Gran's hair? It would have taken a while for the mucous to dry, and it would have taken longer for someone to decide they should comb it out of Gran's hair. Just how long had Gran been sick before Katie told Chasina?

Chasina faked a smile and tucked gray hair behind Gran's ears. "It's not Katie, Gran. It's me. Chasina."

"Where is Katie?"

"I'm right here, Gran," Katie said, kneeling to squeeze Gran's hand. "Don't worry, I'm here. Do you need something?"

"Water."

The villager returned with Chasina's water ration. Chasina held out her hands for the bowl, but Katie took it and lifted it to Gran's lips. Gran drank slowly, pausing several times to gasp for air.

Chasina counted the gasps, and suddenly, the blisters on her palms throbbed with unreal pain. She had already dug three graves and expected to dig more, but she couldn't dig one for Gran. The person who had sung Chasina to sleep every night after adopting her could not die.

Chasina leaned against the wall, feeling for vibrations. Every time a giant moved, their footsteps sent vibrations racing through the earth. Four weeks ago, she had felt those vibrations and herded everyone into the cavern. Even though no one had felt any vibrations since then, that didn't mean the giants had gone. The giants were probably hiding in the forest, studying the empty village and wondering where all the humans were hiding.

Fresh air would clear Gran's lungs and help her recover, but sending sick people aboveground was ridiculous. Giants would flock to the sound of coughing humans, discover the underground cavern and capture everyone. Sick people would get everyone killed. But one healthy person? That might save everyone.

Chasina locked her gaze on the narrow shaft ascending from the cavern. After weeks of watching the village, the giants were likely less vigilant. They might not notice one petite human running into the forest.

"I'll be back, Gran." Chasina brushed her thumb along Gran's cheekbone. She turned and strode toward the ladder, but Katie caught her arm.

"What are you doing?" Katie demanded, wiping tears from her face. "Gran is dying. I know you don't really care, but you could at least pretend for her sake."

Chasina rounded on Katie. "How long was she sick before you decided to tell me? She's my grandmother, Katie. I should have been the first to know."

"Really? I assumed you were too busy interrogating people to check on Gran. She's been sick for hours, and you never visited her."

Chasina leaned closer until their faces brushed, but Katie didn't recoil. "Firstly, I thought she was busy healing people, and I didn't

9

want to interrupt her. If you weren't as thickheaded as everyone else, you would know that nobody cares more about the people in this village than me. And secondly, she's my grandmother, not yours. Stop calling her 'Gran.'"

Katie's eyebrows lowered into a flat line. "If you cared about us, you wouldn't trap us down here for weeks for no reason. We have not heard or sensed a giant since we've been down here. No noises. No vibrations. There haven't been giants around the village for weeks, so if Gran dies, it's your fault for not letting us out of the cavern."

Burns scarred the inside of Chasina's throat and made her voice a harsh rasp. People tended to wince when she spoke, especially if the rasp sawed jagged edges into her words, turning them into weapons. Those were good days. Now, Chasina's voice was even more guttural than usual. An animal's growl.

"I'm going to collect plants for medicine. Get out of my way."

Chasina shoved Katie aside and marched to the ladder, springing lightly up the rungs. Just before she entered the narrow shaft that extended vertically another fifteen feet to the surface, a warm hand circled her ankle.

"I'm coming with you," Katie said.

Chasina squinted down the ladder and found Katie hanging from the rungs below her. "What are you doing? Get back in the cavern."

"I will help you get medicinal plants," Katie said. "I know where to find the plants, and I'm faster than you at harvesting them. Why keep me here? Are you afraid your short legs won't be able to keep up with me?"

Someday, I will find your weakness and dig my thumb into it. Sadly, as Chasina had learned six months ago, spara sap revealed nothing about Katie's weakness. Unlike most villagers, Katie had no shameful secrets. She was an herbwoman apprentice dedicated to overthrowing Chasina with the power of snark, but right now, Katie had some good points. Katie harvested quickly and knew where to find the best plants. As tempting as it was to throw her into a latrine, it was ultimately best for the village that Katie helped harvest plants.

Chasina climbed into the narrow shaft until her head bumped the stone hiding the entrance. "Once we are out of the cavern, stay low to the ground and do exactly as I say. Do you understand? I will not hesitate to beat you into submission if you endanger either of us."

A pause. Then, Katie nodded, and Chasina lifted the stone.

Chapter Three

C hasina poked her head from the shaft and blinked in the silvery moonlight. Nighttime. That was good. Giants would have difficulty spotting two lone humans running into Brundar, the colossal forest that bordered Tarrken on three sides. Everything in Brundar grew in proportion to giants: animals, plants, insects, and even inanimate objects like rocks. Giants hid among the trees while preying on human villages.

Brundar's enormous trees surrounded Tarrken on three sides, and a river capped the fourth side. Tarrken's huts slouched in the moonlight, camouflaged with vines. Any giant who took a second look at the camouflaged huts would notice the narrow dirt paths snaking between them and the stone pillar rising from the center of town. The vines provided minimal protection from giants, but the pungent juice leaking from the vines repelled all of the giant-sized animals that prowled Brundar.

No animals lived in Tarrken. Even though everything in Tarrken's meadow grew in proportion to humans, human-sized animals were extremely rare. There hadn't been any such animals in Tarrken for

12

almost a century. To cope, farmers harnessed themselves to plows when they planted and harvested fields.

A wave of foul air enveloped Chasina as she climbed onto solid ground. Katie followed her, and Chasina replaced the stone that hid the cavern's opening. She motioned for Katie to follow her and crawled to the nearest hut. Chasina pressed against the vines that tumbled down the hut's walls. She searched Brundar for the magical spheres that heralded approaching giants. Magic was a giant's life force, their aura, and each giant possessed a uniquely colored aura.

Right now, no colorful spheres illuminated the forest. But with an abundance of trees hundreds of feet tall and sixty feet in girth, giants could hide until they attacked. Even though she saw no magic, that didn't mean giants weren't hiding in the trees, waiting to pounce

Cutting a slit in one of the vines, Chasina squeezed foul-smelling juice into a small pile of dirt until it turned into mud. She slathered the putrid mixture on her face, scraping the nest of scars on the left side of her face. She slowed, methodically pasting mud in every ridge and crease from hairline to jaw.

"Where are the medicinal plants?" Chasina asked.

Katie blinked back tears as she rubbed mud on her face. It might smell worse than a dead animal, but it kept Brundar's animals from eating humans.

"On the river bank, two miles inside Brundar," Katie said.

Chasina jerked, hissing quietly when she accidentally stabbed herself in the eye. The river was a notorious gathering place for giants because it was the only water source near Tarrken.

"You're not serious. Giants love the river. Is there another place to find the plants?"

"No. And you're assuming that there are giants nearby."

Chasina stole down the dirt paths, ducking from shadow to shadow with Katie at her heels. She reached the river, slid to shore, and rolled beneath the outcropping that jutted from the bank. It created a small crawlspace that kept giants from noticing humans crawling into the forest.

Chasina's chest pinched when she squeezed into the crawlspace. Her breaths came faster, and she smelled smoke. Her hand dipped to the knife in her boot, squeezing the handle until the carved roses printed themselves on her palm. Slowly, her breathing evened.

Katie knocked on Chasina's boot. "Are you having another panic attack? Gran said you even have them at night when she's trying to sleep. Yet another way you made her get sick: she can't sleep."

"Do you smell smoke?" Chasina asked, though she knew the smoke wasn't real. It never was.

"No. And hurry up. Gran's counting on me."

Chasina crawled forward. "Gran is counting on you? That's funny. Tell me another joke."

Chasina shuddered when they entered Brundar. No matter how many times she transitioned from Tarrken's meadow, where everything grew in proportion to humans, to Brundar, the strangeness always caught her off guard. Rocks bigger than her home piled in the river collecting slime. Tree roots had the same girth as a human-sized tree. Even the sand changed texture, turning into hard pebbles that only giants mistook for sand. Unnaturally large fish swam in the river, underscoring rustling brush as predators dragged fresh kills through the trees.

Two miles into Brundar, Katie pulled Chasina's ankle and pointed at the thick patch of green plants ahead. No animals or giants roamed this little section of the river. They were alone.

Chasina rolled from the crawlspace. "Harvest enough leaves for extra medicine. Hurry before some giants show up. I'll stand guard."

She turned in circles, searching the trees for thirsty giants without finding any. *Odd.* Even at night, giants flocked to the river like wolves to the cries of an injured deer. No flickering torches or magical spheres glowed through the darkness, and the tracks on the sandy shore belonged to animals.

Chasina knelt on the shore and kneaded her ear into the ground, feeling for vibrations. Everything was quiet, and the stillness made something slip sideways in Chasina's chest. She stood and searched the bank for footprints, identifying each one: bobcat, coyote, rabbit, and raccoon. A full spectrum of prints tracked along the shore, but none of them belonged to giants.

Giants hadn't visited the river in a long time. So long that water had dissolved their prints. One month ago, she had felt vibrations in the ground and confined everyone to the cavern for safety. And for what? The giants had come and gone.

Katie joined Chasina, her arms full of dark green leaves. She'd piled more leaves on the ground behind her.

"What are you doing?" Katie asked.

"There aren't any giants. There haven't been any for weeks."

"I knew it! How will you tell everyone that they all got lung rot and that three of them died for no reason?"

Chapter Four

Humans worked all day in fields shaded by Brundar's enormous trees. Everyone paused their daily routines when vibrations trembled the dirt, just in case giants attacked. And even with these everyday realities, no one understood one simple truth: it was better to die in an underground cavern than in a giant's hand.

Chasina had made the best possible decision in the circumstances. One month locked inside the cavern was a sad but necessary miscalculation. Three people were dead, but they died a good death. She was proud of them. They were obedient to the end.

Chasina picked up the remaining leaves and started downriver. "There were excellent reasons, Katie, even if you don't understand them."

When Chasina arrived in Tarrken, sent Katie to make medicine, and told everyone to leave the cavern, most people directed their hate-filled stares at the ground. A little boy viciously dismembered a straw doll that looked suspiciously like Chasina.

The boy caught Chasina studying him and ducked behind his

mother's leg, but Chasina still heard the soft swishing of a straw doll crumbling in angry little hands. As if the boy had supernatural power, that was the exact moment four people rushed Chasina.

She tripped the first and punched the second, but the other two people pinned her to the ground. One of them squeezed her throat. Black spots danced in Chasina's vision. She struggled, but she was small, and three people knelt on her arms, legs, and chest.

Chasina recognized the person standing over her. He wielded the shovel she had given him to dig a new latrine. He swung the shovel at Chasina's face. Theodoric caught the shovel and shoved the man aside.

"She has the plow harnesses," Theodoric said, wrapping massive arms around the person choking Chasina. "You know you can't kill her. If she dies, so do we. Let her go."

The attackers released Chasina. She choked on the first breath, coughing as air pumped into her lungs. Slowly, the blackness receded, and she rubbed her throat. She knew from experience that a lovely ring of bruises would decorate her throat for at least two weeks.

This wasn't the first time people had tried killing her. When Chasina began blackmailing people a year ago through secrets she learned by drugging them, retaliation came in the form of attempted assassinations. Chasina had resorted to stealing and hiding the villagers' plow harnesses. If she died, everyone faced starvation because they couldn't grow or harvest crops without plow harnesses. No one risked killing Chasina and losing their plow harnesses forever, especially since leather and metal were scarce resources—except, obviously, for the four farmers in front of Chasina.

Chasina climbed slowly to her feet, leaning against the cavern's straight wall. Six healthy farmers restrained the four people who had tried to kill her.

Chasina pointed at each attacker in turn. "Thief, liar, coward, thief.

Throw them in the common pit, and I'll tell everyone the messy details tomorrow."

Six farmers hustled the four attackers from the cavern. As everyone formed a shuffling line to the ladder, Chasina searched for Gran. Raucous coughing enveloped her as she moved quickly through the cavern and found Gran leaning against the wall. Was it her imagination, or was Gran breathing slower than before?

Chasina slipped an arm around Gran and helped her stand. Gran wheezed as Chasina helped her walk to the back of the line.

Gran tried to shrug off Chasina's arm.

"Don't...want your help," Gran panted, out of breath merely from walking across the cavern. "Where...is...Katie? If you hurt her..." Gran started coughing. Droplets of blood flew from her mouth and sprayed the ground.

As an herbwoman, Gran saved lives every day. Keeping her alive meant more lives saved in the future.

Instead of waiting for the coughing fit to subside, Chasina picked up her grandmother and trotted to the front of the line. Exclamations unfurled in her wake, most of them snide, but she didn't silence anyone. Insults were a small price to pay to keep everyone safe from their own foolishness.

Chasina helped Gran up the ladder and carried her home. It doubled as the medicine hut. Villagers formed a long line outside the door, but they moved aside for Chasina. She entered the hut and laid Gran on the stone table used for examinations.

"How long until Gran recovers?" Chasina asked.

Katie finished brewing the medicine and dipped two fingers into a brown salve, smearing it on Gran's chest. "Not long. The fresh air will speed her recovery."

Chasina carried Gran to her pallet and pulled the blanket to her chin. She kissed Gran's forehead and left the hut, ignoring the crowd's frantic shuffling to get out of her way. They dropped their heads but not before she saw the fear on their faces. Ever since she took their worst secrets, no one looked her in the eye. And no matter how many times she saved their lives, no one had a kind word for her.

Heavy weights hung on Chasina's shoulders, and unbidden, her feet carried her to the stone pillar in the center of the village. Each human village had a similar pillar, and they all shared the same name: the Naridi Pillar. No one born in the last seven decades would have built such noticeable monuments to human life. At twenty feet tall and intricately carved with roses, it was almost like the builders were begging giants to glance from the forest and think, *Hello, there's a human village, and I'm hungry.*

Humanity built the Naridi Pillars centuries ago. The rose-carved pillars warned that villages were protected with magic and that attacking giants would die. Giants enjoyed killing hapless prey. They did not enjoy hunting humans who used magic to set them ablaze or break their necks.

Once, Tarrken's Naridi Pillar was a warning sign. Now, Chasina debated every day whether or not to tear it down because it endangered the village. People shouldn't have to hide underground like animals in their holes, but humanity no longer had magic to protect themselves. Unlike giants, whose magic lived within them, humans did not have inherent magic. Theirs came from an outside source: a rose-shaped rock named the Naridi Stone. That was the second purpose of the Naridi Pillars: they acted as vessels, storing magic from the Naridi Stone and enabling all human villages to protect themselves.

Seven decades ago, everything changed. A group of giants called the Undying attacked Falla, the village that guarded the Naridi Stone. The Undying stole the Naridi Stone, slaughtered most of its guardians, and traveled from village to village draining magic from the Naridi Pillars. The Undying rendered humankind helpless against all giants, who hunted humans without consequences.

Chasina knelt at the Naridi Pillar's base and brushed her lips against a rose. Faces of the loved ones she had lost passed through her mind, and she lingered on each face, committing the details to memory. Tonight, she added three faces to her memory.

"Give us back the Naridi Stone," she whispered, knowing that the Undying could not hear but saying the words anyway. "Don't you think we have suffered enough?"

Da had told her that the Naridi Stone had been a gift from the gods, and anyone who wanted to access its magic must be grateful. A kiss bestowed on the stone rose was also necessary. The kiss reminded people of everyone who had died before the Naridi Stone bestowed power on the human race. Now, kissing a rose was a reminder of everyone who kept dying. Not past deaths. Present ones.

Chasina privately thought it more likely that humans had somehow stolen magic from giants and created the Naridi Stone themselves. If gods were real, they had clearly forgotten the human race.

Theodoric knelt beside Chasina. "It's creepy that you kiss roses all the time. Just because your home village used to kiss roses doesn't mean you have to keep the tradition. No one else does it."

Chasina had been born in the guardian village, but it meant nothing special. Her memories of Falla were a vague collection of dilapidated huts, thievery, and rose-kissing. So much rose-kissing, actually, that it was both Chasina's earliest memory and a custom she'd introduced to Tarrken after Gran adopted her.

The custom hadn't taken root.

"We could get the Naridi Stone back someday," Theodoric said. "Maybe one of the Undying has a conscience."

Chasina knew little about the giants who called themselves Undying, except they were supposedly immortal, but the Undying were giants, and giants did not have consciences. The Naridi Stone was probably faraway, collecting dust in an Undying's hoard where it would never see daylight again.

But it wouldn't hurt Theodoric to feel a little hope, especially since he would have to conduct three funerals the next day.

Chasina rested both palms on her thighs, the lie flowing easily from her lips. "One of them will return it."

"How do you know?"

"Because I said so."

Theodoric snorted and left, heading toward Gran's hut. The line of people was gone. Everyone must have gone home with their families, doubtless happy to be away from Chasina's watchful gaze.

She drew her knife and kissed one of the roses Da had carved into the handle so many years ago.

A gentle vibration trembled through the ground, and the hair rose on her neck.

Giant.

Chapter Five

Chasina started to sound the alarm but choked when she saw a sphere of bright blue magic glimmering from Brundar. The hut-sized sphere floated among the dark trees, throwing the giant into shaded relief. At sixty feet tall, the top of his head almost reached the first branch on the tree beside him. His hands were as large as a single human, and his beard was thick enough to thatch a home. He wore ragged clothes and mismatched quilted armor.

Chasina crawled to the nearest hut and spied on the giant from around the corner. The giant was too close for the villagers to safely move into the cavern. Right now, he might not even see the village because it was dark, and the vines provided some camouflage. But the moment villagers flooded the streets, coughing and shuffling, the giant would attack them.

A dull pain throbbed in Chasina's thumb, and she looked down to see she was squeezing her knife's carved handle. She took a deep breath, sheathed the knife, and dropped to her belly, wriggling down the street until she reached Gran's hut. Only three people remained inside when Chasina entered. Gran snored on her pallet, and Theodoric and Katie pressed their ears to the ground.

Theodoric stood. "We have to evacuate the village."

Chasina blocked the door. "If the giant sees people panicking, he'll know that we've discovered him and attack us immediately. No evacuation. No cavern."

"Get out of my way."

Theodoric's record as an elder was checkered with avoidable deaths. He had not excavated a cavern, posted guards, or placed buckets around the village to put out fires. Theodoric's incompetence and the villagers' staggering inability to take the simplest precautions had convinced Chasina to assume control a year ago.

What happened after she took command? She excavated a cavern, posted guards, and oversaw a year without casualties. Obedience kept everyone safe, but chaos constantly rippled through the village, taking the form of people who incited disobedience. Tonight, chaos wore Theodoric's face.

Chasina held Theodoric's gaze. He maintained the stare longer than usual but eventually looked away. Like most villagers, Theodoric kept a secret he didn't want anyone to know.

"Do you have a better idea?" Theodoric asked.

"I'll kill the giant."

Katie and Theodoric gaped. "You'll do what?"

Chasina locked her hand around Katie's elbow. "You're going to use your heartwords to lull the giant to sleep so I can kill him. Sleeping giants are killable giants."

Heartwords spoke on an emotional level, a language from herb-woman to patient. Herbwomen used them to diagnose illnesses, temporarily soothe pain, and influence emotions and bodily functions.

Katie's voice squeaked. "Me? I still have three years left on my apprenticeship. What if my heartwords aren't powerful enough to work on a giant? It's smarter to abandon the village before the giant notices it."

"Katie is right," Theodoric said. "The giant has not noticed the village. Otherwise, he would have attacked us already, so the best idea is to quietly evacuate everyone."

"We have to kill the monster before he kills us. You can either come willingly, or Theodoric will carry you," Chasina said.

Katie raised her hands in surrender. "I'll go. But I think you're going to get us all killed."

Chasina exited the hut and led Katie to the river, where they squeezed into the crawlspace. Chasina crawled into Brundar. She kept moving until she felt the heavy vibrations that signaled a walking giant. Motioning for Katie to follow her, Chasina rolled from the crawlspace and climbed up the river bank. She hid in a thicket of cattails and peered through the stalks.

The giant crouched beside a tree, bathed in magical blue light, fiddling with a box-shaped trap meant to catch humans. Even crouching, he was enormous, with shoulders twelve feet wide and a sword belted at his waist that could skewer a hut and roast it over a hellish inferno. Average humans stood above a giant's ankle, but Chasina was shorter and slighter than most humans. The top of her head crested even with the giant's ankle.

The giant's blue sphere swerved into a tree and disappeared. The giant raised his fist, and magic appeared at his elbow, sliding across his forearm to his fist like a sheet of blue water. Blue magic coalesced in his palm. He moved his hand like he was tossing a rock, and the blue sphere shot into the air. It hovered above the metal box.

Katie sucked her lip, her face white. "I need skin-on-skin contact."

Chasina pushed through the cattails with Katie at her back. They approached the giant from behind. Drawing her knife, Chasina slid around the tree to the giant's right leg. The giant wore short leather boots that protected his ankles, but the only thing protecting his legs was coarse, tightly fitting trousers—the same hose that Chasina wore. Chasina reached up and ripped a hole above the giant's boot.

Katie slipped her hand through the rip and murmured quiet heartwords. *Peace. Sleep.*

The giant scooped dirt onto the metal box, hiding it beneath a thin layer of earth and leaves. He dusted his hands, and his muscles tensed to make him rise to his feet.

Peace. Sleep.

The giant muttered irritably and shook his head, fighting a yawn.

Peace. Sleep.

Relaxation spread through the giant's body, and he rocked back on his heels. "What in the Hero's name? Heartwords. Finally. There must be a human village nearby."

Chasina threw Katie out of sight a split second before the giant patted his ankles. The blue sphere lowered close to the ground, bathing Chasina in light. Chasina dove into a patch of weeds as the giant cackled delightedly. She ran low to the ground, ducking to each side whenever the giant raked the weeds.

Chasina broke through the weeds and ran face-first into a tree. She staggered backward and fell on her bottom. The world jostled on its hinges, popping in and out of focus as she cradled her head and blinked. She stood, tearing a gash in her forearm when a six-inch thorn caught her arm.

Get up.

Run.

Keep him away from the village.

A blue sphere crashed into the tree beside Chasina, and all the hair on her arms stood upright. She staggered blindly around the tree and ran away from Tarrken. She swerved erratically through the brush, partly to avoid the giant's massive hands, partly because her knees wobbled and her sense of balance slipped through her grasp.

25

After what seemed like an eternity, she tumbled from the trees into a meadow.

Not just any meadow. Tarrken's meadow.

Chasina windmilled to a halt and looked around. She would have bet her dying breath that Tarrken was at least half a mile behind her, but here it was, swimming before her like a nightmarish vision.

The ground shook beneath Chasina's feet, signaling the giant stopping behind her. Chasina half-turned and saw the giant cup his mouth and shout into Brundar.

"Found a village! Found a village! Everyone, I found a village!"

A dozen magical spheres appeared far away in Brundar, each a different color. They looked like bubbles from a child's dream: pretty, colorful, and flying far above the ground. The spheres started fires, captured escaping humans, and illuminated villages. A dozen spheres meant twelve hungry giants.

A horde.

Chapter Six

The giant turned, and Chasina spotted Katie clinging to his boot.

Katie's hand pressed firmly to his skin while her lips moved gently. Katie's heartwords skimmed across his conscious, but the giant was too busy counting huts to notice.

The giant yawned so wide his jaw popped. He crumbled to the ground, and the whole clearing shook when he landed. Katie detached herself from the giant's boot and hurried toward the medicine hut.

Chasina ran into Tarrken before the giant's first snore ripped through the meadow. She yanked open the nearest hut and dragged its occupants into the street, propelling them toward Brundar.

"Evacuate into Brundar," Chasina said.

Chasina kicked open several doors and shouted until everyone understood. Groups of people limped, staggered, and ran toward Brundar, depending on their level of sickness. Theodoric carried people too weak to walk, including Gran.

"I don't care if you're half-dressed," Chasina said, deepening the natural growl in her voice as she pushed a man into the street. He was one of the last people to evacuate. Nearly everyone was either hiding in Brundar or running toward it.

Chasina scouted the streets for stragglers. She picked up a toddler and settled him on her right hip.

"Mama," the little boy said, his hands flailing as he looked around the last group heading into Brundar. "Where's Mama?"

"We'll find your mama," Chasina said, brushing tears from his face. "Do you see those colorful spheres in the trees?"

"Pretty bubbles."

"Those pretty bubbles will kill you. They'll kill your mama and your da, and all your brothers. If you ever see one, run away."

The toddler started crying again, and the sound thudded dully against Chasina's heart as she hurried into Brundar. Scared toddlers grew into wary adults. More importantly, they lived long enough to grow into wary adults, something many children never achieved.

Chasina found the child's mother corralling six other children in a cluster of tree roots. She handed the crying toddler to his mother and moved to the edge of Brundar.

Three giants stepped into Tarrken's meadow. Ratty clothes hung from their bodies, and mud soaked their short boots. Orange, red, and violet spheres hovered at their shoulders.

Orange Giant kicked the sleeping giant. "Four weeks dodging a soldier patrol, setting traps on the sly, and he picks now to take a nap? Those soldiers will catch up soon. We better make quick work of this village before we're caught poaching humans."

Poaching. As though humans were a commodity to be regulated, raised, and slaughtered within reasonable laws.

Chasina turned away as the rest of the horde emerged from Brundar and surrounded Tarrken. They would start by smashing the huts. After the humans ran into the streets to avoid being crushed in their homes, the other stages of a raid began: the screaming, begging, and fire.

Chasina wasn't worried about the first two stages because Tarrken was empty. The villagers had melted beautifully into Brundar's undergrowth, and everything was quiet except for forest noises. Even the toddler had stopped crying. Any giant—*poacher*—who searched Brundar probably wouldn't find any villagers.

Stage three was different because it involved fire. Fire always found its victims.

Chasina whispered Theodoric's name until he emerged from a thicket of weeds.

"We need to move deeper into Brundar before the giants start fires," Chasina said.

"Didn't you hear what the orange giant said about soldiers?" Theodoric asked. "They're afraid to get caught poaching, and a fire would draw those soldiers to the clearing. They won't burn anything."

"We are leaving. Pass the word, Theodoric."

"Everyone is sick, Chasina. They won't be able to march, and if they come out of their hiding place while the giants are searching for us, we will die."

"Go."

Theodoric snapped his mouth shut, sighed, and began whispering the orders to everyone. People emerged from their hiding places, soothing their children as giants crushed their homes.

Sharp pain in her left forearm reminded Chasina that she needed healing. She couldn't expect sick people to march for miles if she dropped from losing too much blood. It would take at least two minutes for the villagers to ready themselves, so Chasina used the time to find Katie.

Katie's face tensed when she saw Chasina. "I was looking for you. We need to talk privately."

"Heal me while you talk."

Katie raked her gaze over the long gash on Chasina's forearm, one hand straying to the bulging pouches tied around her hips.

Katie cleaned the wound and threaded a bone needle. "We need privacy for what I'm going to say."

"No one will repeat a word of what you say. I'm sure it's not too important."

The needle jabbed into Chasina's skin—she should have expected that—but she masked the pain with a horrifying smile, jagged scars tightening across her lips. "Try again."

Katie finished stitching the wound and wrapped it with a clean bandage. "Please."

It was probably important if Katie asked nicely. Chasina led Katie into a thick shadow away from the villagers.

Katie took Chasina's hand. "I just want you to know that I will take care of Gran. Not because she means something to you but because I love her more than you can understand."

Before Chasina gave life to the heat flickering in her belly, Katie whispered softly. "Sleep."

The heartword sank into Chasina's body, and she fell asleep.

Chapter Seven

C hasina awoke to a heavy snap. She jumped to her feet, vision swimming dizzily as she assessed the situation. She didn't hear giants smashing village huts, so either the giants had disbanded, or they'd found the villagers. Either way, Chasina should be with everyone else, not facing Katie on the other side of a hole-punched wall.

"Rise and shine, Chasina," Katie said.

Visions of breaking Katie's nose flooded Chasina's imagination. They evaporated when Chasina finally recognized her surroundings. She stood inside a human trap, the one she'd watched the blue-magicked giant set.

Eight sharp spikes held the trap closed. Four spikes attached on the outside of each wall fit snugly into holes on the opposite side. A locking mechanism squatted on top of the box, far out of reach.

The box's length and breadth measured three strides each way. The top of her head brushed the ceiling, and pain pinched Chasina's chest.

The box was tiny.

Chasina's world slowed to single heartbeats. *Thud.* This trap was not real. *Thud.* It was too small. *Thud.* Smoke seeped through the holes and burned her throat.

The hut was collapsing.

Chasina's screams finally registered in her ears, and she fell against the metal, hands throbbing from beating against the walls. Moonlight pierced the trees and illuminated her bruised hands. Fog, not smoke, rolled between the trees.

She breathed deeply. *Just moonlight. No smoke, just fog. None of it was real.*

Chasina pulled herself up using rows of tiny holes punched into the metal. "Is everyone safe?"

Katie pressed her lips together. "We both know that isn't your primary concern right now, but no, the poachers left over an hour ago without finding anyone."

That was good news. Now, Chasina could focus on getting out of this trap without worrying about her villagers.

"Do you have any idea what you have done?" Chasina asked. "The village will not survive without me."

Katie curled her lip. "Amusing, coming from the person who brought an entire horde of giants into our village and killed three people in an underground cavern. No, Chasina, we probably *won't* survive. How could we?"

"Plow harnesses."

The threat never failed to produce results. No one knew whether or not Chasina was spiteful enough to die without telling them where she'd hidden the plow harnesses. However, everyone agreed that they didn't want to take a chance. It was time to see if Katie believed likewise.

Katie smirked. "You mean the ones hidden in the sand on the river bank? Or the ones you stashed in four different trees? Or maybe you mean the ones buried inside the cavern? At least you thought to hide them where giants couldn't destroy them."

There was only one way Katie could have learned that information. Chasina reached into her left boot and confirmed there were no more spara leaves. Katie had put her to sleep and squeezed spara sap in her mouth, interrogating her like Chasina had done with so many unsuspecting villagers.

Tonight, chaos wore Katie's body. And it was walking away.

Chasina slammed her palms against the metal wall. Half-formed words choked out of her mouth. *Obey me. Save me. Don't leave me.*

Tremors vibrated the ground. Twigs snapped, and two giants' voices grew as they approached from deeper in the forest. The giants came toward Tarrken, not from it, indicating they belonged to a different group than the poachers. Perhaps some of the soldiers Orange Giant was worried about?

Two giants emerged from the fog: one with brown magic and one with honey-colored magic. They were definitely soldiers. Both had good clothes, tall boots, and yellow armbands embroidered with spiders. Brown Giant spotted Katie and dove to catch her.

Katie bolted. A brown magical sphere shot through the air and engulfed her. The sphere returned to Brown Giant, depositing Katie in his outstretched hands.

Abruptly, Brown Giant spotted Chasina's trap and picked it up. "This is our lucky day."

Honey Giant whistled slowly. "I know that look on your face, Elric. We can't keep the humans. It's illegal."

"We're not really poaching. We're just repossessing the goods of an actual poacher. You don't seriously want to let these humans go free?"

Honey Giant shifted. "Shouldn't we look around for the poachers? Silversmith has been tracking these poachers for weeks. Their traps are here. They can't be far away."

"If the poachers aren't stupid enough to shamble across our path, I don't care how many human villages they raze. You shouldn't have to have a license just to hunt humans." Elric held up a placating hand. "We can pretend to find this trap tomorrow on patrol, and then we can tell Silversmith."

Honey Giant pushed Elric's hand away. "Fine, we can sell the humans. The boys won't care how we got them as long as Silversmith doesn't find out."

Elric snorted. "You've got more to fear from your shadow than that gutless knucklehead."

Chasina looked at the faraway ground as the giants hurried through the forest. Her trap hung from Elric's right hand, Katie from his left, at least twenty feet from the ground. A twig thicker than her body crunched beneath his boot. He kicked it aside, striding to the edge of a small clearing where white fog slithered around four lonely tents. The snores rumbled all the way across the clearing.

"You get to your shift change. I'll sell these humans and split the money with you later," Elric said. He ducked inside the nearest tent. A square of moonlight fell across five snoring men wrapped to the chin in fraying blankets.

"Everyone up. I have goods to sell."

A slurred voice broke through the groaning. "Hero's name, Elric. Get out before I slit you from throat to belly and tell Silversmith I caught a poacher."

"I caught humans," Elric said.

Blankets flew from half-naked bodies shoving each other to poke their faces inches from the trap. One of the giants remained asleep.

Someone poked the man's side. "Wake up, Kraihaim."

Kraihaim bolted upright and grabbed the man's throat. Two giants pried Kraihaim's fingers from their comrade's throat and held him on the ground. One giant slapped Kraihaim until he awoke.

Kraihaim relaxed. "Sorry. Nightmares, again. I thought an Undying was draining my aura. I was thinking about their attack on District Three before falling asleep."

"Cheer up," Elric said as the soldiers released Kraihaim. "Buy a human. Tonight, I'm only charging double."

"Double? For those skinny humans?"

The giants crowded around Chasina and Katie, and the complaints blended into a steady stream: too skinny, short, and small. The giants haggled over Katie, but no one seemed willing to pay double for her. Only one person glanced twice at Chasina.

"Where did you find this one?" Kraihaim asked dubiously, pointing at Chasina. "She must be the smallest human I've ever seen. Probably tough eating, too. Look at all those scars."

After a few minutes, all the giants huddled back under their blankets after declining to buy either human. Elric visited the other three tents and faced the same problems. At last, he walked to a tree at the edge of the camp, where Honey Giant stood guard.

"The humans are too small," Elric said. He scowled at Chasina like it was her fault. She blinked innocently, hunching, so her five-foot-zero-inches body looked even smaller.

Honey giant scratched his head. "I guess we get to eat them. Flip a coin for the taller one?"

Chapter Eight

Honey Giant won the coin toss and took Katie.

Chasina mouthed at Katie, *"I'll come for you."*

Katie opened her mouth, but Honey Giant covered her with both hands before she mouthed a reply. He didn't seem happy that his prey was too skinny. Hopefully, it would be enough to protect Katie until Chasina escaped.

It's another hour until dawn. He won't want to eat her while he's on guard duty. Chasina flexed her jaw. *She'll be fine until I get there.*

Elric backtracked through the clearing to his tent. The giant's swaying stride played itself on the ground beside him, where starlight elongated his shadow.

"Please tell me that's not what I think it is," someone said. The person slid from the shadow of a tent and faced Elric at an angle, trying to make himself small.

Elric jumped in surprise and dropped the trap. "Silversmith."

Silversmith caught the trap. "How many times have I asked you to stop hunting humans? You don't have a license, and poaching is illegal. We have to release the human."

Elric snatched the trap from Silversmith, sending Chasina careening into the trap's wall. She barely avoided skewering herself on the spikes.

Silversmith seemed shorter than Elric, or was that because his chin dipped forward and created a triangle with his hunched shoulders? It didn't really matter either way. Theodoric was the biggest person in Tarrken, yet he was a pushover. Chasina smelled the same weakness rolling from Silversmith in sheets.

Elric shoved Silversmith. "This is my human. What are you going to do about it?"

Silversmith touched his neck, tucking fingers behind a curtain of greasy hair. "It's illegal to hunt humans without a license, that's all. It might be smarter to let her go so that someone doesn't report us when we get back to Kavalu. We could all hang."

"Only if someone reports us. Are you going to report me?"

"Of course not. Just think about it." Silversmith backpedaled into the trees.

Elric ducked inside the nearest tent, stepped over four snoring giants, and set Chasina's trap against the tent wall. He pulled a blanket to his chin and quickly fell asleep.

The tent flap fluttered shut and blocked out the starlight, leaving Chasina in almost total darkness, sticky with the body heat of five giants. Chasina squinted at the metal spikes. The trap would fall open if she dislodged them.

Chasina drew her knife and aimed the hilt at the nearest spike, but someone pulled the trap sharply from behind. Chasina pitched forward. She hit the wall and watched the ground drop beneath her as a giant picked up the trap.

The trap tilted back and forth, and Chasina slid around the floor until she anchored herself on one of the walls. She looked through the holes. It was Silversmith. The vibrations of his footsteps must have been masked by the giants tossing in their sleep.

Silversmith tucked her trap under one arm and left the tent. He walked out of the clearing and into Brundar, moving like a silent shadow between the trees. When the camp disappeared behind them, Silversmith stopped. He set the trap down and unlocked it.

Silversmith pointed through the brush. "Go east until you find a wide stream—it will look like a river to you—and follow it downstream through the forest. It will take you home."

He rose to his feet, a massive figure looking down at her from a great height. Was he hungry? Chasina didn't doubt it. She stood very still, knowing that his first instinct would be to catch her if she ran. His second instinct would be to cut off her head and eat her.

"Go home," Silversmith said and melted into the shadows. His vibrations quickly faded, but Chasina didn't believe he was gone until she counted twenty. It seemed Silversmith's desire to avoid a noose for poaching was stronger than his desire to eat a human.

Picking her way through the fog, Chasina found the campsite again. She kept to the brush, wisps of fog caressing her skin as she found Honey Giant. He was stationed at the same tree, yawning and rubbing his face. His hands were empty. Maybe Katie had lulled him asleep and escaped?

A flash of yellow and red caught Chasina's eye. Something oval nestled near the roots of a tree, and when Chasina took a second look, she almost lifted from the ground.

It was Katie's disembodied head. Her mouth hung open, her face frozen in a moment of terror.

Chasina's shoulders sagged. An entire year had passed since a giant had killed a villager. Katie should have known better than to stray from the safe boundaries of obedience. She should have known what it would cost.

Chasina and Katie were enemies, but enemies or not, Katie was still a human who deserved justice for her murder.

Chasina slipped her knife from its sheath and stole from the weeds. Craggy bark scraped her nails and wrists as she scaled the tree, fitting hands and feet into cracks splitting the bark. She anchored herself just above Honey Giant's head, where a nest of spiny twigs scraped the top of his helmet.

Chasina chose a twig and sawed at its base. When she sufficiently weakened it, she wiped the remnants of stinking mud from her face.

"I hope you die in fire," Chasina said.

Honey Giant spun around. His eyes barely had time to narrow before Chasina threw her ball of mud into the left one. The muddy vine juice caused instant tears to stream down his face. While he cried out and scrubbed his face, Chasina heaved at the weakened twig.

Silversmith stepped around the tree and spotted Honey Giant rubbing his face. "Please, no. I thought you promised to stop sleeping on duty?"

Honey Giant choked. "My eye."

"Your eye," Silversmith repeated, looking confused until he saw Chasina.

Silversmith crossed the distance in two paces and reached for her. His fingers brushed her back just as the twig snapped. Chasina kicked from the tree and plunged the sharp twig into Honey Giant's blind eye.

Chasina fell with the body, relishing the horrible scream that died when they hit the ground. Chasina dove from the body and ducked into a tangle of gnarled roots. Her gaze flickered to the clearing behind Silversmith. Soldiers emerged from their tents, tightening their sword belts and chewing dried meat.

Silversmith knelt above Honey Giant. Silversmith had a deep crease between his eyebrows when he turned toward Chasina's hiding place. The ground trembled beneath Chasina's feet when he crossed to her hiding place and knelt, leather boots creaking. Silversmith slipped his hand between the roots, and Chasina backed away. If she gave him something he wanted, maybe Silversmith wouldn't be so intent on catching her.

"I can help you find the poachers," Chasina said, keeping several sharp roots between her and his searching hand. "None of these soldiers respect you, do they? Wouldn't that change if you knew where to find all the poachers?"

Chasina laid one muddied hand on the damp root beside her, blending into the environment to avoid Silversmith's detection. His crisp brown eyes searched the roots and dirt around her, analyzing and discarding the shapes.

"Why would you kill my guard? He hadn't done anything to you."

"Do you want to know where the poachers are or not? They attacked my village less than two hours ago, so I can tell you where to find their trail." Her voice faded with the last words. Silversmith moved closer, his fingers inches from her shoulder.

Silversmith brushed her curly hair, but before he lunged to grab her, a panicked voice called from the camp.

"Poachers!"

A single arrow arced into camp and buried itself in a random soldier's throat.

Chapter Nine

C haos erupted in the camp. Soldiers fumbled with their swords and spun around, searching for the poachers. Some managed a few steps before falling with arrows sprouting from gaps in their armor.

Silversmith cut himself on the roots in his hurry to disentangle his hand. Instead of joining the fight, he hovered just outside the clearing, clearly torn between fighting and running.

While Silversmith teetered on the brink of battle, a poacher attacked him from behind. The poacher swung his sword at Silversmith's neck, and Chasina mentally crossed Silversmith off her enemies list.

She and the poacher miscalculated. Somehow, Silversmith sensed the danger a moment before decapitation. He ducked, grabbed the poacher's wrist, and disarmed him in one clean movement. Silversmith crouched behind the sword like it was the most natural thing in the world.

Then Silversmith frowned at the sword, blinking like he wasn't sure why he was holding it. In that moment of confusion, the poacher drew his knife and dove at Silversmith. Silversmith stepped neatly back, cut off the poacher's hand, and stabbed him in the chest.

The poacher dropped dead.

Silversmith fell to his knees and inexplicably began staunching the poacher's wound. It didn't do any good. Silversmith stood, blood dripping from his hands, and ran away. He disappeared into the battle.

Despite their ratty clothes and mismatched weaponry, the poachers were clearly superior fighters to the soldiers. Maybe because they loved poaching humans. Maybe because they were simply more used to fighting for their lives. Either way, Chasina grimaced each time a soldier fell. If the soldiers fought a little harder, they could kill more poachers and ensure mutual destruction.

A few soldiers escaped into the forest, but most bled freely on the ground, their wounded cries tangling the air. Weak hands pleaded for mercy only to be cut down. The poachers dragged dead soldiers into a pile.

Chasina recognized the poacher's leader, Orange Giant.

Orange Giant finished wiping his sword on a tent and stooped to pick up a metal trap. "This is one of our traps. We must have caught some humans, and the soldiers decided to steal them. Search the camp. Some of the humans might have escaped during the fight."

The poachers began crawling around on hands and knees, slowly approaching Chasina's hiding place. She prepared to worm deeper into the roots but paused when she noticed a human nearby. He slumped fifty feet away, unconscious. A thorn protruded from his thigh.

Where had he come from? Maybe other soldiers had found different traps and brought this human into camp.

Slithering from the roots, Chasina dashed to the human and dragged him into her hiding place just as a poacher crawled past. The thorn sticking from the man's thigh touched a root, prompting heavy groans.

Chasina clamped a hand over his mouth, barely breathing as giants swarmed around their hiding place.

After a few minutes, Orange Giant straightened. "There aren't any humans here. Scavenge what you want from the soldiers so we can move on to another village. Hero knows the last one was disappointing."

Clinking weapons and jingling chainmail filled the camp as poachers rushed to strip the soldiers' bodies.

Chasina shifted, blood from the man's wound chafing her thighs. She tried easing him into a more comfortable position, but the thorn was too long. Much longer than a normal thorn, in fact. It also seemed a bit too uniform for something in nature.

Chasina blinked. It wasn't a thorn; it was an arrow. Who would have shot this man? A few people in Tarrken used bows to hunt frogs or shrews, but those villagers were hiding. No one could have shot this man. Where was he from? Who was he?

Snapping commands to faces distorted with barely-checked rage had sharpened Chasina's ability to recognize people. The man was not from her village. She bit her lip and brushed the black hair from his face.

Chasina gasped.

Silversmith's face was different when it was her own size. His greasy hair framed a sharp chin and dusted the thick scar on his neck.

She'd never seen this kind of magic. Was it common? How many giants walked among her villagers as humans? How many of her little ones followed a kind stranger into the forest and never returned?

Chasina's hand strayed to her knife, but she didn't draw it. No one knew how many humans Silversmith had killed masquerading as one of them, so it was only fair that he felt this death.

Chasina's fingers crooked into claws that circled Silversmith's neck. She felt his pulse drumming beneath her fingertips, but he was unconscious. He was human. She couldn't just kill him, even though she knew his true identity.

Fine. She'd let nature run its course if she couldn't kill him. He was already unconscious. Judging from the amount of blood soaking her legs, he wouldn't live to see another day.

Good riddance.

When the poachers left, Chasina dumped Silversmith from her legs and maneuvered from the roots. The breeze ruffled her hair and brought the smell of unwashed bodies, coppery blood, and filth. It did not take long to find Katie's disembodied head. Blood slicked her hair and stained her frost-white cheeks.

Chasina puked in the weeds and wiped her mouth, glancing at the disembodied head before stumbling back to Silversmith. One dead human was enough for today.

She rolled Silversmith onto his stomach and gently wrapped fingers around the arrow in his thigh. She paused. Blood welled around the wound, but the arrow probably kept some of the blood inside his body. If she extracted it, Silversmith risked bleeding out even faster.

Chasina cut a sleeve from her tunic. She wrapped it above the arrow in his thigh and twisted the ends around her knife handle, cutting off the circulation to his thigh. She knotted it. Her other sleeve went in Silversmith's mouth to stop the groaning while she laid Katie to rest.

Chasina recited the Death Blessing. "My heart knows you, and it will not forget. Be at peace, for you were loved. You are missed and forever in my heart."

Chasina carefully tied the disembodied head in a leaf, securing it so Katie's family could burn her remains and scatter the ashes on the river. They would give Katie a formal Death Blessing, which Chasina would not attend because it would be recited among the burning embers of Katie's pyre.

Dirt scraped beneath Chasina's boots as she turned from the bloody leaf and crouched beside Silversmith's prone figure.

She tapped his cheek. "Say something. Silversmith? Can you hear me?"

He groaned when she tried pulling him to his feet, slipped, and dropped him.

She grunted. "Sweet Naridi roses."

Silversmith's eyelids fluttered. "Naridi Stone."

Chapter Ten

Chasina instinctively reached for her knife to kiss the roses carved on its handle. "Why are you talking about the Naridi Stone?"

Silversmith's eyelids fluttered open. "Made a deal."

"What deal?"

"Trade the Naridi Stone for the…" he sighed, and Chasina shook him for an answer. "The Hero."

"What Hero? Where is the Naridi Stone? Tell me." She snapped her fingers in Silversmith's face, but he didn't answer.

She put a hand on his forehead and winced at the fever burning his skin. The arrow was poisoned.

Chasina gingerly tucked the bloody leaf under one arm and helped Silversmith stand. She pulled his arm over her shoulder.

"Come on, stand up. No one dies around here unless I give permission."

Chasina struggled beneath his weight as they swerved through the forest in senseless loops. They'd barely left the soldiers' camp when Silversmith fell. Chasina dropped behind him and cupped his chin, pulling his head up until his body followed.

"I made a deal," he mumbled. "Trade the Naridi Stone."

The hair rose on Chasina's neck. Since the Undying had stolen the Naridi Stone decades ago, giants mercilessly plundered human villages without consequences or hesitation. If Silversmith knew where to find the Naridi Stone, she needed to know too.

"Gramercy, what deal? Where is the Naridi Stone?" Chasina asked, gasping from the effort of supporting Silversmith.

Silversmith's head lolled. He did not answer.

Chasina dragged Silversmith through the last weeds into Tarrken's clearing, where sunlight laid the devastation bare. The giants had crushed all the huts, leaving nothing but piles of splintered wood and pulped vines. Beams stuck from the wreckage like bodies with punctured ribs, and a cloud of dust hung in the air.

No smoke. No embers. No ash floating in the breeze to suffocate anyone. Theodoric was right; the poachers hadn't burned anything for fear of attracting soldiers. Or maybe they had decided it wasn't worth it because the village was already deserted. Where was the sport in burning someone's home if they weren't available to scream in despair?

Chasina waved at the people filling barrels of water from the river. She collapsed beneath Silversmith's weight. Something popped in her spine, and the disembodied head rolled away.

Concerned murmurs congregated above her head. Someone pulled Silversmith's heavy body off her back. Chasina groaned and rolled over, but before she blinked, Gran was in her face.

Gran shook Chasina. "Where is Katie? Where is my girl?"

Unbidden, she glanced at the leaf. It had opened a few feet away to reveal a shock of blood-streaked hair.

Parents pulled their children behind them. A few screams burst from the crowd.

Chasina slowly stood, careful not to spook her grandmother. The medicine and fresh air had rejuvenated Gran, but she hadn't fully recovered.

"I tried to save her," Chasina said.

"My girl."

"I'm so sorry."

Tears coursed down Gran's wrinkled face. "Were you so jealous of her that you needed to kill her? What did I do to deserve your madness? You took my baby girl."

Chasina recoiled from the hatred spilling from her own grandmother. "Katie tried to kill me."

"Liar. Katie never would have hurt another person. She wasn't like you." Gran stood tall and trembling, clutching the leaf to her chest as she addressed the crowd. "We wanted to do it for so long, but no one ever succeeded. Will someone please drive a stake through Chasina's chest and leave her body for the giants?"

No one moved, and it occurred to Chasina that they still didn't know where to find their plow harnesses. Katie hadn't told them.

Chasina raised both hands. "I avenged her. The giant who killed Katie is dead."

"The Death Blessing is tonight," Gran said and stumbled down the hill. Two farmers followed her with Silversmith.

The crowd melted away without a word. No one attempted to ease the hurt throbbing inside Chasina's chest. *Grief hurts.* It was that simple. Gran was out of her mind with pain when she urged people to kill her own granddaughter.

I thought I was your baby girl.

Chasina pawed Da's knife from its sheath and wrapped both hands around the hilt. Da had loved her. Why didn't Gran? Even after Chasina saved Gran's life, Gran refused to care.

Doesn't matter. You have a job to do. Chasina tamped down her shoulders and kept her footsteps firm as she walked along the river bank to inspect the damage. A young girl ran up to Chasina. Tears streaked her face, but she had the hollow expression of someone too young to understand why she was crying. It was Katie's younger sister, Ella.

Chasina's tongue turned to ash in the absence of comforting words. "Ella, I'm so sorry."

Ella rubbed her tear-streaked face. "Was Katie afraid?"

Bloody hair and a face frozen in terror flashed in Chasina's mind. Giants cooked human bodies with magic, heating up the spheres to impossible temperatures, so they devoured their prey without needing to light a fire. Katie wouldn't have been human without being terrified, but Ella didn't need to know that.

"No," Chasina said softly. "She was very brave."

Ella's lip quivered uncontrollably. "The man you brought from Brundar is dying. Gran needs your help. She's up the river."

Ella ran away, hopefully, to find someone better at comforting than Chasina.

Chasina found Gran farther along the bank. Gran had pulled her gray hair into a skin-peeling bun with several surgical instruments stuck through it like spokes on a wheel.

"How can I help?" Chasina asked.

"The poison won't flush from his system. I need two people pushing the heartwords into his body to purge the poison from him." Gran wheezed as she moved, but not too severely. Her lungs were much clearer with medicine and fresh air.

"How? I don't know how to use heartwords." Chasina dunked her hands in the river and scrubbed the mud and blood from her skin.

"Repeat the words I tell you and push the poison from his magical aura. Yes, I know you saved a monster," Gran said as Chasina took Silversmith's hand. "I sensed his magical aura when I used heartwords

49

to diagnose the poison. Be prepared to live with the consequences like I have for the last twelve years."

Chasina flinched. "What heartwords do I say?"

Gran gripped Chasina's arm and murmured quiet heartwords. The heartwords fell on Chasina's ears, but since Gran had skin-on-skin contact with her, they also spoke directly to Chasina's subconscious in dulcet tones. *Fuse. One. Unity.*

The heartwords pushed Chasina's mind toward another presence, someone distinctly silver. She touched Silversmith's silver aura and instantly felt the poison leeching life from his body. The magical aura was fading.

Chasina slipped inside the silver waves and pushed heartwords into the aura. *Fuse. One. Unity.* The silver magic surrounded her mind and heart and pulled her close. It probed her thoughts and emotions, trying to slip inside of her innermost being.

Chasina resisted the silver magic. She wrestled with it, feeding it heartwords but keeping it away from her mind and heart.

Then she realized.

Everywhere the silver aura touched her, it grew brighter. Chasina stopped fighting and opened herself to meet the magic. Silver aura poured into her mind and suffused the core of her being.

Fuse. One. Unity. She fed the silver magic with heartwords, and when the magic shone brightly, she tried leaving. It hugged her greedily, and Chasina had the distinct feeling of being owned. The silver aura smothered her more tightly every time she tried escaping.

Pulling away from the silver aura was like breaching a living river. Silver droplets pulled at her mind and soul, unwilling to let her leave. Chasina twisted free of the magic's grip and opened her eyes to find herself slumped on the ground.

Chasina wobbled as she stood. "Will he be all right?"

Gran listened to Silversmith's chest and whispered a heartword.

"You cured him. So this is how it works? You chose to save a giant and leave Katie to die. Why did you bother coming out of the forest?"

"I never killed Katie. She tried to kill me."

"Stop insulting me with your lies."

Heat flamed in Chasina's belly, but she held her tongue despite wanting to flay Katie's reputation. Gran needed to believe Katie was good and innocent. Otherwise, it would destroy her. It wasn't fair, but so what? If Gran preferred fantasy to truth and it helped her grieve, Chasina would bear it.

Chasina shifted stray hair to hide her face as she looked away. "I love you, Gran. I have from the moment I hugged your leg twelve years ago. Isn't there part of you that's glad I escaped Brundar today?"

Gran stilled, her hand resting on Silversmith's forehead. "You were a curly-headed little girl when I adopted you. You were the image of your father at the same age. He was such a sweet little boy. I thought that raising you would be like raising a piece of my son again.

"You came out of the smoke and fire a twisted image of your father. Do you have any idea what it feels like to look at you? To look at someone who has been nothing but a curse to me? And for that person to say she loves me, only to blackmail all of my neighbors, steal our plow harnesses, threaten us every day and lock us in a cavern where we slowly died?" Gran dragged fingers down her cheeks. "It is unbearable."

Chasina reached out to touch Gran's shoulder, but Gran slapped the hand away.

Gran took Silversmith's twitching hand and planted it in his stomach. "If I had known what you would turn into, I would have peeled you from my leg and chucked you straight into Brundar."

Chapter Eleven

*S*he does not mean that. The words rebounded against Chasina's skull, but they lacked conviction. She stood rooted to the spot for several eternities, waiting for the part where Gran apologized.

A heavy groan gave Chasina the courage to move her feet. She put one knee in the grass and leaned into Silversmith's face.

"Tell me about the Naridi Stone," she said.

His eyelids flickered in the gray realms of semi-unconsciousness. "I found it. Going to use it to find the Hero."

Either the Undying had lost the Naridi Stone after stealing it, or they kept it hidden from other giants. If Silversmith knew where to find the Naridi Stone, did that make him an Undying? She doubted it. The Undying perpetuated violence on other giants, attacking and destroying entire cities. Silversmith hadn't shown the capability for that level of destruction.

"Are you an Undying?" Chasina asked.

Silversmith shrieked girlishly, and the hair stood up on Chasina's arms. Chasina rubbed her ears, accepting Silversmith's shriek as a 'no.'

"Do you know where the Naridi Stone is?" Chasina asked.

He mumbled incoherently, and Chasina patted her boot for spara leaves. It was empty. Spara leaves grew several miles inside Brundar. Only she knew their location, and she didn't have time to fetch more.

Chasina settled for plucking smelling salts from a nearby basket and waving them beneath Silversmith's nose.

Silversmith inhaled sharply. "Where am I?"

"Where did you say the Naridi Stone was hidden?"

"It's in the...the-the what now?" Silversmith shut his runaway mouth.

Chasina grabbed a bone needle from the basket and leaped on top of Silversmith, straddling him. She gripped his neck and pressed the needle to the corner of one eye.

"Tell me where the Naridi Stone is hidden," she said. "Or I swear by everything in your unholy world, I will sew your eyes shut."

The whitish needle nestled in one of the creases seaming Silversmith's face. They made him look older, but she couldn't be more than five years younger than him.

Silversmith licked his lips. "Please get off me."

"If you want to go free, tell me where to find the Naridi Stone. You know where it is. And if you think I won't sew your eyes shut"—she licked the end of the needle and bared her teeth—"think again."

He squeaked and shoved her. "Get off."

Silver light flashed behind Chasina's eyes. The light pulsed around her spine an instant before searing pain gushed through her body.

Chasina rolled onto the grass, and the silver light receded along with the pain. She stifled a scream when she saw the glowing silver circle stamped on the back of her right hand.

Chasina scrubbed her hand in the river, but the silver circle remained. Somehow, Silversmith had managed to curse her moments after regaining consciousness.

Silversmith climbed to his feet and nodded at Gran. "Thank you for healing me."

When Silversmith stooped to drink from the river, Chasina jumped on his back and pressed her knife against his throat. "Remove my curse."

Silversmith grabbed her wrist and twisted it, forcing her to drop the knife. He shrugged elegantly, shucking Chasina from his back. She landed in the dirt with a bruised wrist.

Silversmith returned her knife. "That must have hurt. Is your wrist all right?" his voice trailed away when he saw the silver circle glowing on Chasina's hand like a miniature moon. "I'm not sure how that happened. I cannot use magic while trapped in a human body, so I shouldn't have been able to turn you into my vessel."

"Vessel?"

Silversmith winced apologetically. "My servant. I cannot remove my magic from you until I return to being a giant."

Chasina's hand itched beneath the mark. Servitude? No wonder the magic had forced her off of him. It compelled her to obey his command to 'get off.'

Did Silversmith honestly believe she was stupid enough to trust him? He had released her once because the other option was a hangman's noose. Now, without any other giants to report him, he likely planned on capturing all the villagers once he transformed into a giant.

Chasina flexed her fingers around her knife. "I won't risk having you change into a monster in the middle of my village. You have thirty seconds to lift my curse."

Silversmith blinked and raised his hands in surrender, and Chasina simply stared.

"You can't do that," she said.

"What?"

"Surrender. There is no surrender. There's only winning or dying. You don't seriously expect me to throw you in the common pits instead of killing you?"

Gran stepped between them and whispered in Silversmith's ear.

Silversmith's mouth slowly thinned. "Why?"

Gran whispered again. She stepped back and spoke normally. "We've tried everything: poison, throat-slitting, hanging, but she just won't die. This is the only way we'll ever be rid of her."

"Are you sure you couldn't just cut off her head? That way, you know she died quickly. You don't want her to suffer, do you?"

"I do."

Silversmith shifted to see Chasina, and she recognized the universal disgust people displayed when they thought she wasn't looking. Typically, she would have raised an eyebrow or bared her teeth, but her mind was too full. What had Gran done? Why was she having this conversation with a giant? And why did the words, even if Chasina didn't understand them, feel like poison in her stomach?

"What did you do, Gran?" Chasina asked.

Gran turned, and there was no remorse in the sweet old face Chasina had loved all her life. "I used my heartwords to siphon a bit of magic from his aura into your body and seal it inside of you. I made you his vessel. Even when he becomes a giant, he will not be able to remove his magic from you. You belong to him for life."

Chasina's hand fell open. The world shifted beneath her feet, echoing silence reverberating through her body. *Fuse. One. Unity.*

She had welcomed the silver aura into her heart and mind, and Gran had sealed it inside her. *Fuse. One. Unity.*

"Gran. Please. You are grieving, and you don't know what you're doing."

Gran lifted her chin. "I know exactly what I am doing. I could not throw you into Brundar as a child, so I'm doing it now."

"How could you do this to me? Your own granddaughter?"

Gran curled her lip. "You have two hours to rest before I expect you to leave."

Chasina ran, but Silversmith caught her around the middle. He touched her hand, and silver light breached the ocean inside Chasina.

"Keep my secret. Tell no one that I am a giant and transform between being human and giant," Silversmith said.

Chasina wrestled free, bolted from the river, and hid behind the boulders at the edge of a field. She hugged her knees and tried desperately to erase the last ten minutes, just as she would with a panic attack. When it didn't work, she started crying.

Chasina shared her food, chores, and living space with Gran. She shared blood. Apparently, none of that mattered. Gran wished Silversmith luck with all the horrors he'd inflict on Chasina.

It didn't even matter to Gran what might happen to Tarrken without Chasina. Who would command the villagers? How would they rebuild their lives? Who would force everyone to survive even if they'd rather give up and die? It did not matter if Gran rejected her own flesh and blood or that Tarrken hated her. They needed Chasina's protection.

Silversmith was probably sleeping since he only had two hours to recover from blood loss and poison. She could easily slit his throat and free herself from servitude, but Silversmith was not the main issue. Gran's machinations proved that Tarrken would never stop hating Chasina. The villagers would never stop trying to kill her because they wanted freedom, not safety, and Chasina couldn't provide both. Or could she?

Her villagers would be safe if she brought back the Naridi Stone and restored magic to the human race. The villagers' gratitude would roll over her invisible bruises and cuts like a sweet balm. Everyone would love her, even Gran.

Chasina had to follow Silversmith if she wanted to find the Naridi

Stone. He wanted to steal the Naridi Stone and knew where to find it.

Chasina dried her face and headed into Brundar, grabbing the leather satchel she kept near the forest for scavenging. Time to harvest some spara leaves. Spara leaves served her purpose twofold: they would help her get answers from Silversmith and addict him to spara sap. She could use his addiction to leverage control over him and keep herself alive.

It took almost an hour to find the underground cavern where the spara plants grew far from sunlight. Sweet fumes clogged the air as Chasina harvested the spara, cut it into pieces, and rolled it in the dirt to preserve the thick sap.

Chasina covered the spara leaves with the food and bandages she kept in her satchel for emergencies. She hurried back to the river where Silversmith rested on the riverbank.

"Did you come to kill me?" Silversmith asked.

"Of course not."

He slowly clenched his fist. "Whatever happens to you will be well-deserved."

Chasina kept her facial muscles relaxed and hid behind her mask of scars. Even if the idea of traveling with a hungry giant made her stomach flop like a dying fish, she wasn't going to let him see it in her face. Fear created a master and servant, and though she bore his mark, she didn't belong to him.

Chasina recognized the heavy footfalls approaching from behind. "Theodoric, I wanted to talk to you before leaving. I will not be here to take responsibility for all the lives in Tarrken. That falls to you, so listen carefully." Chasina told Theodoric where to find the plow harnesses. Afterward, she said, "The village needs rebuilding, and the cavern needs to be resupplied. How are you going to manage until I return?"

Theodoric grabbed her shoulders and spun her around. "You little sprat. Even after Gran enslaves you to a giant, you dare to pretend you're in charge?"

Silversmith might be able to command Chasina's silence, but he didn't control Gran. She must have told everyone about Chasina's demise.

Chasina shrugged Theodoric's hands from her shoulders. "This is my home, Theodoric, and only a fool would think I am leaving for good. There are one hundred and five people in this village. I expect the number to be the same when I return."

He grabbed the satchel slung across Chasina's shoulders. "We are not sending supplies with you."

"Let go."

"Make me."

Chasina punched Theodoric in the center of his chest and twisted his arm, pulling the satchel from his grip as he stumbled into the gathering crowd. It looked like every villager came to see the exile—not exactly touching, but not surprising.

Theodoric righted himself and gestured at the crowd. "No one will burn flowers to grieve you. We all hope your death is long and painful."

A few villagers threw dirt clods at Chasina. She ignored the sharp thumps, only shielding her face when everyone began throwing dirt clods.

Gran appeared from the crowd. She snapped at Chasina standing calmly amid a storm of dirt clods.

"Get going. Now," Gran said.

"I promise you right now, everyone, that I am coming back for you. You have my word," Chasina said and turned to Gran. "Is there anything you want to say before I go into Brundar with a giant, Gran?"

Gran slapped Chasina across the face.

Chasina stumbled in shock. She opened her mouth, willing the perfect words onto her tongue, but nothing encompassed what she wanted Gran to know. Hadn't she already said everything?

Chasina helped Silversmith stand. Hefting his beefy arm across her shoulders, Chasina walked through the crowd toward Brundar. Every person stood aside to let her pass. Their jeers pounded the dirt at her heels, and she entered Brundar to tumultuous roars.

Silversmith's breath seeped onto the crown of her head in laughter. "The first time I've ever been cheered on my way is with a banished criminal. I hate my life."

Chapter Twelve

Chasina followed Silversmith's directions, traveling through deep shadows that pooled between roots and around boulders. The miles slowly lengthened behind them.

She itched to dose Silversmith with spara sap, but she placed the drugs second on her priority list. She was chiefly concerned with the glowing silver circle on her right hand. It represented the magic sealed inside her and marked her as a servant.

How far could Silversmith command her? Was there anything she could disobey, and how invasive was his influence? Could he force her body to move of its own accord, or were his commands chiefly enforced with magical pain? If she wanted to successfully addict Silversmith to spara sap, she needed to know how the mark on her hand worked.

That's why it was time for a bit of token resistance. Silversmith's reaction should give her all the answers she needed.

Chasina spotted a bend in the river. Once they reached the sand, she dropped Silversmith on the shore and backed away.

"You're a scout, smarter than you look and familiar with Brundar.

Tell me about this river."

"We have a long way to go."

Chasina crossed her arms and leaned against the bank. "See the tracks on the ground? This river is busy with all sorts of dangerous animals."

He wiped his forehead. "Then we can leave? Good."

One long stare confirmed that Silversmith was absolutely serious. He really thought that she had compunction about leaving him where cats, foxes, owls, and other animals could hunt him.

Chasina snapped her fingers in his direction. "I am leaving you to suffer a horrible death like the ones you've inflicted on humans. Understand?"

Silversmith tried climbing to his feet by digging his hands into the bank's soft soil, but his injured leg buckled. "I saved you from Elric. Would you really leave me here to die?"

"Absolutely. What are you going to do about it?"

Silversmith stared at her for a long minute, his face slowly hardening. "Help me stand."

Chasina braced herself for a wave of silver agony, but it never came. She sorted through every command Silversmith had given her and realized that he had been touching her each time. Like herbwomen, his orders needed skin-on-skin contact to work.

"You cannot make me do anything if you aren't touching me."

Muscles flexed in Silversmith's jaw, confirming her theory. "A sliver of my magic lives inside of you, which means you cannot be farther than a mile from me at all times. You want to run away? Fine. I'll be waiting for you."

"A human mile or a giant's mile?"

"Guess," Silversmith said crossly, so Chasina assumed he meant the giant's mile. It didn't make much difference. Short or long, it still tethered her to Silversmith.

"Unimpressive. If an animal eats you, my problem is solved." Chasina waited for Silversmith's response, but he did not answer. She had pumped him dry.

Chasina mentally cataloged her discoveries.

Silversmith cannot command me when he isn't touching me. Doubtless, she could put that to great use in the coming weeks.

I cannot stray farther than a mile from him. Chasina couldn't abandon him, which meant she needed the Naridi Stone's magic to free herself. Until then, she was a prisoner.

Silversmith cannot force my body to move. That was the easiest discovery. If he could control her body, he would have done it by now. He needed skin-on-skin contact to command her, and he relied on pain compliance to ensure her obedience.

That took care of all she needed to know about the mark and how it would affect her plans. It was time to move on to interrogating Silversmith and addicting him to spara sap.

The best thing she could do was get his bandage wet, giving her an excuse to change it, and in the process, slather it with spara sap. The sap would enter his body through the wound and begin the addiction.

A sparrow dove through the branches overhead, and the sudden noise made Chasina narrow her gaze at Silversmith. He remained unflinching beneath a glare that often made children cry. The person who had cringed before Elric was willing to sit here all day while an enemy stared at him with bared hostility.

"I give up. Let's go," Chasina said.

She helped Silversmith stand and followed his directions to cross the river. Silversmith wanted to cross on the rocks. He tightly gripped Chasina's neck to keep her from dropping him again, but she still managed to slip from beneath him and dump him in the cold water.

Chasina removed her satchel, jumped into the river, and pulled Silversmith ashore.

She fetched her satchel. "Cut off your old bandage. I'll see if I can find some of that ointment Gran packed for your wound."

Chasina positioned her body so that Silversmith couldn't see the satchel's contents when she opened it. She pulled out a clean bandage and soaked it with spara sap. Burying the used spara leaf in the sand, Chasina closed her satchel and turned back to Silversmith.

Silversmith had buried his wet bandage and was lightly tracing the line of neat stitches in his leg. The wound was small and red but not infected, thanks to Gran's purifying heartwords. Injuries treated by herbwomen did not become infected.

Silversmith accepted the fresh bandage and sniffed it. "This smells strange."

"Gran's ointment. She told me to put it on all of your bandages."

Chasina rubbed her wounded forearm and waited while Silversmith wrapped the bandage tightly around his leg. Most of the spara sap ended up on his unbroken skin. Was he utterly incompetent at everything?

"You're doing it wrong. Let me help," Chasina said, bending to adjust the bandage, pressing the largest deposit of spara sap directly on the wound. "The last thing you want is an infection, so let's change that bandage regularly."

Chapter Thirteen

Chasina hauled Silversmith through Brundar until blue-black twilight swathed the trees, and she felt seconds away from folding beneath his weight. He'd gotten heavier throughout the day as the spara sap slowly entered his body and relaxed him. It should have worked faster. Gran's tight stitches slowed the absorption and extended the amount of time it took to create an addiction.

Then there was the little matter of Silversmith's *condition*. Exactly when would he become a giant again? The moment he was monstrous again was the moment he ceased needing her help. If she didn't have him addicted to spara sap by then, things would get very tricky. He hadn't mentioned how long he expected to remain a human, but maybe he could tell her something. She had a limited supply of spara leaves, so it was worth trying to glean some answers without drugging him.

When Silversmith pointed at a comfortable niche between two roots, she gladly lifted his arm from her neck and rolled her aching shoulders.

He gripped her hand. "Get me a walking stick."

Chasina retrieved a walking stick and rested against a rock while Silversmith tested it. "So, how long have you had this condition? I've never seen a giant transform into a human until now. Are there many of you?"

Silversmith scraped his thumbnail against the stick. "You're a criminal."

"So? I need to know how many giants are walking around human villages and kidnapping people."

Silversmith stopped scraping the stick and studied her for a long minute. "I am the only giant with this curse, and I don't kidnap humans."

"Who cursed you?"

"Someone called an Undying."

The Undying were busy giants, weren't they? Stealing the Naridi Stone, attacking giants' cities, and laying curses that transformed people from giant to human.

"What else can you tell me?"

Silversmith clutched his stick like a safety blanket. "You can't fool me, Chasina. Your grandmother told me all about your crimes, and pretending to care about humans isn't going to change anything."

Chasina circled the tree and leaned her aching body against the bark. She'd survived countless attempted assassinations for over a year: poison, strangling, drowning, and more creative endeavors. Surely she could survive one giant until she stole the Naridi Stone.

Silvery light made patterns on her arms as she climbed the tree, fitting her hands and feet between the bark to anchor herself. The first branch sprouted from the trunk sixty feet above the ground. Silversmith wouldn't have trouble climbing these trees once he transformed into a giant, and the knowledge made Chasina shudder.

Sweat dribbled down Chasina's back as she reached the first high branch. It was thicker than the medicine hut and wide enough for

Chasina to roll over twice without falling. The roots were far, far away, and if she fell, she would burst against the ground like rotten fruit.

Chasina spotted Silversmith in the tree roots, still awake. She couldn't interrogate him until he fell asleep, so she rested against the trunk. When she checked on him ten minutes later, he was missing.

The last thing she needed was for a wild animal to have eaten Silversmith before he took her to the Naridi Stone.

Chasina ran to the trunk and started climbing to the ground. Halfway down the tree, she saw Silversmith lurking around the roots, using his walking stick to move. Starlight reflected from the knife in his hand.

He must think she'd fallen asleep in the roots.

Chasina froze, the dried mud on her clothes camouflaging her against the tree. She waited for Silversmith to return to his sleeping area and then climbed to the ground. Peering around the tree, she watched Silversmith fall asleep and carefully approached him. She drew a spara leaf from her satchel, gently parted Silversmith's lips, and squeezed the sap into his mouth.

Silversmith jerked, his eyelids fluttering open, but she pinched his nose and forced him to swallow before he realized what was happening. He sagged as the spara crawled up his throat and wrapped loving arms around his mind.

Using her thumb, Chasina wiped the corner of Silversmith's mouth where a stray droplet of spara sap winked in the moonlight. Feeding him spara sap worked faster than absorption through wounds, but it had the unhappy side-effect of rotting his teeth over a long period.

Unhappy for some people. He was welcome to all the rotted stumps in the world as far as she was concerned.

"Silversmith? Can you hear me?" she asked.

Silversmith mumbled incoherently. A happy smile drooped on his lips.

Chasina tapped his hand. "How long until you turn back into a giant?"

"I don't know. Any day."

Silversmith's chances of successfully killing her were significantly higher as a giant. She needed to addict him to spara before that happened.

"How often do you turn into a human?"

"Three or four times a year, or sometimes more. I never know."

"Why do you need the Naridi Stone?"

"I'm trading it to find the Vault of Eternal Sleep."

"Who are you trading it to?"

"A woman named Bemea. She says she knows where to find the Vault, but she wants the Naridi Stone in exchange for a map to the Vault. I'm supposed to meet her in the Watchhills after I steal it."

Why did Silversmith want to find the Vault in the first place? Silversmith kept mentioning something about a hero—no, Hero, as though it was someone's title.

"Something about the Hero?" Chasina asked and received a confused groan in reply. If she didn't ask straightforward questions, spara users got lost in meandering thoughts and could not form an answer.

"Is the Hero inside the Vault of Eternal Sleep?"

"Yes."

"Wouldn't your leader already have traded the Naridi Stone to find your Hero?"

Silversmith rolled his head to one side. "Lord Kemer believes my mission is futile. I asked him to give me the Naridi Stone so I could trade it and find the Hero, but Lord Kemer thinks it's too dangerous to let the Naridi Stone out of his tower vault and risk it falling into the wrong hands. But you know what I think? I think he might be a heretic. He doesn't believe in the Hero, so he won't trade the Naridi Stone."

Silversmith wanted to trade the Naridi Stone to find the Hero, who, judging from his name, would save giants from something. But what did giants need to be saved from? The Undying? The Undying were destroying giants' cities, and destroyed cities certainly called for a Hero.

"Where is the Naridi Stone being kept?" she asked.

Silversmith clapped his tongue around the inside of his mouth and shivered, tucking himself deeper into the crevice between tree roots. He was falling asleep.

Chasina snapped her fingers in his face. "Silversmith, wake up. Tell me where to find the Naridi Stone."

But it was too late. The spara sap had finished squeezing Silversmith's mind and was busy sinking into it, dragging him into a deep sleep.

Chasina settled cross-legged across from Silversmith and studied his face. Fully relaxed, he looked younger. Vulnerable. Like she could stab him in the throat and he wouldn't defend himself.

No wonder he needed a Hero.

Chapter Fourteen

Chasina awoke before Silversmith the next day. She used the scant few minutes to check the spara stashed in her satchel. She had four leaves remaining. She would have packed more leaves if she had known how slowly the spara would absorb into Silversmith's body.

Silversmith cracked open one eye. "Human."

"I am," Chasina said. "And you are not. The sky is blue. Your hair is disgustingly greasy. Any other observations?"

"You weren't here last night when I needed you."

"I was stretching my legs. What exactly did you need me for that couldn't wait until daylight?"

Silversmith took several seconds to reply, and when Chasina looked inquisitively up at him, he hunched sullenly.

"Never mind. It can wait. Please help me stand?"

"The walking stick didn't work?"

He winced. "Definitely not as well as I had hoped. Maybe I will try it again later."

Chasina changed Silversmith's dressing, wringing spara sap onto the fresh bandage before wrapping it around his wound. She helped him stand, grimacing because he seemed heavier than yesterday. Was he pushing down on her shoulders? Sweet Naridi roses, he was.

Silversmith gave her a side-long glance like he didn't know why she struggled to support him. "We have a lot of ground to cover before reaching the stone bridge. You're not too tired, are you? Because I saw a snake's den nearby. They kill rather painlessly if you're interested." Silversmith's tone was part hopeful, part helpful, and his face fell when Chasina politely declined.

Chasina looked behind them. She'd managed to carry Silversmith approximately twenty feet. If he kept punishing her, they wouldn't make it a mile.

"There is the alternative," Silversmith said. "Humans never last long in Maelenthra, and some of the deaths are downright disturbing. I've seen people torture butterflies with more empathy. You don't want that to happen to you, do you?"

Chasina twisted gracefully to one side and sent Silversmith stumbling face-first into a rock. She bent double, catching her breath while Silversmith peeled himself from the rock.

"Sorry, that was an accident," Chasina said and helped Silversmith stand. "You were talking about a Hero while Gran was healing you. Did he save a lot of people?"

"He saved everyone. The Hero is the greatest magician who ever lived, and one day, he will return and destroy the Undying."

"Do you think the Hero would suggest that I feed myself to a snake?"

"He probably would have purged your repulsive presence from the Earth seconds after learning the extent of your crimes." Silversmith sighed. "Unfortunately, I am not him."

The weight on her shoulders returned to normal.

Silversmith's stride loosened later in the day and allowed him to carry more of his own weight. Sometimes, his gaze lingered thoughtfully on bird nests and animal dens, but he didn't try killing her.

Evening soon clothed Brundar with shadows. The sun hung low in the sky, painting the back of Chasina's legs with sweat as she clawed her way up a ravine with Silversmith in tow. She paused when the ground began trembling, and then she dragged Silversmith onto a ledge and pressed her cheek against the dirt.

She recognized the steady vibrations caused by walking giants. Six? Seven? Dirt squished beneath her fingernails as she quickly crawled up the ravine and poked her head above the ridge.

The trees thinned in a peninsula of land surrounded by the steep ravine. The stone bridge started on the other side of the peninsula, and according to Silversmith, it spanned a ravine that would take them over a week to circle.

A horde of male, female, and young giants moved steadily into the peninsula. Everyone carried packs that rattled with tools, cookware, and food. Many of the refugees hefted objects that had no place in a forest: basket cradles, panes of stained glass, and even a table suspended between three giantesses.

Silversmith appeared beside Chasina, and she glanced pointedly at his injured thigh. Earlier, it had 'throbbed' too much for him to climb unaided.

"No more problems climbing the ravine?" she asked.

He ignored her observation. "Those are the refugees from District Three."

Chasina lost count of them at one hundred. "Whoever they're running from didn't do an outstanding job of killing everyone."

Silversmith thrust his head in her face. "We do not speak disrespectfully of anyone who survives the Undying. Those brave people are the only survivors from District Three after the Undying attacked it."

There was something almost respectable about the Undyings'

bloodthirstiness. They cursed and murdered humans and giants alike without bias. In contrast, how many of the 'brave' refugees had killed a helpless human in the last week? Giants regularly destroyed human villages but saw the destruction of their own cities as violent attacks and the survivors as heroes.

If Silversmith had any empathy for human struggles, he wouldn't praise these refugees. He'd obviously never watched a giant smash his village.

Physically, Silversmith was a human. The similarities ended there.

"How did you know the refugees would be here?" Chasina asked.

Silversmith relaxed. "We were supposed to escort them after finding the poachers. I knew the route they were taking through Brundar, but I'd hoped they had either already passed the stone bridge or were far behind us."

The horde finished gathering in the peninsula, settling around the stone bridge. The refugees loosened their packs and assembled wood for fires.

"Sweet Naridi roses. We have to cross the bridge before they start the fires. We'll asphyxiate from the smoke." Chasina started to climb onto the peninsula, but Silversmith gripped her elbow.

"We are in the forest," he said. "How in the Hero's name do you think we would even come close to dying from the smoke?"

"... Fire is dangerous."

"It's not the only thing that could get us killed out here. Two humans cannot sneak through a camp of over a hundred giants without dying."

Heat rushed up Chasina's spine and glowed like embers in her face. They were not going to stay here for the fires. *No. Way.*

"We are going to climb to the top of the ridge. You will follow me through the camp on your newly healed legs, and we will cross the stone bridge before sundown. Understand?" Chasina asked.

Silversmith's chin dropped, creating a triangle with his sloped shoulders. "I think it would be smarter to wait until nighttime when everyone is sleeping."

Chasina gripped his chin. "I don't care what you think. Are you ready?"

Silversmith used one trembling hand to peel her fingers from his face. "I can walk by myself, for the most part, so I don't have to obey a criminal. I don't even have to tolerate your presence." He gripped her wrist. "Throw yourself off the ravine. Aim for the sharp rocks. Do it while I'm not watching."

Silver magic seized every muscle in Chasina's body. She did not move, so the magic punished her. She dropped to the ground and clutched her knees, screaming freely. Her thoughts dissolved into silver threads whirling around her mind, tearing chunks from the soft lining of her skull.

Fighting to her feet, she jumped onto Silversmith's back. "If I jump, you're coming with me." Chasina kicked his wounded thigh.

Silversmith dropped to his knees, squealing. "Let go. Stop kicking me."

Silver magic was already eating her organs, so the new commands added nothing to the pain. She felt nothing when Silversmith landed a blow to her head, but her muscles relaxed anyway. She fell from his back.

Without an anchor, her body moved inexorably toward the ravine's edge. She didn't want to move, but she could no longer endure the agony.

I need the Naridi Stone to go home.

I need to go home.

I need.

A clammy hand touched Chasina's arm. "Don't jump off the ravine."

Instantly, the magical agony receded. Chasina touched her chest and found a steady heartbeat. Her body functioned completely normally, right down to her aches from bearing Silversmith's weight.

Silversmith had hinted all day that she should end her suffering by feeding herself to wildlife. Then he tried to force her to commit suicide, only to save her at the last second.

It was terribly confusing.

Chasina drew her knife and held it to her throat, staring at Silversmith. "Ask me to slit my throat."

"What?"

"Either you want me dead, or you want me alive. I'm giving you a chance right now to decide. If we're going to be together for the foreseeable future, I need to know where we stand. Live or die?"

Silversmith furrowed his brow. "I heard you talking about going home while you were delirious. Exiles do not deserve a home."

Chasina kept the knife steady at her throat. "I deserve a home. People just haven't realized it yet."

Silversmith smothered Chasina's free hand in something deceptively like a handshake. "Tell me the truth: did you deserve to be kicked out of the village?"

Silver light flowed into Chasina's mouth. It tasted like snow and metallic water.

"What did you do to me?" Chasina asked.

"I commanded you to tell the truth."

"I did not deserve exile."

The silver magic in her heated until it felt like molten metal in her mouth. Something like terror spawned in Chasina's chest, layers and layers peeling away to reveal the truth.

"I made decisions that made people miserable, but I regret nothing. I would not change a single decision I made for Tarrken."

The silver light returned to Chasina's spine.

Silversmith released her hand. "You can live, but only because I don't have the courage to kill you."

Silversmith turned on his heel and walked away.

"I have done nothing wrong!" Chasina shouted at Silversmith's back.

Chasina sheathed Da's knife and laced her hands together until they stopped shaking. Her exile and Silversmith's disgust did not matter. Stealing the Naridi Stone mattered. As long as she came home with a gift, everyone would love her.

Love me. The words crooned softly in Chasina's ears, and she repeated them until they were stronger and truer than her magical confession.

At least she had learned one useful thing: she was free to lie as long as she couldn't taste Silversmith's magic.

How did she know?

The last thing she said to Silversmith was a lie.

Chapter Fifteen

C hasina climbed up the ravine and found a ledge away from Silversmith. Several flickering fires cast weird shadows on the trees in the peninsula above her. Smoke tendrils curled above her head.

Chasina clutched Da's knife in both hands. She pressed her face against the dirt, blocking out the smell of smoke. Eventually, the fires quieted, and the orange glow died. Snores rattled the overhead trees.

Silversmith joined Chasina on her ledge. "We should probably go now."

Chasina climbed onto the peninsula. She took shallow breaths as they navigated between sleeping giants, just in case the smoke hadn't completely dissipated.

A nearby giantess awakened. The giantess squinted in their direction and began patting the ground.

Chasina pulled Silversmith to the ground and whispered in his ear. "Disguise us with magic."

"I can't access my magic as a human, so I cannot cast an illusion," Silversmith said. After a moment, he touched the back of her neck.

"You are my magical vessel. Maybe I can use the magic inside of you to cast an illusion and hide us from that woman."

Silver light rose inside of Chasina. The magic rushed through her body, collecting where Silversmith touched the back of her neck. He tapped her neck, and the magic rippled like a pool of water.

Magic lived inside Chaisna, but it responded only to Silversmith. The sensation made her skin crawl.

Chasina batted Silversmith's hand away. "I have a better idea. Follow me."

The shadows layering the ground provided cover as Chasina crawled to the nearest sleeping giant. She tucked herself beneath the giant's half-curled hand. Silversmith joined Chasina. Bits of him stuck out, but hopefully, the giantess wouldn't notice it in the darkness.

The giantess patted the ground nearby, sending vibrations through the dirt. She searched the area around Chasina's hiding place and then moved back to her sleeping space.

Chasina waited ten minutes before crawling from beneath the giant's hand. She motioned for Silversmith to lead the way and followed him around the sleeping giants and across the stone bridge.

They found a thick tree and settled in its roots for the night. Silversmith fell asleep immediately, and Chasina squeezed spara sap into his mouth and discarded the leaf.

He instantly drooped into a trance, proof of the addiction growing within him.

"Where are we going?" Chasina asked.

"Kavalu, the Thirteenth District."

"Is that where the Naridi Stone is?"

"It's in Shilist Castle, just outside Kavalu. Lord Kemer keeps it in his vault tower."

A twig snapped nearby. The unexpected stimuli startled Silversmith from the trance, and he looked wildly around the woods.

"What was that? Was I sleeping? What are you doing?"

She showed her empty hands. "Nothing. Did you hear that noise?"

Chasina peeked above the tree root and scanned the area. A giant dressed in a white robe staggered toward the stone bridge. Black circles embroidered his robe, and a hood covered his face. Blood seeped from a wound just beneath the giant's ribs, staining his embroidered robe deep crimson.

The embroidered robe fluttered in the wind, catching around the giant's legs as he crossed the bridge toward the refugees. He bent double, clutching his injury.

Silversmith tracked the wounded giant, lips quivering. "Duck."

"He can't see us."

Silversmith dragged Chasina into the nook beside him, where steady vibrations shook the hard bones in her pelvis.

"Who is that giant in the embroidered robe?" Chasina asked. Silversmith drew both knees to his chest and shook his head mutely.

"You don't know? Or you can't say?" she grabbed his chin, surprised at the tension stored in his face. "One word. Tell me its name."

"Undying."

One of the giants who had stolen the Naridi Stone and terrorized giants' cities? The refugees might stampede. In that case, she and Silversmith needed a safer hiding place.

Slapping away Silversmith's hand, Chasina climbed the tree root again and saw the Undying exiting the refugee camp.

The Undying moved smoothly, unlike his pained staggering five minutes ago. He opened his robe to sheathe his knife, revealing unbroken skin. No wound. Somehow, the Undying had healed himself inside the refugee camp.

The Undying disappeared into the forest.

Even skilled herbwomen could not outright heal wounds, but somehow, Undying giants could heal themselves completely.

Chasina skidded down the tree root and crouched next to Silversmith. "The Undying walked into the camp with a horrific wound, and he walked out completely healed. Did he make a sacrifice? Drink someone's blood?"

Silversmith took a deep, shivering breath. "The Undying got what he wanted in the refugee camp, so he won't be coming back." Silversmith closed his eyes and sank into himself.

An Undying near Kavalu meant the monsters were preparing to attack the city. Even though she wished them luck, it could interfere with finding and stealing the Naridi Stone. She needed to know more about them.

"I killed your soldier. If you tell me about the Undying, if their weaknesses are any different from normal giants, I can kill them, too. Then you wouldn't have to be scared."

A muscle twitched in Silversmith's cheek.

"Pretending to be asleep is childish," Chasina said.

Silversmith's calloused hand flashed out and gripped her arm. "Go to sleep."

Chasina instantly yielded to her exhaustion, falling asleep before incurring magical punishment.

Chapter Sixteen

Chasina awoke to the sound of a screaming giant. A chorus of screams joined the single voice, shaking the leaves. The screams came from the refugee camp, doubtless something to do with the Undying last night. *One dead body? Two? A horrible, horrific mess?*

She blinked and noticed Silversmith sitting nearby, his throat bobbing as the refugees' screaming grew louder.

Silversmith touched Chasina's arm. "Be fully awake."

Chasina sat up and growled at Silversmith. "Why did you tell me to go to sleep? I was going to stand guard so no one killed us in our sleep."

"We have to run. And it could have happened, anyway, because it's not like you could have stopped Brundar's animals from eating us."

Chasina jumped to her feet and helped Silversmith jog. "I was going to keep us safe if that Undying returned and *this* happened, thank you very much. I take it they found a dead body."

"Ten of them. A few minutes ago."

"Ten? Busy night."

A sheen of sweat already covered his face from the effort of moving his wounded leg. "The Undying enjoy their worship."

"So, he sacrificed ten people?" she asked quietly, sensing an answer from Silversmith. Maybe the morning light gave him courage.

Silversmith swallowed hard. "The Hero killed their leader centuries ago, right before he committed himself to the Vault of Eternal Sleep. The Undying hunt giants to avenge their fallen leader. In their minds, every giant who dies is a victory against the Hero."

"And that's why they attack cities."

"Yes. The Undying have increased their war against giants in the last few years and conquered eleven of our thirteen Districts."

"Don't you have armies to stop them?"

"We do, but they are not effective against the Undying. Undying are extremely powerful magicians. They kill giants by draining their magical auras, which heals the Undying and adds years to their lives. It's how they maintain their immortality. In a group, the Undying kill twenty soldiers at a time until they deplete any army sent against them."

"So, how did the refugees escape?" Chasina asked.

A bead of sweat rolled down Silversmith's temple. "The Undying are not powerful enough to trap people inside a city. They lock the gates and kill as many people as possible, but many refugees escape over the walls."

"How can I kill an Undying?"

"They have the same weaknesses as any mortal. Their advantages lie in powerful magic and centuries of fighting experience."

No wonder the Undying had taken the Naridi Stone so easily from humankind. A group of Undying killed twenty giants at once, laughably outmatching a human village armed with magic. After Chasina brought the Naridi Stone home, she would take serious measures to protect it.

However, she needed to steal the Naridi Stone before worrying about defending it, which meant she needed to know how Silversmith planned to steal it. A fifth exposure to spara sap should give her the answers she needed.

The trees thinned around Chasina and Silversmith, replaced with thick brush. Fist-sized insects dropped on Chasina's shoulders as she and Silversmith beat a path through the undergrowth. They parted the brush, and golden sunlight hit Chasina in the face.

Brundar was behind them. Ahead of them, endless hills spanned the earth. Hilltops blocked the sky, feathered with grass taller than Chasina.

A chunk of ice settled in Chasina's stomach. Scavenging in Brundar, a forest where people considered weasels deadly, should have prepared her to exit Brundar and find more monstrosities.

Even the flowers vining across the hills had blossoms bigger than her face, and that was nothing compared to the citadel nestled in the valley below them.

Stone walls three hundred feet tall protected the city on the east and west, built directly into the hillsides. Several steeples rose above the sturdy timber buildings crowding the streets. The timber buildings stacked on top of each other like enormous wooden blocks painted in every color from blackberry to sunshine yellow.

"Kavalu, the Thirteenth District," Silversmith said. "See the castle? I was stationed there for three years. That's where they keep the Naridi Stone."

Soldiers patrolled a massive fortress dominating a hill to the north. A circular outer wall made the fortress look like a crown, and behind the circular walls, secondary rectangular walls rose twice as high. The last walls, the inner ones, stood behind the secondary walls. Round towers jutted from deep inside the castle like ancient dark trees wreathed with heavy crenelation.

82

Chasina steadied herself. She hadn't counted on Kavalu to make her feel so small, but she needed to get over it and learn Silversmith's plan.

Chasina leaned into her raspy voice to disguise any lingering awe. "Do you honestly think you're going to make it inside?"

Silversmith grimaced. "I'm recruiting help."

"Who? And what is your plan?"

"None of your business."

Chasina dipped her hand inside her satchel and found two remaining spara leaves. She squeezed spara sap into Silversmith's mouth, and he coughed, swallowing and sinking to his knees.

Chasina tipped his chin. "What is your plan to steal the Naridi Stone?"

He smiled blissfully. "I need my sister's help to find a secret passage into the castle, and I need my mentor's help to defeat the soldiers guarding the Naridi Stone."

Chasina frowned. She didn't like the idea of other giants meddling in the heist. It would be challenging enough to control Silversmith without worrying about managing two other giants.

"Can you steal the Naridi Stone without their help?" Chasina asked.

"Without their help, I will die before making it inside the castle."

Chasina left Silversmith drooling happily on the ground and crossed to the hill's edge, studying the castle. She needed to piggyback on Silversmith's plan. Allow him to infiltrate the castle and steal the Naridi Stone, and then steal it from him afterward.

She had addicted Silversmith to spara sap. One spara leaf was enough to put him into a trance even after transforming into a giant. Altogether, it created a neat little plan with three simple steps.

Step One: Allow Silversmith to steal the Naridi Stone.

Step Two: Drug Silversmith with her last spara leaf and take the Naridi Stone.

Step Three: Use the Naridi Stone's magic to break her curse and escape before Silversmith awakes.

Chasina only had one spara leaf, and it only worked on established addicts. That meant anyone who joined Silversmith's team wouldn't be affected by the spara leaf, and they'd kill her before she escaped with the Naridi Stone.

Since Silversmith couldn't steal the Naridi Stone without help from other giants, she altered the plan: allow Silversmith to recruit help and then discard them after they served their purpose.

Silversmith spoke unsteadily. "What did you do to me?"

Chasina whirled and saw Silversmith flickering into consciousness, his gaze focused on the spara leaf in Chasina's hand.

"Spara leaves? I can't believe anyone would do that to another person," Silversmith panted, sweat glistening on his brow.

What had awakened him from the trance? An overdose? Chasina squinted from afar, checking his eyeballs for the green tendrils that indicated an overdose. They were crisp, clear, and wide with incredulous anger.

Silversmith launched himself from the ground, the spara sap deadening any pain he felt from his wound. He grabbed Chasina's hand.

"Let me go."

He snarled. "Make me."

Silver aura engulfed his body like a cocoon. He collapsed, stifling screams as his limbs stretched and grew, transforming him into a giant.

Chasina dug in her heels. She yanked her arm free, but he caught her leg. His fingers stretched until they formed a dome that squished her into a ball.

Chasina's knees jutted against her chin. She couldn't take full breaths. Pain pinched her chest, and her nostrils flexed.

She curled against the dirt and covered her head. Smoke seeped through the cracks overhead, between the slats of her crushed home. Embers fell in her hair and sizzled against the wetness on her face.

When was Da coming back?

A deep voice rumbled nearby. It was not Da's voice.

Chapter Seventeen

Silversmith contemplated her with a curled lip. His clothes had grown with him, and his sleeve tightened around the knife strapped to his arm.

His inanimate possessions must grow and shrink with him during his transformations.

"Tell me how often you gave me spara sap," Silversmith said, wording his question as a command.

Silver light sparked within Chasina. "Every time I changed your bandage, and three times orally."

Silversmith gasped. They both knew it was enough to transform him into an addict. The withdrawals would begin in the next few hours if he didn't indulge the addiction.

Silversmith pressed Chasina belly-first against the ground. He drew the knife hidden in his sleeve and rested the blade on Chasina's neck.

Silversmith wouldn't kill her. She'd already gifted him the opportunity, and he'd chosen to keep her alive.

He might want to kill her, but he didn't have the guts to do it.

After a moment, Silversmith sheathed his knife and lifted Chasina from the ground. From wrist to fingertips, his hand was as tall as Chasina. He made a fist around her waist, leaving her head and shoulders poking above his hand and her legs dangling below it. He limped down the hill and joined the crowd of giants moving toward Kavalu.

Wagons trundled through Kavalu's gate, carrying enough grain to feed everyone in Tarrken until they died. The wagons were pulled by giant-sized, four-legged creatures that Chasina had seen only twice: horses. Their barrel chests were thicker than Brundar's trees, and their hooves left tracks half the size of human huts.

Silversmith entered Kavalu between the two stone towers that formed a gate. A wide street stretched in front of them, skinny wooden buildings on either side of the road rising four stories into the sky, each story a hundred feet tall. The skinny buildings had wooden shutters that folded into tables to show wares for sale, and craftsmen behind the tables braided leather, pounded metal, or fashioned weapons.

Silversmith stumbled on the uneven cobblestones and caught himself on a wooden table spread with tooled knives. He pushed away from the blacksmith's shop and supported himself on the next shopkeeper's table and the next, moving down the street until he stopped at one particular shop.

Chasina inhaled deeply, breathing the familiar sweet and musty herbs. This must be the giants' equivalent of an herbwoman.

Stone bowls filled with opaque liquid haphazardly dotted the floor, table, and shelves, and a cauldron bubbled over the fire, orange fumes lacing the air. Earthworms poked from a jar of dirt on the table.

"Surgeon," Silversmith called. "I need help."

A thin man with a drooping mustache dashed from the back of his shop and dragged Silversmith inside. He seated Silversmith on a stool next to a table and examined Silversmith's empty hand.

The surgeon licked Silversmith's palm and traced the veins. "Your excess blood is unbalancing your humors, so I'll have to bleed you."

Silversmith shivered when the surgeon produced a glass bowl and began heating it over the fire. "My humors are fine. I just need some yaira paste because I'm craving spara sap."

The surgeon set down the bowl. "You're a Ramerian scout?"

"Army scout."

"Out in the field for long periods, you get wounded, you need to numb the pain…" the surgeon ran a finger along his eyebrow. "It happens. Spara is highly addictive."

"It is. Incredibly so," Silversmith said, squeezing Chasina. Her ribs creaked.

The surgeon scooped soil into an empty jar and added other ingredients, including a lock of hair. His mustache flopped as he whisked the concoction.

The surgeon sealed the jar and gave it to Silversmith. "The paste reduces the craving, but it won't eradicate it, and it cannot lessen the withdrawal symptoms."

Silversmith paid the surgeon and wobbled back into the crowd. He passed a few buildings and tripped several times before reaching a tavern.

An overhead sign smacked against wooden slats. It depicted a colorful bird with its beak lodged in the side of a frothing tankard.

The tavern's heavy door creaked when Silversmith pushed it open. Empty tables crowded the interior. A giantess occupied a table at the rear, where she wrote in a ledger. A small stack of coins stood on one side of the ledger. A row of ten humans stood on the other side, heads bowed, hands loose.

The giantess tapped one human on the head. "Stupid human licenses. How am I going to get rid of you? Get out of my sight."

All ten humans shimmied down the table leg and disappeared into a crack in the wall.

Silversmith approached the giantess. "You wouldn't have such a hard time selling humans if you did it legally, Muriel."

Muriel's soft ivory dress rippled as she jumped to her feet and hugged Silversmith. "Vorce, what are you doing? The town criers said you'd been killed by poachers."

Although she was shorter than Silversmith, Muriel had the same straight nose and sharp chin framed with soft dark hair. Wasn't there some sort of natural law that made it illegal for giants to have twins?

"You're not wearing mourning clothes," Silversmith said and collapsed on the bench across from Muriel.

"I burned the appropriate number of flowers if that's what you're asking. Grief does not rule my life. Business goes on, Brother."

Silversmith regarded the ledger disdainfully. "I see that Lord Kemer's laws about licenses to hunt and sell humans haven't crimped your business. You know he made those laws for a reason, right? Without regulating how many humans we catch and from which villages, the human population would be wiped out in months. You need to buy from licensed hunters who register their catches, and you need a license to sell humans."

Muriel sniffed. "Very noble of you. Is your human registered? Did you catch her, trot down to the castle, and report which village she's from? No. Because more than likely, Lord Kemer would have taken her from you on some pretense of controlling the market."

Giants treated humans like wild animals, and catching too many of them would deplete resources. According to giants, the most immoral part of the process was illegally trapping humans. As though legally capturing humans made murder and enslavement perfectly acceptable.

"Do you know where I can find Cormac? I need his help," Silversmith said.

Muriel brushed a lock of hair behind her ear and pushed the ledger aside. "He'll be at the cathedral this time of day. He's gotten pious since you refused to take the Ramerian test, always volunteering to guard the priests. Cormac will love to hear how you survived the poachers. Did you kill anyone?"

"No, I had some help escaping. I was lucky." Silversmith shrugged and almost sent Chasina toppling to the table. Lucky? That's what he called it when she dragged his half-dead carcass through Brundar and used her own sleeves to bind his wound?

"Lucky?" Muriel wagged a finger at Chasina. "Does it have anything to do with why you suddenly own a human?"

"Only if it's bad luck. She addicted me to spara sap. I'm seeing double right now and feeling happy despite where I am," Silversmith said, gesturing at the tavern.

Muriel leaned across the table, pooching her lower lip as she contemplated Chasina. "She's an ugly little thing. Are you sure she's smart enough to drug you? I would have snapped her neck. Why didn't you kill her?"

Silversmith did not answer.

Muriel huffed and helped Silversmith stand. "The service will start soon, but we might find Cormac before it begins."

Chasina steadied herself with one hand on Silversmith's shoulder as they left the tavern and squeezed into the throngs of giants. Chasina could easily fit all of Tarrken's winding paths and huts in Kavalu's streets, but the streets were still too skinny for more than three giants to walk abreast. Crowds skinned past each other with smiled apologies. Chunks floated in buckets of rancid water, and gutters funneled filth down both sides of the street.

Chasina shied closer to Silversmith's neck when he turned a corner, avoiding collision with a low building whose beams jutted over the street. She brushed his ear, and he twitched reflexively. Uneven cobblestone paved an open courtyard where a massive cathedral rose above the other buildings. It was at least half a mile tall. Spires arched from the stone building, painted brilliant blue, gold, and green.

Incense floated through the cathedral's open doors and coated Chasina's tongue. She covered her nose as Silversmith shuffled through the jostling crowd. Two groups of barefoot pilgrims chanted prayers as they approached the peaked doors.

A young giant with a little scar on his right hand ran up to Muriel and held out a purse.

"See what I stole!" he said proudly. He looked about ten years old.

Muriel snatched one of his hands. "Chewing your nails, again? What did I tell you about that? The ragged edges catch on purses, Oscar. And once you get caught, it's the common pits or worse."

"You'd come to save me."

Muriel ruffled his hair, spun him around, and lightly smacked his bottom. "Not the point, Oscar. The trick is to never get caught, isn't it? Now, go on. Good luck."

Oscar dashed into the crowd, expertly bumping into people and stealing their purses.

"I see you've adopted another street urchin," Silversmith said.

"He'll be the best pickpocket in Kavalu if he learns to stop chewing his nails. Come on, Cormac will be inside the cathedral."

Suddenly, the crowd stopped moving. It seized in place, vibrating with eagerness as a voice hailed them.

"Make way for Lord Kemer!"

Chapter Eighteen

A group of brightly dressed noblemen trailed behind a single man making his way to the doors. A forked beard poked from his hood, and blue-gold eyes sparkled like the sapphires embroidered on his cloak.

Lord Kemer raised a hand to the crowd. "Hero bless you."

Silversmith ducked as Kemer's gaze swept over the assembled giants. Chasina lurched forward, digging her fingers into Silversmith's shoulder until she regained her balance.

Muriel struggled beneath Silversmith's weight. "What in the Hero's name are you doing?"

"If Lord Kemer sees me alive, he'll know I deserted my unit and execute me," Silversmith whispered. "He will put my head on a pike. It's better if he thinks I'm dead."

"Maybe you shouldn't have abandoned them."

Chasina waited for Silversmith to tell Muriel that his curse had transformed him into a human and prevented him from helping his soldiers.

Silversmith remained silent.

Interesting. Muriel doesn't know about his curse. Does anyone else know besides me? Chasina doubted it. If Silversmith kept his curse a secret from his family, he wasn't likely to tell anyone else. In a world where giants viewed humans as lesser animals, Silversmith might become a target if people learned of his curse.

Could she use that secret against him? Probably not. Silversmith had commanded her to keep his curse a secret, and even if she exposed him, no one would believe her. One way or another, Silversmith's secret was safe with Chasina.

Lord Kemer and his entourage entered the cathedral, allowing the crowd to move again. The pilgrims resumed chanting, and the regular attendees filed through the doors.

An enormous gold statue of the Hero stood on a spire above the cathedral's main doors, stretching out his hand to bless the giants passing through the doors.

Silversmith and Muriel stood and joined the attendees entering the cathedral. Silversmith bowed his head as he passed through the doors.

The cathedral's interior was shaped like a cross. A long, east-west chamber stretched ahead of them. A word chiseled on a stone arch labeled the east-west chamber as the Nave. An unlabeled hall crossed the Nave from north to south, creating the cross.

While the pilgrims and attendees entered the Nave, Silversmith and Muriel entered a small offshoot corridor. It led downstairs.

"What are we doing here? Cormac is a veteran Ramerian scout," Muriel said impatiently.

"I know," Silversmith said.

"Then you should know that Cormac will be guarding the priest. The priest is in the Sacristy, preparing for the service, donning his vestments and other baubles."

"The only other way to the Sacristy is through the Nave and the Quire," Silversmith said, pointing at the ceiling where vibrations from a thousand feet made the dust shake free. "Do you think we'd make it through the crowd in time?"

Muriel conjured a light blue magical sphere and illuminated the lonely corridor. They turned several more corners before finding an ornately carved door.

Silversmith knocked on the door. No one answered.

Muriel cracked the door and poked her head inside while Silversmith repeatedly slapped her arm.

"You can't behold a Sacristy without a blessing," Silversmith said. "Neither of us is worthy of looking inside. Just shut the door, Muriel. Please!"

Muriel shut the door, and they retraced their path to the main entrance and entered the Nave.

Stone arches rose above both sides of the room and met in graceful peaks overhead. Sculptures of the Hero were carved between arches, and pilgrims knelt before stained glass windows depicting the Hero as a golden giant in various poses: wielding a sword, blessing a crowd, and melting a shadowy figure with sunlight.

Town criers flanked Lord Kemer at the head of the Nave, where he stood in front of a stone door.

"Hero bless you," Lord Kemer said as he dropped his jeweled hood. "Our prayers are with the refugees from District Two today. Every generous donation for their food and clothing cares for the Hero's followers."

Muriel hissed in her brother's ear. "What would really help the refugees is our army liberating Districts from the Undying."

"Lord Kemer is the only reason those refugees have a place to run to after escaping their city," Silversmith said. "It's easier for an army to fight the Undying from a defensible position than on a battlefield. That's why we keep the army stationed in Shilist Castle."

"The Lord isn't sheltering refugees outside the city's walls. He's locking them up like prisoners. I've tried to smuggle some of my goods into the refugee camp, and even I can't sneak inside."

Muriel bumped two passing noblemen, stealing their purses in quick succession. Once they left, she held up two leather purses jingling with coins.

Silversmith grabbed the purses and pushed them out of sight. "Please, not in a cathedral, Muriel. It's sacrilegious."

Muriel pulled the purses into plain sight. "What's wrong with stealing? Go on. Say it."

"You know... it's just not something—"

"Nice? Good? Maybe I should have asked before taking them. Would that make you feel better? Last I checked, I'm good at thievery even though it's 'wrong.' You can't even become a Ramerian scout. Until that changes"—she dropped both purses in the collection plate—"stealing feeds people."

Silversmith shuffled to one side, creating a buffer of empty space between the two siblings. "Just let me concentrate on the service."

Lord Kemer stepped back into the crowd, and town criers exited the cathedral, their strong voices raised to impart news to Kavalu.

Twelve acolytes attached a chain to one side of the stone door at the far end of the Nave. They pulled the chain over their shoulders and opened the door. An engraving above the door read, 'Quire.'

Everyone in the Nave moved into the Quire. Silversmith and Muriel found seats on the long oak pews spanning the Quire in rows, stopping at the feet of polished stone steps leading up to an altar.

Muriel poked her brother. "Why do you need to talk to Cormac?"

Silversmith peeked at Muriel from his peripheral vision. "I need his help, and I need your help, too. I found the Vault this time."

"You have a location?"

"Not exactly, but I've found someone named Bemea who says she can tell me where to find it."

Muriel put her hands on her hips. "You're never going to find the Hero, so if you really want to kill the Undying, become a Ramerian scout. Chasing the Hero is a fool's errand."

Bells reverberated through the cathedral and drowned everyone's conversations. When the brassy noise subsided, the hooded priest ascended to the altar. Several people flanked him, weapons visible beneath their robes—probably the veterans who guarded the priests.

The priest placed a small object on the altar.

It sat up.

Chapter Nineteen

The human climbed to his feet, his clean white robe shimmering like milk in the priest's shadow. The priest drew a thin knife from beneath his belted robes and held it across both palms.

"Hero bless you, Number Fourteen."

Chasina stepped backward onto the wooden pew. She slid to the ground and ran beneath the pews. Reaching the wall, she hoisted herself onto the carved friezes that decorated it. Stone scraped against the mud on her hands as she climbed up the wall. She moved quickly, the priest's voice droning in the background, but her muscles burned furiously after a while. If not for a lifetime spent climbing Brundar's massive trees, she would have fallen before nearing the ceiling. She reached an arched doorway and shimmied to the arch's tip, her arms and legs wobbling from exertion.

Sweat dripped from her face as she looked down. Far below, a thousand giants bobbed along with the priest's chanting. Only one of them noticed Chasina crawling on the wall like an insect: Silversmith. He stood beneath the arch where Chasina clung for her life, gesturing frantically for her to come down. His premature wrinkles squeezed into an expression that said, *"Please, please come down."*

Gravity yanked at Chasina's stomach, and she stopped looking down. She'd never been bothered by heights before, but she was so far from the ground that if she fell, there wouldn't be enough left of her body for a giant to lick off the floor.

Using the friezes for handholds, Chasina moved toward the next arch. A single statue decorated each space between the arches and created a pattern of arch, statue, arch.

Chasina reached the nearest statue. She crawled up its golden arm, along its shoulder, and onto the wall beside it. She repeated the pattern of crawling, climbing, and crawling, all the way around the cathedral.

Chasina reached the Hero's statue behind the altar and balanced on its head, which was probably sacrilegious. Far below and across the Quire, Silversmith dove onto his seat on the pew.

Definitely sacrilegious.

The priest raised his hands to the congregation. "Long ago, humankind betrayed the Hero to the Undying, but in return, the wicked Undying cursed all humankind to follow their will. Humans spread lies, spy, sabotage, and obey the Undyings' every command." The priest switched his attention to the human on the altar. "Number Fourteen, like all humans, you were stripped of your name and suffered our righteous wrath, but now your fate changes. Sacrificing your life to the Hero honors him and frees you from the Undyings' curse. You may speak your given name."

The human spoke in a thin voice. "I am Bartholomew, and I am ready to be freed from the Undying's curse."

As soon as Bartholomew fell silent, the priest launched into more nonsense about curses. None of it was true, but at least it explained why giants were so comfortable persecuting humans. They treated humans as justified prey, and now, Bartholomew was about to be

98

sacrificed for those false beliefs.

Chasina judged the distance between the altar and the exit as approximately a mile. Bartholomew needed at least ten minutes to run that distance, but she couldn't supply him with it. She needed to give him five or six minutes to climb down the altar and hide, after which he could escape. She needed to cause a big distraction.

Chasina inched her fingers into the uneven mortar and lifted herself onto the ceiling. She crawled parallel to the faraway floor, hair floating weightless at her shoulders, and wiggled her knife into the mortar holding the mosaic tiles to the ceiling.

The tile came loose, quickly followed by three more tiles that she worked free from the grout. Surprised shouts quickly smothered the sound of stone tiles smashing against the floor.

Dust stuck to the sweat on her face as she slid her knife against more tiles and sent them smashing around the altar. Tight pain curled around Chasina's stomach from the effort of keeping herself suspended from the ceiling.

She readjusted her grip on the mortar and dislodged more tiles. The outraged shouts assured her that the confusion was working.

Palms sweating, slipping on the grout, Chasina crawled back to the Hero's statue and dropped gratefully onto his head. Far below, giants milled like angry ants, touching bloody wounds on their heads and shoulders. They pointed at the ceiling, where a sizable empty spot marred the mosaic.

Chasina smiled. She had completely removed the Hero's right eye. No one wanted a mosaic staring at them with two eyes, right?

"Get the human off the Hero's statue!"

Chasina ducked a magical sphere. It evaporated against the stone statue, and she raised her head to see a veteran glaring at her from below. He rubbed his bloody scalp with one hand and clenched Bartholomew in the other.

Sweet Naridi roses. Chasina searched the crowd and found Silversmith. They locked gazes.

If she threatened to expose Silversmith to Lord Kemer as alive and well, it might pressure Silversmith into rescuing Bartholomew. She couldn't actually expose him because she needed his help stealing the Naridi Stone, but Silversmith didn't know that.

"Everyone, listen to me!" Chasina's guttural voice sawed through the noise, and she repeated herself until a horde of rigid fingers pointed to where she stood on the Hero's outstretched hand. "I have a secret my Master doesn't want Lord Kemer to know. Master, you have five minutes to free Bartholomew before I tell Lord Kemer."

Muriel shot a sphere of light blue magic at Chasina. It missed. Chasina scrambled up the Hero's arm and ducked behind his head.

A rock sailed gracefully over the Hero's neck. Chasina twisted to avoid it and slipped from her perch. She fell. Colors streamed past her, and all her limbs bent backward as she dropped hundreds of feet through the air.

A yellow sphere caught her halfway to the floor. It was transparent, breathable, but just as solid as the statue she'd fallen from. It was a cage. Before Chasina's panic grew from the bubble in her chest, she landed in Lord Kemer's hand, and he absorbed the yellow sphere into his skin.

Lord Kemer crooked his fingers around Chasina. A deep cut slashed across one cheekbone, and the remains of a mosaic tile crumbled around his feet.

Lord Kemer shielded his catch from the advisers crowding around them. "What is your Master's secret?"

Chasina resisted the urge to touch the dried mud that hid the silver mark on her hand. If Lord Kemer saw it, he'd realize that Silversmith was alive and hunt him down.

Chasina did not answer, and the advisers simultaneously leaned forward and swatted the air above her head.

"Kill her for defiling our cathedral. The statue!"

"The mosaic!"

"My Lord, if you release her, she will run back to her Master."

Lord Kemer snapped his fingers, and the advisers immediately fell away. He turned his back on them.

"I'd rather not resort to torture," Kemer said quietly, his voice only for Chasina. "So if you tell me the secret that's so important, I will kill your Master and send you home to your village."

Lord Kemer was offering to kill a giant and let her go free? What a beautiful opportunity. He must be dumber than most of his brethren.

Chasina pointed at a random giant. "That is my Master. He's a criminal who poaches human villages."

Lord Kemer glanced at the stranger. "You're lying to me."

"You asked for my Master's secret, and I gave it to you," Chasina said, keeping her face slack behind her mask of scars. She didn't meet many people who saw through her lies.

Kemer glanced pointedly at the stranger, who trembled but didn't move. "If he was actually your Master and a criminal, he'd be running right now. Guilty people run. Innocent people just look scared. Tell me the truth."

Apparently, Lord Kemer was smarter than his brethren, not dumber than them. Highly unfortunate. But if she couldn't lie her way to freedom, maybe she could demand Bartholomew's way to safety.

"I want Bartholomew freed," Chasina said.

A shadow passed over Lord Kemer's face. "Once a human volunteers as a sacrifice, his life is forfeit."

"You're the Lord. Free Bartholomew."

Lord Kemer held her close to his mouth. "Just so you know, I love what you did to the Hero's mosaic. Now he can only stare at me with one eye."

Kemer abruptly swung around and approached the altar. The horde of advisers stayed away from the polished stone steps, but Kemer took them in two leaps and gripped a short veteran's shoulder. He was the same veteran holding Bartholomew.

"I have always admired your style of torture," Kemer said. "Since the Quire isn't an appropriate place for it, would you mind taking the human elsewhere and torturing the secret from her?"

The short veteran swept back his bloody hood to reveal thick gray eyebrows highlighting his square face. "Promises and threats are usually empty coming from humans, but I'll have the secret in moments if she isn't lying."

Chasina favored the short veteran with a repulsive smile. "You'd best be creative," she said, tilting her face to show the ugly scars. "I don't have all day to get tortured, and I doubt anything you do to me will tender results."

Lord Kemer handed Chasina to the veteran, who carried her from the Quire and down a narrow set of stairs. They entered a small room with melted candles sitting in niches along the walls. Stonework crawled up the walls and overhead, meeting in the center of the room like eight different plants growing on the walls in sinuous patterns.

The veteran dropped Chasina on the table and lit the candles. Smoke curled from the candlewicks.

Hair shot upright on the nape of Chasina's neck, and she moved away from the nearest smoke tendrils. The veteran drew a knife from beneath his robes and twirled it between his fingers.

Chapter Twenty

C hasina ducked to one side, but the veteran flattened her against the table and forced the air from her lungs. Her face swelled with blood.

The veteran relaxed his grip, allowing Chasina to cough air into her lungs. Her vision blurred, settled, and turned black as he forced the air from her lungs again. Her ribs creaked.

"What is your secret?" the veteran asked.

Smoke permeated the room. It trailed delicate tendrils from shallow niches in the wall, floating thin arms toward Chasina, silently seeking to wrap around her heart and break her mind.

Chasina squeezed her wounded arm, and searing pain shot straight to the center of her mind, clearing the panicked haze.

The veteran rolled Chasina onto her stomach and twisted her head, exposing the scarred half of her face.

"Lovely scars," he said. "I bet you are afraid of fire."

Chasina stiffened but said nothing. She focused on the veteran's blurry form as he crossed to a niche. He grabbed a candle.

"What is your secret?" he asked, calmly stroking the candle with the edge of his knife.

Ash-colored smoke twisted from the flickering candle and writhed through the small room. Unwanted memories rose from the silt of Chasina's memories.

"Nothing," Chasina said.

The veteran tipped the candle and dribbled a single drop of hot tallow onto Chasina's face. Not enough to drown her. Just enough for her world to explode in agony. Hungry pain oozed over her skin, licking the scars like liquid fire. Smoke rushed into her mouth and nose when she cried out, and the room disappeared.

Chasina writhed as fire licked her face. Smoke filled the tiny hole in the ground, and she coughed, unable to breathe.

Sooty spittle dribbled down her chin. "Da, save me!"

Cold water splashed her face, bringing her abruptly from the memories. Gasping, Chasina rolled into a ball around her knife. *It's not real. Da is gone.*

Chasina buried her face in her shoulder until all she smelled was skin and sweat.

The veteran's voice rumbled beneath her skin. "She's yours?"

"She got away from me, Cormac," Silversmith said. "If I had any idea she would interrupt the sacrifice, I wouldn't have brought her."

Cormac?

Silversmith and Muriel stood across from Cormac, the veteran, arguing. Silversmith's eyes were squeezed shut, and Muriel had hooked her arm through his to guide him into the Sacristy.

Evidently, Silversmith could enter the Sacristy so long as he did not view it.

Cormac twirled his knife without bothering to look at it. "She defiled the cathedral, desecrated a mosaic, and attacked a priest. She deserves to have all her limbs cut off and fed to a dog. You understand that, don't you?"

Silversmith did not reply.

Cormac wrung out a wet cloth and dabbed the wound on his head. "Lord Kemer is expecting me to return your slave and tell him all the secrets she sobbed. If I do, he'll know you are alive. He will stick your head on a pike for desertion. Desertion, Vorce. What do you want me to do about that? What are you even doing here?"

"I found the Hero, Cormac."

Cormac froze, the cloth still pressed against his head. "You found him? Where is he?"

"I met a woman called Bemea, and she will tell me where to find the Vault of Eternal Sleep if I give her the Naridi Stone. I need you and Muriel to help me steal it from Kemer's vault tower."

"Did you ask Lord Kemer for the Naridi Stone?"

"He refused and instructed me to tell no one about the conversation." Silversmith pressed his lips together. "I think he's a heretic."

Cormac threw the bloodied cloth onto the table. "Another foolish errand. None of this is real, Silversmith. Bemea is probably trying to take advantage of a devout follower, and Lord Kemer was smart enough to realize it."

"I know I let you down before, Cormac. I know it. I have never been confident in many things, but this time it's real."

"And if it is? You allowed your slave to defile a cathedral. If you can't control one little human, what makes you think you could steal something from Lord Kemer's tower vault?" Cormac wrenched his knife from the wood. "You deserted your unit, Vorce. You left your soldiers to fight and die without you. You're the weakest apprentice I ever trained, and today just proved it more than ever."

Chasina flinched when Cormac scooped her off the table and headed toward the door.

Cormac jerked his head at Muriel. "Muriel, I'll need your help if we want Lord Kemer to believe I tortured information from the human.

Pretend to be her Master." Cormac settled his gaze on Silversmith. "We will lie for you, Vorce, but it's more than you deserve."

Cormac slammed the door shut and escorted Muriel through the narrow corridors. Muriel hung back when they came to the stairway leading into the Quire while Cormac entered.

The Quire was empty, save for Kemer and his bobbing advisers. All the other worshipers mingled in the Nave, staring at the stained glass and stroking the statues.

Lord Kemer crossed his legs, one arm flung across the back of the pew. "What did she sing about?"

"She was lying, Lord Kemer. The cursed little monster wanted to save the human sacrifice and didn't have any secrets to tell."

"Who owns her?"

Cormac whistled.

Muriel entered the Quire and curtsied. "The human is mine, Lord Kemer."

"I don't see her mark," Lord Kemer said. "Is it beneath the mud? Let's see it."

Muriel couldn't show Chasina's mark without revealing Silversmith as a deserter.

Muriel hesitated for the barest second before forcing a smile. "I run a small trade in humans. The human is unmarked because she is for sale."

Lord Kemer relaxed. "Now, everything makes sense. Is it possible that you sell illegally poached humans? That you refuse to register which villages you or your suppliers raid?"

"Of course not, my Lord. I adhere to all of the laws."

"You won't mind if I send the sheriff to your business, do you? Of course not. The sheriff will check your license and search for humans on the premises. Just a formality, of course." Lord Kemer leaned forward an inch and smiled patronizingly. "I'm sure everything is

106

perfectly legal and that I won't have your head on a pike by the end of the week. Carry on, Cormac."

Lord Kemer exited the cathedral, somehow avoiding tripping over the advisers mobbing his steps.

Chasina looked around for Bartholomew, hoping to see him somewhere. She studied the altar.

It was bloodstained.

Chapter Twenty-One

My *heart knows you, and it will not forget.* Chasina had recited the words so many times they were etched in the soft lining of her heart alongside a list of names. One more name crowded beside the others: Bartholomew.

According to Lord Kemer, humans weren't forced to become sacrifices. They volunteered. Since no one was stupid enough to volunteer, giants probably coerced hapless humans like Bartholomew to volunteer. How many human sacrifices happened in this cathedral in a year? A month?

Chasina kissed a rose on her knife. *When I find the Naridi Stone, there will be a reckoning for all these murders.*

Silversmith entered the Quire and took Chasina from Muriel.

Muriel shoved Silversmith. "The sheriff is coming to check my license to sell humans. I don't have a license! What am I supposed to show the sheriff? A blank piece of paper? If he finds a single human on the premises, he will hang me."

Silversmith rubbed his forearm. "I'm so sorry, Muriel. Will you be all right?"

"No. And you can steal the Naridi Stone yourself because I will not help you. All you've ever done your whole life is run and hide. How do I know you wouldn't desert Cormac and me just like you deserted your unit and left them to die?"

"Muriel's right," Cormac said. "We cannot trust you. You're too soft and weak, and allowing your human to defile the cathedral proves it."

Cormac and Muriel exited the cathedral.

Silversmith set Chasina on the back of the pew, and she braced herself for whatever happened next. She had defiled a cathedral, and there were bound to be consequences from a pious giant like Silversmith.

Silversmith gripped the pew ahead of him. "I'm sorry. I never should have brought you here. No human should have to witness another human be sacrificed to our god, and I don't blame you for trying to stop it."

Chasina's jaw dropped. "You're not angry?"

"Just with myself. I don't know how to steal the Naridi Stone without Muriel and Cormac's help."

As much as it galled her, especially after Cormac had tortured her and kept Bartholomew from escaping, Chasina needed to recruit Cormac and Muriel. Silversmith couldn't steal the Naridi Stone without them.

"Let me apologize to your friends," Chasina said. "They will come back to you if I am penitent."

Silversmith studied the one-eyed mosaic overhead. "Chasina, I don't blame you for panicking and trying to save Bartholomew, but I had the distinct impression that your only regret was not burning down the cathedral."

"I can grovel."

Silversmith chuckled sadly. "You. Grovel. I would bet my suspended promotion that you couldn't grovel to save your life. Why are you trying to help me?"

Chasina held out both palms. "It's the least I can do after addicting you to spara."

"Or maybe you're trying to sabotage me." Silversmith put his finger on Chasina's forehead. "Tell me the truth: will you do your best to help me steal the Naridi Stone?"

A familiar metallic taste flooded Chasina's mouth. She planned to help Silversmith steal the Naridi Stone, but she also planned to steal it from him afterward. Would that count as the truth?

"I will," Chasina said, and the silver light left her mouth because it was true. "Your friends are upset because you didn't control me in the cathedral. It will show them you've rectified that mistake if I grovel."

Silversmith grunted, unconvinced. "Cormac will expect you to know all the protocol associated with being a slave. Can you bow?"

For a few critical moments, Chasina's muscles refused to work. These monsters had burned her villages, killed her villagers, and kept them in constant fear every moment of her life.

I can do anything for a few days, even weeks. Chasina bowed.

Silversmith clicked his tongue disapprovingly. "I'm sensing your discomfort just by looking at you. Try again."

Silversmith approved the next attempt and set Chasina on his shoulder, limping from the cathedral into the street. When they reached Muriel's tavern, he crouched by the back door.

Silversmith set Chasina on the ground. "When you speak to Cormac and Muriel, refer to them as 'Drasta.' It's a term of respect. Cormac likes humans to be properly afraid of him, so try knocking your knees together if he looks angry. It might keep him from maiming you."

Maim me? She hadn't counted on that possibility, but what if Cormac took it further?

"What if he kills me?" Chasina asked.

"You are a vessel for my magic. Killing you would be an illegal assault on my person, so Cormac cannot kill you. However, he can still injure you. Minor injuries are legal because they cannot hurt the Master. Are you sure I shouldn't go with you?"

"It will look a lot more genuine if I go alone."

"It would sound a lot more genuine if you actually meant it," he pointed out. "You don't feel sorry for defiling a cathedral? Not even a little bit?"

Chasina shrugged helplessly. "Maybe if there had been another way to rescue Bartholomew."

"I guess that makes this less like lying," Silversmith muttered. "Cormac and Muriel are probably sharing a table near the back, complaining about me. Cormac likes to wear orange pointed boots, which, unfortunately, are impossible to ignore."

Silversmith opened the door, and Chasina stepped inside the tavern. Tables and bodies blocked the light that filtered through oiled parchment stuffed in the windows. Coins dropped to the floor, and giants gambled with knuckle-bone dice.

Spotting a pair of garish orange boots at the back of the room, Chasina moved from the door and carefully crept beneath the tables. She tripped across the bronze coins and avoided slender hands reaching for the money.

Chasina reached the orange boots tucked beneath a table at the back. She shimmied up the table leg and hesitated beneath the ledge, her facial scars throbbing from the memory of hot tallow sizzling down her skin.

Chasina gritted her teeth. *You know what would make me feel better? Magic. Get up, get moving.*

Chasina rolled onto the table and saw another human standing nearby. The woman was tall with broad shoulders and hands, and purplish-yellow tattoos swirled up both arms. A brilliant green symbol marked her forehead, and an herbwoman's belt slung around her waist.

"What are you doing here, human?" Cormac asked.

Chasina gracefully bowed. "I came to apologize for defiling the cathedral. My Master commanded me to inform you that I have been properly punished." Chasina touched her ribs and winced, pretending that Silversmith had beaten her.

Cormac relaxed and nudged Muriel. "Vorce beat his human and sent her to grovel. Maybe Lord Kemer was wrong. Maybe Vorce has really found the Hero this time, and it's making him bold."

Muriel tapped her chin. "You think this is a chance to change him from being a fanatical weakling."

"Fanatical?"

Muriel smiled and waved her hands. "So you're pious, and I'm not. If Vorce is correct about the Hero, we can help him and use the opportunity to wring the weakness from him. Human," Muriel said, tapping a long nail next to Chasina, "tell your Master that I have a cargo of unregistered humans in the cellar, and if the sheriff finds them, I will hang. If he helps me smuggle those humans into the refugee camp to sell them, I will help him."

"I'm sorry, Drasta Muriel, but my Master won't be able to smuggle humans into the refugee camp," Chasina said. "Is there something else he can do to earn your help?"

"How dare you speak for your Master," Muriel said. "Tell him those are the only terms I will accept."

"Those are unacceptable terms."

Muriel swelled, nostrils flaring, but Cormac intervened before she said anything.

"You refuse to report those terms to your Master?" Cormac asked.

Chasina chose her words carefully. "I will report whatever terms my Master can fulfill. He is not a smuggler."

"You do not think. You obey," Cormac snapped. "Clearly, your tiny mind doesn't learn through physical punishments, so let's try something else. You risked your life to save Bartholomew. I'm betting you care more about watching others' pain than feeling your own."

Cormac focused his gaze on the tall herbwoman. In a moment, the green mark on her forehead began pulsing like a heartbeat. She started pinching her tattoos—no, they weren't tattoos. They were bruises. Huge bruises, running from shoulder to wrist, broken only by thin bands of undamaged skin.

So much casual abuse.

Heat spread across Chasina's chest, and she moved toward the herbwoman.

Cormac pushed Chasina away with a single finger. "You will convey Muriel's terms to your Master, and you will tell him that I will help him if he stops burning flowers for his parents."

"Yes, Drasta Cormac," Chasina said, dropping her gaze. Since she couldn't win this fight now, she'd have to agree and weasel from the agreement later.

Cormac stopped focusing on the herbwoman, and her mark dimmed to an average glow. She stopped hurting herself. How did Cormac control his slave without touching her? It must have something to do with the mark on her forehead. Perhaps it carried more power than a simple mark on the hand.

"If your Master agrees to our terms, he can meet us in the back of the tavern tomorrow morning," Cormac said.

Chasina climbed down from the table. She dashed through the tavern without a backward glance and rapped on the thick wooden door until it cracked open.

Silversmith greeted her with a quick once-over. "All your bones are in the same place. You must have done a good job of convincing Cormac."

Chapter Twenty-Two

Silversmith scooped Chasina from the ground and let her stagger on his shoulder. "Odd. I owe you an apology for underestimating the power of an apology."

Chasina spread her arms for balance. "Cormac and Muriel will help you on two conditions."

"I take back the apology."

"Muriel says she cannot help you unless you smuggle humans into the refugee camp, where she can sell them."

Silversmith's shoulders sagged, but he didn't respond.

Chasina continued with the second demand. "Cormac wants you to stop burning flowers in remembrance of your family."

Silversmith crossed the street, ducking a stream of foul-smelling liquid cascading from a window. "He wants... What did you say?"

A wagon trundled past, forcing Chasina to speak over the noise. "He saw that Muriel was getting something from helping you, and he wanted something, too."

Silversmith wobbled and nearly fell into another filthy stream pouring from an overhead window. "How people mourn their parents is nobody's business but their own. Not Cormac's, or Muriel's, or yours. I never said you could bargain on my behalf. We'll just have to find another way to steal the Naridi Stone."

Silversmith entered his home and deposited Chasina on the table. He proceeded to untie and retie the strings of meat hanging from the beams.

Chasina chose her words carefully. "Your mother and father would be so proud to see all the hard work you've done to find the Hero. He is immortal?"

Silversmith's hands shook slightly, possibly from emotion or spara withdrawals beginning to tax his body. "The Vault of Eternal Sleep keeps him preserved at the age he was laid to rest, so yes, he's immortal."

"When you find him and tell him your parents' names, he will remember them forever. That's better than burned flowers."

"Is it?" he asked, cinching a knot tight enough to pinch his fingers. "Human poachers come to Muriel from across Maelenthra to unload their traps, and she turns right around and sells those humans for a song. Hundreds of songs. If I have to give up burning flowers, you have to help smuggle humans into the refugee camp."

"Tell Muriel that you will help her do something else in exchange for her help," Chasina said. "I saved your life. Refusing to smuggle humans is the least you can do to repay me."

Silversmith pressed his lips together. "Believe me, I've tried to get Muriel to shut down her business. I've tried appealing to her in every way I know: money, legality, morality. I tried telling my sister that humans are sentient creatures, and she laughed at me."

Chasina inclined her head. "I thought you approved of licenses to hunt and sell humans."

"They're the next best thing to eradicating the human trade. I'll make you a deal," Silversmith said, fetching a map from the wall and placing it on the table. "If you devise a way to steal the Naridi Stone without Muriel and Cormac's help, we won't smuggle humans."

Chasina paced around the map. Neat handwriting labeled it 'Shilist Castle.' Shilist Castle crowned the northern hill outside Kavalu. Three walls separated the inner courtyard from the outside hills. Bridges connected the walls to each other so that soldiers could traverse from the outermost wall to the inner courtyard.

Chasina pointed at the small rectangle at the center of three walls. "This is the inner castle?"

"Yes," Silversmith said. "The keep, vault tower, and barracks are arranged diagonally from one side to the other."

Chasina studied the gates. "You were stationed in Shilist for three years. Is there any way inside the castle except through those gates?"

"All the District castles have a secret tunnel leading out of the fortress in case of a siege. They're called Suicide Tunnels."

"Do you know where it is?"

"People speculate that it leads into the hills, but only the ruling Lord knows for certain. Muriel always knows how to learn those kinds of secrets." Silversmith leaned forward and pointed at the outermost wall. "I regularly patrolled that wall, and I've seen people killed because they wandered too close. Sneaking over the walls is a good way to die, but if we found the Suicide Tunnel, we could get in and out of the castle without anyone detecting us."

Chasina walked around the map's border until she found two drawings labeled 'keystone.' The first drawing detailed a spherical rock the size of a giant's fist. Its twin drawing showed the same rock broken into twenty-five pieces.

"The keystone unlocks the vault?" Chasina asked, continuing when Silversmith nodded. "So, I'm guessing it's hidden somewhere in the castle? Do we know where?"

"Lord Kemer hides it somewhere in the keep. I was stationed there

116

for three years and never saw the keystone."

Chasina traced the castle with her fingertips. Three significant obstacles separated them from the Naridi Stone: getting inside Shilist Castle, finding the keystone, and breaking into the tower.

After they found the Suicide Tunnel, they could use it to enter the castle and search for the keystone. Then all they had to do was break into the vault, steal the Naridi Stone, and escape through the Suicide Tunnel.

Alone, in a human-sized castle, Chasina could devise a feasible plan. But in a giant-sized castle with Silversmith? On his own? Failure was the only outcome. They needed Muriel and Cormac's help, which meant Chasina needed to smuggle humans into the refugee camp.

Chasina imaged the three giants as pieces in a game. If she played the game correctly, she could recruit Cormac and Muriel *and* free the smuggled humans.

After all, possessing illegal humans was a hanging offense, which meant that unwary giants would rather free those humans than get caught and hanged. Chasina simply needed to ensure that the smuggled humans made it into unwary hands. To do that, she needed some special equipment.

Chasina straightened from the map. "We definitely need Cormac and Muriel's help."

Silversmith's face fell, but he nodded like he'd been expecting as much. "Do you have a plan?"

"Yes. We'll need four barrels, two of them with false bottoms, a bribe for the soldiers at the camp, and a wagon."

Chapter Twenty-Three

The following morning, Silversmith drove a wagon through the cobblestone streets where merchants and artisans folded out their shutters and arranged wares. Four barrels jostled in the back of the wagon. Two barrels were equipped with false bottoms, and two of them stank of mulwell fish, which Silversmith assured Chasina made an excellent bribe.

Silversmith stopped the wagon outside Muriel's tavern and tied the horses to a nearby post. Before entering the tavern, he fell twice and grabbed his head—probably from the intense headaches that accompanied spara withdrawals. He wove around empty tables toward the bar.

Chasina inhaled the scent of spiced wine and baking bread, clinging to Silversmith's tunic as he limped behind the bar and into the back room.

Cormac leaned against one of the enormous casks stocked in the back room. His slave did push-ups on top of the cask. Sweat dripped down her face, but she never bothered wiping it away.

"Why do you do that?" Silversmith asked, fixating on the human.

"It's not like she can help you work with anything."

"She's an herbwoman. Her job is to fix me if I'm injured, and whether it happens on the battlefield or in a castle, nothing can stop her from getting to me. She needs to be a rat." Cormac stepped forward. "You agree to our terms?"

Silversmith shook Cormac's hand. "I will stop burning flowers for my mother and father, and I'm here to help smuggle humans into the refugee camp."

Muriel was stirring a cask with a wooden paddle big enough to squash a human hut.

She set aside her paddle and hugged Silversmith. "You're getting less squeamish about selling humans all the time, aren't you, Brother? I'm so proud. This is going to be like when we were children. Remember?"

"You always had more fun than I did," Silversmith said.

"Don't I always?"

Silversmith released his sister. "If I help you smuggle these humans into the refugee camp, you will help me find the Suicide Tunnel. Right?"

Muriel grinned wickedly. "I know someone who can tell us where to find the Suicide Tunnel. His name is Jason, and as it happens, he likes to hang around the refugee camp and fleece the refugees. Let's get started, shall we?"

Muriel scooted aside one of the casks and opened a hidden trapdoor. Silversmith and Cormac carried the two false-bottomed barrels into the cellar.

Cormac conjured a green sphere around his fist and illuminated the cramped cellar. Dozens of cages were stacked against the walls, some of them little more than buckets with breathing holes.

Silversmith positioned a board in front of the first shelf of cages. He unlatched the cages, allowing the humans to shuffle onto the board where Cormac trussed their feet before packaging them inside the barrel. Cormac's hands were surprisingly nimble for someone tying the hands and feet of creatures much smaller than him.

Chasina whispered in Silversmith's ear. "Let me help tie them up. Cormac is hurting them."

Silversmith silently obliged, taking her from his shoulder and setting her on the board. Chasina cut some thread and approached the human next in line for Cormac. She tied the man's legs tightly, aware of Cormac scrutinizing her work.

Cormac looked away, and the human whispered in Chasina's ear. "Give me your knife."

"Don't panic. I've got this under control."

"No one has a giant under control," he said. "Give it to me so I can free everyone."

"Shut up."

Chasina worked quickly, saving as many humans as possible from Cormac's cruel knots. She spotted Cormac's slave efficiently trussing humans.

Chasina purposefully bumped the woman and whispered, "I'm Chasina."

The herbwoman slowly turned her heavy gaze to Chasina. "I am Seven."

"How long has Cormac owned you?"

"I am Seven."

"You already said that. What is your name?"

"I am Seven." Seven's hand strayed to the bruises on her forearm, the green symbol on her forehead pulsing steadily.

Chasina backed away before Seven started pinching herself. Apparently, Cormac didn't want his slave exchanging names with other humans—if 'Seven' even counted as a name. Honestly, if Chasina didn't need Cormac's help stealing the Naridi Stone, she'd stick a knife in his eye right now.

The last human disappeared inside the false-bottomed barrels. Muriel set the false bottoms in place, hiding the humans, and she filled the barrels with a mixture of sawdust, straw, and vegetables. Anyone who looked inside would see only vegetables.

Muriel shut the barrels and labeled them with an etching of a vegetable on the lids.

Cormac and Silversmith carried the barrels from the cellar and through the tavern, loading them into the wagon alongside the fish barrels. Crude fish drawings labeled the fish barrels.

Chasina gagged. The smell of dead fish oozed from the barrels, and it didn't help that Silversmith climbed into the back. He crouched beside the barrels while Muriel and Cormac sat in the front.

Cormac drove the wagon out of Kavalu and toward the city of tents camped above Kavalu.

Eleven flags waved above the camp. Each bore a different insignia: a bird, a shield, and a thin spear, among others. Remembering the spider insignia worn by Kavalu's soldiers, Chasina realized the flags must represent different conquered cities.

Chasina counted the flags. "The Undying have conquered eleven different cities?"

Silversmith nodded. "All but Kavalu and the capital, although there's speculation that the Undying will attack King Omar's District next."

"The old coward will get his aura sucked out of him pretty soon," Cormac said.

"Like a snail out of its shell," Muriel added.

"Not exactly what I meant to say but close enough," Silversmith said. "What's a little treason thrown in with everything else we're planning to do?"

"This is your plan, remember?" Muriel said. "You are the reason we're out here."

"It doesn't mean I enjoy breaking the law."

"Except for desertion, obviously. You don't mind breaking that law when it comes to saving your own life. Unless you want to get captured by the soldiers at the camp, I suggest you wear an illusion."

Silversmith flinched at his sister's words, but he didn't tell her about his curse. He settled himself and breathed slowly. Silver aura shimmered over his face. It gradually changed color and lost its shine, fitting over his face like a mask. His cheekbones softened, his face rounded, and his hair changed color from black to red.

Cormac glanced at Silversmith's illusion. "Can you hold it until we get past the guards?"

Sweat beaded on Silversmith's forehead. "Hurry."

Cormac drove the wagon to the back of the line awaiting inspection. Two soldiers inspected the first wagon in line. After a rigorous inspection of poking, prodding, and peeking inside the barrels, they allowed the wagon into camp.

While Muriel, Cormac, and Silversmith focused on the soldiers, Chasina carefully dropped from Silversmith's shoulder onto a fish barrel. Using her knife, she altered the fish drawing until it resembled a vegetable. A gentle breeze took the wood shavings as Chasina jumped to the second barrel and repeated the process. She switched the labels on all four barrels. Fish barrels bore a vegetable, and the false-bottomed barrels bore a fish.

Chasina returned to Silversmith's shoulder when the wagon rolled to second in line. Soldiers inspected the wagon ahead of them.

A soldier dipped his hand into the wine cask and fished out a handful of ornate combs. "Smugglers," the soldier said, motioning to his comrades.

Two soldiers hustled the smugglers to a large pit and unceremoniously dumped them inside. Four other soldiers removed the contraband from the casks and delivered the wine to camp.

A soldier motioned Cormac forward.

"Hero bless you, soldier," Muriel said as the wagon rolled to a stop in front of him. "We have some food we'd like to distribute among the refugees."

The soldier's yellow armband crinkled as he leaned on the wagon and glanced keenly at the barrels. "What will you give me to let you pass without searching?"

A half-smile appeared on Muriel's lips. "We bring the Hero's blessings to the refugees."

"Only to them?"

Muriel's smile turned upward at the corners. "I hear the Lord's soldiers love mulwell fish? It seemed fitting to bring blessings to more than the refugees. One barrel."

The soldier snapped his fingers. "Two barrels or we empty all of them."

"Can't argue with the Lord's loyal soldiers. Help yourself."

The soldier whistled to his comrades, who quickly unloaded the two barrels labeled as fish. In reality, they took the barrels loaded with humans.

Either the soldiers freed the humans, or they hanged because illegally poaching humans carried a death sentence. This close to Kavalu, a seat of authority, the soldiers weren't likely to break the law because they'd probably get caught.

Afraid of getting hanged, the soldiers would release the humans.

"Do you smell that?" Cormac asked, sniffing the air. He stiffened and called to the soldiers. "Wait a moment. I think you have the wrong barrels."

Chapter Twenty-Four

Cormac caught up to the soldiers.

The lead soldier tapped the fish drawing on the barrel lid. "Are you blind, old man?"

Cormac sniffed the air. "It doesn't smell like fish. The fish smell is coming from the wagon, see? We must have mislabeled our barrels."

Sweet Naridi roses. Chasina smoothed the front of her tunic, covertly wiping the sweat from her palms as the soldiers swapped the barrels. Her plan could not be defeated because of a smell. But if she told the soldiers to search the false-bottomed barrels, they would hang Silversmith for poaching. She had to wait.

Cormac guided the wagon through the camp. Silversmith dropped his illusion when the soldiers disappeared behind them.

A few wide trails cut swathes through the maze of tents, joining the narrow dirt paths to create a makeshift city. Refugees dressed in rags or once-fine clothes cleared the way for their wagon.

Cormac stopped the wagon outside a blue-striped tent. Muriel inspected the tent while Cormac and Silversmith unloaded the wagons and carried them inside.

Silversmith set a barrel near the tent wall, and Chasina reached out and slid her fingers against the coarse fabric. If she escaped and found soldiers before Muriel sold the humans, what would she tell them? How could she expose Muriel without hurting the giants? She needed Muriel and Cormac alive to help steal the Naridi Stone.

Cormac's voice startled Chasina from her thoughts. It took her a moment to realize he spoke directly to her.

"What?" she asked reflexively.

Cormac held up a vegetable. "Surprised to see something?"

Chasina did her best to look confused. "What do you mean, Drasta?"

"What would be surprising?" Silversmith asked.

"Your slave tried to switch the barrels. The guards would have ended up with two barrels of illegally poached humans, and we'd have nothing to sell but fish."

"You're lying," Chasina said.

"Am I?" Cormac held up the barrel's lid. "Those scratches are fresh and too fine for a giant's knife. That only leaves you."

"No, Chasina, please tell me he's wrong," Silversmith said, touching Chasina's forehead. "Tell me the truth: did you sabotage the barrels?"

"Yes."

Cormac began assembling a wooden table in the center of the tent. "Tell her to stay on your shoulder and make no mischief while we sell her friends."

Chasina bit the inside of her cheek as Silversmith repeated the words and laid invisible constraints on her will. Could she attract a guard or burn down the tent?

It was almost a relief to feel the silver cords tightening around her spine, telling her that fire was out of the question. As for guards, magical pain spread through her body when she tried yelling.

Cormac finished erecting the table. It had a high border too tall for an average human to climb, but Cormac greased the walls anyway.

He emptied the humans onto the table, and Muriel swished from the tent to gather customers.

Even though Chasina hated bowing and scraping to these giants, she did it for a purpose. Muriel's humans didn't have the same choice. Chasina had taken responsibility for them and tried to save everyone, only for Cormac to foil her plan.

Chasina's gaze bored holes into Cormac. Instead of growling at her, Cormac simply reached into the crowd of humans, selected one, and snapped the woman's neck. The sickening noise punched Chasina in the gut.

"Cormac," Silversmith said, rebuking.

"There are consequences for disobedience," Cormac said, still holding Chasina's gaze. "For sabotage, underhandedness, and rudeness. Stop looking at my face."

Chasina instantly dropped her gaze, but she wasn't fast enough. Another sickening snap made Chasina gasp. She didn't look up. She didn't move.

Silversmith stepped forward. "Cormac, please stop. Control yourself."

"You need to stop letting these things bother you, Vorce," Cormac said. "It is disconcerting. How do you expect to kill Undying if you can't stomach killing pests?"

Muriel returned through the tent flap, followed by a gaggle of giants. Their ragged clothes belied the gold coins clutched in sweaty fists.

Muriel lightly smacked her brother's shoulder. "I knew the refugees escaped with more than their lives. Look at all this money. I'll stay here and get rid of any evidence the sheriff can use to hang me," she said, motioning at the table filled with humans. "And you can look for Jason. He's lean, green-eyed with messy blond hair, and he has an ego bigger than the whole city. You can probably find him stealing from the patients in the hospital ward."

The tent flap rustled over Chasina's shoulders as Silversmith exited the tent. She tuned out the refugees' chattering voices.

Chasina silently recited the Death Blessing for Cormac's two victims. The words tasted like ash.

She was responsible for keeping those humans safe, and she had failed. If she had given her knife to the human who had asked for it, all the humans might be free. At the very least, they might have a chance to escape.

Chasina slipped Da's knife from its sheath and ran her palm across the blade. It had heard her whispered secrets, felt her tears. It had saved her life countless times, but today, she had not allowed it to save anyone else.

Cormac had killed two humans to punish Chasina. What kind of monster did that? Chasina had tightly controlled Tarrken, but she never silenced them. Curses, baleful stares, and death wishes had all fallen like hail, but she never stopped it. It would have been pointless.

Cormac was different. Apparently, staring at him was an equal crime to sabotage, and he'd killed a human for each offense.

Nausea rolled through Chasina. Those deaths were her fault. All of it was her fault, one way or another.

Silversmith stumbled and caught himself on a nearby tent. He remained stationary, clinging to the tent while spara withdrawals wracked his body with shivers. The shivers passed, and Silversmith walked into the crowd again.

Silversmith twisted his neck at an awkward angle to look at Chasina standing on his shoulder. "You're not really a murderer, are you?"

Chapter Twenty-Five

The question caught Chasina off guard. "What?"

"Your Gran told me that you murdered a girl named Katie, and that's why the village exiled you." Silversmith glanced over his shoulder at Muriel's tent. "But from what I have seen of you, you would rather die than put another human in danger."

Chasina breathed short, fast breaths. Gran had told Silversmith that Chasina was a murderer? That explained why Silversmith went from rescuing Chasina in Brundar to actively trying to kill her.

"Gran lied," Chasina said. "Katie tried to kill me. She left me for dead in Brundar, but I tried to save her."

Silversmith turned a corner and side-stepped a giantess and her three children. "If you didn't kill her, who did?"

"Remember when we first met, you had to steal me from Elric? He and his friend also captured Katie. So when you let me go, I went back to save her. I was too late. Someone had already killed her. So I killed him."

"The soldier you killed was the one who killed Katie?"

"Yes."

Silversmith stumbled on his injured leg. He regained his balance and headed down a narrow alley between rows of tents.

"Your Gran was very sincere. She was convinced that you decapitated Katie."

"I never laid a finger on Katie. If I could have traded my life for hers, I would have." Chasina blinked hard. "Gran would have done anything to kill me herself. I guess having a giant kill me was the next best thing."

Silversmith fell quiet, doubtless wondering what unearthly things Chasina had done to earn such hatred from her family.

"I'm sorry I didn't listen to your side of the story," Silversmith said eventually. "I'm sorry I tried to kill you multiple times. I thought you were a murderer."

Another apology. It might have good intentions, but it didn't ease the knot in Chasina's chest. All she'd ever done was protect Gran, care for her, and Gran repaid the debt by convincing a giant to kill Chasina. Even if Chasina came home with the Naridi Stone, would Gran ever love her?

"Where are we going?" Chasina asked briskly, using her raspy voice to disguise the emotion clogging her throat.

Silversmith looked up at the triangular flags snapping in the breeze. "See the lion? I think that's where they keep the hospital ward."

They entered a street of tents devoted to surgeons tending their patients. Patients gasped for breath on sickbeds made of sweet-smelling rushes, and black cauldrons bubbled over nearby fires. One surgeon added a dead cat to the brew while another spat drops of orange liquid into a different pot.

"Ask one of the surgeons about Jason," Chasina said. "If Jason has been stealing from dying patients, the surgeons have probably seen him lurking nearby."

Silversmith approached one of the surgeons stirring a bubbling cauldron.

"Are you family?" the surgeon asked, gesturing to the patient lying on a rush mat. "An Undying attacked him when he tried escaping the Fourth District. Luckily, a Ramerian scout intervened and fended off the Undying before he finished draining this man's aura."

Chasina sensed the tension spreading through Silversmith's shoulders and neck. Any mention of an Undying sent Silversmith into an intense emotional struggle, and she didn't need that right now. She needed to find Jason so she could steal the Naridi Stone, free herself, and earn Gran's love.

"Ask him about Jason," Chasina said.

Silversmith jerked his head like a horse scaring flies from its coat, silently telling her to shut up.

The patient stretched unconscious on the ground. Bandages on his arms showed where the surgeon had taken blood to balance his humors.

"Is he going to live?" Silversmith asked, kneeling beside the patient.

"The Undying drained almost all of his magic. He's barely alive. See his aura?" the surgeon asked.

"No."

The surgeon touched his patient's neck, fingers gloved with lavender magic. "Now?"

A faint earth-brown aura flickered around the patient's body. Giants' auras varied in thickness depending on their magical strength, but Chasina had never seen a weaker aura.

The surgeon produced a vial of colored glass and pulled out the stopper, pouring mysterious contents into the cauldron. "Lord Kemer comes every evening to bless them. He blessed this one last night, but he seems even weaker. My patients keep dying."

While Silversmith talked with the surgeon, Chasina scanned the nearby tents for a green-eyed giant named Jason. Her gaze caught on someone kneeling beside a sickbed ten patients away. The giant fit Muriel's description, and while Chasina watched, he discreetly stole the patient's purse.

Chasina tapped Silversmith's cheek. "I found Jason."

Silversmith squeezed the patient's hand, stood, and limped toward Jason.

Jason saw Silversmith heading toward him and bolted between rows of tents. Silversmith ran after him, heavily favoring his injured leg. They reached the spot where Jason disappeared and ran straight into a ruckus.

Refugees threw themselves from the dirt path, scrambling to clear the way for the nobles walking through the camp. Sunlight sparkled off their jeweled hoods and tunics.

Chasina recognized some of the nobles. "It's the Lord and his entourage. He's coming early today."

Silversmith ducked into a threadbare tent. Shadows flickered across the tent as nobles marched past. Silversmith opened the flap an inch, and Chasina saw Jason swanning among the nobles like he owned the world. Jason's clothes signified wealth, if not nobility, and he completed the disguise by snapping at anyone who looked sideways at him.

It was a smart move. No one expected a petty thief to hide among nobles, and the nobles themselves provided protection. Chasina and Silversmith couldn't approach Jason until the nobles left.

The bobbing nobles parted for Lord Kemer, who had his back toward Chasina and Silversmith's hiding place. Lord Kemer knelt over a sickbed and blessed the patient.

All this fuss for a dying giant. Two humans had died not twenty minutes ago, and no one even knew. Even Silversmith, who should know better, didn't take a moment to honor the murdered humans.

Sad murmurs rippled through the crowd of giants. Everyone bowed their heads while Lord Kemer closed the patient's eyes.

"Sometimes they recover," Silversmith whispered. "If the Undying doesn't drain the entire aura, sometimes the victim heals and regains his life force." He waited for a long minute and sighed. "No recovery this time. I hope he didn't have any children."

"Me too." The last thing Chasina needed was more giants plaguing the earth.

Lord Kemer turned around, and Chasina noticed he didn't have a cut on his cheek. She'd injured him yesterday. How many herbwomen had it taken to heal his face so quickly? At least two.

She was going to explode if she stayed any longer. "We should go. The nobles are leaving, and we don't want to lose Jason."

Silversmith struggled to his feet. His withdrawals kept worsening, evidenced in his shaky limbs. Soon, the withdrawal symptoms would include fever, cramps, and intense nausea.

They left the tent and followed the nobles at a distance. Lord Kemer and his entourage neared the camp's entrance, where a group of horses waited for them. As soon as the entourage mounted their horses and realized they had one too many nobles, Jason would be forced into the open where Silversmith could catch him.

Silversmith hid behind a tent near Jason.

The nobles mounted their horses, and Jason bolted. He ran past Silversmith's hiding place. Silversmith caught Jason by the tunic.

Jason elbowed Silversmith in the chest. Silversmith effortlessly blocked the blow and then froze. Uncontrollable shivers wracked his body. He crumpled to the ground, and the collision rattled Chasina's body even though she landed safely on his shoulder.

Jason straightened his tunic and sneered at Silversmith. He thumped Silversmith in the stomach, stole his purse, and strolled from the camp.

Chapter Twenty-Six

Silversmith started spasming. Chasina slid from his shoulder and fetched Cormac and Muriel. They returned, and Silversmith's spasms worsened.

Chasina stood back to watch everyone. She would have gotten closer to Silversmith, but he might accidentally crush her while spasming. Spara withdrawals commonly came with spasms, and though they weren't fatal, Silversmith needed someone to take him home where he could safely undergo the misery.

She didn't regret addicting him to spara. She *didn't*. How else could she steal the Naridi Stone and go home? The addiction was necessary, but it didn't mean she liked watching Silversmith suffer. Any reasonably capable person would have killed her upon learning she'd addicted them to spara sap, but Silversmith had let her live. He'd made a mistake thinking she couldn't hurt him again. That sort of naivety, that mercy, would make Silversmith's world crash and burn.

Silversmith's spasms finally calmed. He floated in semi-consciousness even when Cormac flicked the greasy hair from his face.

"Muriel told me your slave addicted you to spara sap," Cormac said. "Why didn't you kill your slave?"

"She was scared. She wants to go home," Silversmith said, eyelids fluttering like leaves in the wind.

Chasina willed herself to not react, even as Silversmith's words made a chunk of ice freeze in her chest.

"She is cursed," Cormac said, leaning forward like he was trying to speak through a wall. "Cursed. Do you honestly think anything goes through her tiny mind except for the Undyings' commands?"

"She's not evil."

And just like that, the block of ice shattered into a million shards that speared Chasina's flesh. *I do not regret addicting him to spara. I do not regret addicting him to spara.*

Cormac and Muriel exchanged twin snorts of disgust. They started lifting Silversmith from the ground, and Chasina quickly latched herself to his shoulder. She was safer with him than either of the other giants.

Muriel and Cormac laid Silversmith in the wagon and drove him home. They carried him inside and tucked him into the pallet on the floor, and Chasina slipped away and hid beneath the colorful cabinet before they turned their attention to her.

Dust tickled Chasina's cheeks and stuck in her hair, and spiderwebs shimmered in the darkness.

Chasina covered her face in both hands. The day replayed in her mind repeatedly, each time like fresh salt scrubbing an internal wound.

She wished she could forget the day, but she couldn't. She should have given her knife away, but how could she have known that Cormac would notice a smell?

Muriel's voice broke Chasina's thoughts. "I'll be back tomorrow."

The door slammed shut, and seconds later, Cormac's shadow engulfed the dusty ground outside Chasina's hiding place. Seven appeared in front of the cabinet. Seven dropped to her knees and faced Chasina. She pointed a rigid finger at the brightly pulsing mark on her forehead, signifying that Cormac controlled her actions.

Seven smashed her face against the ground. She worked efficiently, managing several more smashes without a cry. Not even a groan. Just droplets of blood spraying from her nose.

Chasina hurriedly crawled from beneath the cabinet. "I'm here, Drasta Cormac. Please stop hurting Seven."

Cormac knelt beside the cabinet. He focused on Seven as she smashed her face mercilessly against the ground. He didn't stop.

Chasina bowed deeply. "Forgive me, Drasta."

Cormac relaxed his focus on Seven, and her green mark dimmed. He set Seven on his shoulder and exited the house with Chasina. He moved along the wall to a corner wrapped with shadows, where he halted and checked the surroundings.

A few passersby strode down the muddy alley, but no one gave Cormac and the humans a second look, probably because whatever Cormac planned to do with them wasn't uncommon.

Shocking.

Chasina must have hidden beneath the cabinet longer than she thought because late afternoon sunlight turned the streets dark orange. Even if the passersby cared what Cormac did to her and Seven, they'd be difficult to spot in the dark shadows provided by the waning light and warped buildings.

Cormac crouched and dropped Chasina. She staggered.

Chasina steadied herself. "What do you want, Drasta Cormac?"

Cormac flicked her in the ribs.

Chasina yelped. She tried to suck the noise back down her throat, but it split the air before she stopped it.

"Humankind has sought to hurt and destroy giants ever since the Undying cursed them. Have you heard the Undying voices in your mind?" Cormac asked.

Cormac was utterly mad. Humans didn't persecute giants. What about giants who pillaged human villages? What about the two people Cormac had murdered today?

"There aren't any voices in my head. You're afraid of a curse that isn't real, Drasta Cormac," Chasina said.

Cormac studied Chasina shrewdly. "I believe there's a spark of free will within you that the Undying have not smothered. I've seen you use it to manipulate Vorce. You gave him that plan to smuggle humans into the refugee camp, didn't you? It was too cunning for Vorce. If the soldiers had seen those humans today, they would have hanged all of us."

"I didn't—"

"You addicted Vorce to spara sap. You are perfectly comfortable endangering his life, yet he refuses to kill you."

Chasina rubbed her ribs. Cormac could not kill or seriously maim her. He could only frighten her, and she didn't scare easily.

"Why are you here?" she asked.

"To tell you two things. Firstly, you will stop manipulating my apprentice. Don't suggest plans. Don't interject ideas. Don't even offer an opinion. And secondly, did you really think you would get away with addicting my apprentice to drugs?" Cormac drew a human-sized coffin from a pocket in his cloak. "I'm testing a theory. You panicked when Lord Kemer trapped you inside a magical sphere. You flinch every time Vorce wraps his hand around you. You're afraid of small spaces, aren't you?"

Chasina bolted, but Cormac caught her and stuffed her inside the coffin. She briefly turned upside down as Cormac handled the coffin, and then dirt scraped the outer walls. Footsteps vibrated through her body, then faded, leaving her alone.

Chasina curled around her knees, keeping as much space as possible on all sides. The world faded into quick breaths that never ended. Smoke rose from the depths of her memories and engulfed her world.

Screams ripped her home apart, but little Chasina knew that Mama and Bea never screamed. Now, they wouldn't stop screaming. *Da, you promised to come back. Tell me you are coming for me.*

Smoke burned her throat. Sparks fell on her bare arms and neck, and fire ate the skin on her face until it met bone. Each breath came harder, slower, but they never ceased.

Chasina screamed. For one moment, her noise pierced the suffocating walls. Her raw throat bucked and closed, and she silently sobbed. *Gramercy, just let me die.*

Chapter Twenty-Seven

After several eternities, a deep female voice broke through Chasina's sobbing. "Is someone there?"

Chasina scratched at the casket with bloody fingernails. "Yes! Someone's here. Let me out!"

The casket opened, and Chasina barely glimpsed Seven's face before diving past her onto the ground. She breathed deeply and stared at the sky.

It was morning. Sunlight banished the shadows around the coffin, and busy giants herded pigs down the street. Chasina had languished in the coffin all night.

Chasina stood and hugged Seven, pressing hard enough to pour some of her feelings into the emotionless woman. "Thank you."

"Why would my Master put you there?"

"Because he's insane."

Seven detached from the embrace. "Will you obey my Master?"

Seven's mark glowed brightly and pulsed, signifying that Cormac was controlling Seven. He probably wanted to ensure that Chasina had learned her lesson and planned to obey him: don't suggest plans, ideas, or opinions.

"Yes. I will obey Drasta Cormac," Chasina lied.

She would pretend to obey Cormac to keep him from hurting Seven. However, if she did it subtly, she could manipulate Silversmith without Cormac finding out. In the meantime, she could look forward to killing Cormac as soon as he outlived his usefulness.

Chasina put a hand on Seven's back and guided her to Silversmith's door. They entered through a crack near the bottom.

Cormac, Muriel, and Silversmith bent over the table, perhaps studying a map. Large black circles hung beneath Silversmith's eyes, and a faint odor of spara sap clung to him. The smell meant that he'd passed the worst stage of the withdrawals.

Muriel grinned. "The sheriff inspected the tavern this morning. I didn't have a license, but he couldn't convict me of selling illegal humans because weren't any. I'm officially an honest citizen."

Silversmith pointed at the map. "Jason ran in this direction. I can track him while you contact some castle workers to find where Lord Kemer hides the keystone."

"I know some people," Muriel mused. She glanced at Cormac. "But they're a rough bunch. I need someone to watch my back."

"Always," Cormac said. "Vorce, are you well enough to track today?"

Silversmith nodded, and everyone stood.

Muriel stuck her arm through Cormac's. "Escort me to the bowels of this city, will you? There are some people I want you to meet." Muriel laughed and pulled Cormac into the alley. Her laughter faded as they strode down the street.

Silversmith fastened a cape with an iron clasp before settling Chasina on his shoulder. He splashed into the alley. Several young boys tumbled from the neighboring house and pulled a skinny pig by the ears. They flashed a tangle of thin elbows and round faces, running from the alley, pig squealing angrily behind them.

Chasina settled herself more securely on Silversmith's shoulder as he jogged through the alleys, ducking twisted beams and slamming doors until the bumpy cobblestone appeared underfoot. He moved much better than yesterday, his stride steady, his limp diminished.

They reached the city gates. The gates arched between two towers connected by a narrow bridge, where a Hero's statue stood in a niche and blessed the crowd passing beneath.

Silversmith bowed his head, accepting the Hero's blessing as they passed through the gate and entered the hills. He headed toward the refugee camp.

Chasina studied the silver circle glowing on the back of her hand. "Why is Seven's mark on her forehead?"

Silversmith reached for Chasina, and she shied away. He caught her, and she flinched, pain flickering through her ribs where Cormac had beaten her.

Silversmith gestured at her hand. "See how my mark shows up on your hand? That's what happens when I put a tiny bit of magic inside you. If I filled you with magic, it would show up on your forehead."

Chasina rubbed her mark. "Does that have anything to do with the way Seven acts? Emotionless?"

"Seven acts like Cormac. He possessed her."

"How?" Chasina asked.

Greasy hair flopped across Silversmith's forehead. "He filled her with his magic. For giants, magic is our life force. It's why an Undying can kill people by draining their auras. Because magic is our life force, it's also part of our character." He conjured a sphere of silver magic. "This isn't just magic or life force. It is the magical embodiment of my strengths and weaknesses, goals, and dreams: my soul."

Chasina looked aghast at the mark on her hand, and Silversmith laughed.

"There isn't enough of my magic inside you to possess you," he said.

"Just enough to bind you to my will. But if I filled you to the brim with my magic, like Cormac has done with Seven, I would possess you. Your soul would shrink to the tiniest spark inside your body, and you would become a puppet like Seven. On a positive note, you'd at least be able to travel far more than a mile from me."

Chasina's skin crawled. "Can she still feel pain?"

"If she concentrates. I suspect Cormac allows her to feel pain. Otherwise, he wouldn't be so cruel to her. She can think and feel her own emotions, but she has no control over her actions." Silversmith noticed Chasina staring at the silver sphere in his right hand and extinguished it. "Her name isn't really Seven. It's Maria."

"How do you know?"

"I asked her. It was a year ago before Cormac finished possessing her. After you fill a human vessel with magic, there's always an interval where the human and giant fight for control. The length of time varies depending on the human's willpower, and during that time, a giant cannot control himself and the human at the same time. Once the human yields, they become an extension of the Master. Maria fought for a very long time. I will never forget the moment she gave up and allowed Cormac to fully possess her." Silversmith's throat bobbed. "Her eyes lost their spark."

Deep inside the shell of Seven's body, Seven's spirit suffered the torture of being trapped inside her own body. The sooner Chasina killed Cormac, the better.

Silversmith fell silent as he reached the hilltop. He set Chasina on his shoulder and crouched to inspect the general area where Jason had fled after Silversmith collapsed. He searched several areas before picking up a trail and following it down the hill and back into the city.

Of course, Jason would run into the city. He wanted to disappear into a large gathering of people until it was safe to steal from the refugees again. Silversmith couldn't track Jason on cobblestone streets, especially since thousands of giants traveled them daily.

Silversmith stopped inside the city gates and looked around as though Jason might jump from the gatehouse with a bow on his head, shouting, *"You found me!"*

"We have to look for him somewhere else," Chasina said. "Jason isn't going to jump out at us."

"Where do you suggest we look?"

"This is your city. Figure it out."

Silversmith folded his arms and leaned against one of the towers that formed the gatehouse. "Thanks to you, I spent a sleepless night puking in the alley outside my home, and I smell like a spara addict. If you hadn't addicted me to spara sap, I would have caught Jason yesterday. You figure out how to find him."

"That wouldn't even be hard."

Silversmith settled more comfortably against the wall. "Good. Then it shouldn't take too long for you to think of something."

Chapter Twenty-Eight

C hasina imagined herself in Jason's position: she was a thief who had been discovered in the refugee camp by unknown assailants. She disappeared into Kavalu. She didn't have much money, either, or she wouldn't steal from dying giants.

Where would she hide?

A place with a lot of people. Where tradition and silence kept order, and everyone was too busy staring at stained glass windows to notice a thief stealing from them.

"Jason is hiding in a cathedral," Chasina said. "How many cathedrals are in Kavalu?"

Silversmith started down the street. "Just one."

They reached the cathedral. Services were finished for the day, so no one bothered them while they searched. Silversmith moved methodically, searching everything from dense shadows to a tiny cupboard hidden below a pew, but he stopped outside the Sacristy and refused to enter.

"Do you want Jason to get away? What better place to hide than a room no one is allowed to see?" Chasina asked. She whispered in case

Jason was hiding in the Sacristy and overheard her speaking.

"I will not behold the Sacristy without a blessing," Silversmith said quietly.

"Then go get a blessing."

Silversmith clenched his fists. "The priests are gone for the day. I cannot receive a blessing."

"I am sacrificing a lot to help you steal the Naridi Stone. I have effectively betrayed my people by helping you, and now you're too squeamish to look inside a room?"

Silversmith paced in a tight circle, humming deep in his throat. "I don't know."

"Let me search the Sacristy," Chasina suggested. "Cormac tortured me inside the Sacristy, so I've already seen it. How could I break the same rule twice?"

Silversmith stopped pacing and set Chasina on the floor. "Don't touch anything."

Silversmith cracked open the door, and Chasina poked her head inside the Sacristy and saw Jason sitting at the table.

Jason sorted through a pile of purses. His boots leaned against the wall and judging from the muddy stonework, he'd cleaned his shoes on the sacred carvings.

Silversmith might have another seizure if he saw the desecrated stonework.

"Well?" Silversmith asked a bit too loudly.

Jason's attention switched from his booty to the cracked door. He stuffed the stolen purses under his tunic and raced from the Sacristy.

"Go, go, go," Chasina said as Silversmith dropped her onto his shoulder.

Silversmith's jaw tightened, but he closed his eyes and ran into the Sacristy. He collided with the table and backpedaled, groaning.

"You should have told me it was there," Silversmith said, feathering the air with his hands as he circled the table.

"You were going too fast. Left, left, keep going. Turn right, now straight ahead."

Silversmith found the stairway leading up to the Quire and climbed it. They entered the Quire and saw Jason running into the Nave.

Even with a slight limp, Silversmith sprinted and gained on Jason through the Nave, down the cathedral steps, and into the cobblestone streets.

Jason screamed for help. Pockets of the crowd stirred, and soldiers moved toward them. The soldiers chased Silversmith, who cornered Jason in an alley.

Jason kept crying for help until Silversmith clapped a hand over his mouth.

"Sorry, but I just want to talk," Silversmith said.

Several soldiers entered the alley. The yellow, spider-embroidered armbands wrinkled as the soldiers raised their batons.

Chasina waited for the soldiers to recognize Silversmith and capture him, but none of them did. He must not have worked with them in Shilist Castle.

"Release the noble," the shortest soldier said.

Ever obedient, Silversmith released Jason. Jason stumbled toward the soldiers, sobbing in the perfect imitation of a frightened noble.

"He stole my boots and chased me halfway across the city, trying to kill me," Jason said.

"That's not true," Silversmith said, but the soldiers shouted him down. They believed a noble's word over a commoner.

"Take him to the common pits," Jason said. He watched while two soldiers dragged Silversmith down the alley, a smirk hiding behind his quivering lips.

Chasina's guttural voice broke through the noise. "He's not a noble. He's a thief. He stole my Master's purse and ran through the street, and my Master was just trying to catch him. Check beneath the thief's tunic."

"Kill the human. She's lying," Jason said.

Silversmith freed his arms and touched Chasina's forehead. "Tell us the truth: is this man a thief and an impostor?"

Chasina held up her hand, showing everyone her pulsing silver mark. "He is."

The soldiers searched Jason and found the purses stuffed inside his tunic. Jason's precise features twisted into a snobbish scowl.

"Unhand me, peasants," he said, jerking as the soldiers dragged him from the alley.

Chasina grinned. Now, she and Silversmith could interrogate Jason at their leisure. And once she learned where to find the Suicide Tunnel, she could get rid of Muriel.

Silversmith squeezed past Short Soldier just as one of the soldiers escorting Jason ran up the street.

"Did the prisoner escape?" Short Soldier demanded.

"No, but he said that we need to arrest this man, too," he said, pointing at Silversmith. "Says he entered a Sacristy without a blessing."

"I didn't open my eyes," Silversmith said, touching Chasina's arm. "Tell us the truth: did you see me open my eyes?"

"No," Chasina said.

Short Soldier squinted. "The human cannot see your eyes while standing on your shoulder. You could have had your eyes open the whole time, and she'd never know."

"His eyes were definitely closed," Chasina said. "He ran into a table."

Short Soldier ignored Chasina and grabbed Silversmith's arm. Silversmith said nothing. Apparently, he was perfectly content to get dragged along by whoever stuck a ring through his nose and pulled.

"He ran into a table," Chasina said. "Do you know anyone who runs into tables for fun, or are you just stupid?"

Short Soldier scowled. "Excuse me?"

"She didn't mean it," Silversmith said. "It won't happen again, will it, Chasina?"

"Of course not."

"I want an apology," Short Soldier said.

Both giants waited expectantly for Chasina to knock her knees together and beg for forgiveness. She tried. She really tried. Swallowing her dignity one more time shouldn't hurt so badly, but it did. It was like trying to swallow an ear of corn.

"I want an apology, too," Chasina said. "For all the people you've murdered, tortured, and enslaved. I guess we're both out of luck. Let's go, Silversmith."

Instead of reacting like someone with a grain of sense, Silversmith remained passive. He let Short Soldier escort him to the common pits.

Chapter Twenty-Nine

The common pits. Several of these pits dotted the center of Kavalu, two hundred feet deep or the equivalent of approximately three giants standing on top of each other. A grate covered the pits to keep prisoners from escaping.

The soldiers tossed Silversmith and Chasina into a pit with forty other prisoners. Hopefully, Jason was among them. It made sense that the soldiers might throw two criminals arrested simultaneously into the same pit.

Silversmith leaned against the wall and slid to the ground, resting his wrists on his knees. "So that's what it looks like when you grovel. Impressive. I can see why it won over Cormac."

Chasina pressed her lips together. She wasn't sorry for telling off Short Soldier, but it had been tactically unsound.

Not that she would ever admit it to Silversmith.

"We needed to get into the common pits to interrogate Jason. This was the only way," Chasina said.

"Did you realize that I would pay the price for your pride, not you?" He grimaced. "This place is filthy."

"I was trying to stand up for you, so stop being a sprat. We need to find Jason and get out of here," Chasina said.

"No, please don't apologize," Silversmith muttered softly.

Silversmith stood, and Chasina spotted Jason on the other side of the pit. Jason saw Silversmith and started ripping coins from the lining of his clothes. Jason whistled at the prisoners nearest to him. The prisoners saw Jason's money and gathered around him, hiding him from sight.

Chasina pointed at a medium-sized giant chewing his nails a few feet away. "Quick, beat up that prisoner."

Silversmith scoffed. "He's not bothering anyone."

"That's not the point. Jason is paying a group of giants to turn you into meat paste and possibly kill you. If you brutally injure someone before Jason's group attacks, they'll think twice about hurting you."

"Be better than that, Chasina. We're not going to injure an innocent bystander."

"Do you want me to die?" Chasina asked. "If you get into a fight, they'll crush me. It'll be your fault."

Jason's group broke apart. Three people pocketed coins and started toward Silversmith, and Chasina quickly classified them as Bruiser, Crazy, and Dirty Tricks. The trio shoved prisoners aside and ran toward Silversmith.

Silversmith ran. He circled the pit, trying to keep distance between them and the trio.

He ducked behind a group of giants and set Chasina on the ground. "Hide."

Silversmith ran away.

Vibrations crawled up Chasina's legs and rattled her bones as the trio pounded closer. She pressed against the wall. The trio passed and tackled Silversmith.

Silversmith's voice floated through the pit. "I only wanted to talk.

Please stop—"

The trio attacked Silversmith. He begged for them to stop, but it only encouraged them. The smacks of fists-on-flesh brought cheers from the inmates congregating around the fight.

Jason stood with the group, watching the beating with a smirk. He wouldn't be so satisfied if Lord Kemer learned he knew where to find the Suicide Tunnel. Lord Kemer carefully guarded the secret, so the punishment for knowing it could be long-term imprisonment or death.

It was worth a shot.

Chasina jogged across the pit and whistled sharply for Jason's attention. She backed away when he dropped to hands and knees, grabbing for her.

"Do you honestly think my Master came here unprepared?" Chasina demanded, narrowly avoiding Jason's hands. "If he doesn't return, his partner will tell Lord Kemer that you know where to find the Suicide Tunnel. What do you think Kemer will do to keep that secret?"

Jason glanced at the forest of legs surrounding Silversmith. "He would have said something earlier."

"Your thugs cut him off at 'please stop.' Let him go or risk Lord Kemer's wrath." Chasina held Jason's stare until he yielded.

Jason stood and shoved between the cheering inmates. "Fight's over. Let him go."

Chasina dodged feet as giants shuffled away. Finally, she saw Silversmith curled in the fetal position, bleeding at Jason's feet.

Jason waved at Bruiser, Crazy, and Dirty Tricks. "You can protect me from other lowlifes in here."

Bruiser and Crazy followed Jason across the pit, but Dirty Tricks remained. He helped Silversmith stand and brushed him off.

"No hard feelings," Dirty Tricks said.

Instead of replying, Silversmith wiped the blood from his chin and started after Jason.

Dirty Tricks jumped on Silversmith's back and put him in a stranglehold. Silversmith moved so quickly that Chasina only saw flashes of his movement.

Silver-gloved hand.

Silver hand on Dirty Tricks' arm.

Dirty Tricks on the floor.

Silversmith stepped away from Dirty Tricks' unconscious form and rocked on his heels. "Can you hear me? Wake up. I'm sorry."

Chasina hurried to Silversmith and waved her arms for attention, and he wearily dropped to the ground.

"What was that?" Chasina demanded. "Why didn't you do that when three people tried killing you?"

"Sometimes it's hard to suppress the instincts Cormac drilled into me. Unless I'm consciously focused on not fighting back, I react instinctively, and"—he gestured hopelessly at Dirty Tricks—"this happens. I slowed his heartbeats until he fell asleep."

"You let them destroy you without a fight. Do you care that they could have killed you?"

"I got away."

Chasina braced both hands on her hips. "That's because I saved you."

Bloody cuts streaked Silversmith's face, and he winced when he spoke. "Violence does little good for everyone involved."

"Unless you can win. How do you think I survived so long in Tarrken without dying?"

"I assumed it was your charming personality and winning attitude." He sank against the wall. "I'm just going to rest here for a moment."

Silversmith was a useless coward. Why had she felt guilty about addicting him to spara? He might have some good qualities, but she wouldn't feel guilty about using him when he basically invited it.

At least one good thing came of the whole mess. Since Silversmith could use magic to knock out other giants, he didn't need Cormac's help getting past the soldiers guarding the Naridi Stone. Silversmith didn't want to hurt anyone, but if Cormac died, it would force Silversmith to use magic against the soldiers.

She could officially kill Cormac. And once she knew where to find the Suicide Tunnel, she could kill Muriel.

All in all, not a bad trip to the common pits.

"I'll talk to Jason and find the Suicide Tunnel," Chasina said. "Then we can figure out how to escape."

Chapter Thirty

Silversmith sighed, bubbles of bloody saliva popping on his lips. "No need to worry. Cormac will save us. He won't let me forget it, but he'll come."

"How do you know?"

"We always watch for each other's signals in case we need help," Silversmith said. He conjured a large silver sphere and sent it flying through the overhead grate into the sky.

Chasina crossed the pit and found Jason sitting with the trio. He scowled when Chasina waved at him.

Jason jerked his head at the trio, and they disbanded. "Your Master doesn't know what's good for him if he keeps bothering me. What does he want now?"

"He wants to know where to find the Suicide Tunnel."

Jason snatched Chasina from the ground and squeezed her tightly. "Not so loud. Who told you I know where to find it?"

Chasina gasped in pain. "Muriel Silversmith."

"I knew your Master looked familiar. Siblings, aren't they? Muriel Silversmith is wrong. I don't know where to find the Suicide Tunnel."

Muriel might abuse humans and laugh about it, but she wasn't stupid. If she said Jason knew where to find the Suicide Tunnel, Jason knew. He just didn't want to admit it.

"Liar," Chasina said. "If you don't tell me where to find the Suicide Tunnel, we'll tell Lord Kemer about it. Do you want your head on a pike outside the castle?"

Jason ground his teeth. "Half a mile north of Shilist, there's a little cave in the side of a hill. The Suicide Tunnel is inside the cave. Tell your Master to leave me alone." Jason dropped Chasina into a mud puddle and stalked away.

Chasina crawled from the mud and wiped off the excess filth. She knew the Suicide Tunnel's location, and she knew how to use Silversmith's magic to knock out everyone guarding the Naridi Stone. Once Silversmith stole it, she'd drug him, free herself, and return home.

Cormac and Muriel stood in her way. Only they could stop her from drugging Silversmith and taking the Naridi Stone. Now that Silversmith didn't need their help stealing the Naridi Stone, Chasina needed to kill Cormac and Muriel before they interfered with her plan.

Chasina crossed the pit and joined Silversmith. "How long until Cormac arrives?"

"He just did. He left to bribe the guard."

"For someone who just took a serious beating, you don't sound happy to be rescued."

Silversmith didn't answer. Cormac lowered a ladder ten minutes later, and Silversmith exited the pit and followed Cormac through the city.

"Where is Muriel?" Silversmith asked.

"At the tavern, waiting to meet us. We didn't find the keystone's hiding place," Cormac said. Instead of leading them to the tavern,

154

Cormac led them to Silversmith's house.

Once inside, Cormac shut the door and barred it with his body. "Let me get this straight: instead of tracking Jason, you decided to land in the common pits and take a beating? How many assailants were there?"

Silversmith sank onto the bench and rested his head on the table. He did not answer.

"Over five? Under three?" Cormac asked. "I would have gone myself if I realized you couldn't handle it."

Silversmith lifted his head. "I chose to get these bruises because I didn't want anyone else to be a victim. You always forget there's only one kind of person I want to hurt."

"You don't hate the Undying. You're afraid of them. Why else would you spend your life hiding behind the Hero? He might kill the Undying, but he won't kill your fear."

"Let's go meet Muriel," Silversmith said. "Chasina can tell us what Jason told her about the Suicide Tunnel."

Sensing a pending tirade, Chasina quickly recited the Suicide Tunnel's location. It did not help.

"You allowed your slave to interrogate Jason alone?" Cormac asked. "Don't be stupid, Vorce. The human is completely untrustworthy."

"She saved my life twice. Why wouldn't I trust her?" Silversmith asked.

Cormac seated himself across from Silversmith and allowed Seven to walk on the table. "Your slave nearly killed you when she switched the smuggling barrels. She addicted you to spara sap to control you. Go ahead. Ask her."

Silversmith touched Chasina's forehead and spoke apologetically. "Why did you addict me to spara sap?"

"To control you," Chasina said, quickly adding lies when the silver magic left her mouth. "But I was scared. I didn't know what else to

155

do. I'm sorry you went through withdrawals, but I thought you were going to kill me."

Silversmith wrung his hands and looked away, but Cormac tightened his jaw. Cormac picked up Seven and dangled her by one leg.

Seven's green mark pulsed. Seven shook, eyelids twitching, limbs spasming from the magical pain racking her body.

"Leave her alone," Chasina said.

"Humans are so fragile," Cormac said. "They break so easily. They might cry for each other in the moment, but they're lesser creatures. To us, a dead human is just a meal." Cormac ran the blade of his tongue over his lips and grinned, showing all of his teeth.

Cormac had no restraint in his actions. To him, threatening to kill Seven was casual, something that would eventually happen anyway.

Chasina dropped to her knees. "I haven't done anything to hurt my Master since we entered the city. I never wanted soldiers to hang him. Please don't hurt Seven."

Cormac looked at Silversmith. "Did your slave suggest any plans, opinions, or ideas today?"

"She stayed quiet all day."

"She had nothing to do with why you landed in the common pit?"

"I got in trouble, mishandled it, and they threw me into the pit. What else do you want me to say?"

Instantly, Chasina regretted the bad things she'd thought about Silversmith. For a rule-following coward, he lied convincingly under pressure. Maybe that's how he kept his curse a secret from everyone.

Cormac stopped torturing Seven. He set Seven on his shoulder and pushed the bench away from the table, walking to the door.

"Be a good girl and stay here," Cormac said to Chasina. He walked outside and shut the door.

Chasina stayed on her knees and spoke to Silversmith. "Go without me. He's made it perfectly clear that Seven will pay the price for anything I do, so I'm staying."

Silversmith looked like he wanted to say something, but he swallowed the words and moved to the door. "It's less than a mile between here and the tavern, so I don't see why you can't stay here. Good night."

The door banged shut.

Chasina unsheathed Da's knife and watched the light play across the blade. She couldn't stab Cormac in the eye. He suspected her too much for any tricks to work, so she needed other giants to kill him and Muriel. Perhaps a lot of giants. Cormac was a veteran, after all, and he probably handled himself well in a fight.

If someone caught Cormac and Muriel plotting to steal from the vault tower—a treasonous act—they'd be executed. Chasina just needed to convince an authoritative giant that Cormac and Muriel were traitors.

She needed a chat with Lord Kemer.

Chapter Thirty-One

Lord Kemer visited the refugee camp every night, so Chasina knew where to find him. She just needed to give Silversmith a reason to leave Kavalu and something to pacify his suspicion and keep him occupied while she visited Lord Kemer.

Silversmith needed a story. And an activity.

Chasina finished prepping her plan two hours later when Silversmith walked through the door. A patch of moonlight winked on the floor and disappeared as he shut the door, crawled into his pallet, and pulled the blanket to his chin. Snores soon filled the house.

Chasina slid down the table leg thirty feet to the floor and approached Silversmith's pallet. She pulled his eyelid open.

He jerked upright and sent her skidding backward. "What are you doing? What time is it?" he inhaled deeply through the nose. "Hero's sweet breath. I thought you were trying to stab me through the eye."

Time to tell a story.

Chasina showed him her empty hands. "It's evening. A crescent moon tonight."

Silversmith lay down. "If you woke me up just to tell me that, I might reconsider my stance on eating humans." He cracked open one eye. "I'm joking. Go back to bed."

"But you haven't seen the crescent moon. It's time to remember."

"Remember what? How nice it was to be asleep?"

"I thought you'd know. Haven't you wandered human villages?"

"My curse doesn't keep me as a human for very long at a time. Plus, I never know when it will strike, so I don't always have time to make sure I can hide in a human village."

"It's the crescent moon, which means it is time to remember our loved ones. Look." Chasina scurried from his pallet and pointed at the door.

Sighing, Silversmith dragged himself from his pallet and opened the door. A clean slice of moonlight shone between the buildings and landed between them.

Chasina stuck her hand into the moonlight. "The bright crescent is life, cradling the darkness of death. After we remember our family with burned flowers scattered on the river, the moon grows, our love adding life to the darkness." She turned to Silversmith, who knelt beside her. "You never celebrated as a human?"

Silversmith broke his gaze on the moon and looked at her. "It might have been something only celebrated in your village. I never realized that humans chose certain times to remember their loved ones."

Chasina paused and focused on the thin moon. She would have told a slightly different story for a full moon, perhaps a better one, but it served its purpose. It gave Silversmith a story. Now he needed an activity.

Chasina gentled her voice. "We could sneak out and burn flowers. Cormac would never know that you remembered your parents one last time."

Silversmith looked down at her, his elbow dropping as his grip on the door eased. "You want to burn flowers for your family, don't you?

You should have just asked me."

His offer made the calculated innocence slide from Chasina's face. "Is that all right? You were sleeping."

"I can do that tomorrow." He tugged on his boots, set her on his shoulder, and slipped into the alley.

They navigated the narrow alleys and entered the streets, staying within the town criers' hearing range at all times. Silversmith exited the city and jogged toward the river curling below the refugee hill. A cluster of horses with gilded saddles stood outside the camp, signaling that Lord Kemer hadn't concluded his evening visit.

Chasina pointed to the river where it came closest to the refugees' hill. "Right there is fine. It's late. You shouldn't have to go too far from the city."

Silversmith set Chasina among the blue and white flowers sprouting at the river's edge. He kept glancing at her while he built a fire, foiling her attempts to escape.

Chasina harvested a flower as she looked around the river, hoping for something to distract Silversmith. "Aren't you going to get some flowers to burn? There are some good ones over there."

Silversmith touched the inside of his forearm. "I promised Cormac I wouldn't."

"He won't know you did it," Chasina said impatiently. "It wasn't a reasonable request, anyway. Go get some flowers."

"We came out here for you. Not me."

Silversmith snapped a dry twig into several pieces and conjured a silver sphere around them. The twigs burst into flames.

Silversmith dropped the burning twigs on the firewood, and in moments, a fire lit the river bank. He'd made it too small to warm himself, but the flames still leaped higher than Chasina's head.

"Go ahead," Silversmith said. "It's nice and hot."

Chasina stepped closer to the fire. Red-orange tongues snapped hungrily at her arm, and she fell back, blanching.

The fire cackled gleefully.

Silversmith beckoned her nearer. "Your flower has a long stem. The fire won't touch you."

Chasina couldn't move. She took tiny breaths to avoid smelling smoke. Silversmith's fingers pressed against her back, pushing her toward the fire.

She dug in her heels. "I can't."

Silversmith pushed until Chasina stood rigidly beside the fire. She held out the flower like a peace offering to the fire. *Eat this instead of me.*

Heat toasted her skin.

Silversmith nudged her a shade closer. "You have to open your hand. It doesn't usually work any other way."

Chasina opened her hand.

"Good job," he said, flicking the stem wholly into the flames.

Chasina fetched another flower and waited until a breeze gusted across the hills. She released the flower. It flew down the embankment, providing her with an excuse to escape the unholy fire and find Lord Kemer.

Chasina chased the runaway flower down the riverbank and dove into the river. She sank below the surface and stroked smoothly through the water, fish skimming past her, scales glinting in the moonlight. They weren't big enough to eat her, but they could feed a human family for several meals.

Chasina swam five hundred feet to the other bank and crawled into a thicket of cattails. She searched the opposite bank and found Silversmith bobbing in the river. He called her name.

Was he concerned? Silversmith knew that Tarrken had only been able to exile her by binding her soul to him. Did he honestly think a river could kill her?

She left the cattails and climbed up the embankment, digging her fingers in the dirt. She set a steady jog toward the refugee camp, listening to Silversmith call her name.

Chapter Thirty-Two

Chasina poked her head above the hill's crest. Torches lit the city of tents. The smoke trails thickened deeper in the camp, most likely where Lord Kemer held court.

Chasina crept into the camp, sticking to shadows and pausing whenever a sleepy giant wandered past. She passed six tents, and minimal silver pain needled her body.

Chasina took several steps backward. The pain stopped. She moved forward, and the pain started again. Clearly, she'd neared the end of her one-mile leash, and the magical pain warned her to turn back. It grew with every step.

Chasina gritted her teeth and kept moving. Soon, her whole body ached with silver agony. Magical tendrils radiated pain from her spine and made every step agonizing.

Chasina hobbled around a corner and saw two armored soldiers guarding a red and gold tent. Their torches cast light on the ground and made flickering shadows as giants passed by the tent.

The tent must belong to Lord Kemer. It stood only a hundred yards away—she could make it.

Chasina took three steps toward the tent, and magic split her bones into pain-filled cubes. She gnawed on her fist to stifle her screams.

It's not as bad as the ravine. Take one step. And another. Keep going.

Halfway to Lord Kemer's tent, Chasina fell. She forced herself to her knees and crawled the rest of the way. Her head knocked against something metal.

Chasina looked up and saw a soldier's metal greaves. The soldier didn't notice her, switching his torch between hands, looking supremely bored while guarding the Lord's tent.

Chasina cut some cloth from the tent. She wrapped the cloth around her hand, hiding her silver mark, and crawled inside the tent. She kept to the edges, struggling to focus on the occupants instead of the pain riddling her body.

Lord Kemer sat cross-legged on a thick rug, nodding complacently while a refugee prostrated himself and reeled off an odd mixture of gratitude and complaints. The Lord's bored gaze wandered from the refugee. It passed Chasina once, stopped, and flicked back to her for several moments.

Chasina stood and bowed, and Lord Kemer raised an eyebrow.

Lord Kemer clicked his fingers. "That's enough, refugee. Every effort will be made to satisfy your needs."

The refugee bowed and left the tent.

Lord Kemer poked his head outside the tent and spoke to his guards. "Close the tent. Throw anyone who tries to get past into the cesspit. We'll stay here for the night. That last refugee complained so long that the moon rose behind him."

Lord Kemer closed the tent flap and returned to his thick rug. He beckoned Chasina nearer.

Chasina stepped forward and smoothed her tunic. She had to say everything perfectly, or Kemer wouldn't arrest Cormac and Muriel.

Chasina bowed gracefully. "Hero bless you, Lord. May I have a moment of your time?"

The Lord winked, and the gems decorating his crimson tunic seemed to copy him. "I sent you to the torturers the last time we met. Here we stand once more, and you are doing an admirable job of swallowing your hatred. I think you've earned a moment of my time. What is your name?"

"Chasina, daughter of Ewan."

He rolled one hand in acknowledgment. "Daughter of Ewan, I'm curious. Usually, the people I torture don't ever want to see me again. Assuming you didn't come to poison me, why are you here?"

"I have important information for the safety of Shilist Castle."

He chuckled and stroked his beard. "You angered an entire cathedral of giants to free a single human, and now you're coming to save my castle? You could have thought of something a bit more believable."

"Don't you want to know what's happening at your castle, my Lord?"

"I do, I do," he said, resting his chin on his fist. "Please, go on. I need a good bedtime story after listening to all the Hero-worshipers whine about their hardships."

Obviously, Silversmith had correctly guessed that Lord Kemer was a heretic. The Lord didn't care that Chasina had defiled a cathedral, and he seemed to disdain the 'Hero-worshipers.' He probably hated them for different reasons than Chasina, reasons likely tied to the expense of having them camped outside his District.

Maybe she could use his dislike of Hero-worshipers to her advantage?

Chasina added a touch of disgust to her voice. "Two Hero-worshipers plan to rob the tower vault and steal the Naridi Stone. Cormac and Muriel, my Master."

Kemer clapped. "See? That's a much better story because it is just outlandish enough to be real. Also, lovely touch, using my disdain of religious fanatics to make me more inclined to believe you. But why would Cormac steal the Naridi Stone? He hates humans."

"Cormac and Muriel don't want to give the stone back to humans. They're going to trade it to find the Vault of Eternal Sleep and awaken the Hero."

The mirth faded from Kemer's face, and his lips knotted. "I heard the sheriff found zero illegal humans in Muriel's business. For all I know, your Master commanded you to come here and feed me lies to distract me from investigating her business further."

Chasina pointed toward Kavalu. "If you free Cormac's slave from his magic, she can confirm everything I'm saying. You can find Cormac and Muriel in her tavern."

"You protected Muriel in the cathedral when I offered to kill her in exchange for her secret. Assuming you weren't lying, and this is the secret you were talking about, why did you suddenly change your mind?"

"I thought I could pressure you to free Bartholomew. And when you asked Cormac to torture me, I didn't think he'd do it since he works with my Master. Now I just want both of them to die."

"Why didn't Muriel come forward earlier?"

Chasina opened her mouth to lie again, but silver agony rose like a tsunami within her. In the moment before it destroyed her, Chasina looked around for Silversmith but didn't find him. He must have gone downriver looking for her and inadvertently snapped her one-mile leash.

The tsunami crashed down on Chasina. She bent double, screaming as magic boiled her organs and bones like a stew.

Lord Kemer reached out and pressed a finger to her forehead, and yellow magic blossomed on his fingertip. Yellow magic rippled through Chasina's body and calmed the silver agony. Slowly, the silver magic receded to Chasina's spine.

Chasina touched herself. She felt fine. It always amazed her that she went from a deathbed to perfect health after the magic stopped punishing her.

Chasina bowed. "Thank you, my Lord."

The Lord flexed his fingers, watching yellow magic burgeon on the fingertips. "The magic inside of you is silver. Muriel doesn't own you. It's Vorce, isn't it? He's alive."

Chapter Thirty-Three

C hasina resisted the urge to look toward the river. Silversmith had worked at Shilist Castle for three years, so Kemer must recognize the color of Silversmith's magic. "Who, my Lord?" Chasina asked.

Lord Kemer extinguished his magic. "Silversmith asked to take the Naridi Stone and trade it to find the Hero. He's working with Cormac and Muriel, isn't he? He's just the kind of Hero-worshiper who would steal the Naridi Stone if he thought it would help him find the Hero. That explains why we didn't find his body in Brundar. The cowardly fanatic faked his death and is trying to steal from me. Where is he?"

Chasina said nothing.

"You want Silversmith dead, too," Lord Kemer said, shifting forward until he crouched above Chasina. "His death means your freedom. Where can I find him?"

Chasina slowly inched backward. "He commanded me to keep that a secret."

"His commands won't work until you return to him," Kemer said impatiently. "Tell me where to find him."

"A few miles away, in the hills," she said, pointing in the opposite direction of the river. When Kemer glanced in that direction, she ran.

She barely made it two paces before Lord Kemer caught her leg between two fingers. She struggled, but he rapidly switched his grip, his fingers climbing over her body like spider legs.

Chasina tucked her knife into her sleeve before Kemer finished wrapping his hand around her thin frame.

"You barely have any magic inside of you," Kemer said. "If not for me, you would have died because you were more than a mile from Silversmith. He can't be much more than a mile away."

Lord Kemer rose from his haunches and strode from the tent toward the river. Chasina didn't know what he planned to do with her, but she knew he would execute Silversmith. Silversmith was her only way to steal the Naridi Stone and must be kept safe at all costs.

Plus, anyone gullible enough to believe the lies she spun about the crescent moon was too decent to die young.

Chasina slipped the knife from her sleeve and jammed it beneath Kemer's nail. He cried out, fingers reflexively opening. Chasina fell, caught herself on his jewel-studded tunic, and slid quickly to the ground.

Chasina raced across the camp, dodging a few expertly aimed spheres of yellow magic. The Lord aimed more accurately than most giants, but luckily—*unluckily?*—she had a lot of practice dodging magic.

Rounding a tent, Chasina crouched and felt the ground for the Lord's footsteps. The vibrations faded. Evidently, the Lord wanted to capture Silversmith more than a nuisance human. Unsurprising, but she still had to save Silversmith.

Chasina dashed around the tent and onto the main path. Just ahead, Lord Kemer strode toward the river.

Chasina ran to the nearest giantess, a sleepy woman headed toward the cesspit. "Someone attacked the Lord! He can barely breathe."

The giantess rubbed her face. "The Lord looks like he's walking all right."

"Delusional. Lord Kemer thinks he sees a dead soldier by the river." The Lord tripped over a tent peg, and Chasina pointed triumphantly. "See?"

The giantess hurried to the Lord's side and touched his throat, speaking soothingly.

Chasina scurried up a nearby tent cord and rapped on a soldier's armored shoulder. "That woman came through the back of the tent and attacked Lord Kemer. Look," she said, pointing to Lord Kemer, "he's trying to get away."

Lord Kemer slapped the woman's hands from his throat.

The soldier gasped. "Protect the Lord!"

Quickly, all of the soldiers converged on Lord Kemer, encasing him inside a wall of plated bodies.

Chasina slid down the tent cord and ran to the river. She slid to the river's edge and bobbed in the water while Silversmith inspected the opposite bank. Clothes properly soaked, she waved her arms until he noticed her.

Silversmith dove into the water and stroked to her bank. He stayed chest-deep in the water and looked down at her. "I was afraid the current had taken you downriver. What happened to you?"

Chasina panted. "I chased Da's flower into the water, but I couldn't fight the current. Took me forever to swim ashore. Don't tell me you were worried?"

Silversmith held out the bruised flower Chasina had supposedly chased into the water. "I was afraid I'd miss the chance to ask you about this. Strangely, I found it on the bank, not the water."

"I jumped into the river for nothing? Shame. Can we go home now?"

She glanced up the hill. The confusion would keep Lord Kemer from finding Silversmith tonight, but they needed to get back to Kavalu.

Silversmith pressed his index finger to her forehead. "Did you fall into the water on purpose?"

"Yes." The magic retreated from Chasina's mouth, and she added to her statement before Silversmith asked more questions. "Fire and smoke bring back bad memories."

Silversmith slapped his forehead. "Chasina, you're the one who wanted to burn flowers. Did you think that fire wouldn't be part of it?"

"I know, I'm sorry. Gran had to wait until the ashes were cold before I would sprinkle them on the river."

Silversmith's gaze dropped to her left cheek. "Does that have anything to do with your scars?"

They'd swung from one line of uncomfortable questions to another, but Chasina answered them, maybe because Silversmith hadn't forced her to answer.

Chasina touched her scars. "I had an accident with fire when I was a child. It was long ago, but I still panic around flames." She hugged herself but stopped when her ribs throbbed.

Silversmith leaned his elbows on the bank. "You've been wincing all day whenever I touch your ribs. Did Cormac hurt you because he thinks you're cursed?"

Chasina braced her hands on her hips. "Cormac is an idiot for thinking humans are cursed. The Undying stole our Naridi Stone. Why would Undying allow humans to be exterminated if they also used us to hurt giants?"

Silversmith winced. "Cormac is very pious. Church history records that humans betrayed the Hero when he battled the Undying four centuries ago. The humans poisoned him, but he still killed the Undyings' leader."

Chasina tsked. "And he didn't kill them all? Poor leadership."

"He would have, but he was weakened because humans poisoned him," Silversmith said testily. "Nearly dead, the Hero retreated to the Vault of Eternal Sleep, where he sleeps in a magical coma until someone awakens him. Legend says that the Undying were furious that humans had failed to kill the Hero, so they cursed humankind to obey their every command."

"People believe the legend?"

Silversmith shrugged one shoulder. "It's because there have been many instances of humans helping the Undying kill giants and topple cities."

Chasina raised an eyebrow. "Really? And no one in this enormous world of yours thought that maybe Undying had specifically enslaved those humans, not our entire race? Amazing."

Silversmith shook his head, and water droplets splashed on Chasina's shoulders. "Most people think that humans are the Undyings' minions and have little or no thoughts of their own. Not me, personally, but only because I've lived among humans enough to realize they are sentient people like me. So," he asked, leaning down to peer at her, "did Cormac hurt you?"

"If he knows I told you, he will hurt Seven."

Silversmith dropped the flower into the river, where it spun gently before riding the current. "I promise to be very subtle when I have a word with him. I put out the fire. It's cold now, so you can sprinkle ashes before going home."

Chasina settled in his palm, and he stroked to the opposite shore. She dug handfuls of ash from the cold fire and sprinkled it on the river, silently reciting the Death Blessing.

She didn't have much practice at the remembrance ritual—burning flowers, scattering ashes on the river, and reciting the Death Blessing—since she'd never participated in Tarrken until the fires were cold and everyone had gone home. When Chasina was a little girl, Gran stayed with her to sprinkle the cold ash on the river. A couple years after Gran apprenticed Katie, Gran stopped waiting with Chasina to perform the ritual of remembering loved ones.

Maybe when Chasina brought home the Naridi Stone, Gran would stay with her again. They could sprinkle ashes on the river and share memories together like a loving family.

It sounded like Silversmith constantly sprinkled ash for his parents, but when did Muriel join him? It hadn't bothered Muriel that Cormac wanted Silversmith to stop burning flowers. She'd probably burned 'the appropriate number of flowers' for her parents like she had for Silversmith and then continued selling slaves.

Silversmith didn't have to adhere to Cormac's idiotic rule, but he did. Chasina wouldn't do it—it was stupid—but maybe it was the first sign of strength she'd seen from Silversmith.

It was a spark if nothing else.

Chasina used the last handful of ash for Silversmith's parents. She wouldn't say the Death Blessing for giants, but the ash sufficed.

Chasina dusted her hands clean, and Silversmith took them home. He shut the house door behind them and leaned against it.

"I sprinkled some ash for your parents," Chasina said.

Silversmith inhaled sharply. He pushed himself from the door and left her on the table, rolling himself into his pallet. A quiet 'thank you' floated from the floor.

Chasina pulled her knees to her chest and watched the shadows swim across his face, tangling around the scar on his neck.

Had she ever looked so innocent asleep? Silversmith had no idea that Chasina had sold out his sister and mentor and put him in harm's way. In return, all she did was burn flowers for his parents, and apparently, it was good enough for him.

He smiled in his sleep.

That smile would disappear in the morning. And from there? His life would get much, much worse.

Chapter Thirty-Four

C hasina awoke to Theodoric trying to kill her again.

"Don't make me hurt you, Theodoric," Chasina grunted, twisting madly when Theodoric wrapped five arms around her body and picked her up.

Five arms?

Chasina peeled open her eyes just as she wiggled free from Silversmith's grasp. She fell ten feet and hit the table chest-first.

Theodoric wasn't trying to kill her. Silversmith was trying to...hurt her? Kill her? He'd never grabbed for her quite so desperately. And why take her asleep if he meant no harm?

Silversmith swiped at her again.

A lifetime of instincts honed by close calls took control of Chasina's body. She rolled out of the way and jumped to her feet, assessing the situation.

Cormac stood by the door, blood oozing from a wound across his chest. Something was very, very wrong. Had he learned about her actions in the refugee camp last night? That explained Silversmith's actions.

"Grab her, for Hero's sake," Cormac said. "We have to leave right now."

"She's too fast," Silversmith said. His hands pounced from one spot to the next as Chasina spun and dodged. She ran for her satchel, for the spara leaf that was her only weapon against Silversmith.

Silversmith caught Chasina's legs. She lurched forward, snagging the satchel by two fingers as Silversmith hoisted her into the air. Securing her grip on the satchel, Chasina pawed through its contents.

She fished out the spara leaf as Silversmith hustled to the door with Cormac.

"What's going on, Cormac?" Silversmith asked.

"Someone told Lord Kemer that we planned to steal the Naridi Stone. Two dozen soldiers came to the tavern at midnight and arrested Muriel. They almost got me, too." Cormac checked the alley for passersby and dragged Silversmith from the house. "The town criers are announcing us."

A town crier's voice floated from a few streets to the south. "Muriel Silversmith was apprehended last night preparing to steal from the tower vault. In his wisdom, Lord Kemer has decreed that she shall hang in a cage from the castle wall until her partners yield themselves to justice. Her partners are Cormac, son of Finnian, retired Ramerian scout, and Vorce Silversmith, son of George, army scout."

Chasina released a huge breath, her whole body relaxing. Everything was going according to plan—almost. Soldiers had arrested Muriel but not Cormac, and now soldiers hunted the three of them.

How could she possibly fix this? She needed to keep her betrayal a secret and kill Cormac.

The solutions to both problems lay in Shilist Castle. Firstly, Muriel was the only person besides Lord Kemer who might know about Chasina's betrayal. If Silversmith and Cormac spoke to her, they'd find out that Chasina had betrayed all of them, so Chasina had to get to Muriel first. And secondly, plenty of soldiers patrolled Shilist Castle who'd love to capture Cormac.

Get Silversmith to take me to Shilist Castle to talk to his sister.

Chasina waited until Cormac walked ahead of them, and then she whispered in Silversmith's ear. "You need to make sure Muriel is all right. Can we talk to her and find out what happened?"

Silversmith tensed. "We could send you to talk to her. It might be dangerous, though. Can you handle it?"

"I've spent the last year of my life with people I love trying to kill me. Of course I can handle it."

"Thank you."

Chasina forced a smile into her voice. "You're welcome."

She didn't enjoy outwitting someone as gullible as Silversmith, but that didn't matter. She had to do everything necessary to steal the Naridi Stone, including manipulating a very gullible, well-intentioned giant.

Both giants pulled up their hoods and approached the city gates. Two soldiers tried to stop them, but Cormac put both of them to sleep with the same magical touch Silversmith had used on Dirty Tricks. Cormac led them out of the city, up the hills, and into Brundar, settling on a spot where trees sheltered them from view.

Grimacing, Cormac peeled off his bloody tunic, revealing a deep gash across his chest. It wasn't fatal, but it looked painful, which was some condolence.

Silversmith checked the surrounding trees for pursuers. "We're safe for now. What happened? How did they find out I'm alive?"

"Whoever told the Lord that we planned to steal the Naridi Stone also told him that you're still alive."

Silversmith leaned against a tree. "Muriel might know what happened. We could send Chasina to speak to her and find out who told the Lord. Chasina is so small, none of the soldiers patrolling the wall will notice her."

Cormac balled his bloody tunic in one hand. "We are not sending Chasina to talk to Muriel. Seven will go."

Chasina spent the day wracking her mind for a way to convince Cormac to send her to Shilist instead of Seven, who painstakingly stitched Cormac's wound while he slept. Every idea lacked the cunning to fool Cormac.

Late afternoon, while Silversmith hunted and Cormac slept, Seven approached Chasina. "Is it true?"

Chasina eyed the tall woman. Cormac might not know precisely how sending Seven into Shilist foiled Chasina's plans, but he knew he'd foiled something. Possessing Seven to talk to Chasina was his way of gloating.

"You can't fool me, Drasta Cormac," Chasina said.

Seven laid a hand on her chest. "This is me. Myself. My spirit has limited control over my body while he sleeps. To a certain extent, at least. I cannot violate his standing orders. My Master believes you want to speak with Muriel and that you might have given Drasta Silversmith the idea. Is it true?"

The mark on Seven's forehead maintained its dim glow. Since it didn't pulse like it did when Cormac possessed Seven, Seven must be telling the truth. She controlled herself for the moment.

"I did," Chasina said. "But I cannot change Cormac's mind. He thinks I mean to harm him and Silversmith."

A muscle twitched in Seven's forehead. "I do not wish to harm my Master, nor yours. But if you did...if you had a way to—" she choked. Seven stopped breathing.

Chasina jumped up to hit her on the back, but Seven waved her away. Seven quietly meditated while her face turned blue.

At last, Seven's face blanked, and she inhaled.

"Seven, what happened?" Chasina asked, kneeling in front of her.

"Did you choke?"

Seven's voice was as clear and toneless as spring water. "I thought something bad and was properly punished." She moved the tree and expertly climbed up the bark. Chasina followed. Twenty feet from the ground, Seven started to jump.

Chasina grabbed Seven's arm. "What are you doing?"

"Something that needs to be done. My Master cannot access my memories to see what happened, and since I am choosing to injure myself, you truly have nothing to do with this. He won't be able to prove anything against you."

"This is my plan, understand? I am responsible for it."

"You will talk to Muriel and carry out your plan, whatever it is. And if you hurt someone, make sure it is someone who deserves it."

Chasina kept a tight grip on Seven's arm, looking between Seven and the distant ground. Twenty feet. It wasn't a fatal fall, but bones would break. It wasn't Seven's duty to endure that level of incredible pain; it was Chasina's.

"Unless you are my Master, let go of me," Seven said.

Chasina let go.

Seven jumped from the tree and landed awkwardly, stumbling to the side. Something crunched.

Chasina climbed to the ground and dropped to Seven's side, but the herbwoman was already feeling the break in her leg. No screaming. No crying. The green mark on her forehead glowed more brightly, and Cormac stirred.

Seven swatted Chasina's hand. "He senses my pain. He will come to get me in seconds, and you have to be gone."

Chasina hugged Seven. "Cormac will leave you tonight when we go to the castle. Hide away from the camp. I can't tell you more, so just trust me."

Seven nodded, and Chasina hid in a cluster of rocks, peeking as

179

Cormac rose from his tree and crouched above Seven.

Seven never cried. Not even when Cormac forced her to set her own broken leg.

Chapter Thirty-Five

Chasina balanced on Silversmith's shoulder that night, prepared to speak to Muriel and convince soldiers to capture Cormac.

Seven had wrapped her leg in white linen braced with smooth sticks and slathered with egg whites.

"Seven says your slave had nothing to do with her injury," Cormac told Silversmith.

Silversmith, bless him, sounded genuinely shocked. "Why would Chasina have anything to do with Seven's accident?"

Cormac pinched his nose and sighed. "Hero help me, Silversmith, your slave is smarter than you. She's probably fully possessed by an Undying. It's the only explanation for that much intelligence residing in a human body."

Silversmith picked up a stick and changed the topic. "Are you sure I shouldn't be in charge of the distraction at the castle? You're injured."

Cormac plucked the stick from Silversmith and used it to point out the bruises on Silversmith's face. "I want this mission to be successful, which means the most capable person creates the distraction. If you had passed the trials, it might be you."

"There will be no need for Ramerian scouts when the Hero returns and kills all the Undying."

"So I've heard time and time again. Even if this time is genuine, why haven't you taken the Ramerian trials before now?" He tapped Silversmith's face with the stick. "All of these bruises conveniently landed on the least painful places. You have the skill."

"I don't want to."

"Why not?"

Silversmith snatched the stick from Cormac. "I have no desire to hurt anyone, Cormac. I had no business training to be a Ramerian scout."

"Hogwash. The Undying killed your parents, and you just let them walk away without trying to hunt them down. Are you a coward or not?"

Silversmith silently peeled the bark from his stick.

"Have you thought about what we're going to do after we steal the Naridi Stone?" Cormac asked. "Lord Kemer will hunt us down."

"Lord Kemer does not check the vault very often," Silversmith said, still focused on his stick. "He won't even know the Naridi Stone is missing until the next time he checks the vault. By the time he realizes what happened, we will have awakened the Hero and earned a pardon."

Cormac led them out of the forest toward the castle.

Seven stayed in the camp. Hopefully, she remembered to hide. If everything went according to Chasina's plan, soldiers looking for Cormac would swarm the campsite in less than an hour.

Silversmith and Cormac circled Shilist Castle until they found the gates. Over a dozen decapitated heads rotted on pikes above the gates. Some were fresh, others merely skeletons.

Four rusty iron cages hung from the crenelated wall. Three were empty. Muriel huddled inside the fourth cage, her braids frayed, her feet bare.

Cormac turned to Silversmith. "Give me two minutes to distract the guards, then send your slave to Muriel's cage. I'll meet you back at the camp."

Cormac left their hiding place and circled the castle. In one minute, he disappeared. In one more minute, people started shouting inside the castle. The soldiers standing above Muriel's cage turned toward the commotion on the other side of the castle.

Silversmith conjured a silver sphere around Chasina and sent her toward the wall. She shot through the air and landed on top of Muriel's cage.

Chasina shimmied up the chain suspending the cage from the wall. She counted on being too small and far away for Silversmith to see her deviating from the plan.

Chasina whistled at the soldiers standing on the walkway. "I imagine Lord Kemer would look favorably on you if you caught a traitor."

The two soldiers jostled each other before settling down.

The first soldier cleared his throat and casually lifted one shoulder. "Maybe. What does your Master want in return?"

Chasina didn't want anything in return, but the soldiers were more likely to believe her if she disguised the information as a bribe.

Chasina readjusted her grip on the chain. "Give me two minutes to speak to the prisoner, and I will tell you where to find Cormac, son of Finnian."

The two soldiers looked around and then nodded to Chasina. She climbed down the chain until she hung four chain links above Muriel's cage.

Muriel hissed, pressing her face against the top of the cage. "You little monster. You're the one who told the soldiers where to find Cormac and me."

Chasina gave Muriel a mutilated smile. "Having fun in a cage,

Muriel? That's what some people might call poetic justice."

"Humans deserve to be caged and sold. All I've ever done is turn it profitable," Muriel said, pounding her fist against the rusty bars. "Are you planning to betray my brother, too?"

Chasina bent lower to the cage. "Happy death, Muriel."

Chasina climbed up the chain and spoke to the soldiers. "Cormac is the person making a commotion on the other side of the castle, but you won't catch him. Ambush him when he returns to his camp." Chasina gave the soldiers directions to the campsite.

The two soldiers almost collided when they ran down the walkway. As soon as they killed Cormac, Chasina would help Silversmith steal the Naridi Stone, steal it from him, and return home.

Chasina waited twenty minutes to give the soldiers time to exit the castle and capture Cormac, then she climbed down the rusty chain and jumped into the night. She only fell thirty feet before a silver sphere swallowed and carried her to Silversmith's hiding place.

Silversmith caught Chasina and held her at chest level. "How was Muriel?"

"Hungry but fine," Chasina said. "I told her we would rescue her when we stole the Naridi Stone."

"You aren't serious."

"It's no accident that Kemer put her in a cage instead of executing her. She is bait. If Kemer expects us to save Muriel, his focus will be on her, not on us sneaking into the vault tower. If we work quickly, we can steal the Naridi Stone and save Muriel."

Silversmith wordlessly set Chasina on his shoulder and headed toward the camp. He stopped a hundred feet from the campsite and scented the air like an animal. Slowly, Silversmith moved forward, his footfalls completely silent.

They reached the camp, and Chasina covered her mouth. Eight soldiers sprawled across the campsite, bleeding, broken, and probably dead. Cormac lay in the center of the carnage, bleeding freely from wounds striped across his back.

She had expected some resistance from Cormac, but nothing to this extent.

Chasina tapped Silversmith's jaw. "If a commander sends people looking for these soldiers, we could be overrun in seconds. We need to leave."

Silversmith jerked his shoulder. "Cormac's hurt, Chasina. Shut up. I think he's dead. Hero's name, there's so much blood."

Chapter Thirty-Six

Silversmith checked Cormac's pulse. "He's alive. We need to stop the bleeding."

Chasina examined the deep wounds on Cormac's back. She could kill Cormac in his weakened state, but not with Silversmith watching.

"We need a fire," Chasina told Silversmith. "Heat up your knife and fuse these skin flaps shut. He'll stop bleeding."

Silversmith pressed his wobbling lips together—*Wobbling? Sweet Naridi roses*—and conjured a silver sphere. He inserted his knife into the silver sphere and heated the blade.

Chasina hurried to correct him. "We need a real fire," she lied. "Magic just won't work as well. Hurry! Go get wood."

Silversmith dropped his knife and hurried away, too stricken to question Chasina.

Chasina circled Cormac's body until she stared at his face. Gore matted his gray beard, and blood dripped from the corner of his mouth.

Drawing her knife, Chasina moved behind his beard to his neck. If she slit his throat here, Silversmith would assume Cormac's throat had been cut all along. Silversmith wouldn't ask if Chasina murdered Cormac.

Chasina stabbed Cormac below his jawbone. Before she ripped open his throat, someone grabbed her hand.

Chasina turned and saw Seven. "What are you doing here, Seven? I told you to hide." Another thought struck her. "You can't walk with a broken leg."

Silent tears dripped down Seven's face. "I hid far from camp. I felt my Master's pain and returned to help him."

Seven was here to save Cormac, which meant Chasina had only one option: knock out Seven.

Chasina tried punching Seven in the jaw, but Seven grabbed Chasina's fist, twisted her arm, and kicked her knee. Chasina crumbled to the ground. Chasina grabbed Seven's ankle, but Seven stomped on Chasina's wrist and kicked her ribs. Chasina rolled away, growling as pain flared through her knee, wrist, and ribs.

Seven didn't move like someone suffering the pain of a freshly broken leg. She didn't favor it. Didn't wince. But the pain dripped down Seven's face in silent tears.

Chasina climbed to her feet and charged Seven, but heavy vibrations made her stumble. She looked over her shoulder and saw Silversmith running toward them with a bundle of wood tucked beneath one arm.

"Give me the knife," Chasina said to Seven. Seven threw Chasina's knife to one side, and Chasina retrieved it.

Silversmith dropped the wood. "Maria, thank the Hero you're here. I need you to show me how to do this."

"Use your magic to heat the knife blade," Seven said.

"Chasina said that I needed real fire," Silversmith said.

"Chasina was mistaken."

Chasina fixed an apologetic expression on her face. "I'm sorry. I thought a fire would work better."

Silversmith didn't seem angry, only frightened, so he must not suspect that Chasina had purposefully misinformed him.

Silversmith used magic to heat his blade. Following Seven's instructions, Silversmith waited until the metal almost glowed and pressed it carefully to the wounds on Cormac's back.

Steam curled from Cormac's wet clothes.

Chasina covered her nose until Silversmith finished sealing the wounds. The smell of burning flesh made her want to puke.

"Did it work?" Silversmith asked.

"Yes," Seven said.

Seven began sewing the long gash on Cormac's arm with tiny, precise stitches. Fresh tears coursed down her face each time she put weight on her broken leg, but she said nothing.

Chasina moved to Seven's side and wrapped an arm around her waist, helping her move without putting weight on her injured leg. "What about the Naridi Stone? Now that Seven is here to look after Cormac, it makes sense to use the Suicide Tunnel before anything else goes wrong."

"Do you have a plan?" Silversmith asked.

"We'll find the keystone in the castle, you'll put the guards to sleep like you did in the common pits, and we'll steal the Naridi Stone from the vault."

"And rescue Muriel."

"After we get the Naridi Stone." *By which time, you'll be asleep, and I will have stolen the Naridi Stone from you and left Muriel to die.*

First, though, Chasina needed to speak to Seven alone. "We might need some rope," Chasina said, which sent Silversmith running out of the forest and across the hills.

Seven planted a broad hand on Chasina's chest and whispered a heartword. *"Sleep."*

Chasina yawned, collapsed, and desperately tried to stay awake. She couldn't move. Lifting a finger was like lifting ten rocks.

Seven must not have imbued the heartword with much power because Chasina would already be asleep if she had. Instead, she maintained consciousness by biting her lip.

Seven stood above Chasina. "You betrayed my Master, didn't you?"

"I had to."

"And?"

"You know what happened to Cormac?"

Seven studied the gash on Cormac's arm as though her entire world had been ripped open, not her Master's flesh and blood and tissue. "He has lived inside me for a long time, so I sense his strong emotions. He feels deep anger, though I do not believe he knows exactly how the soldiers found him."

"Are you going to say anything about it?"

"I am bound as my Master's vessel to tell him about plots against his life. My Master will soon wake."

Chasina tried standing, but all she managed was lolling her head to one side. "Will you be safe?"

"I am useful to my Master. I will live, but you will not." Seven began tending Cormac's wound again.

Chasina swallowed. She'd lived with imminent death her entire life. The trick was to keep it from overtaking her life. Catalog the threat, analyze it, and move on. Fearing imminent death wasted time and energy, and right now, she needed both to steal the Naridi Stone.

Once she had the Naridi Stone, imminent death wouldn't be a problem. She'd free herself and Seven and return to Tarrken.

Moments later, Chasina felt the ground vibrating beneath her back. She couldn't see Silversmith from her position on the grass, but he approached quickly.

Seven took Chasina's hand, and a heartword rippled through

Chasina's body. *"Awaken."*

Strength returned to Chasina's body. She stood, and so did Seven. Seven towered above Chasina, impassive but for the tears staining her cheeks.

Chasina reached up and wiped the tears from Seven's face. "Thank you."

In moments, the heavy vibrations beneath their feet reached a pitch and then stopped.

Silversmith spoke from above. "Anything else before we go?"

"No. Let's go find the Suicide Tunnel," Chasina said.

Silversmith set Chasina on his shoulder and loped across several hills. They explored the general area Jason had described to Chasina.

"I think I found the cave," Chasina said, pointing to a hill where a patch of vining flowers hung at an odd angle.

Silversmith hurried to the spot and brushed aside the vines to reveal the mouth of a cave. He ducked inside the cave and followed its downward slope into the earth.

They followed the underground tunnel for several minutes until it finally widened into a small cave. A pool of water glistened in the center of the cave, rippling from Silversmith's footfalls.

"It must feed the castle well," Silversmith said, crouching at the pool's edge. He dropped the rope from his shoulder. "That means I won't need the rope. A bucket already hangs in the well."

Chasina latched herself tightly to Silversmith's shoulder and held her breath as he waded into the pool. Silversmith arced cleanly through the water.

Total darkness engulfed them.

The underground stream moved swiftly, its current tugging at Chasina. Bits of sediment tapped her forehead and arms, but she saw nothing in the darkness.

Chasina struggled to keep her grip on Silversmith's tunic while he

190

swam, his shoulders constantly moving.

Silversmith stroked steadily for ten seconds, then slowed. He hovered aimlessly in the water, lost.

Chapter Thirty-Seven

Silversmith conjured silver light around his hands and illuminated the tunnel. Broken arrows floated in the water along with sediment, a few slimy bricks, and even a skeleton. Silt combed through Silversmith's fingers as he swam around a corner and surfaced.

Chasina broke the water face-first, gulping air. She flung her soaking braids behind her shoulders and blinked through water droplets streaming down her face.

Silversmith treaded water in a well. The cylindrical structure rose to the surface, each slimy brick taller than Chasina.

The silver aura faded from Silversmith's hands, and he pointed at a stone lid covering the mouth of the well. "I think we have a problem."

Chasina slid from Silversmith's shoulder and swam to the bucket knocking against slimy bricks. "You can't lift the lid out of place?"

Droplets streamed from Silversmith's greasy hair. "The stone probably weighs more than me, and I can't push it off without any leverage. Besides, it's probably guarded. The well is Shilist's most important asset."

"Climb up after me," she said. "Pull the soldiers into the well."

Chasina climbed up the rope. Her fingers fit between the fibers, although her legs slipped a few times on the wet rope.

Silversmith whispered harshly below her. "Chasina? Chasina! What if they can't swim?"

There was a small square hole in the stone cover where the giants could fit a metal bar through the hole and push the cover aside. Chasina followed the rope out of that hole, poking her head and shoulders tentatively into plain sight.

Two soldiers guarded the well, one on each side, and the faint screams coming from the other side of the courtyard covered Silversmith's panicked whispers. Obviously, Silversmith couldn't hear the screams through the thick stone cover. He'd probably mess up the whole plan if he heard the screams.

Across the courtyard, ropes secured Muriel to a post while Lord Kemer whipped her. She screamed several more times, sagging against the wooden post.

Lord Kemer let the whip fall at his side. He moved closer to Muriel and asked something too quiet for Chasina to hear. Muriel shook her head. Lord Kemer played with the whip, allowing the tip near Muriel without striking her, before asking her another question.

She shook her head again, and his lips thinned. Lord Kemer untied Muriel and escorted her across the courtyard. Blood spattered his elegant clothes, the same blood that dripped from the whip in his hands and down Muriel's back. He deliberately put his hand on Muriel's shredded back and pushed her past the vault tower.

To Chasina's relief, Kemer and Muriel disappeared inside the keep, probably heading to the dungeons. Chasina didn't need Silversmith seeing his twin sister getting whipped in the courtyard, especially since Chasina had no intention of rescuing Muriel.

Chasina counted to ten, allowing Lord Kemer time to disappear into the dungeons with Muriel. She finished counting and fully emerged from the well, squealing loudly. The two guards jumped, looking around until they spotted Chasina disappearing inside the stone cover.

Chasina dropped onto Silversmith's shoulder.

The stone cover fell from the well, and two giants pushed their heads greedily into the opening.

Silversmith grabbed the first soldier by his tunic and flipped him into the water below, quickly followed by his partner. Silversmith climbed from the well.

"They can't swim," Silversmith said, pulling the rope out of the well so the soldiers couldn't escape.

"Yes, they can. They can hold on to the wall if they get tired, but we have to go before someone sees us." Chasina pointed at the keep. "Let's find the keystone."

Silversmith reluctantly left the well.

Shadows drifted across Silversmith's shoulders, flicking over Chasina as he glided to the keep. Stained glass windows dotted the heavy stone walls, held in place with iron ribbing.

Silversmith opened the great doors and slipped inside. His boots clicked on golden mosaics as he hurried across the spacious entrance to a narrow hall that led to a stairwell.

Two pairs of footsteps descended the stairwell, accompanied by two female voices.

"I tried to stop him," a breathy voice said.

"First, Lord Kemer keeps people in the refugee camp like they're prisoners, and now this," an unhappy voice said.

The voices grew closer as the women descended the stairwell.

Silversmith pushed open the nearest door, closed it behind him, and put his ear to the wood. Chasina copied him.

The unhappy voice continued. "I have been the Chamberlain for decades, and Lord Kemer thinks he can torture people whenever he chooses? I don't care that Muriel Silversmith is accused of treason. Lord Kemer needs a royal court to grant him permission for torture."

The voices faded as the Chamberlain and her assistant passed the floor and kept descending the stairwell. Silversmith left the room ten seconds later and descended the stairwell after them.

Even though she'd never seen a map of Shilist's keep, Chasina knew Silversmith's destination: the dungeon. He wanted to rescue his sister.

Chasina couldn't allow that to happen. "We can't rescue Muriel from the dungeon."

Silversmith did not break stride. "She's my sister."

"We still have to find the keystone and deal with a tower of guards. There's no time."

Silversmith stopped and sagged against the wall. "They're torturing my little sister, Chasina."

Chasina felt a tug of sympathy looking into those pathetically wet eyes. Muriel didn't care that her brother had almost died in Brundar, but he didn't hesitate to throw away his dream of finding the Hero to save her.

And they were twins? Weird. "You can't fight Lord Kemer. He'll have soldiers accompanying him, many more soldiers than in the tower, and we both know that you won't fight them."

"I'm fighting the soldiers in the vault tower."

"You're not fighting them," Chasina said gently. "You're catching them by surprise and putting them to sleep. The soldiers in the dungeon will see you coming and attack you, and you won't fight back. They'll kill you. You can't save your sister."

Silversmith swallowed. "I never could fend for us. After the Undying killed our family, Muriel was heartbroken. She couldn't do anything. Couldn't move, couldn't talk, couldn't even shiver… I nearly let her starve. We both would've died if she hadn't started pickpocketing." He looked down. "I just want to be able to take care of her this time."

195

Chasina touched Silversmith's neck. "After we steal the Naridi Stone and find the Hero, no one will dare hurt her again." She caught his eye. "You will never be able to help Muriel. It's who you are. But you can find the Hero, and he can do everything you cannot."

Silversmith hummed deep in his throat. His Adam's apple wobbled, his fingers twitched, and he turned around.

He climbed the uneven steps two at a time.

Chapter Thirty-Eight

Kemer's chamber stood at the end of the hall and had a bigger door than the other rooms. Intricate carvings decorated the door, so delicate they must have been carved by human hands. The hinges turned smoothly when Silversmith opened the door.

The room was nearly bare, aside from a few pieces of colorful furniture. Silversmith searched the cabinet first, then he sifted through the papers on Kemer's desk and shifted aside the long tunics hanging in the wardrobe.

"Check the window seat," Chasina whispered. Silversmith moved aside the pillows and blankets, searching the window seat and the bricks beside it.

Silversmith slapped the wall. "My sister would have found it by now. We could really use her help."

"Down there," Chasina said, pointing. "What's that crack in the wall?"

"An entrance to the human tunnels. The castle is riddled with them. It barely looks big enough for a keystone."

"Reach inside."

"Kemer probably hid the keystone in a secret compartment in the walls, not in a human tunnel."

"Or he hid it where no giant would ever look. Look inside."

Silversmith knelt and reached inside the tunnel. "I feel something."

Silversmith wiggled his hand deeper into the wall. He felt for a few moments, then pulled out his hand. His arm came away covered with slime and dirt, and a chain tangled around his fingers.

The keystone hung on the chain. It was perfectly round, like a marble. Tiny fractures mottled the keystone's surface, and a heart of pale yellow magic glowed in the center.

Silversmith and Chasina spoke at the same time.

"It's so delicate," Silversmith said.

"It's a boulder," Chasina said.

Clearly, Silversmith forgot how to see things from a human perspective after transforming into a giant. The chain had heavy links thicker than two of her fingers, and the keystone was the size of Silversmith's fist. It would take two humans to lift the keystone, but Silversmith swished it through the air like it was weightless.

While Silversmith studied the keystone, Chasina checked her satchel for the spara leaf. She found it and re-stashed it beneath the bandages. Once Silversmith opened the vault, she'd drug him and steal the Naridi Stone.

Silversmith weighed the keystone on his palm. "It's made from porous rock, so it's lighter than it looks. You could probably roll it fairly easily." Silversmith hung the chain around his neck. "How do we get inside the tower? It's locked."

"I have an idea."

Silversmith sighed. "Of course you do. Promise me it doesn't involve stabbing anyone through the eye."

"No one is getting stabbed."

"Why do I sense that not killing anyone was your second idea?" Silversmith set Chasina on his shoulder and tripped lightly down the stairwell. He exited the keep, staying in the shadows as he crossed the courtyard toward the vault tower.

Chasina pointed to a narrow window near the tower's base. "All you have to do is float me into the vault tower through one of the arrow slits. I'll get the guards to open the door, and then you can put them to sleep."

Arrow slits dotted the vault tower from top to bottom, narrow windows that allowed archers to rain arrows on attackers while maintaining relative safety.

The first arrow slit was one hundred and fifty feet off the ground. Even the tower's great stone blocks were big enough to crush a human without any bits sticking out.

Chasina pressed her lips together. "How high off the ground is that first arrow slit?"

Silversmith gauged the distance. "Maybe fifteen feet."

She'd grown up foraging inside Brundar, so she should feel at home with everything so much bigger than her. So why did the sheer size of everything keep taking her off guard?

Chasina forced herself to stand up straight. She needed something in that mountainous tower, and shrinking in awe wouldn't get the job done.

Silversmith crouched in the shadows beside the vault tower and cupped Chasina in both hands. The heat from his skin lasted only a moment before a silver sphere encased her and flew to the tower.

Chasina landed in the arrow slit. She stepped forward on the wide ledge and looked inside the tower. The stairwell wrapped around the tower in an upward spiral to her left and disappeared. Ten steps below, two soldiers guarded the tower door.

Chasina hoisted herself on the tower's interior wall and climbed down until she reached the landing, standing behind the two soldiers. She whistled sharply.

The soldiers looked down and saw her waving at them, and they nearly head-butted each other when they leaned down to grab Chasina. She slipped from their grasp and wiggled beneath the door.

She joined Silversmith, who stood with his back pressed against the stone beside the door.

Silversmith picked her up. "That was fast."

"Get ready to put them to sleep," Chasina said, crouching on his shoulder.

The door jiggled. It opened.

Two soldiers emerged from the tower. They didn't even see Silversmith, too busy searching the ground for Chasina.

Silversmith gripped each soldier by the wrist, his hand gloved with silver aura. The soldiers dropped to the ground, snoring.

Silversmith dragged the sleeping bodies inside the tower and shut the door. He climbed lightly up the stairs and met two more soldiers. They didn't even draw their weapons before Silversmith dropped them with two silver spheres to the chest.

Stepping over the bodies, Silversmith kept climbing the steps. He reached the top of the tower, a small alcove by giants' standards. The vault door rested against the far wall.

Two soldiers stood in the small space. They jumped, startled when Silversmith stepped into the alcove.

"Vorce?" said the one on the left. "I barely recognized you beneath those bruises. Lord Kemer was right? You're trying to rob the tower vault?"

Silversmith held up his empty hands. "I don't expect you to let me steal the taxes, Hamon, but I need the Naridi Stone to find the Hero. That's all I want."

"I can't let you steal from the vault, Vorce. You know that."

CHAPTER THIRTY-EIGHT

Silversmith lowered his hands. "I know."

In this small space, the soldiers were likelier to hurt each other with swords than kill Silversmith. Both soldiers attacked Silversmith with bare hands.

Silversmith tripped the first soldier, catching him before he fell down the unforgiving stone steps. Silver light bloomed around Silversmith's hands, and the first soldier fell asleep.

Hamon moved quickly, punching Silversmith in the right ear before peppering him with blows to the chest and ribs.

Chasina hunched close to Silversmith's neck, praying Hamon didn't hit her. After a few moments of fighting, she realized that Silversmith intentionally moved to absorb blows in different areas. Whenever a punch might land near her, Silversmith repositioned himself to absorb the attack in his chest or ribs.

Silversmith never fought back. He deflected blows and absorbed them in specific areas, frustrating Hamon's attempts to push him down the stairwell.

Silversmith threw a weak punch—not as an attack, Chasina realized, but as bait. Hamon caught Silversmith's hand. Silver magic instantly blossomed around Silversmith's captured hand.

"Stupid Ramerian trick," Hamon said, his speech slurring.

Hamon wobbled, and Silversmith used the opportunity to plant his other hand over Hamon's heart. Hamon collapsed on the floor, fast asleep.

"Really nice work," Chasina said. "I don't say that often."

"Are you all right?" Silversmith asked.

Chasina pointed at the vault door. "I'm fine. Let's focus on opening the vault."

Chapter Thirty-Nine

The vault door was a solid stone wall without a door, hinges, or frame. Small indentations formed a flower shape in the center of the wall.

Silversmith ignited silver aura around his finger and pressed the keystone's pale yellow center. The keystone broke into pieces.

"The keystone pieces fit in these holes in the vault door," Silversmith explained, examining a keystone piece. "The trick is figuring out which piece fits into which hole. It's a puzzle."

The shards looked roughly the size of Chasina's head and were uncomfortably tiny in Silversmith's hands. He sorted through them, selected one, and tried slotting it into an indentation in the vault wall. His fingers trembled, and it took him several tries to fit the piece into the indentation.

Are his fingers trembling because he thinks we'll get caught, or because I won't let him rescue his pig of a sister? Whether he realized it or not, Muriel's death benefited him. But when Chasina saw the muscle quivering in his jaw, her heart softened.

She had addicted him to spara sap, yet he still trusted her for some reason. Probably because he couldn't imagine doing the things she was about to do to him.

He deserved better from her.

"I never needed the rope," Chasina said. "Back in the hills, you know. I just wanted to talk to Seven alone."

"What did you talk about?" Silversmith pushed another keystone piece into an indentation. Over a dozen yellow stones glowed from the wall.

"That's private." Chasina reached slowly inside her satchel for the spara leaf she'd been saving. "You didn't have to be decent to me, but you were. I will remember it."

Silversmith shook his head, damp hair tumbling across his back as he slipped the last stone into the wall. "Are you going somewhere and haven't told me? I would miss our wonderful conversations."

Chasina fingered her spara leaf. Once she put Silversmith into a trance, he'd sleep until soldiers awakened and arrested him. And while he languished in the dungeon awaiting his execution, he would fight more spara withdrawals, thanks to the reintroduction of drugs into his body.

Silversmith shouldn't have to pay such a heavy price for her freedom and humanity's safety, but she didn't see another way.

"Look at me, Silversmith," Chasina said. She couldn't reach his mouth unless he looked at her.

Silversmith turned his head toward her. Before she drugged him, a giant grabbed her from behind.

"What are you doing?" Chasina's voice trailed away when the giant turned her to face him.

Gray hair. Bloody beard. Stitches rolled up one arm, pointing to the scariest face Chasina had ever seen.

Cormac must have had Seven pump him full of energizing and painkilling heartwords so he could follow Silversmith through the

Suicide Tunnel.

Cormac ripped the spara leaf from Chasina's hand and shoved it in Silversmith's chest. "I told you not to trust her!"

Silversmith pawed at the leaf. "What were you doing with this, Chasina? With the Naridi Stone so close...oh, Hero's bloody sword. You didn't. You wouldn't. What is this, Chasina?"

Chasina split her focus between the two threats. Cormac had the typical fury bleeding from his face, but Silversmith ripped the spara leaf to bits.

Chasina flinched when Silversmith pitched the leaf's remains out the window.

"It was left over from my supply in Brundar," Chasina said.

"And you just happened to be holding it next to my mouth? After you said goodbye. Hero's name." Silversmith gestured with his hands close to his face. "Did you know what they would do to me for robbing a District vault?"

Chasina deepened the growl in her voice. "I risked my life helping you tonight, and now you think I wanted to sabotage you?"

Cormac squeezed her. "You tried to kill me!"

"She tried to kill you?" Silversmith asked. Understanding dawned on his face. "Chasina told the soldiers where to find you. She betrayed us."

Chasina pulled her tongue behind closed lips. Every excuse ticking through her mind either sounded implausible or outright false.

Cormac shoved Chasina into Silversmith's hands. She squirmed, but Silversmith held her tightly.

Cormac stabbed his finger in Silversmith's face. "That little rat is the only one who could have told Kemer that we planned to steal the Naridi Stone. Think. Did she ever have an opportunity to tell Lord Kemer about us?"

Silversmith's face was so tense that it was expressionless. "I let her

204

burn flowers for her poor, dead family, and then she disappeared for a while." He pressed a finger to Chasina's forehead. "Tell me the truth: did you convince Lord Kemer to arrest any of us?"

"Yes," Chasina said, trying and failing to reach her knife. "What were you expecting from me, Silversmith? You're giants. You are my enemies. I would do anything necessary to retrieve the Naridi Stone and give it back to my people."

Silversmith's voice grew louder. "Your people wanted me to kill and eat you, and if I wasn't so squeamish, I would have. Tell me the truth: why did you betray us to Lord Kemer?"

Silver light flooded Chasina's mouth. "Cormac was threatening Seven to control me. He and Muriel both deserve to die. Also, I wouldn't be able to steal the Naridi Stone from you if they were present."

Silversmith tightened his grip on her, and her ribs creaked. "And me? Why would you tell Lord Kemer that I'm alive?"

"I didn't tell him," Chasina said, gasping. "I protected you from Kemer. He found out on his own."

Silversmith dropped Chasina to his side, where she hung upside down in his fist. She glimpsed the vault door. The yellow keystone pieces pulsed rhythmically in their indentations.

Chasina's neck jerked as Silversmith moved to the window. "Cormac, Lord Kemer is coming across the courtyard."

Chapter Forty

"The vault should have opened by now," Cormac said. He tried to pull a keystone piece from its indentation, but yellow magic snapped. He hissed, pulling back his hand and sucking his finger.

"You must have inserted the keystone pieces into the wrong indentations and triggered an alarm," Cormac said. "The keystone is filled with Kemer's magic. He knows someone is trying to steal from his vault."

Silversmith dropped Chasina onto his shoulder and helped Cormac descend the steps. Even though Chasina didn't know if she would live to see another morning, she couldn't help but say something as the giants descended the stairwell.

She was so close to getting the Naridi Stone that admitting defeat wasn't an option.

"We can't just leave the Naridi Stone," Chasina said. "Lord Kemer will hide the keystone in a different place after this. Next time, you won't find it so easily. Kill the Lord and try opening the vault again."

Silversmith jerked his shoulder, sending Chasina to her knees. "Shut up."

"The human has a point, Vorce," Cormac said, and Chasina's heart leaped. It wasn't too late to turn back and steal the Naridi Stone.

"If we stay, we die," Silversmith said. It was only ten steps to the door, and he showed no sign of slowing.

Cormac wheezed, weakened from his brush with death. "Yes, but we can't steal the Naridi Stone without the keystone, and Kemer won't hide it in the same place. We need someone inside the castle to find wherever he hides it, so we can steal it when the time comes."

Silversmith reached the bottom of the steps and exited the tower. Across the courtyard, Kemer moved quickly toward them.

Two wet, unconscious guards sprawled beside the well. They were the same guards that Silversmith had dropped into the well. Cormac must have used them to climb from the well and then knocked them out.

Silversmith tossed Cormac into the well and pulled Chasina from his shoulder.

He pressed his finger to her forehead. "You used me. Now, I'm going to use you."

Silver light exploded behind Chasina's eyelids. It rushed through her body, the magic within her rising to meet its maker. The magic turned her into a star. Every pore shone with silver light.

After a moment, the silver light banded into a heavy coil. The coil settled around Chasina's spine like a snake resting around a tree.

"What did you do to me?" Chasina asked, rubbing her forehead, where a disk of silver light beamed into the courtyard. "Get your magic out of me!"

"I need you to hide in the castle," Silversmith said flatly. "I need you to find the keystone wherever Kemer hides it." Silversmith dropped Chasina beside the well.

Chasina pressed her back against the well's mossy stones, making herself small as Lord Kemer arrived. She'd never seen magic brighter or thicker than the yellow aura roiling around Kemer's arms.

Lord Kemer loosed a yellow sphere toward Silversmith. Silversmith raised both hands, conjuring a silver shield. The yellow sphere struck his shield and rippled the silver magic, but it didn't penetrate.

Striding toward Silversmith, Kemer quickly cast three more spheres. Silversmith caught two spheres on his silver shield and ducked the third.

Kemer closed the distance between them and tackled Silversmith. They went down in a heap. The giants wrestled for a moment, but Kemer ended up on top. He straddled Silversmith and went for the throat.

Silversmith twisted Kemer's hand from his throat. Silver magic gloved his hand as he tried to put Kemer to sleep, but yellow magic welled around Kemer's wrist and protected him.

Lord Kemer produced a knife from beneath his robes and stabbed it at Silversmith's throat. Silversmith caught Lord Kemer's hand before the knife entered his throat, and he punched Kemer in the forehead.

Silversmith bucked his hips and threw Kemer off him. While Kemer rolled several feet, Silversmith stood and jumped in the well.

"Soldiers! Where are my guards?" the Lord shouted. He willed away the magic crawling down his arms.

Chasina crept away from the well and circled the Lord, staying on his blind side. She reached the stone steps leading into the keep, but she paused when something flickered in her peripheral vision. Turning, Chasina saw a large yellow sphere arcing toward her. Chasina dropped to her belly, and the yellow sphere sank into the stone step inches above her head.

Lord Kemer stared at her from across the courtyard. While soldiers spilled from the barracks, answering his call, he conjured another sphere.

Chasina climbed the steps, twisting to avoid another sphere, and she wiggled beneath the castle doors. Chasina climbed one of the sculptures standing in the entrance and hid behind its helmet.

Chasina scrubbed her forehead, pinching, rubbing, and scraping until her fingers came away bloody. The silver mark remained steady, mirroring the silver magic uncoiling within her. The magic embodied Silversmith. A piece of his soul lived inside of her, and it was the only reason she didn't have to stay within a mile of him.

Soldiers shouted in the courtyard, but the shouts didn't register with Chasina. Her entire focus turned inward, trying to cope with having a second person inhabiting her body. She sensed Silversmith's presence like a silver snake roaming her body, nudging her spirit, testing his limits, and she puked.

This was a dream. A nightmare. Any second, she would wake up to Theodoric trying to kill her, and everything would be fine.

Chasina puked again and wiped her mouth. "All right. All right. I can fix this. I just need…a miracle."

Chasina glanced at the entrance as though a miracle might walk through the doors. The great doors opened, but Kemer whirled into the castle instead of a miracle. Twenty soldiers followed him, plus a squat giantess with several parchment scrolls tucked beneath one arm.

"Find the human," Kemer said, directing his soldiers to various spots in the grand entrance. "Silversmith sent her to spy on me."

Chapter Forty-One

C hasina huddled behind the statue's helmet as twenty soldiers searched the entrance. The silver mark on her forehead beamed into the darkness, so she took a bandage from her satchel and tied it around her forehead to smother the light.

Another soldier entered the keep and saluted Lord Kemer. "My Lord, we've searched the courtyard without finding the intruders. We're about to search the hills. Are you certain you didn't see where the intruders fled?"

Obviously, Lord Kemer hadn't told the soldiers to dive into the well after Silversmith and Cormac. He didn't want to reveal the Suicide Tunnel to his soldiers, which made it difficult to help them find Silversmith and Cormac. Silversmith and Cormac suddenly had excellent chances of escaping unscathed.

"No, I didn't see where they went," Lord Kemer snapped. "Search the surrounding hills."

The soldier saluted and exited the keep.

Lord Kemer snapped his fingers at the squat giantess standing beside him. "Chamberlain, what does the register record about Silversmith's slave?"

The Chamberlain unrolled a parchment and searched it. "There are no humans registered to Vorce Silversmith. We don't know what village the human is from or how long she's been Silversmith's slave. She might not know anything about Silversmith's plans, my Lord."

Kemer searched a nearby statue. "Whoever finds the human will be rewarded, but I want her alive and as undamaged as possible. Search the statues."

Chasina climbed down from the statue. She needed to hide in a human tunnel before Kemer discovered her, and she learned what he defined as 'undamaged.'

Even though moonlight came through the open doors, velvety shadows layered the floor. Magical spheres hovered near soldiers' boots. Huge shadows flickered across the golden tiles as soldiers searched with their magical spheres.

Chasina waited for a break in the crowd of boots and dashed to the next statue, heading toward a narrow hall at the back of the entrance. Six statues separated her from the hall.

"I think I saw something," a soldier called.

Chasina froze, flattening herself against a statue's leg as the soldier came nearer. She remained immobile as the soldier conjured some bright blue magic and searched the shadows beside her.

Chasina held her hand close to the blue light so that her shadow stretched long and thin, and she made shadows dance on the ground a dozen yards away. The movement caught the soldier's attention.

"False alarm," he said, moving away. "Just a shadow."

"Confirm that it's worth noticing before you distract everyone," Lord Kemer said, searching the statue behind Chasina.

Chasina made it to the following five statues without incident. She grazed her elbows on some of the boots swishing across the golden mosaics, but nothing serious.

She hid against the last statue. The narrow hallway started just ahead, leading to the left side of the keep.

Lord Kemer whistled. "Guard the hallways to make sure the human doesn't escape."

Chasina bolted toward the hallway. She dodged a dozen magical spheres and skittered around the corner into the hallway. Running down the hall, she searched the wall carvings for an entrance to the tunnels.

Heavy vibrations traveled up and down her legs. The first few soldiers clamored into the hall behind her, and she spun to one side to avoid several magical spheres.

She spotted the tunnel entrance hidden among twisting vines dripping from the overhead carving. It was tiny. Barely more than a gap between stones.

Chasina halted two feet from the minuscule entrance, unable to go inside. It was too small. The walls would close in as smoke uncoiled from the depths of her mind and suffocated her.

The heavy vibrations multiplied. All twenty soldiers converged on Chasina, but she couldn't move.

Six giants pounced on Chasina. She squeezed inside the tunnel entrance a moment before the giants crashed on the spot she occupied a second ago.

Chasina took two small steps into the tunnel. The ceiling was only a foot above her head, and she touched both walls when she stood in the center and reached out. Puddles dotted the ground, black water rippling as giants slapped the floor outside the tunnel.

Chasina counted her heartbeats, struggling to keep a panic attack at bay. She refused to go farther into the tunnel, but she couldn't leave the tunnel, either. How could she steal the Naridi Stone while trapped here? What about water or food? What about the panic ballooning in her chest, and what if it exploded?

Chasina struggled to capture the panic. She boxed it in her chest and concentrated on keeping it from escaping. It didn't help that the soldier never left his post even as minutes stretched into an hour. Evidently, he wouldn't afford her the opportunity to escape unseen into the hallway.

Chasina felt Silversmith fall asleep. The silver snake relaxed around her spine, its scaled sides rising and falling. Waves of uneasiness, like bad dreams, ebbed from the silver snake and into Chasina.

She looked around, unnerved. Were Silversmith's bad dreams infecting her outlook? How soon until he fully possessed her and turned her into Seven? Didn't he know that Chasina's body was too small for two people?

Chasina wrestled her panic back into its box. The panic was slowly dying when she felt Silversmith's silver snake open one glazed eye. The snake rolled, hissed sleepily, and curled more tightly around Chasina's spine.

Something snapped inside of Chasina. The panic burst from its box and exploded in a firestorm.

Orderly thoughts unraveled and descended into the firestorm. Distant screams reached the pit where Chasina crouched, waiting for Da to come back and hold her tight against his chest.

He argued with Mama and Bea. "Get into the pit, *please.* Can't you feel the vibrations? Their footsteps?"

Chasina curled against the shaking ground. Steady vibrations skittered from the earth and sewed needles through her skin. Whimpering, Chasina stood and craned her neck to see into her family's hut.

Da pleaded with Mama while she and Bea gathered the basket cradle. Bea's quick fingers settled their possessions into long baskets.

Dust shook from the thatched ceiling with every massive vibration.

"Mama, it's not worth it," Da said.

"This is our life—"

Chasina felt someone tugging her shoulder. Her hand snapped to the hand on her shoulder, and Chasina looked into a boy's haggard face.

"How long have you been stuck?" the boy asked. "You missed counting."

Chasina looked down and saw she sat against the wall, curled in the fetal position. Her muscles cramped, hinting that she'd spent significant time lost in memories.

Chasina squeezed the boy's hand to keep herself from sinking into her memories. "I'm not sure. What time is it?"

"Morning, though you'd never know it inside the tunnels." The boy looked toward the tunnel entrance. "I'm guessing you had a run-in with the soldier crouching outside the tunnel. It must have been pretty serious."

At first, Chasina didn't know what the boy meant. How would he know if it was serious or not? Then she realized her throat was raw from screaming. He must have heard her screams and come to investigate.

The boy pointed at the tunnel entrance. "When you cause chaos, you need to make sure you're near a tunnel that you know how to navigate. Otherwise, you'll get trapped."

"Thank you," she croaked, her raspy voice harsher than usual. "I'm Chasina."

He clasped her hand and helped her stand, wiry muscles cording his skinny arms. "Keir."

Keir was perhaps eighteen years old, as skinny as he was tall, with sharp features and ragged black hair cut in swathes around his face.

Chasina sensed the silver snake sleeping within her, so the soldiers must not have found Silversmith or Cormac. For the moment, it meant she didn't have to worry about the snake crowding her soul.

Chasina followed Keir down the tunnel. She focused on his back, breathing slowly, focusing her whole willpower on triumphing over a second panic attack. But despite her concentration, smoke rose from the depths of her mind and cast a haze over her vision.

Chasina swatted the phantom smoke, but before it overtook her senses, she heard human voices spooling from the alcove ahead.

Chasina stepped into an alcove filled with humans. The large room instantly eased the pain in her chest.

Chasina relaxed. "What do people do here?"

"Can you not see the contented humans working to beautify the giants' castle?" Keir gestured grandly at more than fifty people sitting cross-legged on the floor, laps filled with colored thread. Across the alcove, more workers dyed thread in sunken vats filled with colorful liquid. Marks glimmered from every person's hand, and everyone worked feverishly, as though their lives depended on their work.

Sadly, they probably did.

A thickly set man with a shiny head hurried over to them. "We don't have time to stand around and gawk. Let's move! Keir, get back to work." He jerked a thumb over his shoulder and turned to Chasina. "What can you do?"

"I'm a basket weaver."

"Basket weaving? That's good. Hey!" he yelled at Keir, striding across the room to stand over him. Chasina followed.

The overseer gestured at the knotted thread in Keir's lap. "Are you trying to get us killed? The tapestry is due in three days. We don't have time for mistakes."

"Sorry."

"Pull your weight, or I swear you'll never return to the painting alcove. And you," the overseer said, rounding on Chasina, "lower your backside on the ground and start weaving before I send you to the cleaning alcove."

After last night's epic failure, Chasina needed time to collect herself and figure out a plan to steal the Naridi Stone. Silversmith wanted her to find the keystone, but he hadn't worded his wishes as commands. She didn't need to obey him. It gave her time to steal the Naridi Stone, and if she stayed in the alcove, she could help the castle slaves while creating a plan.

Chasina sat down beside Keir. "Let me help you."

Chapter Forty-Two

Keir gave Chasina the knotted thread. It was the same thickness and strength as rope, but giants classified it as thread.

Chasina began untangling the knot with deliberate strokes. The overseer hovered behind her like a thundercloud for several seconds before grunting and moving away.

"I'm still learning," Keir said quietly, glancing at the overseer's back. "I was walking to clear my head when I heard you screaming."

Chasina finished untangling the thread and laid it neatly on the ground. "What is this place?"

His brow knit together. "This alcove is in charge of tapestries. They're behind schedule, so my overseer from the painting alcove assigned a dozen of us to help weave."

"When do you go back to the painting alcove?"

"Not for a few more days, but I'll probably help the mosaic alcove next." He sighed. "Mosaics are always behind."

The threads trailed across the floor to a massive nest of material that filled half of the spacious room. A lobe of pale yellow magic glowed above the enormous pile, illuminating the room with delicate light.

"How did the giants put magic down here?" Chasina asked, nodding at the yellow orb.

"That isn't magic; it's our invention. The Masters can't push their magic through stone to light the alcoves for us, so we make do on our own." Keir pointed at the orb. "We dug holes through the wall and caught the light in a lantern. The sunlight makes the room glow at this time of day. It's almost alive, isn't it?"

Chasina reached out and trailed her fingers through beams of sunshine. Other people around the room tilted their faces toward the light, including Keir.

"You've been outside, haven't you?" Keir asked. "With the grass and the sunlight and the sky. What's it like?"

For the first time, Chasina noticed that Keir's skin was so pale that it was almost luminescent. He'd obviously never set foot outside the castle, perhaps even outside the tunnels, and no amount of description would replace that.

Chasina faltered for words. She wasn't good at this sort of thing. "It's beautiful. I lived near fields that my neighbors tilled, and when the wind swept across them, the crops rustled. I liked the noise."

Keir leaned forward hungrily. "You must be wild-caught. Sometimes, I see things from my window. Feel the sunlight on my skin. What's it like to touch a flower?"

"The petals are very soft," Chasina said. She spotted the overseer moving closer and hurried to look busy. "What are we making?"

Keir grimaced at the thread Chasina had untangled. "It's supposed to be a tassel braid for the tapestry they're working on. Honestly, I'm not even sure what a tassel braid is. I just know the weavers need lots of them."

Chasina showed Keir how to pass the threads back and forth without tangling them. Soon, Keir hunched over a new tassel braid, eyebrows twitching in concentration.

Chasina lost herself in the familiarity of weaving. How could she steal the Naridi Stone? She couldn't break into the vault. She was one human against six guards and a vault door, which made stealing the Naridi Stone physically impossible.

Even if she somehow managed to extricate herself from Silversmith's magic without the Naridi Stone, Chasina couldn't go home empty-handed. The villagers would simply hang her if she went home without a gift like the Naridi Stone. Gran would still look at her like...*like she wishes Da had never saved me. Like I'm the one mistake he ever made.*

She couldn't assail the vault tower. Instead of overcoming the tower's defenses, what if she convinced Lord Kemer to give her the Naridi Stone?

True, Kemer hadn't given Silversmith the Naridi Stone. In fact, Kemer seemed genuinely outraged that Silversmith had even asked—probably due to Kemer's heretical beliefs. If he didn't believe in the Hero, why waste a powerful magical totem looking for him?

However, Silversmith hadn't had any leverage to pressure Kemer into relinquishing the Naridi Stone.

She'd investigate Kemer, find his weakness, and leverage it until he yielded the Naridi Stone.

"What do you know about Lord Kemer?" Chasina asked Keir as she started on her fifteenth tassel. Her harsh voice carried around the alcove, and other weavers tossed answers at her.

"He hates the refugees. No one knows why he goes to the camp every day and blesses them since he despises them."

"Lord Kemer is a heretic."

"People hate his laws on hunting humans, but he doesn't care. He's getting rich."

The last voice rang loudest. "Don't go into the Lord's room unless summoned."

The weavers all murmured their agreement and turned back to their tassels.

The weavers had given Chasina a couple places to start her investigation. Unfortunately, knowing that Kemer was a heretic who grew wealthier by controlling the market on humans wasn't enough. She needed specific crimes. More importantly, she needed proof.

"Anything else, Keir?" Chasina asked.

Keir squinted at his knotted tassel. "I think they covered everything. The last bit of advice was the most important, but only if you enjoy being alive, something that's always debatable in the tunnels."

Chasina finished her tassel and started another. "Does Kemer have a slave? One who serves him personally, not just a castle slave?"

"No. Why do you want to know so badly?" Keir asked, still trying to untangle his tassel.

"Just curious."

The heavy magical snake shifted around Chasina's spine, still sleeping, and Silversmith's restless dreams effused from it. The snake quieted a moment later, and Chasina did her best to ignore it.

She held Silversmith's restless dreams. She held his aura, the embodiment of his soul. Surely, such a small vessel couldn't hold much more. How long until she overflowed with everything but her own spirit?

Keir broke Chasina's thoughts. "Can you help me with this knot?"

She pointed at a thread. "Try pulling on that one."

Keir pulled the thread, and the knot unfurled like a spring flower.

Beaming, he shifted the threads and looked at the lantern. "It's bedtime."

Chapter Forty-Three

Chasina's hands ached. She hadn't realized they had weaved all day, so Keir's proclamation surprised her.

The lantern dimmed, and darkness came as silently and suddenly as the folding of a crow's wing. Two torches sputtered into life. Haggard faces appeared in the firelight, unnaturally sharp where shadows pooled beneath their cheekbones.

Everyone in the tapestry alcove split into groups of men and women. Keir joined the men shuffling into a tunnel.

"I'll see you tomorrow," Keir said over his shoulder, pointing at the women filing into the tunnel. "Follow them to the women's dormitory."

Instead of joining the women, Chasina rested against the nearest wall until the alcove emptied. Alone, she picked her way around tassels to the massive pile of string. She settled behind the pile, hidden from the rest of the room.

Lord Kemer might not have a personal slave, but the giants who occupied the rooms closest to Kemer's might have personal slaves. She would start by interviewing them for any secrets she could use to blackmail Kemer.

Chasina shuffled to her knees and yanked some thread from the pile. She arranged it in a rough schematic of the castle keep, trying to remember how to get to Kemer's room.

Soft footsteps made Chasina look up. Keir came around the pile of thread, his huge blue eyes widening when he saw Chasina occupying the hiding place.

"What are you doing here?" Chasina asked.

The painter put a finger to his lips, jerking his head toward the footsteps stalking across the room. As soon as the footsteps left the room, Keir grinned and slumped against the threads.

"I spilled a bucket of salt in the bread for tomorrow's feast. The chef is going to have some explaining to do. What?" Keir asked, catching Chasina's stern expression.

"You put yourself in danger for no good reason."

He shrugged, chest rising and falling with laughter. "We don't get to eat good bread, anyway. Why should giants get to eat it?"

"Did you really think it through?"

Keir's laughter dried up like a stream beneath the searing heat of her stare. "We can't all enter a room and instantly become the wisest person there. Aren't you supposed to be in the women's dormitories?"

"Aren't you supposed to be in the men's dormitories?" Chasina turned back to her outline of the castle keep.

Keir leaned over her shoulder. "What's this?"

"Nothing."

"You're missing two corridors, see? They run parallel to each other for a while before splitting in different directions." Keir rearranged the threads to show the new corridors. Once he finished, he pointed at the approximation. "What are you doing with this map?"

Chasina studied him for a long moment before leaning against the thread pile. "Kemer has the Naridi Stone locked inside the tower vault.

I'm trying to make him give it to me. To do that, I have to investigate him, find his weakness, and exploit it until he yields the Naridi Stone. I need to talk to the humans around Kemer and see if they know anything I can use to blackmail him."

A cold draft blew ragged hair from Keir's bony face. "The Naridi Stone? That sounds like fun. Every ten years or so, there are always a few people who try to steal the Naridi Stone. Blackmailing Kemer is a new strategy, though probably not one I would have chosen."

Chasina knew she shouldn't ask, but she couldn't help herself. "What happens to the people who try to steal the Naridi Stone?"

"The usual. Burning, mutilation, crushing. There's a whole list of things that happen to them—us, I guess, now that we're planning on stealing it from Lord Kemer."

Chasina bit her tongue. *We?* There was zero room in her plans for a second person to endanger themselves.

"Absolutely not," Chasina said.

"I don't care."

"What?"

"I won't accept 'no' for an answer."

She could tie Keir's hands and feet and leave him behind if necessary. It wouldn't be difficult because she easily outweighed him despite the fourteen inches height difference.

Then again, if Keir wanted to help, maybe she should let him? She'd effectively imprisoned Tarrken, and they'd bound her soul to a giant hoping that he'd eat her. Obviously, the villagers had lost their senses, but she didn't want Keir to follow suit. Plus, she might need his help.

If necessary, she'd put herself between Keir and danger, but she wouldn't stop him from helping.

"You understand that it's dangerous?" Chasina asked.

Keir gestured at the stone walls. "I grew up in this godforsaken castle. I know more dangers than you could possibly guess."

"Then we'd better start planning. Kemer doesn't have a slave who can tell us about any dirty secrets."

"Aldith does," Keir said. "Or at least, she used to have a personal slave. Aldith maimed Regina and then discarded her as useless. We'll talk to Regina and see if she can communicate anything to us."

"What did Aldith do to Regina?" Chasina asked, bracing herself for the answer.

Keir lowered his voice. "Regina delivered a message from Lord Kemer that Aldith didn't like, so Aldith had Regina cut out her own tongue. None of the castle slaves speak sign language, so Regina can't communicate very well."

Chasina resisted the urge to smash something against the nearest wall. She needed answers Regina might not be able to communicate, and yet another act of brutality against humans went unanswered. If Regina gave Chasina answers, it wouldn't be long before humans in Shilist Castle wreaked vengeance with the Naridi Stone.

Keir stood, and Chasina followed him to one of the many tunnels leading away from the alcove.

Chasina stopped on the tunnel's threshold. "Is there a bigger tunnel we can take? Maybe we could use the corridors in the castle?"

Keir dismissed the idea with a flick of his hand. "That soldier is still looking for you, remember? I saw other soldiers patrolling the corridors, and if they catch us, say goodnight."

"A lot of soldiers?"

"They will catch and eat us. Coming?"

Chasina inched into the tunnel. The darkness was almost complete, but she still glimpsed the faintest hint of the stifling rock walls.

Chasina fell back a step. "I can't do this. It's too small."

Keir looked back at her. "Is this a wild-caught thing? You can't deal with small spaces, so you stayed in the alcove tonight."

"Go ahead without me."

Keir took Chasina's hand and pulled her forward. Chasina blindly followed him through Shilist's tunnels, knees wobbling with each step. She splashed through cold puddles, listened to dripping water, and coughed whenever a fresh breeze drifted through drafts in the mortar.

Chasina sensed when they exited the tunnel. She felt air expand around her and heard wind rattling panes of glass.

Keir released Chasina's hand. "Welcome to the Great Hall."

Chapter Forty-Four

Rows of tables stood in two rows on either side of the Great Hall. Twenty-five metal spikes jutted from both walls. Half-melted candles wept on the metal spikes, and dried tallow spotted the floor beneath them. The candles probably provided enough light to eat during feasts. After all, giants might wear themselves out if they conjured magical spheres to light the room while eating.

At the head of the room, stone steps led to a dais. A single table stood on the dais, and a rich velvet curtain hung behind it.

At least a hundred humans worked at the foot of the dais. Judging from the piles of obsidian, gold, and silver tiles, these must be the mosaic workers Keir talked about. Didn't they get to sleep at the same time as the weavers? If they were behind schedule like Keir said, they probably worked later than the other alcoves.

Keir and Chasina entered the Great Hall. They jogged beneath several benches and tables and across a long stretch of open space before reaching the workers. Some workers supplied tilers with tools, mortar, and tiles, but most stood ankle-deep in a depression that pooled before the dais. They laid tiles in the depression, creating an incomplete mosaic.

Keir approached a girl laying tiles in the depression. She looked around thirteen years old and had dried mortar in her hair.

"Regina, I have someone I want you to meet," Keir said. "This is Chasina. She'd like to ask you some questions about Aldith and Kemer."

Regina tilted her head to the side and gestured for Chasina to speak.

Chasina jumped into the depression. "Can you tell me about Lord Kemer's heresy? Has he committed heretical crimes?"

Regina pursed her lips and thought for several moments. She shook her head. Evidently, aside from hating refugees and enjoying the cathedral's defilement, Lord Kemer hadn't committed any heinous acts against the giants' religion.

"Is there any proof that Lord Kemer is financially benefiting from controlling the human market?" Chasina asked.

Regina grabbed a chisel and mallet and used them to etch a message in the depression. It took a long time, and Regina had to take breaks to flex her fingers and readjust her grip.

The finished message said: EVERYONE KNOWS.

Chasina read the message and resisted the urge to voice a growing concern. What if Kemer didn't have any dark secrets? His potential weaknesses turned out to be dead ends, and while people rarely hadn't committed a shameful act, it wasn't impossible. Plus, Chasina couldn't settle for just any nefarious deed. It had to be a provable crime that would threaten Kemer's power.

Chasina tried again. "What about Aldith? She is Kemer's Chamberlain. Could she know something about Kemer that no one else knows?"

Regina flexed her hands, which were red and swollen from laying tiles all day, and she chiseled another message.

The message read: HATES KEMER.

"Aldith hates Kemer?" Chasina asked.

Regina nodded emphatically and rubbed her swollen hands.

It wasn't enough to blackmail Kemer. After all, why would the Lord of Kavalu care that his Chamberlain hated him? He wouldn't.

"Is there anything else you can tell me about Lord Kemer? Anything he might not want people to know?" Chasina asked.

Regina nodded. She dropped her tools and stood, motioning with her hands. She drew a box in the air and reached inside, pretending to pocket the contents.

Chasina and Keir tried guessing what it meant.

"A container?" Chasina asked.

Regina pointed at her, nodding. Regina mimed opening a door and reaching inside the container.

"It's hidden," Chasina guessed. "A secret compartment where Kemer hides things."

Regina nodded again.

"In Kemer's room?" Chasina asked.

Regina nodded.

"What does Kemer hide inside of it?" Chasina asked, but Regina shrugged and shook her head.

"How do you know about the secret compartment but not what's inside?" Chasina asked.

Regina pressed both hands over her lips, thinking. She jumped, waving her arms and running in place.

"Too dangerous?" Keir asked. "Kemer would find you?"

Regina lifted one shoulder. Keir was partially correct, but they were missing the point.

Regina picked up her tools and etched another message: BOOBY TRAP.

Chasina connected Regina's previous fake-running with the new message. "As soon as we open the compartment, Kemer will come running to find us?"

A big nod and two thumbs-up.

Perfect. Whatever Kemer kept hidden in the compartment was so sensitive that he'd booby-trapped it. If Chasina made it in and out of Kemer's room without incident, she'd have the perfect blackmail material.

"Is there anything else you can tell us about Kemer or his compartment?" Chasina asked.

Regina shook her head and started tiling again.

Chasina thanked Regina and jogged toward the tunnel, Keir close behind. Opening a booby-trapped compartment was very dangerous, so this was an excellent opportunity to dissuade Keir from helping her.

"We are going to Kemer's room to open the compartment," Chasina said.

"Kemer's room? I don't think so. My feet officially stop moving halfway down that particular tunnel," Keir said.

Good. She didn't need Keir putting himself in harm's way. "I will see you tomorrow. Good night."

Chasina turned away from the tunnels and toward the corridors in the castle proper. To her chagrin, Keir jogged beside her.

The painter stared at the stained glass windows, where moonlight dripped into the Great Hall. "I've heard the Naridi Stone is carved in the shape of a rose. It flashes different colors from the magic inside it, and it's warm to the touch. It endows power." He never stopped gazing at the soft rays of moonlight, his expression hungry. "I'm coming with you."

Chasina stopped jogging and faced Keir. "It doesn't make sense for more than one person to endanger themselves."

"Or maybe you need someone to watch your back, so we both make it out alive. Let's go."

Keir headed toward the tunnels, and after a moment, Chasina followed.

Chapter Forty-Five

I t didn't take long to arrive at Kemer's room. The room was shaped like a rectangle, the neat bed tucked beneath a deep blue canopy in the far corner. The bed was empty. Moonlight slanted through the narrow windows and cut scythes from the enormous shadows pooling on the floor.

Keir pointed at the velvet rope hanging next to the bed. "Aldith's room has one just like it. One pull brings a servant, but two pulls bring a horde of soldiers. As soon as you find the secret compartment, I'll pull the cord in Aldith's room. Hopefully, it's a big enough distraction to fill the halls with soldiers and keep Lord Kemer busy while we escape."

"Wait by the door," Chasina said. "I'll tell you when I find the compartment."

Chasina assessed the room while Keir ran to the door. A bed, table and benches, wardrobe, and a cabinet comprised all the furniture. The limited furniture meant Lord Kemer had very few places to hide his secret compartment, so it shouldn't take long to find.

Chasina moved to the wardrobe. Lord Kemer had left the door ajar, and it squeaked as Chasina pulled it open. Jumping, Chasina grabbed the bottom of the wardrobe and hauled herself inside.

Purple and green tunics glowed in the darkness, rustling as Chasina moved inside. Pointed boots stood neatly arranged beneath the tunics.

Ducking beneath the hems, Chasina explored the walls. Her hand caught on something nearly invisible at face level, a seam in the wood barely wider than her finger.

Chasina poked her head from the wardrobe and called to Keir. "I found the secret compartment. I won't open it until I hear soldiers in the hallway. Are you sure you will be safe?"

Keir answered with an eye roll and wiggled beneath the door.

She'd taken charge of Tarrken because of people like Keir. People who didn't care about their lives and seemed incapable of making good decisions. If Keir didn't start making safer choices, Chasina would have to make them for him.

But...nothing terrible had happened to Keir in a lifetime of making his own choices, so it probably wouldn't happen tonight.

When Chasina heard giants' footsteps thundering down the hallway, she used her knife to wiggle open the panel. The panel tipped forward. She caught it, rested it on a pair of spotless yellow boots, and crawled inside the secret compartment. Unable to see in the darkness, Chasina tugged the bandage from her forehead and let her silver mark illuminate the compartment.

She gaped at the folded robe stashed inside the compartment. It was a robe, the same ceremonial robe the Undying in Brundar had worn.

No wonder Kemer was a heretic. No wonder he hadn't wanted Silversmith to use the Naridi Stone to find the Hero. Kemer was an Undying who hated the Hero, and he'd fight against any attempt to awaken him.

It explained how the cut on his face had healed so quickly after she injured him in the cathedral. He didn't visit the refugee camp to bless people; he visited the camp to drain their auras, which healed him and added to his immortality. The sick patients kept dying because Lord Kemer stole their life force.

Was Kemer the Undying she had seen in Brundar?

Chasina searched the robe, crawling through dozens of yards of fabric until she found a neatly sewn rip. The rip perfectly aligned with the wound she'd seen on the Undying in Brundar.

Why had Lord Kemer gone into Brundar? Was he hunting the refugees on purpose, or was he after something else in Brundar and gotten attacked? And why bother masquerading as a Lord when other Undying openly conquered cities? Perhaps he preferred the subtle approach.

How was she supposed to blackmail an Undying? They had already stolen humanity's magic and laid waste to the guardian village, her home. They'd only grown more powerful in the seventy years since then, conquering cities and destroying armies.

Chasina squared her shoulders. She possessed Kemer's greatest secret, and now she had to figure out how to use it against him without exposing herself to his wrath.

In the hallway outside Kemer's room, the thunderous footsteps quieted. Aldith raised her voice, yelling at the soldiers for coming to her room when she didn't need help. She screamed at them until their footsteps retreated down the hall.

Chasina shook herself. Kemer might return any second and find her gawking at his Undying robe, so she needed to hurry.

She climbed from the secret compartment, sealed it, and exited the wardrobe. Chasina retied the bandage around her head and started for the tunnel. She only took two steps before she felt the silver snake awaken.

The silver snake lifted its head and nosed her emotions. It understood what she felt. Whether it understood that Chasina wanted to steal the Naridi Stone or only felt her inner conflict, she didn't know.

Since Silversmith lived within her, he might hear her speaking to him.

"Get away from me, Silversmith," Chasina said.

The snake opened its mouth and spoke with Silversmith's voice. "I'm not leaving." He talked inside Chasina's mind. If anyone stood around her, they wouldn't hear anything.

"You told me about what happened to Seven when Cormac possessed her body," Chasina said, starting toward the tunnel again. "You were horrified. Stop pretending that you'll do the same to me, and get out of my body."

"Have you found the keystone yet?" Silversmith asked, his voice clipped. "Have you looked? Tell me truthfully."

"No."

The silver snake hissed. "It has been an entire day, and you haven't even looked. You're stalling on purpose."

"No, I'm not," Chasina lied since he hadn't commanded her to tell the truth.

The silver snake hissed. "Stop whatever you're doing right now and look for the keystone."

Chasina tried to take another step toward the safety of the tunnel, but the silver snake wrapped around her legs. Her legs became numb from the knee down. She stood frozen in the middle of the room, totally vulnerable if Kemer arrived.

Tipping forward, Chasina crashed to the floor and tried crawling. The snake wrapped its tail around her arms, numbing them. Silver scales rippled as the snake glided behind Chasina's eyes. It aligned itself with her vision so that she saw everything through a silver film.

"You're in Kemer's room?" Silversmith asked, and Chasina swallowed a shriek. He saw through her eyes. He was taking control of her body.

"I learned he had a secret compartment, and I came to search it," Chasina said, telling parts of the truth.

"Tell me the truth: what was inside?"

"An Undying robe."

Pure terror ebbed from the silver snake. Chasina whimpered, unable to separate Silversmith's emotions from her own. Did she feel vibrations? Was Kemer approaching? All the horrific deaths she'd seen in her lifetime played through her mind.

Silversmith stuttered. "Lord Kemer is an Undying?"

"Yes."

She felt the snake turn dormant as Silversmith withdrew his attention. He didn't fall asleep. He simply focused on something other than Chasina, which meant she regained control over her body.

Chasina tried running toward the tunnel, but pain cascaded through her body. She tried crawling to the tunnel, but her mind stopped working, splitting into a hundred disconnected thoughts.

Silversmith's last commands played in her mind: "Stop whatever you're doing right now and look for the keystone."

Chasina tried standing again, concentrating on her intention to obey Silversmith. The pain receded, and she faced the room. Silversmith wouldn't let her run to safety until she searched for the keystone.

Where would Kemer hide the keystone?

Chapter Forty-Six

Chasina crossed to the bed and inspected it. Criss-crossed ropes supported a soft mattress without rips, tears, or bulges. Clearly, Kemer hadn't hidden the keystone in his mattress. A bench nestled in an alcove beneath the window, piled with soft white cushions trimmed in gold brocade. Chasina stepped behind the draped blanket and pressed her face into a gap between bricks.

The keystone wouldn't fit in the gap.

Vibrations traveled beneath Chasina's feet. Hurried footsteps approached the Lord's chamber.

Chasina whirled, but the blanket blocked her view of the room. She squeezed into the gap beneath the window seat.

The door swung open. One pair of footsteps halted at the wardrobe. The wardrobe squeaked open, and Chasina heard Lord Kemer rustling his tunics and boots as he checked the secret compartment. Nothing was missing or disturbed, so he'd probably dismiss it as a false alarm.

Someone knocked on the door. Lord Kemer's footsteps moved, and the heavy oak doors creaked open.

"We caught the pickpocket, my Lord," someone said. "What should we do with him? He's only a boy."

"His mentor is a traitor," Kemer replied crisply. "Keep him in an iron cage where Muriel cannot see him. I want to save him as a surprise for her."

Lord Kemer meant Oscar, the boy training as Muriel's apprentice.

"Yes, Lord," the soldier replied.

Boots tramped into the hallway, the door boomed shut, and silence draped the room. Chasina counted to thirty, straining to hear the slightest noise. She heard nothing.

Breathless, Chasina wriggled from the gap and pushed the blanket aside.

And there was Kemer, on hands and knees, searching beneath his bed. Lord. Undying. Murderer. Lord Kemer had spun more lies in his unnaturally long lifetime than she had for a year controlling Tarrken.

Chasina locked eyes with him. The Lord leaped.

Chasina shoved herself back inside the gap, squeezing until she scraped her calves.

Lord Kemer crouched and looked at her with one enormous blue-gold eye. "You're smaller than most humans who try hiding in there. You know that none of them ever succeed, don't you?"

Lord Kemer rose and exited Chasina's line of sight. She heard him whistling around the room, but she couldn't see him.

Silversmith's voice emanated from the silver snake wrapped around her spine. "Chasina, what is happening?"

"I'm trapped. Kemer's got me."

"Tell me everything you see."

"I'm wedged in a gap between stones. No way out." She glanced up, listening to Kemer's cheerful whistling. "I think he's planning something."

"Can you run?"

"No."

"We smuggled Jason into the castle," Silversmith said. "He's undercover as a soldier, so he can steal the keystone as soon as you find it. He can help you, but it would take me at least two hours to contact him. Will you be safe that long?"

"I seriously doubt it."

The silver snake exploded, and magic flooded Chasina's mind. It glazed her senses, shoving them deep inside her mind where she felt nothing, saw nothing, and heard nothing. A surge of panic twisted like smoke around her courage as she drowned in the magic.

Chasina fought the magic, and her eyesight flickered in and out of focus. Her body tingled, split between two souls trying to control the same body.

A wave of artificial calm flowed from the silver light and soothed Chasina's panic.

"Stop resisting," Silversmith said. "If I can hit Kemer with magic, maybe that will give you enough time to run to the tunnel."

"Get out of me," Chasina said, desperately trying to regain control over her body. "I don't want your help."

Lord Kemer appeared outside the gap again, and a sphere of silver light burst from Chasina's forehead. Lord Kemer barely conjured a shield in time to block the attack.

He raised his eyebrows. "That's what I get for my hospitality? I allow you in my castle, and you try to hurt me. Rude."

The Lord conjured a shield outside the gap. He teased a wire through the yellow shield and into the gap. The wire slipped around Chasina's waist. Her arm scraped the stone as Kemer yanked her from the gap and flattened her against the floor.

Chasina fought Silversmith's overwhelming presence, barely aware of the Lord's smooth voice or that he'd engulfed her in a sphere.

"Go. Away," Chasina growled, clutching her ears as though she could physically remove Silversmith from her mind.

Chasina saw Lord Kemer's face through a silver sheen.

Kemer waved. "Hello, Silversmith. I know you can see me, so please come and yield to justice. I'm getting tired of torturing your sister. It's exhausting, and honestly, I'm not enjoying it very much anymore. So come to the castle and surrender before your sister sucks all the joy out of my life, all right? Goodbye."

Kemer plucked Chasina from the yellow sphere, rolled her onto her belly, and spaced his fingers along her spine. Kemer's yellow aura sank into Chasina's spine and surrounded the silver magic. The yellow magic bullied the silver magic until it retreated and curled around Chasina's spine.

Heat rushed through Chasina's body as she regained control over herself.

Lord Kemer dusted his fingers. "I assume the other slaves told you what happens to people who try to steal the Naridi Stone?"

Chasina stood and squared her shoulders. "Yes."

"What about people who look inside my secret compartment?"

"What secret compartment?"

A dimple appeared in Kemer's cheek. "That's very good. Not so much as a flinch. Physical pain really doesn't deter you, does it? I have lived long enough to know that you're either crazy or...well, less crazy. You are a certain level of crazy, shall we say?"

Chasina said nothing.

Lord Kemer tapped the floor near Chasina. "I know you learned my secret, but I'm not going to kill you because I believe you can help me."

He wanted to know where to find Silversmith, something Chasina refused to tell him. She prepared to deceive an ancient Undying who had lied for centuries. Challenging, but not impossible.

"I don't know if you're working for yourself or your Master," Kemer said. "It seems unlikely that a human could navigate their slavery and turn it for their own gain, but some of your actions suggest you've managed to do it. Either way, Silversmith has no power over you right now. I made his magic go dormant inside of you. Until you leave this room, you are safe from him." Kemer casually rested his wrist on one knee like they were two friends conversing. "Tell me about yourself. Where are you from?"

Surprise made Chasina drop her reservation. "Don't you want to know about Silversmith? Where he's hiding or something?"

"Silversmith is inconsequential compared to you."

"Why? He is trying to steal from you. I'm just working for him. I'm not important. You kidnapped and tortured his sister, so you must feel threatened by Silversmith. What game are you playing?"

"A long game," Lord Kemer said, wrinkling his brow. "A game where Silversmith is a threat, but you are my winning piece unless I'm greatly mistaken. Where were you born?"

Behind Lord Kemer, Keir sneaked from the tunnel and grabbed the velvet rope beside the bed. Keir pulled the rope twice and ran back to the tunnel.

Keir had summoned soldiers. She just needed to stall until they arrived.

Chasina lifted her chin. "I was born in Falla. We have a long and illustrious history of killing giants."

She'd hoped to rattle Kemer, but it had the opposite effect.

Kemer clenched a triumphant fist and pounded his chest. "I knew it! I couldn't place you immediately, but I realized why you look so familiar after our second meeting. You are so small, so delicate. You look exactly like the humans in Falla. When Aldith told me you were not registered, I suspected you were the one I've been hoping to find. Tell me, how do I use the Naridi Stone?"

Chasina countered with another question. "Why do you want to know?"

Before Kemer answered, the door burst open. Armed soldiers rushed into the room, prepared to save Lord Kemer from attackers.

"What are you doing here?" demanded Kemer, reaching for Chasina. She bolted to the tunnel and dove inside.

Chapter Forty-Seven

A soldier's boot passed in front of the tunnel entrance. "Lord Kemer, we heard the emergency bell. Were you attacked?" The giants' voices dissolved into concern, washing over Chasina as she panted inside the tunnel.

If she hadn't allowed Keir to come along, she'd be imprisoned right now. He'd endangered himself, and she'd allowed it, but nothing horrendous had happened. They were both alive and safe.

"Are you all right?" Keir asked.

Chasina nodded. "Good idea, summoning the soldiers."

She took Keir's proffered arm and closed her eyes. While they walked, she shared everything she had learned about Kemer: he was an Undying, he had been hunting for something in Brundar, and he wanted to know how to use the Naridi Stone.

"What would an Undying want with the Naridi Stone?" Keir asked, pulling Chasina around a corner.

Chasina wrinkled her nose. She'd been wondering the same thing, and it only made sense when paired with what Kemer wanted most: to kill giants. Like all his Undying brethren, Kemer killed giants to

242

avenge their leader's death at the Hero's hands.

Chasina stepped in a puddle. "Can he use the Naridi Stone to kill giants, somehow? Humans have used the Naridi Stone's power to kill giants for centuries. Kemer could be planning to do the same."

If Lord Kemer wanted to use the Naridi Stone's power to kill giants, it explained why he hadn't destroyed the Naridi Stone to keep Silversmith from using it to find the Hero.

Keir's voice echoed down the tunnel. "How would Kemer use the Naridi Stone?"

"He wants me to tell him how to use it. You have to be grateful and kiss the stone before you can access the magic."

"I've never heard of that before," Keir said thoughtfully.

"Falla villagers passed down the knowledge from generation to generation," Chasina said. "After we failed to protect the Naridi Stone, we still passed down the knowledge of how to use it."

"And other villages didn't?"

"No point. The Naridi Stone was gone, never coming back, and it was easier to forget."

"So you're the only person who knows how to use the Naridi Stone?" Keir asked.

"It's the only explanation," Chasina said. "Otherwise, Kemer would have already accessed its magic and killed masses of giants."

Keir guided her down a steep passage. "If all this is true, and the Lord wants to kill a bunch of giants, why not let him?"

Chasina bumped against a slimy wall. "The Undying drain magic into themselves. It adds years to their lives, heals them, and gives them more power. That's what Kemer will do to the Naridi Stone. When he unlocks its power, he will feed on the magic and destroy the Naridi Stone."

Chasina felt Silversmith's attention focus on her. The silver snake expanded, locked eyes with her, and her whole body went numb. All her senses flickered out of existence, and Chasina dropped into an ocean of silver magic.

Chasina stood in the silver ocean. Warm water lapped around her knees, the temperature of fresh blood.

Chasina slapped the water. It sprayed her face, drops landing in her mouth. It tasted like Silversmith's magic when it flooded her mouth and forced her to tell the truth.

The ocean spanned as far as the eye could see, meeting with silver horizons at the edge of the world. The waves crashed against a tiny, barren island behind Chasina. Silver sand covered the shores.

Farther from shore, something swam beneath the waves. The creature stayed below the waves, but water rippled around its massive body.

"Let me go," Chasina said, and her voice sounded terribly small in the vast silver ocean.

A massive silver sea snake rose from the waves. Its head was bigger than Chasina's body, and when it opened its mouth, a long tongue flicked around teeth the size of Chasina's hand.

The snake spoke with Silversmith's voice. "Tell me the truth: have you tried finding the keystone—truly tried, not simply making the least effort to obey my commands?"

"No."

The snake hissed. "You hurt my sister, my mentor, and used me, and somehow, you keep finding ways to hinder me. Not this time."

"You can't possess my body. It's not something you're capable of doing," Chasina said.

"You can have it back when I find the keystone." The sea snake dove below the waves and disappeared.

The water rose to Chasina's hips. Her waist. The higher it rose, the more control Silversmith gained over her body and spirit. If she drowned, he won.

Chasina tried swimming, but her feet were glued to the sand beneath the waves. She focused on the silver sky and willed herself to see.

Her vision flickered. The silver ocean disappeared, and Shilist Castle appeared in its place. A slimy tunnel burrowed through the rock, and water dripped on her boots as she crept along.

Chasina tried moving her arm. It did not respond. She shared her vision with Silversmith, but he still controlled her body.

"Stop possessing me," Chasina said, but her voice didn't come out of her mouth. She was a little voice inside her own mind, and only Silversmith heard her.

Silversmith answered aloud, using Chasina's guttural voice. "Not until I find the keystone."

They turned a corner and exited the tunnel, stepping into a giant's bedroom. It looked exactly like Lord Kemer's bedroom, save for the open wardrobe full of gowns and Aldith sleeping on the bed.

"What are you doing?" Chasina asked as they headed into the room.

Silversmith started searching the room using Chasina's body. "Aldith is the next highest official in the castle, after Lord Kemer. Soldiers obey her if Lord Kemer is unfit to lead. If the keystone isn't in Lord Kemer's room, it might be here."

While Silversmith searched, Chasina tried regaining control over her body. Warmth briefly flashed in her fingertips, but aside from that, she felt nothing.

Over a hundred villagers obeyed her commands, but her own body rebelled. She couldn't blackmail Silversmith or physically punish him until he relinquished his control. She was a prisoner in her own body, and the swelling panic threatened to drown her if the smoke didn't suffocate her first.

"Listen," Chasina said, her voice breaking, "if you stop possessing me, I'll genuinely look for the keystone all night. I will go wherever you want to go, I swear. Just let me go."

Silversmith ignored Chasina and jumped into the wardrobe, searching inside the shoes.

A burst of warmth flowed from Chasina's fingers. She grabbed the sensation, anchoring herself against Silversmith's control.

Give me back my body.

Chapter Forty-Eight

Silversmith finished searching Aldith's room and reentered the tunnel. Instantly, the smell of slime and stagnant water filled Chasina's nostrils.

Good. She could smell again. She focused on the foul smell as Silversmith traveled through the narrow tunnels, but he took a long time. With every passing second, the walls threatened to suffocate her.

"How do you know how to navigate the tunnels?" Chasina asked, distracting herself from the tunnel.

"I used to hide in these tunnels whenever my curse transformed me into a human. How did you meet Keir?"

"I taught him how to weave," Chasina said, genuinely surprised. "How do you know him?"

Silversmith jogged down another passage. He mistimed a jump and twisted an ankle in a deep puddle, and Chasina felt the pain. For a brief second, warmth blossomed in her leg, and she regained control.

A moment later, everything went numb again.

Silversmith rubbed the ankle. "Hero's bloody sword! I'm not used to controlling this little body." He limped for a few steps and then jogged again. "Keir dragged me into helping him start a fire in the kitchen. The fire burned half of the chef's equipment, and the bricks are still charred. I thought we were going to die, but Keir thoroughly enjoyed himself."

Making chaos, recklessly endangering his life, and enjoying it. Yes, that sounded like Keir.

"How did you get us away from Keir? Does he know about your curse?" Chasina asked.

Silversmith snorted. "Do you think any human in the castle would associate with me if they knew I was a giant? Of course Keir doesn't know. And don't worry about him. I told him you were going to the women's dormitory and that you'd see him tomorrow."

Silversmith exited the tunnel and entered the Great Hall, where the mosaic workers laboriously tiled a mosaic below the dais.

Silversmith stopped at the foot of the raised dais and jumped, catching the step's edge and pulling himself up. He climbed the other steps, and though Chasina didn't feel her body panting, she heard Silversmith breathing hard.

So creepy.

Silversmith reached the top of the dais. He walked to the curtain, slipped beneath it, and stepped into a small alcove. A statue of the Hero stood on a narrow table that smelled like lavender.

"This alcove is reserved for Lord Kemer's worship," Silversmith said. "Since he's an Undying, it's possible he's using this off-limits space to hide the keystone." Silversmith looked up at the towering table and sighed. "I hate climbing."

Chasina saw an opportunity. "Let me climb the table for you. I have a lot more experience."

"I'm not that stupid."

"If you fall, it's my body that will die. Will you even feel it?"

Silversmith started climbing the table leg. "I would, but don't worry. I might not like climbing, but I'm very good at it."

Silversmith reached the tabletop. It was bare except for the statue and crushed flower petals scattered around it.

Chasina couldn't see anything beyond the curtain, but she heard a giant walk into the Great Hall. The human voices ceased.

"All these humans are behind on their work?" Lord Kemer asked, his rich voice carrying easily around the Great Hall.

At the sound of Lord Kemer's voice, Silversmith hid behind the Hero's statue.

Chasina struggled to regain control over her body. There wasn't a doubt in her mind that she was infinitely more qualified to keep herself safe from Kemer than Silversmith.

"Yes, my Lord, they're behind schedule," said Aldith sleepily. Kemer must have dragged her out of bed to answer his questions.

"They're all on the death list?" Kemer asked.

"Unless they finish this mosaic in seven days, yes. They will be killed and cooked for tardy work," Aldith said.

"I see," Lord Kemer mused. "Are there any other alcoves operating behind schedule?"

"The tapestry alcove got back on schedule, so everyone is on time except for the mosaics alcove," Aldith said.

"Tell the mosaic workers they can quit for the night. I am extending their deadline by another two weeks. And Aldith? I want you to make an announcement when you brief the human slaves tomorrow."

Lord Kemer's voice faded. He and Aldith walked away, talking quietly. Chasina wanted to move nearer and eavesdrop, but her body refused to obey.

She focused all her willpower on curling her fingers. It was like trying to make a fist with a frozen hand.

Heat flashed through her fingers. She made a fist.

"Chasina," Silversmith warned. "Do not fight me."

She braced herself for the magical agony that accompanied disobedience, but it never came. Silversmith fully inhabited her body, so he'd share her suffering. Once she regained control, however, he could torture her with impunity.

Chasina continued fighting his control, and heat bloomed in her legs and arms. She stood slowly, every movement a battle with silver magic. She inhaled deeply. Sweet relief flooded her as she breathed, strengthening herself with the sensation of air in her lungs.

Silversmith's silver snake curled around her abdomen and squeezed. "Give me control, or I will flood your body with magical agony."

"Give me a moment to think," Chasina said, buying herself some time.

Silversmith would torture her. It was already a fact and one she accepted. However, she needed to find a safe place to endure the agony.

Chasina climbed down the table leg and peeked from behind the curtain. Kemer, Aldith, and most humans had left the Great Hall.

Chasina ran toward the tunnel. Halfway there, she collapsed as silver agony rose within her. It boiled her organs, tissue, blood, and bone in the silver ocean.

Chasina clutched her head and then her stomach, trying to comfort herself. "No, no, no."

She repeated the word over and over to herself and Silversmith. Her body was failing. But it was hers.

Chapter Forty-Nine

The agony faded somewhere between Chasina's tears and the word 'no.' It was good, too, because Chasina almost reached her breaking point.

After the pain stopped, Chasina crashed into a bottomless abyss where even smoke-filled nightmares couldn't find her. She awoke to someone dragging her across the stone floor. Chasina blindly grabbed the attacker's hand and brought him crashing to the ground.

Blinking quickly, Chasina straddled the skinny attacker and pinned his pale arms. "Keir?"

The painter wrenched one arm free and covered his face. "Don't hit me!"

"What are you doing?" she asked, rolling off him and helping him stand.

Keir brushed his paint-spattered vest as though a few extra spots mattered. "I've been trying to find you. I thought you said you were going to the women's dormitory?"

Chasina quickly explained that Silversmith had possessed her body the previous night. She left out Silversmith's name because she was still under orders to keep his curse a secret, and after a torturous night, she wasn't eager to disobey again.

Keir shuddered. "I came to bring you to counting, but maybe you should rest after last night. People who miss counting are put on the death list, but the Chamberlain won't know if you skip since she hasn't marked your hand."

"What is counting?"

"Counting happens every morning so the Chamberlain can count the slaves and get briefed on our work progress.

Chasina remembered Kemer's conversation with Aldith. She told Keir about it. "I have to go. Kemer is planning something with the mosaic workers, and I need to know what it is."

Chasina took Keir's hand and followed him into a tunnel.

The silver snake shifted inside of her, sleeping. Had Silversmith pitied her or simply fallen asleep, too tired to keep torturing her? He had always seemed decent. It was one of the qualities that made her regret the necessity of addicting him to spara sap, but she'd pushed him too far. She had crossed some of Silversmith's sacred boundaries.

She couldn't blame him for reacting as he had. She'd told Silversmith they were enemies, and he'd finally learned to treat her like one.

It made sense because she and Silversmith were enemies. Not like Gran or everyone in Tarrken, who mindlessly hated her.

"Do you hate me?" Chasina asked Keir.

"Well, you don't have a very good sense of humor," he said, stopping when she sighed. "No. Why would I hate you?"

"There's not something about me that makes you want to kill me? Or bind my soul to a giant?" Chasina slitted one eye open to see Keir's reaction.

Keir glanced at their entwined hands, where Chasina squeezed his hand so tightly that white spots speckled her knuckles.

He wiggled his fingers. "Now that you mention it—"

Chasina released his hand. "Whatever you hate me for, I'm sorry. I was probably just trying to help."

Keir laughed, his voice echoing off the slimy walls. "I was going to say, 'now that you mention it, no.' Nothing about you makes me want to kill you."

"Really?"

"Really. Hey, we're going this way." He tugged Chasina's hand when she tried to take the lead. "Wild-caught humans are most likely to get lost and starve in the tunnels."

Light filtered into the tunnel through the same cracks responsible for water and cold drafts. It provided barely enough light for Chasina to see Keir's amused smile.

He knew how to survive in the tunnels, but he was reckless and chaotic. One day, he would do something foolish and get himself killed. Should she allow that to happen?

"We're here," Keir said, releasing Chasina's hand.

Chasina stepped onto a wide ledge high over the ground. She and Keir stood beside each other.

The room didn't have any windows, and barrels stood against two walls. Woven rush mats dotted the floor. Crushed lavender and rose petals scattered the mats and scented the air.

Aldith sat at a table in the center of the room. "Report."

One human stepped forward and cleared his throat. "Tapestries, cleaners, sculptors, and painters are on schedule for completion. Mosaics are one week behind schedule.

The Chamberlain scratched a note on her parchment. "Lord Kemer extended the Mosaics' deadline by two weeks. Births and deaths?"

"Twelve newborns. Four girls and eight boys." The human waved an arm, and twelve mothers stepped forward, clutching their babies tightly. Aldith marked each child's left hand and then returned to the table.

"Deaths?" Aldith asked, barely glancing up.

"Eighteen. We buried the bodies and performed the Death Blessing."

The long sleeves on Aldith's gown trailed across the parchment as she wrote. Silence descended on the humans.

"She never counted us," Chasina whispered to Keir.

Keir leaned down and whispered in her ear. "The Chamberlain's magic keeps us from escaping the castle. The Chamberlain cannot tell us apart by magic alone, but she can sense if all of us are gathered in the same room."

Aldith spoke again. "Lord Kemer wanted me to announce an opportunity for five humans to earn their freedom."

The humans chattered excitedly.

Aldith silenced the humans with a glare. "Lord Kemer wants to speak to a human named Chasina hiding in the tunnels. The Lord will free five humans and their families if they bring him Chasina."

Chasina shrank as Aldith recited an uncomfortably accurate description of her: slight build, short stature, curly hair, and scars mutilating the left half of her face.

"If you find Chasina, bring her directly to Lord Kemer. You have permission to enter his personal chamber. Counting dismissed," Aldith said, sliding a fresh sheet of parchment from a small stack.

All the humans stampeded into the tunnels, separating Chasina from Keir. She bounced off of several people, shielding her scars with a hand.

A heavyset woman grabbed Chasina's wrist and dragged her into the tunnel. Chasina twisted free and tried escaping from the tunnel, but another woman grabbed her.

The woman looked at Chasina's scars and laughed deliriously with her four friends.

"We're free," the woman laughed, covering her mouth. "Free."

The five people herded Chasina into an empty tunnel.

Chapter Fifty

The leader wrestled Chasina's arms behind her back. "We don't want to hurt you."

The leader had a beard and closely resembled the other four people. Obviously, a team of siblings.

Footsteps trotted up the passage behind them. Chasina twisted her head and saw another team of five people carrying a girl up the passageway. The girl had a few burns on her face and vaguely resembled Chasina. The girl didn't struggle. Maybe she figured that those five people and their families deserved a chance for freedom.

Chasina inhaled through her nose. "I don't blame you for trying to earn your freedom, but it's better for everyone that I remain free. I'm trying to steal the Naridi Stone."

The bearded leader readjusted his grip on Chasina's arms. "Everyone who tries to steal the Naridi Stone ends up horribly murdered. Right now, the five of us have a chance to free ourselves and our families. I am truly sorry to betray a fellow human, but we will not risk losing our chance at freedom."

Chasina shouted. "My name is Chasina, and I am the person Kemer wants to find. Look at my scars!"

She planted her feet and twisted her head, showing her face to the team behind them. The team gasped collectively, dropped the innocent girl, and ran toward Chasina.

"Move, move, move!" the bearded team leader roared. He threw Chasina over his shoulder and ran toward Kemer's room.

Chasina punched the bearded man in the kidney. He grunted and loosened his grip on Chasina's legs, giving her enough freedom to jam her knee in his neck.

The bearded man choked and collapsed.

Chasina hit the ground, rolled, and came up running. She jumped over puddles and made tight corners, but her pursuers still gained. Rounding a corner, she saw Kemer's room ahead.

She had nowhere else to run. If she entered Kemer's room, maybe she could escape out the door before Kemer captured her.

Chasina shot into Kemer's room at full speed. She skidded to a halt when she saw Kemer facing the door, his back toward her. If she blew past him into the hall, Kemer would easily catch her. The hall was too long and straight for her to outrun a giant.

Chasina climbed the velvet rope beside Kemer's bed. Her head brushed the ceiling, and she twisted her knees around the rope. Hopefully, no one would see her this far above the ground, especially since she perched above Kemer's head height.

Ten humans ran from the tunnel just as Kemer opened the door to reveal three more giants. The humans backpedaled into the tunnel. Evidently, they didn't want to bother Lord Kemer when he was busy.

Muriel stood with two soldiers on Kemer's threshold. Dungeon filth stained Muriel's clothes, and torn silk bunched around her upper arm where one soldier held her fast.

"You summoned Muriel of Kavalu, my Lord," the soldier said. "Tavern keeper, alewife, and thief, charged with treason."

Lord Kemer nodded sharply at the soldiers. "Wait outside."

Muriel gave a wobbly curtsy and plastered a fake smile on her face. "Hero bless you, Lord."

The Lord inclined his head. "I have a high tolerance for many things, alewife. Murder and lies are all part of the"—he tilted his shoulders—"*delicacy* of the office. But you tried to steal from me. That is one of the very few laws I actually care about."

Muriel flinched, angry wounds showing through the tears in her dress. "I told you, I do not know where my brother is hiding. Torture doesn't change reality."

"I no longer care where your brother is hiding," Lord Kemer said. "I'm more interested in his slave, Chasina. Has she ever mentioned the Naridi Stone?"

Chasina's chin hit her chest. She hadn't ever mentioned the Naridi Stone to Muriel, had she?

Muriel tilted her head. "The slave?"

"Chasina."

"Chasina. Why do you care about her?"

Lord Kemer covered Muriel's mouth. "I do not care about your curiosity. I care about answers. Give them to me, and disembowelment is off the list of possible executions."

Muriel paled. "Why should I know anything about Vorce's slave? I'm not going to waste time paying attention to a human."

Obviously, she needn't have bothered worrying about revealing her plans to Muriel since Muriel wasn't smart enough to pay attention to them.

Huffing, Chasina wrapped her legs more tightly around the velvet rope. Her muscles burned. She wouldn't make it if Lord Kemer talked much longer.

Lord Kemer seated Muriel at the table and produced a parcel wrapped in bright red silk.

He slid the parcel toward Muriel. "Go ahead. Open it."

Muriel laid her hand flat on the table. "I don't know anything about my brother's slave."

Kemer settled lazily on a seat across the table. "Muriel, darling, you can do better than that. Maybe you need some help remembering? That's why I brought you a present. I'll tell you a story, and you can guess what I got you." The Lord rolled his knuckles on the table, chewing his cheek as he sought the right beginning. "Once, there was a little boy named Oscar whose mentor committed treason."

Muriel gasped and snatched the parcel, tearing off the ribbon. Kemer appeared at her side to stifle her scream when she saw the contents.

"Choke it down. Swallow. Very good," Kemer purred. "I saw the little scar on his hand and knew that you would recognize it. He is a pickpocket, yes? Well, he was a pickpocket."

Muriel dropped the parcel, and a severed hand flopped onto the floor. It was mottled black from days without blood, and the fingernails were chewed ragged.

"Is he all right? Take me to see him!" Muriel stammered. She tried running, but Kemer wrapped an arm around her ribs.

"Tell me about Chasina, or I will take Oscar's other hand and his feet, followed by his ears," Kemer said.

Muriel covered her mouth, shaking. "The slave only ever mentioned the Naridi Stone when she was helping us steal it."

"Nothing that wasn't common knowledge?"

"No."

Lord Kemer inhaled deeply through his nose, exhaled, and spoke in Muriel's ear. "What about tics? Does Chasina have any odd habits?"

Muriel licked her lips. "She kisses her knife."

Lord Kemer spun Muriel around to face him. "She kisses it. Are you sure?"

"Yes. I've seen Chasina rubbing it like there are carvings on the handle. Maybe shapes. They are too small to see clearly."

Lord Kemer's expression relaxed as the puzzle piece clicked in his mind. He knew to kiss the Naridi Stone.

Kemer knew he had to kiss the Naridi Stone, but he didn't know to be grateful at the same time. Kiss the stone and be grateful. One didn't matter without the other.

Lord Kemer snagged the severed hand from the floor and escorted Muriel to the door.

He pressed the severed hand against Muriel's belly. "Take this as a keepsake. It can keep you company in the dungeon."

Lord Kemer gave Muriel to the awaiting soldiers and closed the door. He faced the door, absentmindedly combing his hair.

"She kisses it," he mused softly. "Do I remember that?"

Chasina shook freely. Every burning muscle trembled beyond her control, and slowly, she slipped down the velvet rope.

Chapter Fifty-One

Chasina relaxed her grip and finished sliding to the ground. She ran toward the door, keeping herself in Lord Kemer's blind spot.

Ten yards from the door, Chasina heard noises from the tunnel. The freedom-hungry humans entered Lord Kemer's room.

"It must be my birthday," Lord Kemer said, walking to the tunnel where ten humans shifted nervously. "Where is Chasina?"

Chasina sprinted the last ten yards and rolled beneath the door. She chased Muriel and the two soldiers, following them down the corridor.

Keir detached from the wall halfway down the hall and ran alongside her. "You're all right. I lost you in the crowd after Aldith made the announcement, but I figured you would probably end up in Kemer's room eventually."

They reached the end of the hall and started descending the steps. Muriel and her escort were already near the bottom.

Keir pointed to a spot at the bottom of the steps. "There is a tunnel entrance. We can get lost inside the tunnel and figure out our next step to blackmailing Kemer."

Behind them, Kemer's door slammed shut. Heavy footsteps ran down the hallway toward the stairs, sending vibrations through Chasina's body.

Chasina doubled the pace. Ten stone steps separated her and Keir from the tunnel. If they forgot about bodily injury and hurried, they might make it to the tunnel in time.

The vibrations from Lord Kemer's footsteps buzzed up Chasina's spine.

"If Kemer catches us, pretend that you were trying to catch me," Chasina said. "Turn me over to him. It'll keep you safe."

"Don't be stupid," Keir grunted, dropping to another step.

Six steps to the bottom.

Chasina's twisted ankle twinged every time she jumped down a step. It was fine. She was more worried about Keir, whose skinny body looked like it might snap if he landed awkwardly.

Two steps to the bottom.

A yellow sphere fizzled against the stone step above Chasina. She glanced over her shoulder and saw Kemer rapidly descending the stairs toward them.

Chasina and Keir reached the bottom of the stairs. Keir ducked inside the tunnel, but Chasina froze as the silver snake within her rose and locked eyes with her.

Silversmith shared her vision just in time to see Muriel crying as she walked down the hall in filthy rags.

"What are you doing?" Keir asked.

"Run," Chasina said woodenly, unable to move.

Keir dashed from the passage and grabbed Chasina beneath the arms, pulling her to safety just as Kemer's boot crashed outside the tunnel.

Chasina shivered. The silver virus spread from her spine to infect her body. "What has Kemer done to my sister?" Silversmith shouted in Chasina's mind.

"Let me go," Chasina said.

"You betrayed Muriel and got her captured. Whatever happens to her is your fault."

Chasina shook from the effort of keeping control of her body. She rolled onto her stomach, gasping.

"I will save my sister," Silversmith said coldly.

"Save her…another…way. What can…I do?"

"I am taking your body to the dungeon so I can talk to Muriel."

Chasina lost control of herself and dropped into the silver ocean. She floundered helplessly, struggling to keep her head above water because she knew Silversmith would own her if she drowned. She'd be trapped on the lonely little island and never control herself again.

"Let me go. Do you hear me?" Chasina shouted. "Let me go!"

There was no answer, but the ocean turned choppy. A riptide pulled her beneath the waves. She flailed underwater. The longer she stayed beneath the water, the more confusion roared in her mind. Wasn't she a creature of this sea? Didn't she live here?

Chasina kicked free of the riptide and swam to the surface. The silver ocean fought back, tides pulling her back and forth like a piece of seaweed.

A memory swam from the ocean floor, skimming the waves and unfolding with a bright snap of color.

Da's sweaty hand chafed Chasina's wrist. "Duck against the ground, Chasina," he said, dropping her into the pit they'd excavated over the summer. "I'll be right back with Mama and Bea. Stay"

The memory yawned and folded shut abruptly, leaving Chasina desperately treading water in the silver ocean.

The silver ocean rippled, and a single thought floated through Chasina's mind before everything went black.

She had stayed. No one else in the hut had obeyed Da, too busy screaming at each other to collect the heirlooms.

I stayed.

Chapter Fifty-Two

Cold water dripped down Chasina's cheek. She stared blindly for a moment before recognizing Keir's gaunt face.

Keir knuckled the mark on Chasina's forehead. "Your Master was getting the best of you, so I knocked you out. Luckily, that drove him out."

Chasina touched her chest. As though it sensed her quiet searching, the silver snake rose and hissed.

"Stop resisting me," Silversmith said. "I wouldn't have to possess your body if you would obey me."

"I do obey you."

"You do everything except obey me, but not this time. It's only a matter of time before you cannot resist me anymore. Until then, tell my sister I am coming to rescue her. Tell her tonight."

Silversmith turned his attention elsewhere, and the snake went dormant.

Silversmith was right. It was only a matter of time before he fully possessed her. A week ago, she would have said that Silversmith was incapable of possessing a human. Maybe she'd been so eager to manipulate him because she thought he wouldn't fight back.

A pang kicked Chasina square in the chest, and it had nothing to do with magic. She had destroyed Silversmith's naivety, and though she'd never say it aloud, it had been endearing. People born innocent were ordinary. People who stayed that way were special.

"Are you all right?" Keir asked. "You were whimpering right before I knocked you out."

Was that concern in his voice? "I don't whimper."

"Yes, you do. Was it something your Master said?"

Chasina shrugged noncommittally and rubbed the inside of her wrist. If Da were alive, his hand would probably still swallow hers up to the wrist. She felt the sweat from his palm all those years ago, smelled the fresh dirt, and heard Bea and Mama rushing around the hut. Even after years of trying to forget, she still remembered every detail about the attack, even the way Bea snapped at her for trying to help weave baskets half an hour before it happened.

Phantom smoke rose from Chasina's memories. "I need out of here, Keir," Chasina said, her guttural voice rising quickly. "Now."

Keir rose and started down the passage, and Chasina followed.

The passage narrowed, and she felt it shoot deep inside her chest. She pressed her face against the wall, hands on either side of her face, blocking out the tunnel closing in on all sides.

"Chasina, calm down. We're almost there," Keir said.

Chasina hunched against the wall, babbling things that only she understood. "Let me help with the basket. Leave the heirlooms. Da, help me!"

Keir wrestled Chasina's hand from the wall and forced something into her palm. Her fingers snapped shut around Da's knife, and Chasina instantly breathed more deeply.

Keir tugged on the knife, and, unable to release it, Chasina followed him with her eyes closed. It felt like eons until he released the knife.

"You can look, now," Keir said. "We're in an abandoned room. I've painted here for almost two years."

Chasina blinked and saw an empty bedchamber. Golden sunlight slid over the window ledge and caressed the bedroom, fondling the fireplace and dusty stools. Dead insects and cobwebs cluttered the corners, and mildew slowly devoured the falcon perch beside the bed.

They stood on the sill of a ribbed window. Rivulets of freshwater gathered beneath a shattered pane. Colorful paintings decorated both sides of the window.

A horse with the wind in its mane.

A single flower, dewdrops sparkling in rays of sunlight.

A tree, boughs dripping with arrow-shaped leaves, home to a flock of ravens.

The tension eased from Chasina's shoulders, and she stroked the horse's neck. "They're beautiful, Keir."

A hint of color touched Keir's cheeks. He leaned against the wall and crossed his arms, scratching his neck. "How are we going to get the Naridi Stone? Kemer is an Undying. If we meet him to blackmail him, he'll just capture you and kill me."

The whole situation was far messier than Chasina liked. And why was she dragging Keir into it? She didn't want him ending up on Aldith's death list if they got caught. Keir was the first human to express concern about her well-being since she was young.

"Why are you helping me? It's dangerous." Chasina asked, stooping to breathe the fresh air wafting into the room through the shattered pane.

"I like making chaos."

Chasina raised an eyebrow. "That can get you killed."

"Shilist is the single most godforsaken place on Earth. It's a dead body, see?" He scraped fingernails against the bricks. "And everyone who lives here are maggots crawling in its veins. If you told me we

266

had to jump from a window to steal the Naridi Stone, I'd do it. I'd do anything to escape."

"Anything except turn me over to Lord Kemer."

Keir grinned, revealing a lot of teeth crammed inside his bony face. "Even an agent of chaos has rules. So how do we blackmail Kemer?"

Investigating Kemer and using his secrets against him had seemed like a great idea until Chasina discovered he was an Undying. How would she blackmail someone who wouldn't be intimidated by it? Kemer was an immortal who had walked the Earth for centuries. Blackmail was nothing new to him.

Silversmith wanted the Naridi Stone to trade to Bemea and awaken the Hero, who slept in the Vault of Eternal Sleep.

She wanted the Naridi Stone because it rightfully belonged to humankind. Because people like Keir deserved a better life and because she wanted to go home.

Lord Kemer wanted to absorb the Naridi Stone's power and use it to destroy giants, his sworn enemies who worshiped the Hero. But that wasn't all he wanted, was it?

Blackmail wasn't the only way to get the Naridi Stone. She could bargain with Kemer using all the information she'd gathered, plus the one thing she knew Lord Kemer wanted: her.

Chapter Fifty-Three

C hasina climbed onto Aldith's sturdy table in the counting room, listening to Keir's panting as he joined her. Thick black clouds rolled outside the peaked windows and made her shadow almost invisible.

Ink stained her hands as she twisted off the inkwell's lid and dipped her finger in the thick liquid.

Lord Kemer,

Bring the Naridi Stone to your chamber at sunrise. I want it. You want my information. We will trade. If I don't see the Naridi Stone in your room, I won't come.

—Chasina

"You really think he'll come?" Keir asked, leaning over Chasina's shoulder and reading the letter while the ink dried.

"Lord Kemer wants me too badly to refuse."

"He wants you to help him access the Naridi Stone's power. He's not going to give you the Naridi Stone; he will double-cross you."

Chasina wrote a second later and addressed it to the Chamberlain. "That's why I have to double-cross him first. The Chamberlain is the second highest ranking official in the castle, so soldiers will obey her if Lord Kemer is unfit to lead. Let's make sure she brings some soldiers to Kemer's room."

Chasina left the Chamberlain's letter on the table and pushed Kemer's letter off of the table. It floated to the ground while Chasina closed the inkwell and wiped the ink from her hands.

Keir read the letter addressed to the Chamberlain. "You really think Aldith will believe the allegations in this letter? Kemer knows you opened his compartment. He will have moved his Undying robe, so you don't have any proof."

"Aldith hates Lord Kemer. Even if she doesn't believe the accusations in this letter, she will pretend to believe them so she can harass him. I need Aldith to show up, but I don't need her to arrest Kemer. Proof isn't necessary."

Chasina and Keir slid down the table leg and entered the tunnels. She held Keir's hand as they navigated the tunnels to Kemer's room. They arrived, and Chasina entered Kemer's room with the letter.

Rain slashed against the stained glass like thousands of desperate hands, but it did not bother Lord Kemer. He snored lightly on his bed.

Chasina quickly scaled the table and left the letter in plain sight. She rejoined Keir, and they headed to the dungeon. Silversmith had commanded her to talk to Muriel tonight, and she obeyed.

The tunnels leading to the dungeon arced steeply through the stone. Keir did his best to lead her steadily, but sometimes her foot landed in the wrong hole or twisted on rubble. When Keir told her to open her eyes, Chasina felt like she had skidded down a dozen tunnels and had the scrapes to prove them.

Chasina peeked inside the dungeon, covering her nose against the foul odor permeating the air. A hall cut the dungeon from left to right.

To the left, several guards sat around a table. Torchlight flickered over their faces, and the crackling fire provided a steady undercurrent to their voices.

Cells lined one side of the hall to the right, and chains hung from the other.

Keir glanced at the chatting guards. "They keep important prisoners in their own cells. To the right, around the corner."

Chasina followed Keir out of the tunnel, glancing over her shoulder to ensure the guards didn't see them. They walked down the right hall, following the moans floating around the corner. Heavy wooden doors lined the right side of the hall. Prisoners on the opposite side of the aisle were thrown together and chained to the wall.

Chasina noticed the rats crawling on the filthy prisoners. "Are those rats? We didn't bring anything to keep them away."

Keir glanced at the rats, most of which had more muscle and flesh than both humans put together. "They're usually not interested in humans. Just keep walking."

Chasina reached for Da's knife just in case.

"Muriel isn't in any of these cells?" Chasina asked, whispering even though none of the giants could reach them.

Keir jerked his chin at the far end of the hall. "Lord Kemer always keeps his most valuable prisoner in that cell. We'll start there."

Water dribbled from patches of oozing moss stuck to the walls and fed rivulets that splashed across Chasina's boots. She wrinkled her nose. How long did it take giants to mete out justice? Long enough for dark clumps of fungus to feed on the decay shoved in corners.

Chasina wiggled under the door at the end of the hall. The cell was roomy enough for the various torture implements to have their own space on the wall. Dried blood streaked the wall beneath whips, saws, and strange metal devices.

Opposite the torture wall, Muriel curled on a pile of moldy hay with both manacled hands tucked under her head.

Muriel snarled at Chasina. "You. Rat. I'm going to kill you."

"Do that," Chasina said. "I'd love to see how far you can move with those chains. Besides, you'd never hear what I came to say."

Keir rolled under the door. He jumped up beside Chasina, and she subtly moved in front of him. Even chained, Muriel was dangerous and might pounce if Keir moved too close.

Muriel tilted her head, and dried blood cracked on her face. "Come closer. I cannot hear your little voice."

"How stupid do you think I am?" Chasina asked. Killing her would be like assaulting Silversmith, but Muriel might not mind assaulting her brother if it meant killing Chasina.

Muriel sat back. "I see my brother finally filled you with magic. How much longer do you think you can keep control of your body?"

"Why has Kemer allowed you to keep living? I would have killed you already," Chasina said.

Muriel tested the length of her chain, eyeing the distance between her and Chasina. "Since I'm accused of treason, he has to hold me for royal trial. A messenger arrived two hours ago with the news that multiple Undying murdered King Omar yesterday when they attacked District One."

"How do you know that?"

"The guards won't shut up about the refugees coming from District One or that the Undying finally killed King Omar. There's no monarch to preside over a royal trial unless the Prince comes forward from hiding, so Lord Kemer cannot execute me."

Since Lord Kemer masqueraded as a proper Lord, he probably didn't want to break too many rules by executing Muriel without a trial. He wouldn't want the hens to discover a fox in the henhouse.

"What did my brother send you to tell me?" Muriel asked.

"He is coming to rescue you."

Muriel rattled her chains. "That's it? He didn't share any plans or ideas to get me out of here? They're putting me back in a cage tomorrow."

Chasina smiled, showing her bottom teeth. "What? Afraid he's not competent enough to save you?"

Muriel's silence told the story.

Chasina spared Muriel a last baleful glance before following Keir under the door and through the dungeon.

Chapter Fifty-Four

One or two prisoners clawed at the end of their chains, trying to grab Keir and Chasina. Chasina put herself between Keir and the prisoners.

Keir guided Chasina through the tunnels, stopping in a relatively dry passage. It was roomier than other tunnels, but Chasina still felt the walls closing in from all sides.

It made sense to sleep here. People still hunted for her, hoping to free themselves and their families.

The necessity didn't comfort her very much.

"I'll be fine," Chasina said to Keir. "You should go to the men's dormitories and get some sleep."

Keir folded his skinny frame beneath him and sank against the wall. He looked like a collapsed scarecrow.

"I'm sleeping here," Keir said.

Chasina slowly slid down the wall. She had never shared a sleeping area with someone who hadn't hated her, even Gran.

"I get panic attacks," Chasina said. "I don't allow fires in the winter. If you wake me, I'll attack you before realizing what's happening. Are you sure you want to stay here?"

"Do you want me to leave?"

"No."

"Then I'll stay. I'm curious, though. How do you survive winter without a fire?"

Chasina massaged her palm with a thumb. "Gran moves in with another family. If it gets too cold, I build an igloo. Otherwise, I rub a thick layer of animal fat on my skin, wrap myself in rabbit fur, and sleep beneath a layer of decaying leaves."

Keir grimaced. "I bet you're not a popular person until spring. Can you smell yourself?"

Chasina dug a rock from beneath her leg and threw it against the wall. "At first. After the first week, I'm just happy to be moderately warm."

Keir used his hand for a pillow and fell asleep.

Chasina tried sleeping, but the silver snake didn't let her rest. She felt it expanding inside her, shifting its silver coils and nosing her emotions.

It was only a matter of time before Silversmith won. Unless she freed herself with the Naridi Stone before the snake grew too powerful, her spirit would drown in a silver ocean while Silversmith possessed her body.

Chasina never slept. When Keir awoke, he told Chasina it was sunrise, instinctively knowing the sun's position.

Chasina took Keir's hand and allowed him to guide her to Kemer's room. "How can you tell where we are going if you don't have a torch?"

Keir splashed through a puddle. "Every tunnel has a personality. Color, smell, and shape. I sense the tunnels more than I see them."

Keir stopped suddenly, and she collided against him. Keir was so gaunt that his spine stuck from his back like rocks half-buried in the dirt.

"We're here," Keir said.

She carefully approached the exit and peeked inside Lord Kemer's room. Kemer sat cross-legged on the floor. A rose-shaped stone lay on the floor before him, glowing briefly with every imaginable color from white to black.

Kemer noticed Chasina studying him from the tunnel. He raised an eyebrow.

"I'm not going to wait all day, Chasina," Lord Kemer said. "Either come out or run away."

Keir and Chasina backed down the tunnel until Lord Kemer couldn't see them.

Keir's whispered nervously. "Isn't Aldith supposed to be here by now?"

"She must be running late," Chasina said.

"Late to accuse Lord Kemer of being an Undying? She'd jump at the chance. Chasina, I don't think Aldith is coming."

"She has to come. Maybe she just needs more time."

If Chasina stalled Kemer until Aldith arrived, the plan would still work. When Aldith arrived, Chasina would snatch the Naridi Stone and leave.

Chasina kissed a rose on her knife, squared her shoulders, and strode into Kemer's room. "I'm glad to see you came, Lord Kemer."

Kemer tilted his head. "I'm the one we were worried about not showing? I'm not the one who's been hiding in the castle tunnels. The Naridi Stone is here, as you can see."

"Excuse me if I authenticate it."

"Of course."

Chasina stood in front of the Naridi Stone, ignoring Kemer towering above her. The Naridi Stone was twice as large as her head. It glowed hot pink before fading to pale green.

"Go ahead and touch it," Kemer said, utterly relaxed, "Make sure

I'm not trying to fool you with an elaborate illusion."

A subtle smirk crossed Kemer's face, buried beneath layers of courtesy. He wanted to know how to use the Naridi Stone, and if Chasina showed him while authenticating it, so much the better. If she accessed the magic, Kemer might squish her before she killed him.

Chasina touched the Naridi Stone. It was pleasantly warm and throbbed like a stone heart, ready to pump power into the human race.

Chasina removed her hand before she yielded to temptation. "It seems authentic. How do you sleep at night knowing you slaughtered hundreds of humans to get it?"

"It's a long tale of betrayal and bloodshed," Kemer said. "I shall regale you with the story one day when we're not busy manipulating each other."

"Manipulating?"

Kemer winked. "Let's be honest, shall we? There is no scenario where both of us get what we want. I want to access the Naridi Stone's magic, and you want to spirit it away. You know I will capture you, yet you came anyway, which means you're going to double-cross me. Is this your Master's plan, or have you outfoxed him?"

Chasina didn't even bother trying to look innocent. "What now?"

"Play the game, Chasina. Always play the game."

Kemer reached out to pick up Chasina, but several giants slamming against the door saved her. Bright axes split the oak panels, and beyond them, a shadowed battalion attacked the door.

"I win," Chasina said. She picked up the Naridi Stone and ran while Kemer stared at the door in shock.

Kemer's hand locked around her body. "Not this time, darling," he said, standing and ripping the Naridi Stone from her arms. "We're going to have a very long discussion later."

Lord Kemer stood beside the table and faced the door. While he assessed the scenario, Chasina eased her knife from its sheath. She ripped the blade through his palm and felt something snap. He gasped in pain; she fell through his spasming fingers. Chasina caught the table's edge, her chin slamming against the wood.

She tasted blood.

The oak panels split.

Soldiers exploded through the door.

Chapter Fifty-Five

Two soldiers tackled Kemer and pinned him to the floor, a dagger at his throat. They conjured magic around their hands to protect themselves from Kemer's magic if he attacked.

Four men flanked the Chamberlain as she stepped through the ruined doorway. One of the four soldiers wore a chainmail hauberk embroidered with Lord Kemer's coat of arms: a black spider on a yellow background. It marked the soldier as the sergeant-at-arms.

The sergeant nodded at the other soldiers. "Search the room."

Grunting, Chasina struggled onto the table and crawled to the nearest leg, sweaty fingers slipping in the delicate carvings. She climbed to the ground and ducked inside the tunnel. A bloody swathe stained her thigh as she cleaned her knife.

"Are you hurt?" Keir asked.

"No. As soon as Kemer dumps the Naridi Stone and leaves, we can steal it."

"Why would he drop the Naridi Stone and leave?"

Chasina nodded at the unfolding chaos. "He won't want to get caught with it. He will hide it in the room, and then Aldith will take him to search the vault tower. You'll see. Just watch the chaos."

Keir grinned and dropped to his belly on the passage floor. "My favorite part."

Vibrations rumbled through Chasina's stomach as she joined Keir on the floor and watched the sergeant march across the room to inspect the wardrobe. The letter Chasina had left Aldith detailed where to find the Undying robe.

The Chamberlain planted stout legs above Kemer. "We know what you've done."

Chasina glimpsed Kemer's expression between the forest of legs and chuckled softly. It looked like he was trying to swallow a rock.

"What in Hero's name are you talking about?" Kemer asked.

The Chamberlain waved Chasina's letter. "My informant says that you are an Undying planning to attack Kavalu, and you were trying to absorb power from the Naridi Stone. Where is it? In the secret compartment where you hide your Undying robe?"

Kemer's expression grew tenser. "I'm disappointed in you, Aldith. You have no idea who sent that letter, do you?"

"In a crisis, we must take every accusation seriously."

"Especially if it dethrones me, eh?"

The sergeant straightened from searching the wardrobe. "Chamberlain, we found nothing. The Lord is innocent. Release him," he said, beckoning to his soldiers.

"Are you certain?" Aldith asked.

"I found the secret compartment, but not the robe indicated in the message. Perhaps the message was mistaken?"

A soldier helped Kemer to his feet. While Aldith argued with the soldiers, Kemer backed to the window and dropped the Naridi Stone. He crossed his ankles, one heel nudging the Naridi Stone into the gap beneath the window seat.

"What about the Naridi Stone?" Aldith asked.

Kemer stepped into the soldiers' nexus. "Search me. I don't have the Naridi Stone."

The Chamberlain eyed Kemer's smooth, tight clothes, and a hint of color receded from her face. "This is not good enough. Lord Kemer, you are unfit to lead under such accusations."

"I'm sorry you didn't face me with them earlier," Kemer interrupted, situating his body so that Aldith bared her neck when she looked up at him. "We could have avoided any repercussions."

Removing his gloves, the sergeant carefully patted Kemer's arms and legs, pausing at his breastbone. He looked questioningly into the Lord's face.

Lord Kemer lifted a long chain over his head and pulled the keystone from beneath his flat clothes.

"Just a little illusion," Kemer said, glancing at Aldith. "Being a Lord requires some finesse."

Aldith rigidly straightened the letter. "My informant tells me to search the tower vault. Whether or not we find the Naridi Stone could determine your innocence."

Chasina imagined the conflict happening in Kemer's mind. He had already hidden the Naridi Stone and couldn't retrieve it in front of everyone, but neither could he accompany everyone to the tower vault. They would see the Naridi Stone was gone. However, if he didn't accompany everyone to inspect the tower vault, it would expose his true identity as an Undying.

Decisions, decisions.

Kemer did not hesitate. He exited his room, followed by a horde of giants marching into the hall.

Standing, Chasina exited the tunnel with Keir at her side. They hurried toward the window seat. Halfway across the room, vibrations rumbled beneath Chasina's feet, and a cold shadow fell across her back.

Chasina shoved Keir aside. He stumbled, regained his balance, and dashed toward the bed.

The giant smashed Chasina against the ground. Muttering angrily, the giant flipped her over. It was Jason. He'd disguised himself as a soldier, complete with the yellow armband around his bicep.

"Oh. It's you," Jason said. "I thought maybe it was someone edible." Jason released her and poked around the room.

Chasina searched for Keir and found him on the canopy above the bed. At least he'd gotten away safely.

"I found the keystone," Chasina said to Jason. "Lord Kemer enchants an illusion on the keystone and wears it around his neck."

Jason glanced at the decimated doorway before checking the bricks around the window. His boot nudged the gap where the Naridi Stone nestled.

Chasina winced. "What are you doing?"

Jason started searching the cabinet. "Where does Kemer keep his valuables?"

"He doesn't have any valuables in here. You need to leave before Kemer returns."

Chasina locked gazes with Keir hiding atop the canopy. She silently communicated with him, pointing at the Naridi Stone's hiding place, herself, and Jason. *I'll distract him while you get the stone.*

Keir nodded.

Chasina moved closer to Jason while he searched the cabinet. "Lord Kemer has a secret compartment in the wardrobe."

He glanced irritatedly at Chasina. "Go away. I don't like humans watching me with their creepy little eyes."

Jason closed the cabinet and moved to the wardrobe. He stuck his head inside.

Keir slid to the ground and ran toward the gap in the wall.

Jason emerged from the wardrobe and spotted Chasina looking across the room at Keir. Jason saw Keir and took three strides to pluck him from the ground.

"You can't kill him. He's a castle slave," Chasina said. "He's marked."

Jason checked Keir's mark and snarled. "Just my luck. Right when I'm hungry, too." He jerked his head at Chasina. "I told you to go away. I cannot kill you, but I can certainly hurt you."

Jason returned to the wardrobe and picked up Chasina. He threw Chasina against the wall beside the wardrobe—fast enough to hurt, not kill.

Chasina covered her head just before she collided against the wall. She crumpled to the floor, ears buzzing. A low whine rose from her lips, and her skull throbbed painfully. A moment later, Keir hit the wall above her and fell onto her back.

New vibrations traveled through the floor. The vibrations moved up the hall, coming steadily closer.

Lord Kemer stepped through the broken doorway. "Thank you for guarding my room, soldier."

Jason replied smoothly, and Kemer dismissed him. Kemer's shadow passed over Chasina as he crouched above her and brushed Keir from her back, picking her up.

"I win," Lord Kemer said.

Chapter Fifty-Six

C hasina blinked, trying to regain her composure. Why did Silversmith find it necessary to work with Jason? Silversmith probably needed someone to steal the keystone after Chasina found it, and Jason was greedy enough to risk Lord Kemer's wrath in exchange for looting the vault tower.

Chasina touched the spot on her ribs where pain blossomed. She'd be surprised if it wasn't broken. Hopefully, Keir had fared better than her. Kemer held Keir's unconscious body in his other hand.

"You're supposed to be under arrest after they didn't find the Naridi Stone," Chasina said bluntly. She couldn't fool Kemer with submissiveness, which worked for her. Cowering went against her nature.

Lord Kemer held her level with his face. "I cast an illusion that looked like the Naridi Stone. Right now, Aldith is languishing in a dungeon cell for sedition."

"I thought she had the power to control the army if you couldn't?"

"She does. She didn't think there'd be consequences for accusing me of being an Undying, but I imagine she's rethinking that since I've arrested her." The Lord glanced at his wardrobe. "I don't look four centuries old, but I am, and somehow you figured out my secret. You found my robe and told Aldith. What gave me away?"

"I investigated you and found the secret compartment," Chasina said, leaving Regina out of the conversation. "What were you doing in Brundar dressed in your robes?"

Kemer raised his eyebrows. "I was looking for someone from Falla. All the humans I have asked about the Naridi Stone point me toward the Falla descendants. Even after years of forcing people to register their human slaves, you're the first Falla descendant I've found."

Lord Kemer had managed to masquerade as Lord and leverage all his office's powers toward finding a specific human. While everyone thought he manipulated the market on human hunting to get rich, he actually used it to find humans who might tell him how to use the Naridi Stone. He required every human to be registered. He limited giants to hunt humans in certain areas, probably villages near Falla's ruins.

"I'm going to save you some time," Chasina lied. "Giants razed Falla when I was five years old, and we didn't make a habit of passing down secrets of the Naridi Stone. Why bother? We'd already lost it once. We wouldn't get a second chance. I have no idea how to access the magic inside the Naridi Stone, so let me and Keir go. We cannot help you."

"An excellent lie," Kemer said. "But I am four hundred years old, so you'll have to try better than that."

Kemer conjured a yellow sphere around Keir, and Chasina's stomach dropped. Magical orbs almost always meant death. That's why she told young children horror stories, so they ran from the magical spheres.

Keir was unconscious. He could not run.

Chasina hid behind her mask of scars. "Is this supposed to

intimidate me? I'm a human. We're immune to intimidation. We've lived with it too long for it to work."

Kemer focused on the yellow orb containing Keir, and the orb pulsed. Sweat beaded on Keir's skin. His face reddened. His hair and clothes caught fire.

"Stop!" Chasina said.

The yellow orb disappeared, and Keir dropped into Kemer's hand. Kemer rubbed his thumb over Keir's smoking clothes and hair, smothering the fire.

"Tell me how to access the Naridi Stone's magic," Kemer said, setting Keir's limp body on the bed and retrieving the Naridi Stone from beneath the window seat. "Lie to me, and I will burn him to ashes."

Should she sacrifice Keir or save him? Saving him meant losing the Naridi Stone. It meant condemning the human race to live the way they'd lived for seventy years without magic. She couldn't make that decision...but neither could she sacrifice Keir. She simply didn't have the strength to watch him die.

"You have to be grateful when you kiss the stone," Chasina said.

Kemer's face cracked with relief. It was like watching a stone split down the center and reveal glittering insides.

"I remember," Kemer said, his voice hushed. "It's been so long. But now I remember."

Kemer acted like he'd once known how to use the Naridi Stone but had forgotten. He had probably learned seventy years ago while attacking Falla.

Kemer kissed the Naridi Stone. The stone glowed even brighter, multicolored petals throwing brilliance across the room. A wave of warmth rolled from the Naridi Stone.

Lord Kemer dropped the Naridi Stone in his purse, sealing away the warmth and brilliance. He hadn't drained its magic. "If you're a good girl for me, I'll let you see it again before I destroy it."

"I hate you."

"You don't know the whole story."

"So tell me," Chasina demanded.

Kemer knelt and pulled a wooden cage from beneath his bed. "I'd love to, darling, but I have refugees arriving tonight and guests to welcome before that, so I don't have time for storytelling." He opened the cage's wooden door and quickly deposited Chasina and Keir inside.

The cage was a square box with wooden slats in the front. A coiled spring held the lock shut. Chasina turned in a circle, her throat closing as she saw all four walls. The walls shimmered like heat over a fire, ribbons of black smoke flowing through the cage and pooling around her ankles. Everything stank of soot and sweat, cinders floating in the open pit where she dug her shoulder into the dirt.

Da pleaded with Mama. "We just need to be alive. Mama. Who cares about the heirlooms? Get in the pit."

"I cannot leave my mother's basket cradle," Mama said.

Vibrations tugged at Chasina's skin like fishhooks. Buildings crashed to the ground, and giants called out above the cacophony.

"Get the torches over here!" a giant yelled. "Smoke the humans out of hiding."

Chasina's hut collapsed. Beams crunched and twisted, falling across Chasina's hiding place. She screamed, digging her fingers into the dirt wall and trying to stand.

The Earth shook. She fell.

Da reached through the splintered beams and dropped his favorite knife. "Stay hidden, Chasina," he said, his face scratched and bloody. "No matter what happens or what you hear, don't come out. I will come back for you."

Someone tore Da away. He didn't scream.

Chasina picked up Da's knife and wrapped her little body around it. *He is coming back,* she told herself, humming to block out the screams of her villagers. *He is coming back. He promised.*

Orange tongues licked at the beams overhead, and black smoke seeped into the tiny pit. Burning splinters fell through the overhead beams. One beam caught fire and cracked. It fell, pinning Chasina to the ground. She wheezed, each breath painful and tiny.

Smoke stung her throat, but she didn't notice it. Nothing compared to the agony of fire eating her face.

Melted skin dripped down her face.

Chapter Fifty-Seven

A voice spoke in Chasina's ear. "Are you all right?"

Chasina cracked open one eye and saw Keir leaning over her. Not Da. Not Mama or Bea, but someone she'd met days ago.

Chasina hugged Keir, digging her fists into his back.

Keir's breath hitched in pain, but he returned the embrace. "I can't say that you're safe, but you're with a friend. Lord Kemer is gone."

Friend. So this was how it felt to be loved. It meant having someone who didn't sneer when she panicked. Someone who remained steady while she clung to them and whispered furiously for the smoke that only she saw to dissipate.

She had always feared losing Gran, but it wasn't until now that Chasina feared losing someone who loved her.

Chasina squeezed Keir one last time and stepped away. "Sorry. I panicked."

"It's all right," Keir said, touching his burnt bangs. "But I'd like to know what happened after I passed out."

Chasina told Keir about her confrontation with Lord Kemer. Every few seconds, Keir's face fell another notch.

How had she fooled herself into believing she could steal the Naridi Stone? It just wasn't possible. Giants, fortresses, and magic versus her, a small human with a knife.

Keir raked his hair. "I was born into this mess, but you weren't. How did the giants enslave you?"

Chasina drew her knife and held it against her belly. "My grandmother bound my soul to a giant, and everyone cheered when he took me into Brundar."

Keir did a double-take. "Why would they do that?"

"Because I am the only person in the village who did anything necessary to keep us alive."

"Like what?"

Chasina thumbed the roses carved on her knife. Her pulse hammered in her neck, and she felt slightly sick.

"I used to drug them. I only did it once or twice to get the information I needed to blackmail everyone into obeying me." She swallowed. "I would never harm my villagers."

Keir stared at Chasina in shock. "You drugged them?"

Chasina blinked hard and fast. "I kept them safe."

"Drugs are safe?"

"Not one of my villagers died when they obeyed my commands. How could no one see that? Everything I did was for them." Hot tears dripped down her face. "Why couldn't they understand?"

Keir moved closer. "Chaos is a beautiful thing, Chasina. Nothing constrains it."

Keir was wrong. Chaos was not beautiful; it was dangerous. Chaos killed her entire family and burned her village to the ground. Chaos meant death, destruction, and heartbreak, but no one realized it except Chasina.

"So that's it," Keir said, sighing as he leaned against one of the wooden bars. "I guess I never wanted to grow old, anyway. I wonder what seasonings Kemer will pair with me? Sage or thyme?"

"Stop talking," Chasina said, too horrified to keep listening. "That isn't funny."

"What?" Keir asked. "These are legitimate questions. If I had a gravestone, I'd want it to say, 'he died with a delicious sauce,' not, 'he was fed rotten food his whole life and poetically turned into rotten food at his death.'"

He was trying to make her laugh. Admirable, but sorely mistimed.

"You are not going to die," Chasina said. "I forbid it."

Keir nodded slowly. "Interesting tactic. What else do you think will happen to us now?"

Chasina clenched her hands. Not knowing their fate was probably the worst part of the whole situation. She dealt with enslavement, torture, and impending death on a daily basis, but she couldn't control ignorance. At least the giants in Shilist Castle had the same problem. What would the giants do when Lord Kemer absorbed the Naridi Stone and started killing everyone?

Lord Kemer probably resented masquerading as a legitimate Lord while his brethren had fun razing cities, killing giants, and draining auras to sustain their immortality. Why masquerade as a Lord? Why not join his brethren? Only one reason explained everything.

Chasina gasped. "It's a trap."

"What is a trap?" Keir asked.

"The refugee camp. Kemer set up Kavalu as a safe haven to draw all the refugees who escape from Undying-controlled cities because he wants to kill them."

That explained the level of security around the refugee camp. Kemer didn't want any of the refugees escaping.

Keir did not blink. "I don't understand."

"Kemer didn't absorb the Naridi Stone's magic when I told him how to access it," Chasina said, quickly assembling the puzzle. "And he said that he might let me see the Naridi Stone before he destroys it. That means he is waiting to absorb its power."

"Why not absorb the magic immediately?"

"There is a lot of magic inside the Naridi Stone," Chasina said. "Just like my forehead glows because Silversmith filled me with his magic, I'm guessing absorbing all the magic from the Naridi Stone would cause a noticeable change in Kemer. Who knows? He might glow like me."

Keir stiffened with realization. "Kemer isn't ready to expose himself as an Undying. But why wait to absorb the magic? Why not immediately destroy the refugee camp?"

Chasina walked in a tight circle, tapping her forehead. "Some of the Undying recently attacked District One and killed King Omar. The refugees from District One are arriving tonight."

"Kemer is waiting until they arrive to kill everyone," Keir said. "That means we have until tonight to steal the Naridi Stone."

Chasina drew her knife and approached the locked door. If she dislodged the spring that held the lock shut, the door would sag open. A wooden casing protected the spring.

Chasina carved a hole in the top of the wooden casing. The blade nicked her finger as she slid the knife tip through a metal loop.

She braced her feet on the bars. Together, she and Keir pulled on the metal spring. It jumped free of the wooden casing, clattering against the bars before falling onto the bed.

The door opened.

Chasina opened the door and stepped from the cage. She turned and closed the door in Keir's face, trapping him inside the cage. She quickly replaced the spring. Without her help, he wasn't strong enough to displace the spring.

Keir stared at Chasina in disbelief. "What did you just do? Kemer will kill me if he comes back."

Keir was mistaken. Until Lord Kemer returned to his room, the cage was the safest place in the castle. No giants or humans entered the room without Kemer's permission, and Lord Kemer himself had said he had a busy day. He wouldn't return to his room until nightfall.

Chasina laid her hand flat on a wooden bar. "Saving the Naridi Stone is a dangerous job, Keir, and I couldn't handle it if you died. People have died around me my whole life, people who hated me, and I cried for them. But if you died?" she shook her head. "It might actually kill me."

Keir licked his lips. "I cannot stay here, Chasina. I have always known that if Lord Kemer caught me, he'd kill me. Please don't take this decision from me."

Chasina started walking away.

Keir reached through the bars after her. "I am coming with you. I choose the danger that goes with it. Would you stay here if I asked you to?"

"I have a duty to perform," Chasina said.

Chasina climbed down from the bed and exited the room, leaving Keir behind.

Chapter Fifty-Eight

Chasina entered the corridor outside Kemer's room and knew instinctively something was wrong. Loud noises echoed from nearby corridors, doors slammed, and humans screaming underscored everything.

Instead of running toward the noises, Chasina gave herself sixty seconds to figure out a plan. Where was the Naridi Stone right now? Unless Lord Kemer had another chain to hang the Naridi Stone around his neck, he had probably returned it to the vault. He wouldn't want people to see him carrying it before he revealed his true identity.

Chasina sucked her bottom lip, frowning. She couldn't climb the tower alone, which meant she needed a giant's help. She couldn't ask Silversmith. Lately, he'd wielded power over her too effectively for her to trust she'd be able to manipulate him without severe consequences.

What about Jason? He didn't seem to care about the Naridi Stone as much as money, something Chasina could use against him. Plus, he was a thief. He could steal the keystone and correctly insert it into the vault door. She just needed to convince him to break into the vault today.

Jason was probably in the barracks or the courtyard. Hopefully, he wouldn't throw her against another wall.

Chasina jogged down the corridor. She climbed down the steps, wincing whenever her injured ribs stretched or scraped against the stone. She reached the bottom of the steps and instantly shrank against the nearest wall.

The corridor ahead traveled in a straight line for five hundred feet before reaching the entryway. Screaming giants filled the hall. Nobles and servants, merchants and soldiers collided in the corridor, mindless of rank. Some giants raced through the corridor, but other giants huddled in small groups.

Humans streamed like water around the giants' feet, a horde of people climbing over each other to reach the tunnel entrances.

Chasina stepped into the melee. She set her shoulders against humans running into her and yielded her path to screaming giants. She passed a group of soldiers and stopped.

The soldiers huddled around a large magical sphere. The sphere contained at least twenty humans, screaming as they pounded against the magical walls. Their hair was on fire.

The soldiers were cooking them alive.

Chasina unsheathed her knife. She found the giant whose rose-colored magic trapped the humans and climbed up his leather boot. She stabbed him beneath the knee, sawing on the tendon until it snapped.

The magic died, and the humans fell while the soldier clutched his knee. The humans broke their fall by catching a giant's tunic and sliding to the floor.

While the giants knelt over their fallen comrade, most of the humans ran toward the tunnel entrance. A few humans couldn't move, too shocked to even stand.

Chasina pulled two boys to their feet and slapped them in the face.

"Breathe," she said, spinning them toward the tunnel and reaching down to help the last human stand.

The woman shook so badly she couldn't move. Chasina slung the woman across her shoulders and jogged to the tunnel. She entered the tunnel and caught one of the boys she'd saved.

"What is happening to the castle?" Chasina asked, easing the woman from her shoulders and seating her against the tunnel wall. The woman started sobbing.

The boy's mouth flapped uselessly.

Chasina gripped the boy's chin. "Speak slowly. Why is everyone panicking?"

"Lord Kemer spotted a large group of Undying near the castle. Then the Undying group fled into Brundar," the boy said slowly. "Lord Kemer is mustering the army outside the castle. Everyone panicked, especially the soldiers. They know they're about to die, so-so-so—"

"So they decided to eat as many humans as possible before dying," Chasina finished, and the boy nodded. Since the soldiers assumed they were about to die, they didn't care about breaking the law by killing marked humans.

The other Undying must be the guests Lord Kemer had mentioned. Their presence gave him an excuse to muster the army outside the castle, making them easy prey. The Undying in Brundar would kill all the soldiers. When Lord Kemer decided to absorb the Naridi Stone's power and kill everyone, there wouldn't be any soldiers left in Shilist to fight him.

It was the perfect trap.

Chasina left the boy with the other survivors and walked to the exit, fighting against the tide of people streaming into the tunnel. She entered the corridor and saw Lord Kemer standing at the top of the steps.

Lord Kemer spread his hands to the panicking crowd. "I sent

messengers to Kavalu telling them that the army is doing drills and that there is nothing to worry about."

Chasina snorted. *Of course you did.* If Kavalu citizens felt safe in the city, they wouldn't leave. When they finally realized Lord Kemer was an Undying, it would be too late to run.

"Everyone remain calm," Lord Kemer said. "I am not frightened. There is no need to panic."

Lord Kemer swept down the steps and through the crowd, passing right in front of Chasina. Humans took advantage of the calm created in Lord Kemer's wake, disappearing into the tunnels until only giants occupied the corridor.

Chasina followed Lord Kemer out of the keep and into the courtyard. She parted ways with him and headed toward the barracks.

Soldiers assembled inside the castle gates, gripping their swords and praying. The barracks were probably empty. Where was Jason? A vantage point might help her locate him.

Chasina headed toward one of the stairways leading up to the walkways that spanned the castle walls. She stopped when she saw Keir exit the keep and walk toward her.

He wasn't wearing his paint-spattered vest. Maybe he'd lost it?

"What are you doing?" Chasina asked, shoving him when he got close enough. "I told you to stay in the cage. Haven't you noticed? Madness rules the castle today."

A strange little smile curled half of Keir's lips. "Why am I not surprised to see you out here? Are you following your Master's orders or your own?"

"Mine," Chasina said.

"I suspected as much, but I couldn't be sure until now. It answers a lot of questions, actually. You simply saw an opportunity to steal the Naridi Stone and took it." He laid a hand on his chest. "You know something, darling? I admire the evil brain crammed inside your little head." Keir snatched Chasina's wrist.

A breeze stirred Keir's dark bangs, revealing a yellow mark pulsing on his forehead.

Chapter Fifty-Nine

Chasina sucked in a deep breath. She searched the courtyard for Lord Kemer and found him standing on a walkway on the opposite end of the courtyard. She caught his eye, but he didn't react. Most likely, the only reason Lord Kemer used Keir was in case she hid in the castle tunnels.

Lord Kemer shouldn't have returned to his room until tonight. How had she miscalculated so badly? Keir was supposed to be safely locked away in Lord Kemer's room. Instead, Chasina had wrapped him in a nice package for Lord Kemer to use at his pleasure.

Keir's spirit drowned in a sea of yellow magic because she'd caged him in Kemer's room. That could not continue. She needed to escape and free him with the Naridi Stone.

"I still can't decide why you left Keir behind," Keir said. His voice was the same, but the cadence belonged to Lord Kemer. "He seemed to feel quite betrayed."

Chasina gripped Keir's shoulder. "Listen to me, Keir. Kemer cannot control you if you fight him."

The glowing yellow mark did not flicker, and Keir began dragging

Chasina toward Lord Kemer.

Chasina leaped on Keir and tackled him. She ducked a fist and planted one of her own on his chin. Flipping him onto his stomach, she put him in a stranglehold.

Chasina looked up at Lord Kemer, expecting to see him running toward her. He didn't move. His brow furrowed in concentration. He and Keir were still fighting for control over Keir's body, which meant that Kemer couldn't control himself and Keir simultaneously. As long as Kemer controlled Keir, he couldn't move his own body.

Keir went limp just as Lord Kemer snapped his concentration and ran down the walkway.

"I am so sorry," Chasina whispered as she rolled Keir to a safe spot where he wouldn't be trampled before Lord Kemer found him.

Chasina quickly lost herself in the crowd of giants rushing around the courtyard. She hid next to the well and watched Lord Kemer pick up Keir and return to the walkway.

It wouldn't take long for Keir to awaken.

Chasina climbed the walkway opposite Lord Kemer, her ribs throbbing. She jogged along the walkway, scanning the courtyard. She spotted Jason standing by the gates, near the assembled soldiers but not quite one of them. He adjusted his sword and checked his armor twice while Chasina watched, pretending to look busy.

Every time a panicked noble entered or exited through the gates, Jason stole their purses. He dropped each purse into the tangle of weeds and vines growing beside the wall.

Amazing. Even though the Undying stood poised to destroy his race, Jason was still greedy enough to rob the nobles blind.

Chasina hurried down the stairs and across the courtyard toward the gates. She dodged several servants and waved at Jason. He glanced at Chasina, checked over his shoulder, and headed over to her.

"What do you want?" Jason asked, snatching Chasina from the

ground. "If Lord Kemer sees me talking to you, you'll blow my cover."

Chasina nodded toward the bushes. "I couldn't help but notice your collection of purses. Silversmith and Cormac must not be paying you very well to help them steal the Naridi Stone."

Jason shrugged. "They promised I could steal whatever I can carry from the vault. The purses are just something to keep my mind off impending doom."

"Do you really think Silversmith will let you steal from the vault?"

Jason's fingers tensed around her body as he wrestled between ending the conversation or listening to her. His fingers relaxed.

Jason held her closer, shielding their conversation from passersby. "Spit it out. What are you trying to say?"

"Silversmith has too much of a conscience to let you steal from the vault tower. Even if he did, you only get what you can carry. Right?"

"Right."

"So why not make sure you can carry more?"

Jason slowly blinked. "You want to steal from the tower right now? While everyone is in the courtyard?" He paused. "It's a good distraction. I could load up a couple of horses and leave, and everyone would think I'm joining the fight against the Undying. What do you get out of it?"

"Buy me from Silversmith and set me free," Chasina said, resisting the urge to roll her eyes when Jason smirked. Did he honestly think she trusted him?

"Yes, I'll do that. Promise. But you have a gaping flaw in your scheme. I have to wait for Lord Kemer to fall asleep so I can steal the keystone from around his neck. How do you suggest I get the Lord to fall asleep in the morning?"

Chasina scanned the courtyard and found Lord Kemer on the walkway. His gaze bored holes in the grass as he concentrated on possessing Keir's body.

300

Kemer might not even feel it when Jason stole the keystone from around his neck.

"Kemer has possessed his slave and is looking for me," Chasina said. "I will find Keir and distract him. While Kemer is paying attention to me via his slave, you steal the keystone from around his neck."

Jason pursed his lips for several seconds, weighing the possible outcomes. "I can do it. Just make sure you engage with the slave verbally and physically. That way, Lord Kemer's entire attention is focused on inhabiting his slave."

Jason started to set Chasina on the grass, but she stopped him with a warning. "So we are clear," Chasina said, "if you enter the tower without me, I will tell Silversmith what you're doing."

"He won't do anything to me."

"Cormac will."

Jason shut his mouth and set Chasina on the ground. He strode to the walkway where Lord Kemer stood.

Chasina climbed on top of the well and waited for Keir to find her. Unfortunately, someone else found her first, in the shape of a silver snake awakening within Chasina.

"What are you doing?" Silversmith asked.

Chapter Sixty

Chasina's voice stuck in her throat, but she recovered quickly. Silversmith hadn't ordered her to tell the truth. She was safe for now.

"I am in the courtyard," Chasina said.

"Have you found the keystone yet? Cormac wants to break into the tower tonight. Some of his Ramerian friends told him about the Undying being spotted in Brundar." Silversmith gulped, and the silver snake reared its head to strike. "Chasina, I need the keystone now, and if you don't have it, I will take your body. Tell me the truth: have you found the keystone?"

"Yes," Chasina said. "Lord Kemer keeps it on a chain around his neck. Didn't Jason tell you? I told him about it."

The silver snake relaxed somewhat, but its tail twitched back and forth. "Jason was only supposed to contact us after he stole it. It was safer that way."

Chasina said nothing, hoping Silversmith would leave.

The silver snake wrapped its coils around Chasina's spine. "You're being unusually quiet. Are you hiding something?"

"Of course not."

"Tell me the truth: are you hiding something from me?"

Silver magic pooled on Chasina's tongue. It heated to molten silver, scalding the inside of her mouth until the truth tumbled out.

"Yes," Chasina said. "I am hiding something."

"Tell me the truth about everything you are hiding," Silversmith commanded.

Chasina fought the command until the pain overwhelmed her. She tried telling the truth in the tiniest possible snippets, but Silversmith squeezed everything from her: her attempts to steal the Naridi Stone, her partnership with Keir, Kemer's plan to destroy the refugee camp by draining the Naridi Stone—everything. When she finished, the silver snake showed its fangs.

"Cormac and I are stealing the Naridi Stone tonight," Silversmith said. "And we'll decide what to do with you later."

The silver snake slithered up Chasina's spine and opened its maw, sinking four fangs into her neck.

Chasina dropped into a raging silver ocean. Tall waves crashed down on her, each one shoving her deeper beneath the surface. Every time she kicked to the surface, another wave attempted to drown her. She tried swimming ashore, but the riptide kept pulling her beneath the waves. The ocean wanted to drown her.

Somehow, she managed to stay afloat.

The ocean roared even louder. In the distance, Chasina saw a tsunami gliding across the waves. It blocked the sky.

She held her breath, but it didn't matter. The tsunami crashed down on her and buried her hundreds of feet below the surface. She didn't die. Only drowning would kill her.

Chasina swirled in the ocean, not knowing which way to swim. Even if she knew, it wouldn't matter. She'd never reach the surface before drowning. Silversmith had won. She never thought anyone could impose their will on her, but Silversmith of all people, a weakling, had done it. Or had he? Her body might contain a silver ocean, but it was still her body. Hers to control. Hers to command.

The massive sea snake opened its mouth beside Chasina. "Keep fighting me, and I will put you in agony."

Chasina ignored Silversmith. Pain was life. Its absence was a luxury she was ready to sacrifice if it meant controlling her body again.

Chasina pulled the silver ocean into herself. She swallowed all the waves and sand and the massive sea snake, and she awakened in the real world. True to his promise, Silversmith greeted her awakening with waves of purest agony. Pain chewed through her bones, hacked at the soft tissue inside her skull, and shredded her muscles.

Chasina fell to her knees and clung to consciousness. She needed to engage with Keir verbally and physically, or Jason wouldn't steal the keystone, and her last chance at stealing the Naridi Stone would disappear forever.

Chasina studied her surroundings. Silversmith hadn't moved her body. She still knelt on top of the well, and two hundred yards away, Keir trotted toward her. His face lit with a curiosity that belonged to Lord Kemer.

Chasina climbed down the well and staggered toward the castle keep. She needed to lure Keir somewhere that Lord Kemer couldn't follow. Otherwise, nothing stopped him from coming directly to capture her.

Chasina had only gone ten feet when she collapsed. Every movement shredded her body as the silver snake tore chunks from her organs, and the silver ocean boiled them with salt.

The pain disconnected her thoughts, stealing her ability to reason. Chasina latched on to a single thought: get inside a tunnel.

She reached out, planted her hand in the dirt, and pulled herself forward a foot. Another foot. She crawled into the castle keep, trusting the courtyard's madness to keep Lord Kemer and Keir at bay.

The castle keep was a madhouse, with servants and nobles forgetting all decorum as they prepared to die. Humans screamed from distant halls. Not everyone had gotten safely into the tunnels before the rioting started, and their tortured screams raked across Chasina's heart.

She crawled inside the nearest tunnel and lay there, panting, until a skinny pair of legs walked in front of her face.

Keir crouched. "Had a little run-in with your Master, I see," Keir said, touching the pulsing mark on Chasina's forehead. "Silversmith never struck me as the kind of person to torture his slave, but evidently, I misjudged him." Keir reached beneath Chasina's armpits and started dragging her from the tunnel.

She weakly slapped his hands. "What about that story you were telling me about? You said I didn't know the whole story behind the Naridi Stone. What were you talking about?"

The hands around her chest loosened. Chasina slipped free, twisted, and yanked Keir to the floor. She crawled on top of him and pinned him with her heavier body.

"I will steal the Naridi Stone," Chasina said, pressing her forehead against Keir's. "And I'm going to free Keir, and there's nothing you can do to stop me."

"I can kill you."

Chasina flexed her jaw. "Go ahead and try. It has never worked out well for others who've tried."

Keir grinned. "Death threats always touch a sore spot. I have everything under control, Chasina. Unlike most giants, I don't have an insatiable need to kill hapless humans."

"Generous of you."

"So much anger. Somebody is trying to blame me for what happened to Keir," he said. He paused, his eyes losing focus. "Keir wants you to know that he would have helped you to the end. And if he died, it would have been a beautiful act of unconstrained chaos." Lord Kemer, possessing Keir's body, shifted beneath Chasina. "'A beautiful act of unconstrained chaos.' I didn't know I had possessed such an artistic soul."

Keir was saying goodbye and reminding her that it wasn't his decision to leave the world this way. It was hers. She'd made that decision by locking him in a cage.

Keir pushed Chasina off of him. He took Chasina's wrists and began dragging her from the tunnel. She rolled from side to side, trying to break free, but the magical punishment weakened her.

She hummed with agony, a deadly song that screeched through bone, marrow, and soul. Even the slightest movement enhanced the excruciating torture and robbed Chasina of her basic strength.

Keir ignored all her attacks, brushing them off as he dragged her into the courtyard. A sphere of green magic swallowed Keir and carried him far away from Chasina.

Chasina recognized the color of Jason's magic. "Don't hurt him. Don't hurt Keir."

Jason appeared above Chasina. "And incur Lord Kemer's wrath? I don't care that much about you." He poked Chasina with his forefinger before picking her up. "Silversmith is punishing you for some reason. Did you tell him about our plan?"

"No," Chasina lied, panting. "He's punishing me for refusing to tell him anything. Did you get the keystone?"

Jason patted a lump beneath his tunic. "Lord Kemer never even felt it. Let's go into the vault before Kemer realizes I stole his necklace."

Chasina searched the courtyard but did not see Lord Kemer. He must have moved from his vantage point after Jason knocked out Keir.

Jason hurried to the vault tower and through the open door. No one guarded the tower. All the soldiers assembled inside the castle gates waiting for the chance to fight the Undying.

Jason climbed the steps. He reached the top and broke the keystone into pieces, carefully inserting them into the vault door. When he inserted the last piece, the keystone's many pieces glowed yellow and shot from their indentations. They hovered in the air, fused into one rock, and dropped to the floor. The keystone rolled aside.

The vault vibrated. Yellow magic outlined a door in the stone wall, and the door swung open.

They stepped inside the vault, a perfectly circular room. Dust sprinkled the evenly spaced shelves built into the stone walls, and heavy chests lined the shelves, each with an iron lock dangling from wooden lips.

Sweet Naridi roses. Chasina's heart hammered against her chest when she saw the table in the center of the room. The Naridi Stone glowed from a glass stand on the table. It was beautiful, but it wasn't what made her heart hammer.

Lord Kemer sat at the table, his feet propped on the table, wearing a soaking wet Undying robe.

He smiled.

Chapter Sixty-One

L ord Kemer's pointed beard dripped water onto his lap, and his robes created a large puddle beneath the table. The mat beneath the table was askew, and Chasina's mind instantly sprang to possibilities. Was it a secret entrance into the tower? Perhaps one connected to the Suicide Tunnel? That explained how Lord Kemer had entered a locked vault without the keystone. He must have hurried into the tower after Jason had dispatched Keir, correctly deducing that Chasina would eventually infiltrate the vault.

Keir stood on the table, looking unharmed except for the bruises from his fight with Chasina. He still didn't have his vest. Lord Kemer must have shed it the moment he possessed Keir's body.

Keir's gaunt face hovered somewhere between terrified and furious. The emotion meant that Lord Kemer wasn't currently possessing Keir, allowing Keir to control his facial expressions.

Keir glared at Chasina from behind his burnt bangs. He opened his mouth and shut it again, unable to speak. Lord Kemer must have commanded him to keep quiet.

Lord Kemer shot Jason in the chest with a yellow sphere. Jason crumbled. Chasina fell from his hand, and Kemer caught her with another sphere before she hit the ground.

The sphere deposited Chasina on the table beside the glass case. She wobbled. It took all of her energy to stand upright while silver agony rushed through her body.

Kemer steadied Chasina with a finger on her back. "We don't have to be enemies, Chasina. Keir and I are getting along fine, and so can you and I."

"The Undying stole the Naridi Stone," Chasina said. "You condemned the human race to be hunted, tortured, and enslaved. You made us your enemies."

Lord Kemer laced his hands behind his neck, boots knocking together. "If I hated humans so much as to condemn their race, why did I help my brethren forge the stone that allows you to use magic? That would be stupid. And I"—he nestled his neck more comfortably into his hands—"am brilliant."

"You didn't make the Naridi Stone," Chasina said.

"No? Don't humans say that the Naridi Stone is a gift from the gods?" Kemer spread his arms, grinning wickedly. "Here I am."

No one actually knew where the Naridi Stone came from or who made it. She'd always assumed humans had created it because it wasn't a gift from the gods, and it certainly wasn't a gift from an Undying.

Chasina thinned her lips. "If Undying made the Naridi Stone for humans, why did you steal it? Why do you keep it hidden in a vault? Give it to me if you're telling the truth."

Lord Kemer raised a finger. "Ah, there we've hit a snag. Give it to you so you can betray me? Of course, I'd kill you with a snap of my fingers, but the betrayal itself would turn my stomach. It seemed despite our generosity, humans believed the Hero's lie that we cursed you. Humans started killing us with the magic we'd gifted to them. Naturally, we took our gift away. It was self-preservation."

"The Undying slaughtered hundreds of people taking back the Naridi Stone and draining the Naridi Pillars."

"War," Kemer said simply. "And not one that we started."

Chasina folded her arms. "If you made the Naridi Stone and gave it to humans, why couldn't you remember how to use it?"

"I keep my immortality by draining the auras of other giants, something never meant to happen. My life is infinite. My memory is finite," Kemer said. "I forget things that happened a long time ago. If I had known seventy years ago that I would plan to slaughter thousands of giants by absorbing the Naridi Stone's magic, I would have written myself a little note reminding me how to use it."

Chasina crossed and uncrossed her arms. She wanted to catch Kemer in a lie, but everything he said rang true. It made sense that the Undying had given humans the Naridi Stone. It shed new light on the fact that humans and Undying worked against giants—not because of a curse but because humans and Undying both hated giants.

Chasina regularly manipulated the truth, so she recognized when other people did it. It wasn't happening right now. Kemer was being honest, and she believed him.

"Give me the Naridi Stone," Chasina said. "I guarantee that humans will not bother you. We just want to protect our villages. No one will care how many giants you and your brethren slaughter. In fact, we will celebrate with you."

Kemer tapped the stone against the table. "How bad is it where you come from? How many raids? Poachers only seem to grow bolder when I enact laws against them."

Chasina studied Kemer's face, wondering if she should swallow the acidic words burning on the back of her tongue. Enemy or not, he never discounted her opinion. He was earnestly asking a question that even Silversmith had never asked.

"Why do you care?" she asked. "I thought you only enacted those laws to find a human from Falla."

Lord Kemer stopped playing with the Naridi Stone. "I enacted those laws when I became the Lord of this District. People assumed I did it to make myself wealthy, but I saw too many humans living miserable lives, and they didn't deserve it. I curbed the market. Later, I reworked the laws to help me find a human from Falla."

"What about the miserable conditions in the castle? Why have castle slaves in the first place if you care so much about humans? Maybe you didn't curse the human race, but you possessed Keir's body. What about him?" Chasina demanded.

Kemer tossed the Naridi Stone and caught it. "I thought you might have hidden in the tunnels, so I needed a human to explore the tunnels for me. You left Keir for me like a birthday gift. What else was I supposed to do? He is safer with me than anyone else in Kavalu." He tossed the Naridi Stone again. "And as for the castle, I have a role to play. I cannot have people thinking I'm an Undying, and that's exactly what people would assume if I was publicly generous toward humans."

"Generous?"

Kemer winked. "You're still alive, aren't you?"

Chasina glanced at the vault door. "Silversmith and Cormac are coming. Cormac specializes in killing Undying. You could die. Plus, you have no way of knowing that one of them won't escape and use the Naridi Stone to awaken the Hero. Give it to me instead."

A dimple appeared in Kemer's left cheek. "You really are relentless, aren't you? How about instead, I make sure you can't make any trouble for me until the party starts?"

Kemer's gaze lost its focus as he possessed Keir. Keir stepped forward and wrapped his skinny arms around Chasina's neck. She struggled, but magical torture had weakened her, and Keir had a good grip.

In a matter of moments, everything went black.

Chapter Sixty-Two

C hasina whimpered when she awoke. The silver snake within her still had its fangs fastened into her soul, pouring magical pain into her body.

She was willing to endure this pain to keep control of her body, but it hurt. It hurt so much.

It was nighttime. Cold, dark shadows layered the floor and painted Kemer's back. He crouched above Jason, who had perfectly spherical burns on his naked torso.

"You're sure there is nothing else I need to know?" Lord Kemer asked. "They're coming through the Suicide Tunnel and into the tower."

Jason's voice had lost all its snark. "I am supposed to bring Chasina with me."

Lord Kemer stood and faced the table, dusting his hands. In the hours while she'd slept, he'd dried his clothes and beard and, amazingly, managed to maintain his elegance even after torturing Jason for hours.

Lord Kemer beckoned for Chasina to climb into his palm, but she

312

was too weak to stand.

Lord Kemer scooped her off the table. "Usually, I would ease your pain, but Silversmith would notice if I interfered with his magical punishment," Lord Kemer said. He clicked his fingers impatiently at Jason, who stood, trembling, and pulled his tunic over his scorched torso.

Lord Kemer placed Chasina on Jason's shoulder, and she leaned against his neck to avoid falling. She tried catching Keir's eye when Kemer put him next to her. Keir avoided her gaze.

"Keir will tell me if you try to warn Silversmith or Cormac," Kemer said to Jason. "And I will be watching from an arrow slit, ready to kill you if you do something wrong. Be a good boy and bring them to me like nothing is wrong. The same goes for you, Chasina."

Chasina clung to Jason's collar as he descended the tower. They reached the bottom and entered the courtyard. Something about the courtyard bothered her, but it took her a moment to figure it out: it was totally empty. No soldiers patrolled the walkways, no nobles swanned across the courtyard, and no servants rushed from place to place.

Lord Kemer had deployed all the soldiers to die while fighting the Undying in Brundar, and the other castle residents were probably cowering inside the keep.

Jason crossed the eerie courtyard and removed the stone lid from the well. In a moment, Silversmith climbed from the well, followed quickly by Cormac.

Silversmith's gaze cut to Chasina. His gaze softened when he saw she didn't have the Naridi Stone, and the silver snake stopped biting her.

Her pain receded. She felt normal again.

"You tried to betray us," Cormac said to Jason.

Cormac stepped smartly into Jason's personal space and punched him. Jason bent double, and Chasina grabbed his collar to keep from falling. She snagged Keir's tunic as he sailed past.

Silversmith caught Chasina and Keir before they fell. "Are you all right?" Silversmith asked.

"You tortured me all day," Chasina snapped. "What makes you think I'd be all right?"

"It was the only way I knew you wouldn't be able to steal the Naridi Stone. I'm sorry, but I had to do it."

Chasina ignored Silversmith and focused on the situation at hand. Could she somehow tell the giants they were walking into a trap?

Chasina glanced at Keir, who sat beside her in Silversmith's hands. Keir minimally shook his head, silently telling her to keep quiet.

"Who is that?" Cormac asked, spotting Keir and plucking him from Silversmith's hands.

Silversmith gasped when he got a good look at Keir. "Keir?"

Keir obviously did not recognize Silversmith, and who could blame him? It wasn't every day that a human acquaintance turned out to be a cursed giant.

Cormac gripped Keir's neck.

Chasina and Silversmith shouted at the same time. "Stop!"

"He cannot hurt anyone," Chasina said. "Drasta Cormac, please don't kill him."

"She's right, Cormac," Silversmith said. "Keir is not a threat."

Cormac conjured a sphere around Keir. "This human is marked with Kemer's magic. That makes him a threat."

Cormac's magical sphere glowed brilliantly, and Keir erupted in flames. He screamed until the fire consumed him. The green sphere disappeared, and ash drifted to the ground.

Numbness spread across Chasina's body. She did not understand the harsh words Silversmith and Cormac exchanged. She didn't utter a sound as Jason led them into the vault and everyone seemed surprised that the Naridi Stone was gone. Kemer closed the vault door. The ambush, the screaming, how she fell and barely managed to catch herself on the table—it all slid over her consciousness like water droplets.

One thing stuck: she needed to give Keir a burial. She needed to scatter his ashes and recite the Death Blessing. It didn't matter if she maimed herself leaving the tower during the fight because Keir's death was her fault.

A block lodged in Chasina's throat. *Keir told me goodbye. Even after everything I did, he still said goodbye to me.*

One of the giants crashed against the table and sent Chasina flying. She hit the chair, and pain wrapped around her torso. Splinters lodged beneath her nails as she slid to the ground, crawling beneath the table.

Chasina patted the mat beneath the table until she felt a bump, confirming her suspicions that a trapdoor led into the vault. She slid beneath the mat of woven rushes, moving forward until she found a metal chain that looped through two holes in the trapdoor.

Chasina wiggled into one of the holes, sucked in her stomach, and fell through the trapdoor.

Chapter Sixty-Three

C hasina fell through the darkness. She pulled her arms over her head to protect herself and hunched against the wind trying to flap her limbs. She hit the water.

Chasina swirled in the water, righted herself, and stroked upward. She broke the surface and swam into the well, shimmying up the rope and climbing onto the mossy stones above the well. Dripping wet, she descended to the ground and knelt among Keir's ashes.

The ashes were still warm.

Chasina ripped the bandage from her forehead and gathered the ashes inside, bundling them with a tight knot. She couldn't scatter Keir's ashes in a well where giants drew water. It would be an unspeakable desecration.

Chasina climbed into the well again. She dropped into the water and swam through the underground stream. She kept her head above water, in the foot of space between the stream and the cavern, and held Keir's ashes overhead.

She surfaced in the cave and climbed from the pool. Hot tears mingled with the cold water on her face, dripping to the dirt as she knelt beside the pool.

"I'm so sorry," she said, squeezing the little bundle containing Keir's ashes. "I shouldn't have caged you."

Untying the bundle, Chasina sprinkled ashes into the pool as she recited the Death Blessing. "My heart knows you, and it will not forget. Be at peace, for you were loved. You are missed and forever in my heart." Chasina finished sprinkling ashes. "Please forgive me."

The silver snake within Chasina opened its mouth. Silversmith spoke very quietly, as though afraid of someone overhearing him.

"Chasina, where are you?" Silversmith asked.

Chasina wiped tears from her face. "I escaped the tower and swam through the Suicide Tunnel. Where are you?"

"Hiding from Lord Kemer. I think he killed Jason."

Chasina shuddered as Silversmith's fear ebbed into her body. "Swim through the Suicide Tunnel. There's nothing left to do."

"I can't just leave Cormac on his own. Kemer dragged him onto the castle walls and dropped him in the cage with Muriel."

"What do you want to do?" Chasina asked. "We can't do anything except make it worse."

Silversmith rumbled deep in his throat. "I am not like you, Chasina. I don't manipulate people to my own ends and then leave them. I don't want to betray Cormac. He deserves a better apprentice than me. What can I do?"

Instead of replying, Chasina drew Da's knife and cradled it. She remembered perfectly the day Da had given it to her. He could have shoved the debris to trap her inside the pit and keep her safe from giants, but he hadn't. Da had given her everything necessary to keep herself safe and trusted her judgment.

Chasina kissed a rose on Da's knife. "I'm coming, Silversmith."

She sheathed her knife and dove into the pool, swimming through the Suicide Tunnel. She passed the dark tunnel that led into the vault tower and surfaced in the well. Water streaming from her clothes, she climbed up the rope and poked her head from the well.

Silversmith crouched beside the vault tower. He spotted Chasina and crawled over to her, taking her from the rope. He huddled beside the well.

Chasina tucked dripping hair behind one ear. "You were right. I manipulated you, used you, and I'm sorry. I wanted to bribe my villagers to care about me, but they wouldn't have wanted me even if I returned with the Naridi Stone. They deserved better from me, and so did you."

Silversmith parted his lips and shut them.

Chasina's palm tingled where Keir had taken her hand and guided her through Shilist's frightening tunnels. "You have every right to kill me. Think carefully about everything I've done to you and decide if justice is served by killing me."

Black hair dusted his shoulders as he shook his head. "I tried to kill you, too. I possessed and magically tortured you, so we don't owe each other anything. We're even."

Chasina nodded sharply. Now that they were clear, they had a lot of work ahead of them. First, she needed to understand precisely what had happened in the tower.

"Where are Cormac and Jason?" Chasina asked.

Silversmith rested his forehead on one knee. "Cormac was trying to pull Jason out of the tower when I ran away. I was going to help him, I swear... But I couldn't."

Chasina looked at her hands to give him some privacy. "Giants sacked my village when I was five. I heard everyone screaming while I huddled inside the pit, and so help me, I have never been more afraid in my whole life. That's how I got my scars."

Silversmith brushed aside his long hair to show the thick scar rippling down his neck. "I got this from the Undying who killed my parents and cursed me. I joined the scouts because I wanted to hunt down the monsters that ruined me and my sister's lives, but the first time Cormac and I found an Undying, I hid behind a tree and cried."

"I'm sorry."

"Me too."

"We wouldn't be here if we didn't want to do anything tonight," Chasina said, pointing to the vault tower. "I have a plan. You have the skill. Can we work together?"

Chapter Sixty-Four

Silversmith bit his lip. "I don't know if I can do this, Chasina. I didn't stop Cormac from killing Keir. I didn't help Cormac fight Lord Kemer. I'm weak. I'm a coward!"

"That's true," Chasina said bluntly. "So let your weakness hide behind your strength."

Silversmith met Chasina's gaze. His shoulders twitched, but there was a hopeful, desperate spark in his eyes. He wouldn't run away this time.

Silversmith looked up at the tower. "I saw the Naridi Stone flicker into existence during the fight. Lord Kemer has cast an illusion to hide it, but it's still in the tower. How would we get it away from him?"

"We get help." Chasina nodded at the farthest walkway, where Cormac and Muriel hung in cages. The cages hung on the outer wall but anchored on the walkway.

"Why would I help you steal the Naridi Stone?" Silversmith asked. "You will probably betray me."

"We can both get what we want. You trade the Naridi Stone to

Bemea to find the Vault of Eternal Sleep, and afterward, we steal it from her so I can return magic to humans." She put a hand on her knife. "No more manipulating. Promise."

Silversmith curled his empty hand into a loose fist. "I agree. We work together."

They hurried across the courtyard and climbed the uneven stone steps leading to the first walkway. They crossed the bridges connecting Shilist's three walls and reached the outermost walkway. Silversmith put his hand on the thick chains wrapping around the crenelation and peered down at the cages swinging against the outer wall.

Cormac and Muriel shared the same cage. Nearby, Oscar huddled in another cage, cradling the stump of his right hand.

Cormac pressed his face against the top of the iron bars and snarled at Silversmith. "You deserted me."

"I came back," Silversmith said.

"But you brought her," Cormac said, shifting his snarl to Chasina. "Don't tell me this is her idea, Silversmith. You know she wants to kill us all and take the Naridi Stone for herself."

Silversmith's gaze shifted to Chasina, heavy and doubtful. He would be a fool to not have reservations.

Chasina held her knife to her throat. "Tell me to slit my own throat if I deceive you."

"If I wanted to kill you, I could do it on my own," Silversmith said.

"If you had better judgment, you would have killed me after I addicted you to spara sap. Do it." She pressed the blade against her throat.

Silversmith grimaced. "Slit your throat if you lie to me."

"You have to say 'deceive.' There's a difference, and I've been using it since Gran enslaved me."

"If you deceive me in any way, slit your own throat immediately."

Chasina lowered her knife and raised an eyebrow at Cormac. "Satisfied?"

Cormac didn't bat an eye. "How do you plan to kill Lord Kemer? Muriel is weak, Silversmith doesn't have the backbone to do it, and I am injured. Kemer will never stop chasing us if we steal the Naridi Stone."

"True," Chasina said. "And that's why we don't want to kill Kemer. We just want to distract him. I need you to cast an illusion on a rock to make it look like the Naridi Stone. I'll switch it with the real one while Silversmith distracts Kemer. By the time Kemer realizes we tricked him, we'll be far away on stolen horses."

"Lord Kemer is an Undying," Cormac said. "Underestimate him at your own peril."

"Meaning?"

Cormac counted on his fingers. "Firstly, he is so powerful that he will sense the fake Naridi Stone holds no magic. Secondly, I cannot use magic in this cage because Kemer enchanted the lock. And lastly," he said, pointing at Silversmith without looking at him, "what makes you think he can distract an Undying?"

"Silversmith will distract Kemer, or we'll fail. Plain and simple." Chasina tapped her chin. "What if you cast an illusion on the keystone? It already has magic inside of it."

Cormac pursed his lips. "It's Kemer's magic, so Kemer will realize it's a fake faster than if we had a stone imbued with foreign power, but it's our only option. I saw the keystone on the floor outside the vault."

That made sense. Lord Kemer had been too busy gloating and torturing Jason all afternoon to retrieve the keystone, especially since he had no desire to keep people out of the vault.

Chasina paced for several minutes and worked out the details. For the plan to work, she needed to retrieve the keystone and free Cormac, allowing him to cast an illusion on the keystone. She'd swap the fake Naridi Stone for the real one while Silversmith distracted Lord Kemer.

"How do I get Kemer to lift the enchantment on the lock?" Chasina asked, studying the yellow magic that enclosed the lock.

"Anything that takes his concentration off maintaining the spell will cause it to falter," Cormac said. "In this case, sudden pain should make him lapse long enough for Vorce to pick the locks." Cormac squinted narrowly at Silversmith. "You remember how to do that, don't you? Or have you decided that it isn't nice to pick locks?"

"Give me thirty seconds," Silversmith said.

Chasina glanced at the tower. Lord Kemer waited in the tower like a spider in its web, knowing that Chasina and Silversmith had to come to him if they wanted the Naridi Stone.

She didn't see any magical glowing to indicate that Lord Kemer was busily draining the Naridi Stone, probably because he didn't want to frighten Silversmith. Lord Kemer wanted Silversmith to have some hope of beating him, even if it was false, and draining the Naridi Stone would destroy Silversmith's hope and prevent him from entering the tower.

To distract Kemer, Chasina needed to cause him some pain. It had to be painful enough to make a disciplined magician lose control of his magic for thirty seconds while Silversmith opened the cage.

Chasina turned to the others. "Does anyone have something flammable?"

Cormac reached inside his tunic and pulled out a flask.

Silversmith took it through the bars and uncorked it, wrinkling his nose at the fermented odor. "This is definitely flammable."

"Send me to the keep," Chasina told Silversmith. "I need to get some supplies from the tunnels."

Silversmith complied, sending her shooting across the courtyard in a silver sphere. She landed neatly in front of the enormous keep doors. Chasina wiggled under the keep door and raced through the magnificently tiled entrance, where moonlight streaked through stained glass windows and made the mosaics on the ceiling glitter like stars. It was empty, which meant the nobles and servants were probably hiding in separate rooms—or perhaps they'd barricaded themselves in the Great Hall.

Chasina found the tunnel entrance she'd first used after entering Shilist Castle. She moved past the twisting vines carved on the wall and squeezed inside the tunnel, waiting while her vision adjusted to the darkness.

A shiver crawled up her spine and tapped her shoulder. *This tunnel is so small.*

She ignored the shiver, feeling her way through the tunnel. Soon, the sharp smell of dyes greeted her, and she entered the tapestry alcove.

Chasina went straight to the pile of thread—rope, to a human. She cut two lengths of it and dyed the last ten feet of each rope a different color: red and blue. Securing the rope around her shoulders, Chasina crossed the alcove and stood before the passage leading to the castle proper.

Instinctively, she reached for Keir's hand. Her hand dropped to her side. *Keir is not alive. Go alone.*

Chasina gripped Da's knife until her palm ached, imagining the carved roses pouring sacred strength into her body. She stepped inside the passage. It led her around corners and past deep pools in the ground. Sickles of moonlight dotted the pools of water.

Ghostly faces fluttered from the depths of her mind and floated down the passage ahead of her. Chasina pressed her face to the tunnel wall, but she felt the surroundings changing, twisted by smoke.

Reality slipped away.

She was a child again, trapped beneath the burning beam. Skin dripped down her face, but no matter how hard she twisted, pulled, and clawed at the earth, she couldn't free herself from the wreckage.

"Somebody help me!" she screamed.

Chasina's screams faded among the snapping fire, and she knew in her bones that no one was coming to help her. Da was gone.

Blood rolled down her little fingers as she grabbed Da's knife by the blade, tugging it from beneath her belly. Blinking embers from her eyes, Chasina sawed at the beam across her back. She sawed for hours until the beam cracked and split, and she dragged herself from the wreckage.

Charred wood burned her hands and feet as she climbed up a burning beam. The only thing left of her home was a pile of ash taller than her head, shafts sticking from it like broken bones. Red embers glowed in the cinders.

Chasina collapsed on the ash pile that used to be her home. Her world turned fuzzy and black around the edges, and ash shifted beneath her torso until the mound swallowed her whole. Whimpering, she inched Da's knife closer.

The roses pressed firmly against her palm. The blade felt solid against her chest. Unable to move, she counted the heartbeats thumping erratically against Da's knife. She breathed.

Chasina breathed. And she awakened.

Chapter Sixty-Five

Chasina took deep breaths and found herself huddled against the tunnel wall. She stared at the nearest puddle while phantom pain licked her face.

Slime coated her fingers as she crawled up the wall to a standing position. Chasina readjusted the ropes on her shoulders and started down the passage again. It only took a few minutes to arrive at the exit.

Chasina paused at the exit. She crouched, fingers trembling as she picked up Keir's paint-spattered vest. Keir's paintings depicted wind, rain, plants, or wildlife—perfectly unconstrained elements or creatures. It seemed fitting that the paint dripped onto his vest.

Chasina laid the vest a few feet from the entrance, where she'd met Keir for the first time. "I am so sorry. This will never happen again."

Chasina left the tunnel and ran through the castle corridor until she reached the grand entrance and squeezed beneath the doors. She told Silversmith that she needed a ride, and he used a silver sphere to carry her back to the third walkway that spanned the outermost wall.

On the walkway, Chasina soaked both ropes with Cormac's alcohol.

Then she had Silversmith transport the three-quarters full flask to a window in the vault tower.

Chasina showed Silversmith the dyed ropes. "When I signal you, ignite the blue rope. Thirty seconds later, ignite the red one."

Silversmith nodded and conjured a sphere around Chasina, transporting her to the vault tower. She landed in the window near the top alongside Cormac's flask. To the left, she saw the open vault door. Lord Kemer relaxed at the table inside the vault, probably waiting for supreme stupidity to overrule Silversmith's good sense and send him into the tower for the Naridi Stone.

Chasina tipped the flask, and alcohol spilled down the wall and steps. She fed the ten feet of blue-tipped rope out the window and trailed the other end down the alcohol-soaked wall.

Chasina tied a lasso in the red-tipped rope, dropped the colorful tail out the window, and secured the lasso around her waist. Moving to the end of the window sill, Chasina fit her hands and feet into cracks in the wall. She climbed the bricks, careful to stay flat against the wall to avoid Kemer's attention. She reached the ceiling.

Chasina's ribs throbbed. Gritting her teeth, Chasina untied the lasso from around her waist and made the loop large enough to fit around Kemer's head.

Chasina spoke to the silver snake wrapped around her spine. "Ignite the blue rope."

Seconds later, a silver sphere crashed into the blue-tipped rope. Fire raced along the blue rope, spreading to the puddle of alcohol. Soon, the wall below the window and two steps were on fire. Heat rose from the flames and embraced Chasina. *We're old friends,* it said. *We know your taste.*

Lord Kemer exited the vault and strode down the steps. Before he stamped out the fire, Chasina dropped her lasso around Kemer's neck and pulled it tight. She released the rope, and before Kemer did more than jerk in surprise, Silversmith set the red-tipped rope on fire.

Red-orange flames birthed along the rope and circled the Lord's neck. Lord Kemer screamed and clawed at his throat, unable to touch the fire or bear its kiss. He stepped into the fire burning on the steps, and it spread to his clothes.

Chasina quickly descended to the floor in front of the vault. She found the keystone by the door and rolled it to the steps. It was lighter than it looked, very porous, some kind of stone whose size didn't equal its weight.

She shoved it down the steps. It rolled like a marble, picking up speed as it clattered down the steps and out of sight. Chasina followed it, jumping down the steps past Kemer, who was too busy screaming to notice when she passed him.

Chasina reached the bottom of the stairwell and rolled the keystone into the courtyard. A silver sphere shot across the yard. It carried her and the keystone to the walkway where Silversmith, Cormac, and Muriel hunkered behind the crenelation. Chasina landed between two stone blocks and stood eye-level with the crouched giants.

Silversmith had found a sword and belted it around his waist, but he seemed so uncomfortable wearing it that Chasina instinctively wanted him to remove it. He might accidentally kill himself if he drew the sword.

Cormac took the keystone and cupped it in both hands. "This will take a moment."

Across the courtyard, Kemer stormed from the tower. Smoke wisped from his clothes. Even at a distance, Chasina spotted the glowing red burn around his neck.

Chasina turned her attention to Muriel. "You know the plan? I will switch the keystone for the real Naridi Stone as soon as Cormac finishes the illusion. Silversmith will send me to the tower, but you will have to carry me back."

Muriel touched the welts on her back. "This isn't my first heist. You're lucky I decided to give you a reprieve from crushing your disgusting little body because I'd rather kill Lord Kemer."

Chasina mock-bowed. "I feel so honored."

Cormac swayed on his heels as he finished enchanting the stone. Delicate petals replaced the keystone's chiseled cracks, and it glowed different colors every few seconds.

Silversmith caught Cormac before he fell. "Ready, Chasina?"

"I'm ready."

Silver light engulfed Chasina's body along with the fake Naridi Stone. It bumped her leg as they shot across the courtyard. She landed in an arrow slit at the top of the tower, but the keystone flew farther. It landed in front of the vault.

Chasina looked down at the courtyard. Kemer flashed beneath her, running toward the walkway. A stairway and three bridges separated him from the three giants clustering together.

Before Kemer made it to the first flight of stairs, Silversmith dropped to the ground behind him.

Silversmith drew his sword.

Chapter Sixty-Six

Chasina climbed down the wall and reached the vault, the noise of metal on metal screeching in her ears. Cormac had faith in Silversmith's abilities. But against an Undying with centuries of practice? He'd probably die.

Chasina rolled the keystone into the vault and stopped it below the table. She climbed the chair and jumped to the table, tipping the glass case. It fell on the floor and shattered into a thousand pieces that crunched beneath her feet when she hit the ground. She swapped the two stones, leaving the fake Naridi Stone nestled in a sea of broken glass.

The authentic Naridi Stone didn't throb like Chasina remembered, and it was rougher than its perfectly shaped petals suggested. The stone's sharp edges cut her skin as she climbed to the arrow slit and waved at Muriel.

Muriel did not see Chasina, too busy watching Silversmith fight Lord Kemer.

Blood trickled down Silversmith's arm, but he held his sword steady as Kemer circled. Kemer bared his teeth and closed the distance between them, his sword darting in and out like a serpent's tongue.

Silversmith bobbed to one side. He flicked his wrist, and a weighted knife split the air toward Kemer.

Kemer conjured a magical shield and caught the knife. Yellow magic sank into the blade, and Kemer hurled the glowing weapon at Silversmith.

Silversmith sloppily dodged. He staggered backward and barely blocked another yellow enchantment. Sweat poured down his face.

This was not going to end well.

Chasina jumped and waved her arms, shouting for Muriel's attention. Muriel finally noticed Chasina and sent a sphere of magic to carry her back to the walkway.

Chasina landed on the crenelation, and Muriel collapsed.

"She overexerted herself with the magic," Cormac said, checking her pulse. "She'll be fine."

Chasina turned to watch the fight in the courtyard. "We need to help Silversmith before he dies. Shoot Lord Kemer with magic."

"It is taking all of my strength to hold an illusion," Cormac said, his jaw barely moving as he gazed unblinkingly into the courtyard.

Chasina cradled the Naridi Stone more closely. She didn't need Cormac's magic to save Silversmith now that she had the Naridi Stone.

Chasina kissed the Naridi Stone, but nothing happened. She summoned her gratitude and kissed the stone again, but nothing happened. Chasina kissed the stone a dozen more times to no avail. What was wrong? Was she just an ingrate? Had Lord Kemer drained all its power already?

The Naridi Stone flashed a myriad of different colors, a testament to the magic inside of it. Lord Kemer had not drained it. She just couldn't access the magic for some reason. But why?

Chasina leaned forward, following the fight.

Silversmith parried an overhand stroke from Kemer and punched him in the chest. Kemer backpedaled a few steps, and Silversmith shot tiny silver spheres at him. The spheres separated like fireflies, coming at him from all directions.

Kemer conjured a shield to absorb most of them, but some of the spheres hit him. They didn't burn or cause any visible harm. What was Silversmith thinking?

A lazy smile swam across Kemer's face, and Chasina realized that Silversmith was trying to put him to sleep. It was a better plan than burning Kemer. Burns brought adrenaline, but sleep ended a fight.

"I thought someone had finally lit a candle in your darkness. I thought you might actually singe me," Kemer said, tracing a nail through the blood dripping from his sword. "But I guess you're still content to mewl quietly at my feet and do nothing like all the other grovelers who worship the Hero."

Kemer started forward but yawned and stumbled. He raised his sword just in time to block a vicious backhanded stroke. As he parried Silversmith's attacks, Kemer backpedaled, metal clanging dully across the yard.

Kemer snarled, dropped his sword, and conjured a thick yellow aura that fit his body like a second skin.

Silversmith's sword touched the aura, and yellow magic sank into the blade. Silversmith dropped his weapon before the yellow magic touched his skin.

Kemer swayed on his feet, blinking from the effort of trying to stay awake. His aura grew thicker, billowing from his body until he looked like a dying sun.

"That was sneaky," Kemer said, his words slurred. He rolled his hands, and a massive sphere of light appeared between them. The yellow sphere shot toward Silversmith.

Silversmith dropped to one knee, the magic flying over his head, and threw a knife at Kemer. It halted an inch from Kemer's heart, suspended in yellow magic.

Silver tendrils spread from the knife's blade. Most of the magic disappeared on contact with the yellow aura, but a few tendrils pierced the shield and sank into Kemer's face.

Raw, red burns scorched Kemer's skin, and the yellow shield died with his scream.

Silversmith closed the distance between them and tackled Kemer. He knelt on Kemer's throat. Kemer struggled, but the yellow magic faded from his hands. Oblivion loomed.

Cormac laughed. He leaned against the crenelation, staring into the courtyard, laughing. "My apprentice is a fighter."

Chasina kissed the Naridi Stone again, but nothing happened. Lord Kemer had immediately accessed the Naridi Stone's magic. Why couldn't she?

Cormac's laughter quieted. "Vorce is too forgiving."

Chasina looked up, confused. "What did you say?"

"Somehow, after everything you did to him, you regained his trust. I am rectifying that mistake."

Cormac's gray eyebrows connected into one furry line as he dropped a level stare on Chasina. His hand flicked out. She spun to one side and crashed into his other hand.

"You can't kill me. I am Silversmith's vessel," she said, wiggling.

"Killing you will physically wound Vorce but not fatally. It's illegal, but I'm already a wanted man who has committed treason."

"We had a deal."

"You are a bloodthirsty little hypocrite. We both know you'd do the same thing in my position to protect someone you care about." Cormac circled one finger around her throat and squeezed.

Chasina's tongue ballooned. Her injured ribs cracked where the Naridi Stone pressed against them.

Vivid memories flashed in her vision.

She saw Gran smile at her when she was young. She wrapped skinny arms around Gran's leg, and she smelled wheat fields on a humid day. Dark earth churned beneath bare feet as she ran with other children.

Those were the old memories. The others were sharp and shiny as a new blade between her ribs.

Chasina tasted poisoned food. She felt Theodoric's big hand on her neck, shoving her face beneath the river while onlookers watched. Chasina's cheeks stung when Katie whipped hair into her face and stalked away with Gran.

Chasina felt the sting of a hundred memories in one second, the burn of a thousand nights spent crying on her pallet, and the ache of intense emptiness swelling inside her chest. The emptiness spread. It crawled over her arms and legs, leaving numbness in its wake. When it spread blackness over her vision, Chasina accepted it. She hung limply and waited for Cormac to rip off her head.

Cormac dropped Chasina. She fell to the stone with a hard slap, flopping like a dying fish. The emptiness receded from her vision as she gasped for air. Coughing, she looked across the dark courtyard.

Somehow, Kemer had switched places with Silversmith and knelt on top of him. Something bright blue flashed around Kemer's wrist and caught Chasina's eye. It was a bracelet. *Odd.* She hadn't noticed it until now. The blue magic gleamed before fading to scarlet, then purple. The multi-colored magic steadily fed Kemer's aura, healing the burns on his neck and making his yellow aura flare even brighter.

Something clicked in Chasina's mind. She dug the Naridi Stone from her side and gaped.

It was not a rose. It didn't even glow. It was a random rock with sharp edges and grit that found its way beneath her nails. When Kemer finished enchanting Silversmith, yellow magic rippled across the stone in Chasina's hands. It turned into a rose again.

An illusion.

Chapter Sixty-Seven

L ord Kemer had swapped the real Naridi Stone with a fake one, disguising both with an illusion. Chasina should have known that Lord Kemer wouldn't leave the Naridi Stone unguarded in the tower. She had swapped a fake Naridi Stone for another fake Naridi Stone.

Now, Lord Kemer was draining the Naridi Stone, healing himself and gaining power. He glowed more brightly with every passing second.

"Hero's sweet breath," breathed Cormac. "What has he done to my apprentice?"

Chasina clutched the fake Naridi Stone, afraid she would find a pile of ashes where Silversmith used to be. A small humanoid figure lay prone at Kemer's feet. Somehow, Lord Kemer had activated Silversmith's curse and turned him into a human.

Chasina covered one eye, waiting for Kemer to incinerate or smash Silversmith. Instead, Kemer reached down and deliberately pressed his finger to Silversmith's chest, squeezing the air from his lungs.

As an Undying, Lord Kemer crusaded to eradicate giants. He

wanted to relish ending Silversmith's life and mark the beginning of a bloodbath.

Chasina dropped the fake Naridi Stone and climbed down the crenelation, whimpering as her ribs shifted like broken glass. Before descending ten feet, Cormac scooped her up from behind and limped across the three bridges and down the steps.

Cormac set Chasina on the grass and crouched beside her. "This has to be an illusion. How can Silversmith be human? You are his slave. Tell me."

Chasina picked her words carefully to dance around Silversmith's command to keep his curse secret. "Does that look like an illusion to you?" she asked, telling Cormac the answer without explicitly revealing Silversmith's secret.

Cormac shot a green sphere across the courtyard. It swallowed Silversmith and flew back toward Cormac, colliding with a yellow sphere. Both spheres disappeared, and Silversmith dropped motionless to the ground ten yards from Kemer.

"I lost four apprentices to the Undying. I can't do it again. Save my boy," Cormac said.

"Keep Kemer away from the center of the courtyard," Chasina said. Cormac nodded briskly, their feud forgotten.

Kemer rose and strolled across the courtyard to meet Cormac. His hand remained clasped around the Naridi Stone to absorb its power. It was a powerful totem, but eventually, Kemer would absorb all the magic and destroy it.

"You seem shocked, my friend," Kemer said, gesturing at Silversmith's motionless human body. "Silversmith never told you about his curse, did he? You two have a lot to discuss if you survive. What are the chances of that, you suppose?"

Cormac sent burning green spheres toward Kemer. None hit their mark, but they forced Kemer to stop draining the Naridi

Stone. Cormac quickly lurched forward, moving jerkily due to his wounds. He tackled Kemer and rolled him away from the center of the courtyard.

Chasina dashed to Silversmith's side. He groaned as she dragged him to the well. He was too weak to climb into the well and too heavy for her to carry. Their best option was to hide until Cormac killed Lord Kemer. Cormac *would* kill him, right? Kemer had already fought several people tonight. He had to be getting tired.

Silversmith interrupted Chasina's thoughts. He tried standing but settled for propping his head against the wet stone.

Quickly, Chasina checked all the spots where blood leaked through his tunic.

"How bad is it?" he asked.

Chasina grimaced. "You probably won't die if Seven tends your wounds in the next hour. Where is she?"

"She got injured in the tower, so we left her with Jason." Silversmith tried standing. This time, he made it halfway to his feet before collapsing.

Across the courtyard, Cormac and Kemer wrestled in a tangle of limbs and flashing knives. Kemer's agonized howl cut across the grass. Cormac was winning.

"Was Seven badly injured?" Chasina asked.

"I think it was her broken leg. Nothing fatal." Silversmith tracked the wrestling giants, covering his mouth when Cormac rebounded from a blow to the head and wrapped sinewy arms around Kemer's throat.

Chasina jostled Silversmith's shoulder. "Can you climb into the well? We need to leave in case something goes wrong and Kemer comes to kill us."

"What about Seven? And where's my sister?"

Chasina bit her lip. "Seven will be fine if she's still alive. If she's dead, you're the only person left to save."

"My sister."

"Let me rephrase." Chasina touched her lips. "You are the only person that I can save. Seven is either dead or perfectly safe, and I physically cannot rescue Muriel. Now...can you stand?"

Wincing, Silversmith climbed slowly to his feet, leaning on Chasina for support. She yelped when his weight strained her broken ribs. He quickly leaned away from Chasina.

Yellow magic gleamed in the corner of Chasina's eye. She turned and saw Lord Kemer straddling Cormac. Green magic flowed from Cormac's chest, feeding Kemer's aura.

Silversmith started toward the two giants.

"Stop," Chasina said. "Kemer won't even look at you before he crushes you. What are you going to do?"

Silversmith looked around at his doomed mentor and Chasina. "I have to do something."

"Use magic."

"I can't use magic in human form. I can't even feel my magic!"

Silversmith lifted his arm from Chasina's shoulders and staggered toward Cormac. He clearly had not spent enough time as a helpless human because he wasn't thinking clearly. Silversmith was one injured human offering himself as easy prey to a giant.

It would be easy to tackle Silversmith and stop him from endangering himself, but he wanted to save Cormac. She would not take that from him.

Chasina caught up to Silversmith. "I am your vessel. Use the magic you've stored inside me to put Kemer to sleep."

"Cormac will have tried that already," Silversmith said.

"Kemer is busy draining the life from Cormac's body. He's distracted, see?" She pointed. "He dropped the illusion on the Naridi Stone."

Silversmith followed her finger to where the Naridi Stone dangled from Kemer's wrist.

Silversmith looked down into Chasina's face. "We've tried this before."

"So let's try again."

Chasina clasped his hand firmly and looked him in the eye. At his touch, the silver snake awakened within her.

Silversmith twitched his fingers, and Chasina stopped breathing for a moment. As the snake rose inside her and she lost control of her senses, she heard Silversmith speak in her ear.

"If you fight me this time, Cormac will die. I need full control."

Chasina dropped into an ocean of silver magic, where she treaded water. The ocean remained calm.

There was another presence in the nexus of the silvery ocean.

Silversmith floated in the ocean of his own magic. A dark blue shape throbbed in his hands. It was the size of her fist, indigo blue, and pumped so fast she thought it might burst any moment.

My heart.

Chapter Sixty-Eight

Silver skies. Silver ocean. All of it warm like an ocean of silver blood, and Chasina treaded water somewhere in its vastness. She patted herself, pausing on her chest. Nothing trembled beneath her hand. No heat, not the steady thump of her heart or the rising and falling of her chest. Nothing.

Yellow light encroached on the silver ocean like a plague trickling into the water. It spread across the ocean in hundreds of interconnecting branches until the silver sea was almost entirely yellow.

Chasina sank lower in the waves until they rose above her head and formed a dome around her and Silversmith. The yellow aura pushed through the waves like an infection. A yellow tendril brushed her skin, and though she felt no pain, she saw herself fade. Silversmith faded.

Silver waves rose around them and surged outward, disappearing beyond glowing horizons. The indigo heart beat faster. It trembled in Silversmith's hands, pumping faster until it turned into an indigo blur...and then stopped.

Chasina stopped swimming, allowing a fierce riptide to pull her deep below the surface. Her lungs burned. She opened her mouth.

Silver light gushed through her mouth and nose, flooding her brain with total numbness. She was a vessel. Nothing more.

Someone grabbed her hand. An indigo thread of light emerged from the deepest recesses of Chasina's mind. Warmth bloomed in her chest, and she remembered her name.

Silversmith pulled Chasina to the surface. They surfaced near the silver island, and Silversmith swam toward the shore, one arm wrapped securely around Chasina's ribs. He released her when they reached shallow water.

Silversmith's apparition seemed solid again, his blue eyes like twin skies as he blinked and shifted his hands. In one moment, his hands were empty. In another, the indigo heart appeared in his hands, beating steadily once again.

Silversmith had purified the silver ocean. The yellow infection was gone.

Chasina stepped closer, silver waves pooling around her thighs. "You're eyes..." she tipped back her head and searched his face. "Those are my eyes."

Silversmith shifted his gaze.

Chasina lifted a hand to her chest, searching for a heartbeat, but she felt nothing. "Does our deal still stand?"

Silversmith nodded, and a web of scars flickered on the left side of his face before disappearing. "After I awaken the Hero, I will help you steal the Naridi Stone and give it back to humans. Do you really think your Gran will take you back?"

"I hope so. But if not, I understand. I oppressed Gran, so what else was she supposed to do but betray me?"

Silversmith's blue eyes lost their focus. "Cormac sees us," he said softly. "I never told him about my curse because he hates humans."

Chasina looked around but only saw the silver island surrounded by a silver ocean and sky. "True, but he doesn't hate you. He was very proud when he saw you fighting Lord Kemer."

A small smile touched Silversmith's face—a mutilated smile that belonged to Chasina. "Did he cry?"

"No, but he laughed, which was a lot more disturbing."

Silversmith's laughter held the same rasp that sanded everything Chasina said. It was warm.

"I saved his life, too," she said, intrigued by the warmth in her laughter that she'd never known existed. "Hopefully, he remembers that before he kills me."

Silversmith's borrowed blue eyes were so intense they flayed Chasina to the bone. "I let him kill Keir. I won't do that again." Silversmith held out her heart. "Thank you for letting me save Cormac."

"You're welcome."

The moment Chasina took her heart, the silver ocean rushed inside her, wrapping itself around her spine in the form of a snake.

Chasina landed in the real world and took a deep breath. The scent of baked stone filled the air, and wet clothes stuck uncomfortably to her body.

Cormac knelt above her and Silversmith, jaw slack, staring at them. "All those weeks, I thought you were skipping training and hiding from me—"

"I was," Silversmith finished.

Chasina struggled to her feet and limped around the well. She spotted Muriel high on the walkway, fiercely hugging Oscar and crying.

Nearby, Lord Kemer snored on the ground. Green magic threaded the ropes tying his hands and feet, ensuring he couldn't escape or use magic.

A lone figure crept from the tower carrying a heavy wooden chest. Jason looked over his shoulder as he approached the castle gate, and that's when Chasina spotted Seven. The herbwoman leaned against Jason's neck, holding her injured leg steady.

Evidently, Jason didn't mind assaulting Cormac by killing Seven. Maybe he figured the heist was over, so he didn't have to worry about hurting Cormac.

Cormac spotted Jason and went to yell at him.

Chasina cut the Naridi Stone from the bracelet around Kemer's wrist and limped back to Silversmith, dropping heavily beside him.

She held the Naridi Stone to her chest and absorbed its gentle throbbing. Even though Kemer had absorbed some of its power, she felt strength in the steady throbs and the heat emanating from it. After seventy years, the Naridi Stone was going to empower humans again.

Sighing, Chasina offered the Naridi Stone to Silversmith. "If I keep holding it, I'm going to kill Cormac and Jason. Take it."

"You don't want to kill them?"

"Until our bargain is complete, I will refrain from harming them. You get to use the Naridi Stone first."

Silversmith took the Naridi Stone and set it on the ground beside him. "Thank you."

"That must have been an awkward conversation with Cormac," Chasina said.

Silversmith coughed. "The Undying are still coming for the refugees. Our soldiers may hold them at bay for a while, but not for long. We need the Hero."

Chasina rested her cheek on her knees. The moon was only halfway across the sky, but her body screamed that it had been at least a week since she had slept. Between Kemer, Silversmith, and the tunnels, she felt like melting into a puddle on the spot.

We did it. But what about the price? Keir was dead, and everyone in their little party would be lucky to maintain a steady jog back to the city.

"How soon do we start for the Vault of Eternal Sleep?" Chasina asked.

Silversmith tensed his jaw. "Tonight."

Chasina kissed the rose on her knife once for every villager and loved one she had ever lost. Her lips hovered over the wood. *My heart will never forget, Keir.* She kissed the rose one last time and sheathed her knife before climbing to her feet.

She offered Silversmith her hand. "We have a Hero to find."

Hi There!

If you enjoyed reading The Stolen Rose, I'd appreciate it if you would rate or review it on Amazon or goodreads. Thank you!

About the Author

Hi Everyone! This is the part of a book where the author talks about themselves in the third person. Because that sounds boring, I'll skip to the good parts before I fall asleep and land on my keyboard.

I am a fun-loving peanut butter addict. I love telling stories and plumbing the depths of human nature (which, ironically, I did not realize would end up with my book being filled with mostly awful people), and my secondary life calling is annoying my brothers. The Stolen Rose is my first story, and I am positively thrilled to share it with you.

Made in the USA
Monee, IL
31 December 2022

23938952R00208